The Resurrection Murders

The Resurrection Murders

Donald Michael Kraig

2014
Galde Press
Lakeville, Minnesota, U.S.A.

The Resurrection Murders

Printed in the United States of America

First Edition, 2009
Second Printing, 2010
Third Printing, 2014

Cover design by Garrett Moore

Galde Press
PO Box 460
Lakeville, Minnesota 55044–0460
www.galdepress.com

Author's Note

The rituals and magical techniques described in this book are based on ancient, traditional methods. Practitioners of magic believe such rituals are effective and can actually work to cause changes in our physical world. However, all of the rituals and magical methods described in this book are incomplete. The author, publisher, distributors, and retailers will not be responsible for the results should any person attempt to perform any of the rituals described in this work. Readers interested in learning the full forms of the rituals presented in this book, along with the theories, techniques, and philosophies behind them, are directed to the author's previous work, *Modern Magick* (St. Paul: Llewellyn Publications, 1988).

The descriptions of some of the locations and sites in this work, as well as the titles of some books mentioned in this work, are real, but are used only to provide a background for the fictitious events and characters in this work. All events, characters and names mentioned in this book (except the use of historical names to provide a background) are imaginary and totally fictitious.

The author would also like to thank Devin O'Branagan, Mike Sheeter, Mary Temkin, and Scott Cunningham for their friendship and invaluable advice.

Prologue

Five Years Ago

SIMON WALKED OUT of the meeting hall. The night glowed mystically from the light of stars as the warm San Diego air greeted him and his anger. *I don't believe it! I don't believe it!* he shouted to himself over and over. *How could they have agreed to it?*

He jogged down Park Boulevard to his car and stood next to it for several moments before he slammed his fist against the roof of the '56 Ford Thunderbird red hardtop convertible. Resigned, he lowered himself to the sparse grass patch by the curb next to his car. *How could they have agreed to it?*

For the past five years Simon studied with AHMOCT, the Arcane, Hermetic, and Magical Order of Christian Templars. For years he had ignored their silly-looking ads that had been running forever in magazines like *Popular Mechanics*, but one day, on a whim, he sent for information and became a member. As he expected, AHMOCT's lessons were little more than pseudo-mystical ramblings from the New Thought teachings popular in the early 1900s and which had evolved from the earlier religion of

Spiritualism. But he was overjoyed when, three years after joining the main Order of Christian Templars in Florida, he joined the local organization. Here was a group of people not like the other "orders" he had joined. For years he drifted from one magical group to another, only to quit each in disgust—they seemed to have egotistical leaders who either wanted power or took monetary or sexual advantage of their students. AHMOCT, or at least the local affiliated group, was different.

For two years he studied with these wonderful people, all of whom had the same goals as he—to study the mystical and to grow in spirituality. For awhile Simon was the lover to one of the women members, a gentle, loving woman with soft, wet lips and just a hint of a southern drawl that filled him with antebellum fantasies. He even kept a painting she had made and gave to him. Simon listened to stories of members, shared their happy times and commiserated with them in their sadnesses.

Two members he especially admired . John was a tall, burly, ex-Marine D.I. He had a severe face and rarely smiled, but when he did its light filled the room. He rarely talked about his past or his wife and three children; indeed, he rarely talked at all. But when he did, it was usually to share a spiritual truth which, in a pithy sentence or two, would clear up questions Simon secretly kept for years.

The other was Diane. Medium in height, she appeared rather mousy when Simon first met her. Shortly thereafter, her divorce became final and she blossomed. Her long, auburn hair took on a glow, and her green eyes sparkled with life and wit. Unlike John, she was quick to smile and even quicker to laugh. She began wearing tighter and more revealing clothes. Diane was one of the most beautiful women in the local group.

During the two-year period that Simon was a member of the local group, he watched Diane grow spiritually. She progressed tremendously, and just months ago became the Head of Rituals for the local group. Simon admired her and considered her a friend even after she made her one mistake. She fell in love.

Diane fell passionately, romantically and spiritually in love with John, and he with her. Simon, who knew John had been unhappy with his home life, was pleased both of them found somebody to love, to care for, to grow with. *Yes, their affair is not "proper,"* Simon thought. *After all, John is still married. But they're both aware of the spiritual consequences of their actions. There's no way these two spiritual people would have decided to start and continue this relationship if they were not positive it was the correct thing to do.* Although Simon was pleased to see his friends so happy and in love, John's wife, Roberta, was not as pleased.

John and Roberta had talked about a divorce several times, but since they had three young children, she refused to consider it. There was no way she would agree to raise them by herself. When she found out about the affair, she exploded.

Roberta did not confront the lovers. Rather, she wrote to the headquarters of AHMOCT in DeLand, Florida. Her letter read, "Your Order is ruining my marriage. What are you going to do about it?"

As a result of the letter AHMOCT panicked. The organization issued an official pronunciamento, a letter, which was read at an emergency general meeting of the San Diego group. It read, "Diane must step down as Head of Rituals and both she and John must not be involved with the local group for a period of at least one year."

Diane stood up and made an impassioned speech. She refused to step down. Simon and some of the younger members applauded her loudly and she began to cry out of thanks for their support. John, in a short but eloquent speech, also refused to leave the San Diego group.

Unfortunately, the board of directors for the local group was composed of elderly, long-time members who were flunkeys of their DeLand masters. They moved to expel both John and Diane.

Simon rose and protested, "How can you do this? We all know and love Diane and John." His short speech was greeted with applause.

Irene, an elderly woman who was a member of AHMOCT for over

twenty years, rose to explain the reality of the situation, "If John and Diane do not leave for at least one year, and if we continue to support them, AHMOCT will withdraw their backing for the San Diego group, close us down and expel each of us." A hush covered the room like a blanket that brought no warmth.

"These are our friends," Simon said. "This is their hour of trial. We mustn't desert them now. We can form our own group…" Simon looked at the faces of the one-hundred-plus people in the room. The ones who cheered him earlier now hung their heads and wouldn't look at him. The other faces were simply grim and cold.

The vote was quickly taken and the inevitable result was announced.

Diane now rose. "I'd like to say one last thing before John and I leave. We've talked it over and we urge each of you to stay with the Order. Do not let any of this cause you to stray from the path. May the light always guide you." She and John left quickly, her sobs filling the silence.

Simon slowly rose and looked at the people. "How could you do this? They love AHMOCT. For them the Order was their true life. These meetings gave them joy. They've helped each of us. Why have you chosen to desert them now?"

A couple of the women started to cry, but no one rose to answer. No one would dare.

Finally, the presiding officer banged her gavel and said, "Now, we must take on the business of electing a new Head of Rituals."

Simon rose, his face set in indignation, filled with anger and disappointment. He stood tall and walked out of the room. No one followed .

Simon gazed into the night sky and watched as a meteor streaked across the darkness, leaving a trail of light. *That's what we need. A magical order filled with honor and respect for its members rather than one that hides with cowardice in order to protect the leaders.* But he had searched for years. He had yet to find such a group, a group that could be warriors of the Light.

Another shooting star sped across the night. *How odd,* he thought. *Shooting stars are rarely seen in the sky here.* Another meteor sped from the horizon and seemed to come right at him before it vanished. *Me?* he thought. *Well, no one else will do it. Why not me?*

Simon stood and looked at the stars. "By all the powers of this universe, known and unknown, and in the presence of the Divine, I hereby vow to start an occult order that will create true Warriors of the Light of God. This order will have but one purpose: to teach real magic and spirituality to all who truly wish to learn the art. Further, I vow to help each and every student become both a powerful magician and a strong, independent person."

He quickly drove home and made plans to move to a new area and begin his magical order. When he finished, it was daylight. Rather than go to sleep, he sat on the floor, curled his legs into the yogic lotus position and began a deep meditation. He felt lifted and good. He knew his decision was right.

This will be an order for the benefit of the members, not the leaders. I will not fail any of them, he thought. When he finally left the meditation, it was dark. Simon assumed he must have meditated for the entire day.

Actually, it had been two days.

Chapter One

First Night

"Why do you put up with me?"

With a silent sigh, Simon's head fell slightly. He raised it quickly, hoping his student did not see his frustration with her. The woman sitting near him, Allenda Henley, had been studying with him for over two years now. Even so, her self-image was incredibly low. He worried she was beginning to idolize him and treat him like a guru *I detest that word!* he thought. *How can I help her to find her strength?*

"It's no good, Simon, I'll never get it right. That's the zillionth time I've tried the Hexagram ritual and I still haven't gotten it. I can't generate the magical power," she said. As she spoke, a bluish haze barely a quarter-inch around her hand faded to nothingness. That blue glow was a visible sign of the magical energy she had generated, and now that slight flicker of energy evaporated from around her fingertips. Tears started to glisten at her eyes, but before they completely formed, she sighed and hung her head. "Simon, I don't know why you put up…"

Simon stared at her. His energy made her look up. His glance, a combination of strength and control, stopped her in mid-sentence. He knew what he said at this moment would be important. He spoke in a calm yet strong voice. "Stop it, Allenda. I never put up with anyone I don't value, and I value you. It's been a long night and I think it's time to stop our practice. I'm sure you'll get it at our next session."

"You've said that before, Simon, but I still feel like a failure. Why do you put up with me?"

"And you've said that before," he laughed, purposely trying to lighten the situation. Like the first time he met her, he had to hide his appreciation of her beauty. Allenda Henley was twenty-three. *She should be coming into her magical and personal power, yet she was always…hmm, what would be the right word…hiding. She hides behind her conservative clothes and large, heavy-framed glasses. She hides behind her ten pounds or so of excess weight. She hides behind her insecurity.*

"Alli, we both know you have quickly gained a deep knowledge of the Kabalah, the theoretical basis of our magic. There is an old Sufi saying, 'Beware of too much study or you may become a scholar.' I, for one, would hate to see you limit yourself to being a scholar, an armchair magician, when you could put your knowledge into use and become a powerful, practicing magical worker. You just need some practical experience. I know that with a little more work you will…"

Crash!

Simon was interrupted by the sound. For a moment, both he and Allenda held their breaths—surprised, shocked. He quickly looked around the familiar room. It was large and circular with a high, conical ceiling crossed by sweeping, open beams. The window filled walls were hidden in shadows created by the few white candles that lit the room. In the darkness, the sound seemed to come from everywhere. Simon quickly made a visual check against his memory of everything in the chamber.

"What was that?" asked Allenda finally, a tinge of fear in her voice. She had seen enough strange things in the magic room to know everything that happened in there meant something, and nothing occurred by chance.

Simon found the cause of the sound and pointed it out to her. "It's nothing, Allenda," he told her, seeking to calm her nerves. "See? A mirror fell off of the wall, that's all. It was probably shaken loose by a microquake or a big truck going by. And you know how bad I am at hanging stuff on the walls."

They were both silent for a second, as if thinking about the fallen mirror. In the silence they heard an eerie crackling sound, like the wrinkling of cellophane when it is being removed from a new toy. The sound sent shivers of fear up Allenda's spine, as if some horrible *thing* was clawing at her, seeking to tear her soul from her body. Simon felt a similar sensation but fought it and brought his attention back to discovering the source of the sound. He found that source in one of the thirteen large windows that filled the walls of the magic room. He watched, fascinated, as an uncanny spider-web of translucent lines crept from the lower, left-hand corner of the window up and across its length and width. When the window was covered with a maze of cracks, the sound stopped for a second. All Simon could hear was their breathing, breaking the silence. Suddenly, the window exploded inward, covering the area around it with shards of glass.

Allenda's voice rose in fear as she called her teacher's name, "Simon…"

The mage closed his eyes and opened his psychic senses. Instantly he felt a familiar, prickly sensation. It ran up and down his body like static electricity. The hair on his arms and on the back of his neck stood almost straight out.

Damn me for being overconfident! He further explored using his psychic senses and saw where someone, or some *thing*, an enemy, had broken though his magical defenses. Simon, caught up in his daily responsibilities, had simply forgotten to regularly strengthen them. *When this is over I'll have to reset the magical wards.* That would protect his home against unwanted intruders. But now there was work to do, magical work. The window to the left of the first one started to make crackling noises and a web of lines started to appear, marring its clarity.

"Okay, Alli," he said in a calming voice, "move into the circle."

Allenda started to grab her notebooks and some papers. *My notes! My notes! I need them so I can help perform the rituals.* The window shattered into the room, covering several tables and the floor around it with sharp blades of glass. A wind whistled through the massive, broken-edged holes which were once two sealed windows. Like walking into a grocer's freezer, the temperature dropped.

Allenda's skin broke out in gooseflesh and her breath became visible in the dim light. "What's happening?" she cried, trying to be heard over the increasing volume of the wind. Loose papers from a desk flew off it and blew across the floor like flat marionettes drawn by invisible strings.

"We're under some sort of magical attack. Get into the circle—now! Let me work."

Another window shattered into the room. Startled by this new crash, Allenda dropped the things she had gathered and bent to pick them up.

"Alli, forget about that stuff and get into the circle."

"But how can I help you if I don't have my notes and..."

"Get in the circle!"

Another window crashed into the room. She could barely hear Simon over the wind that now blew freely from the outside. In all their work he had never raised his voice to her like that. The wind picked up papers all over the room. The worn, leather cover on an ancient book flew open and the pages, as if animated by a controlling mind, flew at her, attacking as if they were alive. They covered her face, suffocating her. Allenda started to scream, but they flew into her mouth, gagging her. She tore them off and threw them aside, but for every one she removed, two took its place. She fell to her knees, struggling for breath. Finally, the pages stopped coming at her and she was able to pull the remaining ones off of her face. Hunched over on her hands and knees, she sucked in air. For some reason, the air smelled bad, like a sour smog. *The air smells...evil.* Allenda rose and followed Simon's order to move into the circle. She moved slowly as the candles had long-since blown out and the room was only lit with distant lights from outside Simon's home. She did not know the room as well as Simon did. She was also worried. *How can I possibly be of any help without my notes?*

Three more windows exploded, one after another, showering the room with glass. A large shard, seemingly a guided missile, struck a glancing blow on Allenda's left calf. She cried out in pain as she fell to the floor. Simon, meanwhile, assembled his tools on the altar in the middle of the room. The altar was formed from two cubes on top of each other, forming a double cube a yard high and eighteen inches wide. The top cube was painted white. The lower cube black. On top of it now were a cup, a couple of daggers razor sharp on both edges, a strangely-shaped wand and something circular under a black piece of cloth. All the items were colorfully painted and had strange symbols on them. When Simon heard Allenda's cry, he turned and looked at her. She waved him off and got to her feet. The cut was painful but she thought it was neither serious nor deep. Even so, she left a trail of large driblets of blackish-red blood as she limped the rest of the way across the floor and entered the circle.

Crash! Crash! Crash! Crash! Crash!

The rest of the windows exploded inward, one after another. Noise from the howling wind made communication between Simon and Allenda virtually impossible. The huge chandelier hanging above the center of the room, swung randomly and ominously, buffeted by the wind which came, it seemed, from all directions.

Allenda looked at Simon as he prepared the magic circle of protection. *He will protect me just as…* Alli gasped as she realized what she was thinking. *…just as daddy always protected me.*

Simon folded both his hands around the handle of one of the daggers and pointed with the tip of it to his forehead. "Ah-tah!" he cried. A bright beam of pure, white, scintillating light came from far above and seemed to glow around his head. He brought the tip of the blade down to his stomach and cried "Mahl-koot!" The beam of light followed the dagger and went past it to the floor. Allenda knew that the spiritual light would descend to the center of the Earth.

He pointed to his right shoulder, then his left shoulder. "Vih-geh-boorah! Vih-geh-doo-lah!" Then he folded his hands at his chest, the tip of the blade pointing upwards. "Lih-oh-lahm, Vah-ed!" Simon was enveloped in a cross of purified, white light. The features on his face seemed to blend in with the light, as if he had united with the Divine. The ends of the bars of the cross of light seemed to extend onward and outward to infinity.

With each of his breaths, the cross of light expanded until it surrounded the mage and his pupil. He moved around the altar to stand at the eastern point of the glow. This was also at the most eastern point of a white circle, nine feet in diameter, which had been painted on the magic room's floor. With the dagger, he drew in the air before him a large, five-pointed star—the sacred pentagram!—with one point upward. The star glowed with the blue light of an electrical spark. The energy-form he created hung in the air crackling and sizzling with magical force and power. He inhaled and drew the dagger up into the air. A reddish glow formed around the tip. As he exhaled he thrust the blade toward the center of the star, shouting, "Yood-Heh-Vahv-Heh!" A torrent of reddish flame burst from the tip of the blade and went through the center of the pentagram to the ends of time and space. When he released his breath, the red line faded, leaving only strange, reddish symbols in the center of the star. The East was sealed with one of the sacred names of God.

Allenda, her pain forgotten, watched in awe. *I've seen Simon in ritual before, but never like this!* He was power incarnate, imbued with energy, self-confidence and strength. She longed to feel that energy, to join with it.

He pointed to the center of the star and moved around the circumference of the circle to the south, always pointing outward with the dagger. A line of blue fire, crackling with energy, followed the tip of the blade. Here he repeated his previous actions, calling, "Ah-doh-nai," another of God's names. The mad wind began to die down.

Simon continued the process to the West and the North, calling "Eh-heh-yeh!" and "Ah-glah!" respectively. Then he completed the circle, connecting with magical energy the northern pentagram to the one at the East. A ring of blue light with bright blue stars at the four directions, each with red symbols in their centers, surrounded them. As Simon concentrated, the ring expanded below and above, forming a sphere of protection. The wind roared once, as if in defiance, and was gone.

The sudden silence was eerie. Their breaths, the creaking of the chandelier as its swaying slowed on its support wire and the occasional rustle of papers as a calm breeze blew through the destroyed windows was almost painfully loud against the silence. The magic room was on the top floor of the turret Simon added to the house and he could almost always count on a breeze coming through ant open windows. Usually the wind was cleansing, purifying, bringing in clean air. Tonight it was stagnant, humid and noxious. All it did was gently move.

Simon opened a side of the altar and pulled out a candle. He placed the candle on the altar and lit it with a Bic lighter also taken from inside the altar. As the flame on the candle grew he peered through the spiritual lights surrounding them.

"Is it over?" Allenda asked.

Simon closed his eyes. He sensed the evil that had invaded his home was even stronger than before. He was furious with himself for being so overconfident. *How could I have forgotten to keep my defenses strong? Why didn't I detect this attack and deflect it long before it arrived?* Simon tried to detect the direction the attack was coming from. Suddenly, his eyes grew big with a thought he had not wanted to face. *Whoever did this is as at least as powerful—maybe even more powerful—than me.*

"Simon, is it over?" Allenda repeated.

He didn't bother to reply to her directly. Instead he used his foot to push aside some glass and sat on the floor. "Sit with me, Allenda. Let's use our strength to increase the power of the circle."

Allenda hobbled over to him, pushed aside some glass, and sat cross-legged, face-to-face with her mentor. Simon sat comfortably in the yogic lotus position. *Damn! I wish I had his flexibility.* She brought her mind back to the point at hand and concentrated with Simon on making the circle strong. Although she knew it was a sphere, tradition made everyone call it a circle. They visualized the energy that protected them grow stronger in their minds. Allenda looked around and took a deep breath. The blue of the circle had grown brighter. The white energy inside the circle was brighter, too.

The candle sputtered and went out. All Allenda could hear was their breathing. *I don't like this. I don't know what's going to happen. I can't stand it when I'm not in control!* She squirmed. Her leg ached. *Why couldn't this be over?* A new sound, unlike anything she had ever heard, assaulted her. It made her think both of an ugly, oleaginous, sticky substance and also the slitheriness of a demonic night creature. She detected some motion near one of the windows. *What's that outside the circle?*

A fog unlike any she had ever seen hovered at the sills of all the smashed windows. Lit up from behind, the fog glowed like a mist from hell. It was on all sides of the room. As if on command, it oozed over the sills of the shattered windows. It slithered and burbled across the floor, moving slowly, inexorably undulating toward the circle—and them.

When it reached their protective sphere it halted. *We'll be safe in the circle,* she thought. Tendrils of the fog, like tentacles of sticky goo, reached out toward the protective blue sphere. Each time one of the tendrils touched the sphere a spark of bluish electricity would dart out. A roar of pain came from the fog and the tendril would retreat back to the main body of the thick mist that had undulated across the floor. Time after time a tendril would reach out, only to be driven back by the circle. To her horror, Allenda realized each time the fog made an attempt to breach the circle and was driven back, the circle lost some of its brightness, some of its strength, some of its power.

The circle's fading! I have to do something, but what? I don't know what to do. She looked at her mentor. Simon sat calmly. His body was drenched in sweat from the mental exertion. The ends of his long, perspiration-slicked hair were white with ice from the cold in the air. *Look at him. In spite of everything going on he's...he looks like he's at peace.* The confidence he showed encouraged her. *It's time for a change. He is* not *my daddy. Simon is my teacher. And I will learn from him.* Alli forgot the fog and its tendrils, she ignored the cold, her discomfort and pain and simply focused on what she needed to do—add her energies to the circle. She inhaled and started a low chant. "Aum" she sang quietly. Imperceptibly, Simon smiled. The circle glimmered, then grew strong.

An inhuman howl came from the fog. The heavy mist had continued to pour over the window sills and the room outside the circle was thick with it. Now it tried a new tactic. Instead of mere tendrils, shapes of unspeakable things appeared to test the circle. Incomplete, tortuous faces with gaping maws filled with rows of sharp teeth and arms with claws or pincers approached, only to be driven back. Jutting beaks and prehensile things with eyes and suckers and other organs Allenda couldn't even describe approached the circle, only to be driven back with something that approached a roar of intense pain, if such sounds could be made with mouths and vocal cords that did not exist on Earth.

Allenda broke her concentration again and looked at the monstrosities outside the circle. It was her downfall. "Simon, stop it! Stop it! Do something, please." Allenda was almost in tears and verging on hysteria.

Simon made sure the circle would last without his attention for a few moments, then rose in a single, fluid motion. He went to the altar and took hold of the object under the cloth which he placed there earlier. The item was a mere disk of wood with a pentagram and some symbols on it. Allenda gasped at the sight. She had heard of it and seen drawings, but she never actually beheld one. Simon never showed this one to her. *It's the Shield of Solomon the King*. A sphere of shimmering white light surrounded it.

Simon moved clockwise around the circle, showing the object in all directions and shouting, "In the name of the most holy Tetragrammaton, and by this sacred symbol which gave King Solomon the wise power over all demons, I *command* all ye demons to be gone! Return now to thy abodes and habitations. Harm none along the way. So mote it be!" As he spoke, the light around the disk of wood spun in an ever-growing circle and expanded until it filled the room. When the light could expand no more it began to sparkle and spin with a blindingly intense brightness. Miniature streaks of something akin to lightning attacked the gooey fog that also filled the room.

The fog reared up, screaming in agony. Allenda closed her eyes and covered her ears to block the sound. In terror, her own screams matched those that filled the night around her. The wind returned, blowing the fog every which way. When she ended her scream the room was enveloped in a peaceful silence. She opened her eyes. The wind had subsided and was now a gentle breeze. The fog was gone.

"Is it over?" Allenda asked. Her voice seemed out of place in the silence.

Simon stood still, sensing, feeling the room. He moved slowly, in a clockwise direction around the edge of the circle. *He moves like a dancer*, Allenda thought. As he moved he examined the psychic nature of the room. When he completed the examination his body visibly relaxed. He turned to her and said, "I think so. Will you dismiss the circle, please?" The Shield of Solomon which he held no longer had a light about it. He started to put it down, but as he tilted it the piece of wood crumbled in his hand, forming a pile of powdery sawdust at his feet. Its magic was gone, but they were safe.

* * * * *

Tiger, Michael and Tom were each twelve years old. By some fortuitous chance their parents all moved onto the same cul-de-sac street in West Los Angeles about ten years earlier. They grew up together and were close friends. They played together and called themselves a gang.

Behind the houses on the west side of their street was a hill with a huge lot. The lot was overgrown with grasses, weeds, bushes and enormous, leaf-laden trees including Elm, Oak and Eucalyptus. To the gang it was a jungle, and as long as they could remember they played there. About seven years ago an Oriental-looking man began building a home on that lot. He worked on weekends and usually worked alone, only calling in help when he came to an aspect of construction he couldn't complete by himself. Sometimes the gang would go out at night, climb over the eight-foot-tall brick wall surrounding the lot and explore the skeleton of the growing house. Once they went in during the day, only to find the builder there. Surprised to see the kids, he yelled at them in Japanese. The gang ran and hid behind some bushes. He went to his car, an old, green, rust-stained Ford Ranchero, and got a rifle from inside. Tiger screamed and all the kids ran. The builder fired his BB gun into the air. The entire gang yelled as they vaulted over the top of the wall and dropped to the safety of the other side, gasping for breath as they crouched, afraid to move. They might get shot at! The builder laughed at their ignominious flight. He hoped it would keep them away so they wouldn't get hurt while trespassing; and also so their parents wouldn't sue him if they did.

The Japanese man finished building the house but never occupied it. No one in the gang knew why, although the rumor was he had died. All they knew was one day a large crew of people came in and worked on the house for six weeks. When they left, the typical Southern California ranch-style house had a very atypical turret. The addition was so big it overshadowed the house to which it was attached. Michael thought it was six stories tall, but Tiger was sure it only had five levels.

One night they decided to take a closer look. After all, they were in sixth grade. Soon they would be starting junior high school. They weren't 'fraid o' nothin'. The gang scrambled over the surrounding wall and looked at each other. None of them wanted to admit the feeling of dread that suddenly came over them. They forced themselves through the woods until they could easily see the house.

"Look," said Tom in awe, "there are thirteen windows in the top of the tower!"

Michael, showing youthly bravado, said, "Aw, it don't mean nothin'. Don't be 'stuperstitious'."

"I ain't 'stuperstitious'," said Tom, defensively. "It's just kinda queer that they would…"

"Shhh," interrupted Tiger. "Look" he said, pointing to the turret.

Inside, the flickering of a candle could be seen. The single light flashed fleeting, weird shadows through the windows. A large, ominous, dark shape crossed a window. Seconds later a caped figure appeared at the window and stared directly at the gang. The boys gasped and froze where they stood, unable to move. The figure raised its arms, the cape forming a batwing behind him. The creature in the window snarled and brought the candle forward, allowing the light to gleam off of huge, fang-like incisors. Then the creature slowly and majestically pointed its left hand directly at the boys.

Pointing at them broke their trance. Once again they ran screaming for safety. In the magic room at the top of the turret, Simon laughed. He had known someday the silly "vampire cape" and plastic "vampire fangs" he purchased in a costume shop would come in handy. He made a mental note to strengthen the magical wards against intruders. He set up the wards two years ago—one week after the turret had been completed—when he moved into his new home. *Perhaps some noisy burglar alarms might help, too,* he thought

The boys never came back. Sometimes Simon wondered how they were doing.

* * * * *

Glass tinkled as Allenda swept the floor. Simon had bandaged her leg that, as she had thought, was not badly cut—it was merely a deep scratch. As he bandaged her leg, Allenda thought about Simon and the attack. *Whatever it was that attacked us almost killed us. I know it! I thought Simon would be able to protect me. Was I wrong?* Allenda had been brought up in wealth, although her mother died when she was young. She traveled all over the world with her father, and the two became very close. Years of therapy helped her realize her dependence on her father was unhealthy for her own well-being. *Daddy had always taken care of me. No matter what happened Daddy's money always seemed to take care of it. I've been on my own for over two years now, refusing any money from my father. Why have I been letting Simon play the role of my father? I don't want him for another daddy. I want him to be my teacher. I want to change, but how do I do it?*

The temperature had returned to normal and Allenda began to perspire from the work. *I wish Simon would let a vacuum cleaner be used in the magic room.* He forbade the use of such a machine in that room, however, as well as the use of any other electrical devices. Even the chandelier used candles. She knew after they swept they would need to mop the floors, too.

Things were calmer now, and even though the work was energetic, she was getting into it. Allenda always hated the thought of doing physical labor, but once she started, she enjoyed the feel of her muscles working and the perspiration coming through her pores. At this moment she envied Simon, both because he seemed to look forward to hard work and because of his location.

Simon worked hard, yet from the expression on his face Allenda knew his mind was elsewhere. She also knew better than to disturb him even though she was eager to ask him questions about what they just experienced. She did not know where his mind was. *Am I feeling jealous because I can't go with him? I have to be able to reach the level he's at.* She looked up toward the skies as if she could see the heavens through the roof. *I will work harder, learn more and do more practicing of magic in the future,* she vowed.

She stopped for a second and looked at Simon as he worked. *How old is he?* she mused. *Thirty-five? Forty-five?* It was hard to tell. His light-brown hair was short in the front and shoulder length and thrown back, falling to either side of a natural, central part. His rectangular face had deep-set, mysterious, hazel eyes. Simon was not quite six-feet tall, yet his physical training left him muscular, so he weighed more than he appeared to weigh. He was also limber from years of yoga. Simon almost always wore black and was a total vegetarian, although he did not require his students to dress or eat as he did. Allenda envied his ability to pick at food rather than gobble it down.

Allenda loved the magic room of Simon's turret. Everything smelled delicious from years of ample use of incense—myrrh, frankincense, cedar, sage, copal, ambergris, sandalwood (red and white), dragon's blood, musk, and aloes wood, as well as many others. The smells were in everything, from the wood of the walls to the books in the glass-fronted bookcases.

Suddenly, Simon turned toward her and said, "Alli, we were attacked by a type of psychic vampire. But unlike most of those creatures, they did not merely want our energy. If they'd succeeded they would have sucked out our souls, leaving our bodies lifeless. Only the power of Solomon's Shield stopped them. When we're finished cleaning up we have to determine who attacked us…and why."

Allenda pondered this as she worked. *I know what psychic vampires are. Hell, everyone in the occult has heard of them. But they're just people with an ability to drain a person of energy. I've never heard of soul-stealing psychic vampires.* Yet she never knew Simon to lie or exaggerate.

Allenda curled her lip in frustration. Here was yet another subject to learn about. She sighed. *Learning real magic is a never-ending process. The more I learn about the magical universe the more, it seems, I need to learn.* Then she came up with another question. *How did Simon learn about them?*

She continued riding on her train of thought until a glimpse of old leather on the floor drew her attention. "Oh Simon! Your original edition of the *Grimoire of Honorius* lost its binding. The pages are all over the place."

"Well, gather them as best you can and I'll try to reassemble it later."

She started picking up the aged, foxing papers and realized these were the same pages which attacked her moments ago. Once again they were lifeless save for the information written on them. She carefully collected all the parts of the valuable book. As she picked up one page she saw a purplish-blue glittering below a small pile of pages. "The beryl crystal is shattered, too," she announced.

"Damn! I'd had that for an awful long time. We were like old friends. Oh well…"

They continued their work for another hour. Simon then declared, "Well, that's good enough for now. I'll put some more effort into it tomorrow. Let's leave and get a bite to…"

"Just a minute, Mr. Simon Raven! I've been damn patient and you know it! I also figure you know more than you're telling me—you've had a run-in with those things before, haven't you? I've been studying occult literature for some time and there's no record of soul-stealing psychic vampires. The only way you could have known what they were is if you dealt with them previously. So let me in. You know who did this, don't you? Why was it done? Why to you? Why to us? Why now? Why…"

Simon held up his hand to quiet her. He pursed his lips, thinking about what he had experienced and what he would say. He went to a large, over-stuffed chair, picked up a shard of glass from the seat, tossed it onto a pile of broken glass, and sat down.

Simon pursed his lips and made a silent, half-laugh. Then he folded his hands, leaned forward and used his legs to support his arms. "You're right, of course. I have dealt with these things before." Allenda smiled triumphantly. "In fact, you're getting pretty smart to have figured so much out," he said with a smile. Then his eyes glazed slightly as he leaned back in the chair and stared out as if reviewing and reliving his past. "It was many years ago. I was a student of magic in Paris, France. My expenses were paid by some American sponsors. Another student, one who claimed to be very talented, was able to conjure up something similar to the things that visited us tonight, although at a far lesser strength than what we just experienced. Even so, we were young and inexperienced. As a result of a miscalculation one student died." Simon sat up on the edge of the chair. "But Alli, I swear I don't know the answers to your questions. I don't know of anyone with as much magical power as our attacker had and who would have any reason to attack me."

Simon paused for a second, his brows knitted in thought. "Hmm. Because of the seriousness of the attack—because of its strength—the threat may not be just against me. It could also be against you and the whole Order. I want you to start the telephone pyramid and assemble the temple. Plan to meet here in three days at 7:30 P.M."

Allenda trekked down the circular stairs which led around the turret to the living room of the house. Her mind was in turmoil. *Someone attacking me? Why would someone do that?* When she reached the main room of the house she went to the phone and called two members of the Order. She told them the time for the meeting. They, in turn, each called two other members. This process of one member calling two continued, and within an hour the entire temple was notified of the emergency meeting. Allenda was sure it would be the most important meeting they ever had.

Later That Night

I'M HERE, MOTHER. Come to me."

Simon stood near the ocean waves, 100 yards north of the pier at Venice beach. It was dark, and Simon looked out across the waters toward the distant stars above the horizon. The Moon shone in his eyes as he looked up at it.

For several years he came here when the crowds were gone. At first it was simply to find peace near the Pacific's waters. His meditations were deep here, and he assumed this was the result of the negative ions produced by the ocean.

But soon he realized there was more here; a presence, a being. This being was a nurturer, a lover of all without limitations. Over months he called out to the being and realized only one name fit: Mother.

It was like Mother Earth, but there was more. He felt it in his meditations. He was comfortable here. He was home. He shared his joys and his sorrows with it. Then one evening She spoke to him.

There was a long pause between waves. The water, pulled back to its source, made a hissing sound as it left the sand. Simon focused on that sound until it obliterated all other sounds. Within that sound She spoke.

Simon never bothered to investigate whether Her voice was real or simply a manifestation of his subconscious. She brought comfort and peace, so he didn't care. Soon She always spoke to Simon. But not tonight.

"Mother, please answer me."

Sand.

Water.

Silence.

"Please, Mother, I need you."

Finally, within the hiss of the retreating waves, he was able to hear sobbing.

"What's wrong, Mother?"

"Simon, my son, my heart aches for the pain you will feel. You will be involved in great evil..."

"Impossible. For my entire life I have fought evil."

"Yet you will have a choice: let evil reign and thousands will die. Fight that evil and hundreds will die, including ones you love."

Simon sat on the sand, stunned. He was quiet for a long time. Only the sounds of the waves caressing the sand broke the silence. "I can't make such decisions," he said.

"You will have no choice. The decisions must be made and you must make them."

"It's unfair."

"I do not recall our ever discussing 'fairness' as being a part of reality. It is not."

Simon's mind was awash in emotions and feelings he never considered. For minutes on end he let his mind run crazy, uncontrolled. He became aware of what he was doing and regained control by slowing his breathing, paying attention to each breath. Then he listened to the universe.

"It's started already, Mother, hasn't it? It started tonight," he said.

"Your participation started tonight. I have been fighting this evil for...for

a long time."

Simon hung his head. "What do I do, Mother? What do I do?

"A warrior is a person who does what he has to do. A hero is merely a person who does the same but gets noticed. You have always been a warrior and I have always been proud of you. That is why you will do what you must."

For a long time Simon said nothing. He was lost in thought. "Mother," he said, "my parents are gone. So are my grandparents, three aunts, an uncle and six close friends. I don't want to lose anyone else. I can't handle that. There's too much death in this world; too much death in my life. I'll leave the country. I'll go where I won't be a part of this. I'll…"

"I have always been proud of you."

"But I…" There was nothing more he could say. He knew what he would do and he dreaded the outcome. Simon stood and brushed off the sand from his Levi 501 jeans. He straightened himself and walked away from the beach without saying goodbye. With each step he felt his shoulders droop, the weight of the lives of loved ones pressing them down. The lights of the city were hidden by a dirty atmosphere. Somewhere he heard the shouts of a man and woman fighting. As he moved forward there was only darkness ahead.

Chapter Two

Second Night

PAUL CHRISTIAN TOOK ONE LOOK at the naked body and rolled his eyes. After twenty-two years on the force he thought he was used to the weird ones. But each one, with its senseless horror and inhumanity, still got to him. He longed for the simple life—whores, traffic, ODs, filth and crimes of passion—he usually found on Hollywood Boulevard. He'd worked the night beat on "The Boulevard" for nine years.

The night was sultry. It was a curious feeling for L.A. where it was often smoggy and shaky, but rarely muggy. Tonight was different. Smog made it tough to breathe, but so did this humidity. There was something strange in the air, and this murder was only part of it. Paul wiped sweat off of his chin with the sleeve of his jacket. *Curious. The jacket was only a couple of years old. They just don't make 'em like they used to.* He sighed, knowing he'd have to buy a new jacket soon. He glanced down at the street. A rainbow had formed from some oil mixed in a puddle of water. He kicked at it, causing it to explode into little slivers of color in the streetlight. Then he reached into his jacket pocket and pulled two Tums antacids from a container. He almost gagged from their chalky taste, but he knew it would help the burning from his peptic ulcer.

Paul turned back to look at the body. *Jesus, she must have been beautiful. What monster could have done this?* Without taking his eyes off the body he called out, "Have the pictures been taken? Is forensics done?"

Darren McCall, dressed in a crisp uniform, was the officer who had originally responded to the phoned-in report of a dead body. He answered Paul in the affirmative. Darren was standing by the yellow police tape which isolated the area and took care of crowd control in spite of the fact there was little need for it at 3:17 A.M. Still, he was glad to do it, just so he could watch Paul Christian work. Everyone knew of Lieutenant Paul Christian and how he broke the strangler case and the murder-for-hire case. Every cop knew Paul wouldn't play the political games necessary to get ahead on the force or he would have made captain or better by now.

He was as tough as a bad steak. His superiors hated him. His co-workers liked him. Criminals feared him. But everyone respected him.

Paul called out that he wanted a full report within twelve hours, then bent to examine the body. *God, I hate stiffs!* This one was a ghastly pale blue. The eyes without a mind stared blankly out into space. There was a large incision across the neck, but there was no blood. *She was dumped here. She was killed, drained of blood, cleaned up and dumped.* And somewhere along the line her breasts had been cut off, leaving only exposed muscle, and were nowhere to be seen. *Oh, the papers are going to have a field day with this one.* He quietly belched and chewed another Tums.

He examined her wrists. There were no signs of cuts. Her arms showed no signs of tracks, but he expected that. Her body did not have the look of a drug user. It was firm, well-toned, and obviously taken care of. Just the opposite of what he usually saw with a junky who had ODed. He looked closely at her clean, shiny hair and caught a scent of perfume. Now here was a physical, tangible clue he could deal with. But he had never smelled that scent before. "McCall," he said, "would you come here for a minute?"

The words were a question but McCall knew it was an order. He walked the fifteen paces and asked the Lieutenant, "What do you need, sir?"

"There's perfume in her hair, but I don't recognize the kind it is. You're younger than me and I thought you might be up on this sort of stuff. Does it smell familiar to you?"

McCall swallowed hard. When he received the forensics lecture at the police academy he had almost passed out. But he wasn't going to let the great Paul Christian see him weak. He closed his eyes and leaned close for a smell.

The scent was thick and heady. It brought back childhood memories of processions and robes, of candles and echoing voices that he didn't understand. McCall stood up, confused. It didn't make sense. Then it clicked. He had assumed Lieutenant Christian had been correct in calling the smell a perfume. It wasn't.

"Sir," said McCall, "I don't think it's perfume."

"Oh?" questioned Paul.

"No sir. I'm pretty sure it's incense. Church incense. It must have been pretty heavy, too, for it to stay this thick in her hair."

"Thank you, McCall," he said, dismissing the young officer. The Lieutenant looked at the body and thought that evidence made it even worse. *The headline mongers will be calling this the "Church Murder."*

The van from the coroner's office arrived and two jump-suited men picked up the corpse to place it in a body bag when Paul saw a glimmer, a flash from a street light against something shiny. "Hold it!" he called to the coroner's officers.

They stopped moving the body and lowered it to the ground. Paul pulled a plastic bag from his left jacket pocket and opened it with a practiced, one-handed shake. He took a pair of tweezers from a pocket inside his jacket then leaned close to the dead woman's pubic hair. The thick patch of curly, black hair had prevented him from seeing it earlier. He grabbed the shiny object with the tweezers and slid it out of her vagina. He put it into the clear bag, but looked at it closely before giving it to an officer who would rush it to forensics.

Somebody had folded a card in half and stuffed it inside her. The card showed the image of a skeleton with a scythe, cutting every living thing in its path. Limbs of dead bodies littered the ground around the skeleton. The figure's skull had a frightening appearance, a grimace that gave the impression the skeleton was smiling. The name of the card was boldly written at the bottom: "Death."

"McCall, do you know what this card is?"

The officer came over and looked at the content of the bag. "Uh, it's a Tarot card, I think. Occultists use a pack of them."

When he moved the victim's legs to retrieve the card he saw something else. A strange design had been painted on her inner thigh. It was a bizarre mixture of circles and lines, curves and curlicues. *Calling this a "Church Murder" may have been an easy label to put on this killing,* he thought.

Paul went to his car and decided to go home. It was going to be a long day tomorrow and he wanted plenty of rest.

He crunched on two more Tums.

* * * * *

Third Day

PAUL CHRISTIAN ARRIVED for work at 1:00 P.M., four hours earlier than usual. The papers, TV and radio were already screaming about the new occult murder, even though they had little information. Every televangelist was screaming about the evils of the occult. Tabloid TV shows culled clips, photos and news bites from their archives and made inflammatory, paranoia-inducing accusations. Paul had a bad feeling about the whole thing. His cop instincts screamed this wasn't over. There were going to be more murders, more deaths. And until he could find the cause for this one there would be nothing he could do to stop it.

He went over all the paper work. The reports from the various investigative departments all listed the same sort of information. A woman, aged about twenty-three, had her throat slashed and her blood drained. The knife was of surgical quality and was probably the same knife used to remove her breasts. She had had sex with different partners during the previous twenty-four hours as indicated by DNA tests of sperm found in her vagina, anus, mouth and stomach.

There was no indication—bruises, rope marks, etc.—that she had been forced into these sexual acts, so Paul guessed she might be a prostitute. Her fingerprints were checked against known Hollywood prostitutes with no result. The fingerprint search was enlarged to include Los Angeles, Ventura, San Gabriel and Orange Counties, as well as all of nearby Nevada with its legal brothels. The results were still negative. The only clues were the Tarot card and the weird blood drawing on her thigh.

Although she had no I.D. on her, when they checked her thumbprint through the D.M.V. they discovered her name, Christy Brown, and her West Hollywood address. Meanwhile, Paul made a call to a friend who was his usual connection for occult information, and set up a time to meet him later that afternoon at the police station. Then he went to the woman's address to search her place. By the time he arrived, it had already been gone over thoroughly by the homicide team. There was no indication of a struggle. No indication of drugs. No indication of an angry boyfriend. Paul hadn't thought there would be.

There were pay stubs, however, indicating his next stop. She apparently worked in a shop called *SACRED Sites* on Sunset Blvd. Paul had never been there but he was familiar with it. It was a New Age store, the current name given to shops where you could buy occult books and paraphernalia.

Twenty minutes later he arrived at *SACRED Sites* on Sunset Boulevard. Paul had never been there but he was familiar with it. It was a New Age store, the current name given to shops where you could buy occult books and paraphernalia.

He walked in and looked at the statuaries, crystals, incenses and Tarot decks. He felt totally out of place. From behind him he heard a voice welcome him to the shop. It was the most obnoxious voice Paul had ever heard.

"You are?" asked Paul.

"My cognomen is White, Arthur White."

Paul already ran a check on the owner of the shop (and of the obnoxious voice) during a previous case. However, the case was solved (there was nothing occult about it) before he had to interview the man. White had a Doctor of Letters degree, but it had taken him almost twice as long as normal to obtain it. The reason for this, according to some of his competitors, was that although White had a wide range of knowledge and a good memory, he really wasn't very smart when it came to using it. He could understand the idea of two and the idea of addition, but when he added two and two he would somehow get five.

In person, White was a stuffy old fart in his fifties. He was graying and balding, yet his face was hardly lined. He was like a very old baby. His appearance was that of a person who was filled with egotism and a false notion of his own self-importance. Paul guessed that when speaking or writing White would always pick a bigger word than necessary. *If White had been a Catholic priest nobody would have wanted to go to him for confession. He's the type who would give out huge punishments that would far outweigh the sin.*

White had thin lips, beady eyes, an overbite and a receding chin. "How might I assuage your needs?" he requested of Paul.

Paul identified himself and verified White was indeed the owner of the shop. "Does a Ms. Christie Brown work here?"

"Well, she did. The girl didn't show up today and didn't call in. I cannot have people working for me at this establishment who do not come in when scheduled. Certainly you can understand that. The business would..."

Paul interrupted the monologue and showed a picture of the dead woman's face to the man. "Is this her?"

White took the picture and sat on a stool behind a glass counter. He shook his head and said, "Oh dear, oh dear." He kept repeating it, over and over, as if it might return life to the dead woman.

"Is that her?" Paul repeated.

"Oh, Yes. Yes, it is. Oh dear, what a terrible, irreplaceable loss. She was so young and beautiful and full of life."

"Did she have any relatives? Friends? Enemies?"

"I'm afraid I really don't know."

"Was she dating anybody who worked in the shop or who came into the shop?"

"I'm afraid I really don't have a clue. Perhaps a member of the Order knows."

"Order? Was she a member of some occult group?"

"Oh, yes. She was a new member of the "Sacred And Ceremonial Religious Ecstasy of the Divine" or SACRED. That's why this rather exemplary establishment of mine is called *SACRED Sites.* If you want to meet members, we're having a ritual that is open to the public tonight. You're welcome to be in attendance and ask questions of the members. Here, I'll give you the address. It's at the Theosophical hall on Beechwood."

As he wrote the address down, Paul said, "Look, Mr. White, don't take offense, but I have to ask you this question. Where were you last night?"

White perked up, his eyes glistening. "Oh this is marvelous! I'm to be a suspect. I'm sorry, Lieutenant, I was teaching a class on Tarot cards in the back room of this very place of business until the hour of 10:00 P.M. Then my dear wife picked me up and drove me home. We were there until about 9:00 this morning."

"Were the people in your Tarot class all members of your SACRED order?"

"Oh, no. They were all just people who wandered into the store over the past few months and decided to take the class. I can give you their names and addresses if you like. We recorded them so we could send flyers and advertisements to them later, and we also wanted to..."

"No, I don't think that will be necessary," Paul interrupted. "I don't really think you are a suspect, but I have to ask all the routine questions."

"Oh," said White, disappointedly.

"Can you tell me the meaning of a Tarot card called 'Death'?"

White's mouth opened in surprise. "I didn't get the impression you were interested in the Occult, Lieutenant. You know, the Tarot has a fascinating history. It dates back to the late 13th century and is the source for our modern-day pack of playing cards and…"

"The meaning of the card, Mr. White?"

"Oh, sorry. Sometimes I get carried away on my little tangents and drone on and on about subjects not directly relevant to the question. I don't know exactly why I do that, but…"

Paul, exasperated, interrupted again. "The card?"

"Yes," responded the shop owner. "It means 'natural evolution.' Old things die so that new things can be born. It's actually a very positive card."

"Thank you. I'll see you later tonight." As Paul left the store and walked to his car he mused over the selection of that particular card. *It wasn't very positive for Christie Brown. Hmmm. I wonder what new things are going to be born?*

* * * * *

As Paul walked into his office at the police station, the buzzer on his intercom sounded. His guest, he was told, was waiting for him. Paul told the clerk to send him in. This was quickly followed by a knock on his door. "Come on in," he said.

Dr. Alexander Gardner, his perfect, shiny white teeth gleaming from behind a perfectly trimmed goatee, entered the door. The two old friends greeted each other warmly. Gardner, a comparative religion and anthropology professor at UCLA, was in his seventies, although he looked much younger. He had silver-grey hair and was slim, but had more than a bit of a tummy paunch. He held his dark, tobacco-stained pipe in his left hand. As usual, it was unlit.

They had known each other for over a decade, although Paul hadn't seen him in a couple of years. Alexander still looked the same. The silver hair was a wild mane; and those eyebrows! *He's still wearing a sweater rather than a suit jacket or sport coat,* thought Paul. *He's probably trying to fit the archetype of the college professor. Huh. He looks a lot like my grandfather.* A newspaper article once said this world-famous author, researcher and professor looked like he might be nothing more than the "bestest storyteller in the whole wide world."

In spite of the man's grandfatherly appearance, however, Paul had a great deal of respect for Dr. Alexander Gardner's knowledge. Alexander had been a consultant to the police force on numerous crimes with occult overtones. Most of the crimes, it turned out, had nothing to do with the occult. Paul had no doubt, however, that without Gardner's help he never would have solved the murder-for-hire case. It was Gardner who had seen a link between the murders and signs of the astrological zodiac.

Paul knew that Alexander would be aware of the reason he had been summoned to the Hollywood police station. They fumbled for words for a few moments, two friends who had grown apart and didn't exactly know what to say now that they had met again. Then Alexander said, "Well, Paul, let's get down to business, shall we? I know you wouldn't have called me unless you needed my…ah…special knowledge. So can we get on with it? I have to get back to campus and finish preparing a lecture for tomorrow. It's a lecture on…"

Paul interrupted him. "Yeah, well, uh, here. Look at these photos." He passed a set of photos to Gardner. The professor pulled some glasses from his shirt pocket. They had curving springs that went around the ears, and after he fumbled them open, and slowly placed them on, one ear at a time. At first he looked at the pictures rather coldly, but as he looked at more of them Paul could see an expression of revulsion and disgust pass over the professor.

Gardner pursed his lips as he continued to look at the photos. Finally he dropped the photos onto Paul's desk, leaned back and did something Paul had never seen him do—he lit his pipe. It filled the air with the sweet and acrid scent of perique. "When…?"

"We're not exactly sure. Our coroner's best guess is last night around eleven or twelve."

"Was anything found with the body?"

"Weirdest damn thing. A card was stuck up her vagina and a strange drawing was on her left thigh. The drawing was made from her own blood."

"Come on, Paul. We've been friends for years. You wouldn't have called me unless you had a special reason. Tell me what's up."

"The card was…"

"Let me guess," said Alexander. "It was a Tarot card. Which one was it?"

"It was called 'Death'."

"Hmm. A positive card. It means positive evolutionary change."

"Yes, I know. But if it's positive, then why was it used here?"

The professor took a puff from his pipe and slowly let out a stream of bluish-grey smoke as he considered the question. "Possibly to scare someone who knows nothing about the Tarot. Someone like a police officer with no knowledge of the occult." Alexander meant nothing by the statement, but Paul bristled at what he perceived as a personal insult.

Alexander picked up the photos again and looked at them more closely. He suddenly went slack-jawed when he looked at the photo of the girl's thigh and saw the strange markings on it. He leaned back for a second, deep in thought. "Paul, let me give it to you straight. We may be in for some very diabolic trouble here, very diabolic indeed. I'll have to check in some rare books at the UCLA art library, of all places, but if what I think has happened and it has gone far enough for there to have been a ritual involving human sacrifice…"

"So you think this was some satanic cult's ritual sacrifice?"

Alexander laughed. "I've heard all about the fantasy of satanic cults running wild around the country, but that's too simple an answer. This was a ritualized murder, yes. But it has nothing to do with any satanic cult.

"Most so-called satanists are just people looking for an excuse to have an orgy of sex or drugs, or kids trying to upset their parents or society in general. They have no theology and use their ersatz satanism as a rationale for their anti-social or merely rebellious behavior." Alexander's voice became strained and he leaned forward in his chair. "But this heinous crime must have been well-planned by people who knew what they were doing. I believe that the symbol on her leg may be from a rare magical book called *The Grimoire of Armadel.* No mere dabbler in the occult would know these things. That book has only been in print twice in the last four hundred years."

"Excuse me, did you say *people?*" asked Paul. "Do you think more than one person was involved?"

"Oh, yes. And from the looks of it this may be the beginning of enough evil to make this single murder look as harmless as a mother and babe."

"Oh come on, Doc! You're a teacher at the university. You don't believe in any of this occult mumbo-jumbo, do you?"

Alexander flushed with anger, but quickly realized this attack from his friend was from someone who had little knowledge on the subject. He took a deep breath and calmed himself. "Look, Paul," he said, using his pipe as a pointer, "it really doesn't matter what I believe. The people who did this believe, and that's enough.

"But look at this from another point of view. Either the occult is real or it's not. If it's not real all you have to worry about is a terrible, brutal crime; a crime which may be repeated in the future. If any of it *is* real, however, we could be in real trouble."

"What do you mean, 'real trouble'?"

"The killers have a reason for their action. They did not kill in this particular way just for a thrill. I don't know what their goal with this murder is, but I have no reason to assume \they have completed what they set out to do. I'll check with some books in the library regarding that symbol. They may give me a better idea as to what's going on. I'll work on this from my end, you do your regular homicide work. Keep me informed and hopefully we will be able to solve this quickly."

They sat in silence for a moment. Paul considered what the professor said. Paul knew he was into this occult crap and was way over his head. He decided to ask his friend for advice. "So tell me, Alex, where do I start?"

"Well, like you said, I'm a college professor. I'm a researcher, not a practical occultist. I don't keep up with the various groups and individuals running around today. But if I were you, I think I'd start by getting information on various local occult groups over at the *Bodhi Tree*."

* * * * *

It was 5:36 P.M. according to Paul's Casio digital watch as he stood in front of the *Bodhi Tree* bookstore. An elegant, dramatic building with a large circular window in front, the bookstore stood guard at a corner on Melrose Boulevard. Paul had heard that it was one of the biggest metaphysically-oriented bookstores in America.

Paul entered through the front door and faced the three constantly ringing registers to the left and racks of magazines and incenses on the right. He saw the store housed tens of thousands of books. He asked a skinny young man with long hair and a tie-dyed tee shirt behind the register where the occult books were.

"They're all around you," beamed the young man.

"Uh, I guess I mean the ones on magic."

"Those are in the room to the left."

Paul sauntered past jewelry, Tarot cards, acupuncture aids, books on death and dying, books on drugs and a variety of biographies. He entered the back room and went past the western religion section and a case of palmistry books until he found the bookcase filled with books on magic.

He was surprised there were not more titles available. He expected row after row of books on black masses and black magic. Instead, there was a single case, eight-feet-tall and six feet wide. There were multiple copies of books on the shelves, making the total number of titles even smaller. He went past titles such as *Ceremonial Magic, The Golden Dawn, The Goetia, Real Magic, Modern Magick, The Encyclopedia of Crystal, Gem and Metal Magic, The Greater Key of Solomon, Transcendental Magic, Magic in Theory and Practice, Planetary Magic,* several histories of magic and many others.

This is not what I need. I don't have time to study old and new books on the occult. Paul returned to the main room and asked the tie-dyed kid where he could get some help. The man pointed to the rear of the central room and told Paul to go through a wide doorway, past a hallway and into a room with some computers.

When Paul made his way to the room where he could find help he discovered several people answering phones and looking up information in files and on computers. He asked for assistance. Another man with long hair (tied neatly into a ponytail), but wearing a jacket and tie, asked what he could do.

"I'm looking for information on magical groups in this area."

"Well, there are a couple of ways you can go. First, in the Wicca section look for *Circle Guide to Resources.* Then also look at the flyers in the hallway to the side of this room. You can look at the ads in some of the freebee newspapers at the front of the store, and finally you can go around the building to the used book annex and look at the flyers on the shelves at their front door."

* * * * *

When Paul returned to the station he was loaded down with flyers, books and notes. Several of the books, by some guy named Crowley, had been kept locked up in a glass case because, he was told, they were the most frequently stolen. A couple of the books now had smears on them from the chili dogs he had stopped off for at *Pink's* on the corner of Melrose and La Brea. He knew he shouldn't have eaten there, but jeez they were good! Blots of their infamous chili that had an orange-colored, oily texture marred his booty of papers. *But damn, they were good*! Still, now he was suffering and even the Tums weren't much help.

A quick look through the papers he collected showed there really wasn't much local information there. He only found five local groups that advertised, one of which was White's SACRED. He did not know how useful any of this information would be. "At least it's a start," he sighed.

* * * * *

Third Night

WHEN PAUL ARRIVED at the address on Beechwood in the Hollywood Hills he bumped into a woman leaving the site. "Are you with SACRED?" he asked.

"Goodness no! I'm a member of a different group and I'm not interested in any other orders," replied the woman. "I was just checking on this Theosophical Lodge as a possible site for our rituals. They rent out their main hall to groups such as SACRED. Oh, I'm sorry. Please pardon my rudeness. My name is Donna, Donna Fortuna."

Paul introduced himself, not saying that he was a cop. He looked at the perky woman in front of him. *She must have been a dazzler a few years ago. She might have even won a beauty contest or two.*

"This is my first time here. What can you tell me about SACRED?" he queried.

"Not much," replied the woman, "except they're all left-brained."

"Excuse me? What do you mean by that?"

"Well, I'm a a student of psychology. Psychologists believe there is a logical and an emotional side to the brain. Logic is associated with the left side of the brain and the emotions come from the right side. This is only a metaphor, of course, but it does give an understanding of the idea. Anyway, White's group is all left brain and logical. There is no emotion. To do magic you need both sides of the brain. Without the passion there is no real magical power. SACRED is missing the passion. I think that as magicians they're sorely lacking.

"Look, I'm sorry, but I have to run. Here's my card and phone number for when you get bored with SACRED. Call any time and I'll give you any information you want, including information about our group, the Silver Moonrise." With that she ran off, vanishing into the darkness.

A goofy dame, he thought, *but I may have to investigate her.*

It was 9:32 P.M. when he entered the building.

"Welcome. Enter. Join us, Lieutenant. Please come in, take off your shoes and enter...the sacred temple of SACRED!" White intoned the last phrase as if it were the most important words ever uttered.

Paul bit his lip to keep from laughing at the pomposity. Then he removed his shoes and followed another man through a small book store or library to a large room. He was shown a place to sit and instructed to wait. As he did so, he observed the room. It was overly ornate with heavy hangings and lots of furniture. There were colorful banners and pseudo-Egyptian illustrations all around. One massive photograph framed the close-up of a large, square-faced woman resting her head on her arms. She seemed to be staring at him and, surprisingly, it unnerved him. After many minutes of having a staring contest with her, a gong sounded.

Paul watched along with a sparse collection of other observers sitting around the perimeter of the lodge room as White led a procession into the hall. He had changed into a white robe covered with occult symbols in blue, green, red and gold. On his head he wore a pseudo-papal crown. He also wore three sashes with all sorts of gewgaws on them and a white cape so long it dragged on the floor. Around his neck was a heavy necklace. A bulky medallion with the image of a sphere with a cross on top of it hung from the chain. Around his waist was a thick red belt with a large tassel on one end. In front was a small square of cloth attached to the belt by strings. *Hmm. I think my uncle used to have an "apron" like that. He'd take it with him to his weekly meeting with the freemasons.*

White walked slowly, and what he must have thought was impressively, across the room. Behind him was a row of people with more silly paraphernalia, all equally robed and carrying lamps, swords, ornate wands and censers belching smoke of frankincense and sandalwood. The ritual that followed was nothing more than harmless recitations of imitation old English, using thees and thous, plus some Greek, Latin and a few other languages sprinkled around.

I may not be an occult expert, thought Paul, *but you don't have to be an expert to know that this is nothing more than a group performing mutual mental masturbation. There was no energy, no strength, no power here. Donna Fortuna was correct.*

Paul thought the whole thing was ridiculous. He almost fell asleep twice. *These people are about as dangerous as cotton candy. Maybe I can get some more information from White.* When the ritual was over, Paul queried White about *The Grimoire of Armadel.*

White looked startled. *How could this police officer, an obvious neophyte in the ways of the occult, know of that book?* "We of the SACRED do not engage in such banal work as the excrescences found in the *Armadel,*" he responded. "The SACRED does not work with that system. Any members of our lodge would be excommunicated if they worked with it."

"Where could I find some people with information on this?"

"There are only a few dabblers in the occult who would qualify, although I would suggest that you turn from this low-class pursuit and turn toward the SACRED. But if you must investigate that worthless rag of a book further, you might contact, uh, let's see now, there's the Fullons in the valley, Simon Raven in West Los Angeles, and Dr. Orlac in Hollywood. You might also try Jim Dodge of the Templars in West Hollywood, The Baron in Venice or Sylvia Scorsi in Tarzana. I think that might be just about everyone who could give you information about that book. Call *SACRED Sites* tomorrow and I'll leave you contact information for them."

When Paul finally got to his car he laughed out loud. *What a pompous idiot,* he thought. But when he called into the station the smile left his face. There had been another murder. *And almost all of those people White named are all out of my jurisdiction.*

* * * * *

It was twelve minutes after one in the morning when Paul arrived on the scene. He worked his way past a small group of onlookers and ducked under the yellow police tape surrounding the site. He came up to the body, took one look and let his shoulders drop. Too much of it was familiar. The slashed throat, the lack of blood, the ghastly blue appearance of the corpse and the heavy smell of incense in her hair. This corpse had the same symbol on her thigh as had the first corpse. He wondered if there was anything to the weird, blue appearance of the body. He had seen over one hundred corpses in his years working the homicide beat, but only two had that color. This was the second one.

Rage filled him. *I don't have the slightest clue as to what's going on. How do I stop these killings?* He turned from the scene and popped two tums into his mouth. He chewed them slowly, allowing the gritty taste to fill his mind and let him calm down. Then he turned back to the site and began his investigation.

When he finished his work he noted there were two differences between this murder and the previous one. The card inserted in her vagina showed a large structure being hit by lightning and two people falling to earth. It was called the "Tower."

Also, this woman had both of her breasts still attached to her body.

Her right arm, however, was neatly severed at the shoulder. It was gone.

Chapter Three

Fourth Night

Alan Crawford knew he was late as he took the arching overpass that let him from the Santa Monica Freeway to the San Diego Freeway. He got his Honda Civic up to seventy-seven miles per hour and almost missed the Venice Boulevard exit. Screeching across three lanes, he made the off ramp, turned up Sawtelle and made a left on Venice. The lights were a blur as he careered through the side streets. With a sigh of relief he drove up the Inglewood Boulevard hill and came to the unmarked driveway which held his goal. He turned in and parked his car next to the row of other vehicles, a silent, metallic line that reminded him of pawns on a chessboard.

Alan grabbed some clothes off the passenger seat and crunched across the gravel lot. His footfalls became silent as he trod over the neatly trimmed Dichondra lawn and went directly to the front door of the large house with the unusual cylindrical addition. When he reached the door he used the massive, antique knocker in the shape of a ram's head to signal his presence. The loud cloong! cloong! cloong! had barely stopped echoing when a small square area in the center of the door creaked opened on a squeaky hinge. He peered through the opening. Behind it, eerily illuminated from below by a single candle, was a beautiful face surrounded in black.

"Who seeks admittance through the outer portal?" came the memorized challenge.

Alan responded from memory. "A brother."

"What is thy name?"

"Outside the portals I am known as Alan Crawford."

"Be ye alone?"

"Aye."

"What is thy purpose in seeking admittance to our holy sanctuary?"

"I am answering a summons from our chief."

"And what is your cause?"

"I seek to improve my ability to be a Warrior of the Light of God, and achieve knowledge of, and conversation with, my Higher Self, my Holy Guardian Angel."

"So mote it be! Enter, brother." The opening in the door was closed and the entire door swung open on its ornate hinges. Behind the door was Eris, his inquisitor. She was dressed in a simple, hooded, black robe that belled out at the arms and skirt. "Hurry and robe yourself,"she said, no longer repeating a memorized speech. "You're the last one here and Simon is anxious to start."

Alan Crawford had grown up in a middle-class family in Chicago. He was an outstanding student and had a supportive family. His sharp mind gave him good grades, but it was also his curse. Most things soon bored him—they just weren't challenging. He became bored with almost every job he ever held. His long resume showed he hadn't held any job for more than three years

By chance, he fell into a position as a typesetter. He took the position just to help a friend out, but quickly discovered setting type for books was something he found intriguing, challenging and even exciting. He would look at a computer screen where the words and esoteric computer codes he entered merged to form a bizarre, secret language. From this glowing hodge-podge he learned to visualize what the final, printed page would look like. Soon this skill became automatic and he excelled in designing beautiful pages. He used this talent to work his way across the country. When he arrived in Southern California he was hired to set type for the *Los Angeles Express* newspaper. He managed to keep this job for the last seven of his thirty-eight years, even though the *Express* had computerized and the monitors showed how the pages would look, ending the need for his visualization abilities.

For Alan the only purpose for the job was to make enough money to pay his minimal bills. Magic and spiritual development were his true goals. Yet because he never had to struggle for anything, he was lazy and overweight. It was Simon's magical lodge, the Warriors of the Light, that really got him moving. Already he lost over 35 pounds and found a reason for being. He loved coming to lodge meetings and he loved the work. He loved the thought that he was helping himself and the world.

And he loved Eris.

Alan was too shy to tell Eris how much he loved her, but he found out all he could about her. As long as anyone could remember, she had had no name other than Eris. She claimed she had been deserted by her Romany parents when she was very small. She had been a wild child, raised by a succession of foster parents, none of whom could tame her. Now, still untamed, she was in her middle to late thirties. She was short, barely five-one, but she knew she had a great figure and liked to show it off with low-cut blouses revealing her full, rounded breasts and long skirts slit up the sides to show her curvaceous legs to her hips.

Alan thought her movements were cat-like. Her high cheekbones and deep-set, green eyes, her smooth, dark skin and reddish-black hair only added to her beauty. And her mystery.

Eris never worked but she always had money. Plenty of money. It was understood by the Warriors of the Light she should never be asked how she earned her money. Alan knew he could never give her everything she wanted or needed, so he was content to watch her and be near her. Sometimes he would sit or stand next to her in ritual. He found her sensuality to be a tangible reality, something so real and so physical that even separated by mere inches or feet it leapt across the chasm of space and affected him, aroused him, made him sweat. It produced passions within him he didn't know existed. If he wanted to he was able to focus that sexual energy toward the magic and make his ritual work more effective. When he practiced in his small temple at home, he would often recall the feelings so he could tap into that energy for his personal magical work.

Other than his job and magic, Alan had nothing. He had no hobbies and no friends outside of the Warriors. Alan was lonely. Often he would look longingly but surreptitiously at Eris and wonder if she were lonely, too.

Alan put on his robe and stood in front of a full-length mirror. *Odd,* he thought, *how if we hold the arms of the robes we wear out to the side, we look like the old Greek Tau cross.* "Let's go," said Eris, and they walked toward the lodge room located at the bottom floor of the turret. Eris threw back a heavy drape to reveal the room. About two dozen people were there, all in black robes, sitting on folding chairs in a large circle. In the center was an altar similar to the one in the magic room, four stories above. Seated to the west of the altar, facing east, was Simon. A plain red sash went from his right shoulder to his left hip over his black robe. He held a three-foot long wand in his right hand. The bottom half of the wand was black and the upper half was white. It was topped with a pointed, golden crown with inlaid gemstones just below each of the crown's five points. The sash and wand were his only signs of authority. Shadows flittered across the room. Alan thought that the dark shapes, the result of the flames surrounding the wicks on the large candles providing the only light in the temple, had a life of their own. *Is fire sentient? Does it have its own, think-*

ing existence?

Eris gave the *Warrior Salute*. She crossed her arms, right over left, touching her shoulders and slightly bowing her head. Then she straightened her arms, with her palms forward, and said, "Hail worthy chief. Our last brother has arrived." As she spoke, Alan repeated the salute and seated himself in an empty chair. "All are accounted for." Alan noticed Allenda, his frequent study partner, was seated in the northwest.

"Thank you, worthy Warrior and Guardian. Is this temple safe and secure from intruders?" asked Simon, as part of the preface to the ritual.

Eris moved back to where she and Alan had entered and swung closed a large, heavy door. It sealed with an airy "vulf" sound. Then she threw the massive bolt that locked the door.

"Aye, it is so!" she cried.

"All is as it should be. Join our circle, Warrior and Guardian, and let us begin," said Simon, in his role as the Chief of the Temple.

Eris, having completed her task, moved clockwise around the circle and took a seat. It was time for the ritual to commence.

* * * * *

Simon stood. He slowly looked around the circle, then made the Warrior Salute. He held his arms away from his body, forming a cross, the crowned wand firmly grasped in his right hand. "Welcome to all Warriors of the Light of God Welcome to this circle of love and strength. Let us be purified and consecrated with Earth, Air, Fire and Water."

Two people, a man and a woman sitting next to one another, rose from their chairs and gave the Warrior Salute. In front of them was a small table holding several items. Before the woman was a small bowl piled with salt and a stemmed goblet filled with water. She took three pinches of salt and added them to the chalice. "Behold!" she cried, "I unite Earth with Water." She stirred the brine with a leafy frond taken earlier from a fern which grew in the yard around Simon's house.

The man lit a small, circular brick of charcoal. Saltpeter mixed with the coal caused it to sputter, shoot out red sparks and burn. Everyone watched as a line of red, showing where the coal was igniting, moved languorously across the coal. Those sitting nearby caught the acrid smell of the burning disk. At the last moment, just before it would have burned his fingers, he placed it in an ornate censer. Then he added a small spoonful of frankincense tears to the glowing coal. The resulting plume of pungent smoke was visible in the candlelight as it meandered fitfully through the still air. "Behold!" he cried, "I unite Fire and Air."

Together they started around the circle in a clockwise direction. As they circled she used the frond to sprinkle the mixed salt and water she carried to outline the circle. He swung the censer as he walked, leaving a thick trail of scented smoke that wafted into the Warriors' nostrils. The smoke filled the room and dimmed the candlelight with its pungent haze.

When they completed the circle and stood in front of their seats once again, they recited a memorized speech.

"Earth," she began.

"Air," he continued.

"Water."

"Fire."

Then together they said, "With these, the four sacred elements of the universe, we have purified and consecrated both this circle and the Warriors of the Light."

"Fidelity," he began.

"Wisdom," she said.

"Honor."

"Love."

Then, again together, they said, "With these four sacred powers we unite both this circle and the Warriors of the Light. So mote it be."

As the two again made the saluting sign and sat in their chairs, the members of the circle responded by saying, "So mote it be."

Now it was Simon's turn. "Purified and consecrated, united in spirit, it is now time to banish the profane, clear away the unwanted, be it physical or immaterial. I call on Frater D.E.D.I. to perform the banishing."

Alan Crawford heard Simon call him by the initials of his magical name and froze; then he rose. When called on in the circle you do what you are told. His magical name—D.E.D.I., short for *Demon Est Deus Inversus*—meant "the devil is the reverse of God." To him it meant that the spiritual world must be looked at carefully. One could never be too sure when dealing with a non-physical entity. It was also the magical name of the great Irish poet William Butler Yeats when he had been the leader of the Victorian magical society, The Hermetic Order of the Golden Dawn.

The banishing was the same ritual Simon had performed with Allenda just a few days ago. Alan, however, did not have to face the rigors which Simon had dealt with. Still, Simon was disappointed with Alan's version of the banishing—it was mechanical and perfunctory. He made a mental note to have a discussion about this with Alan after the ritual. Simon added his own visualizations to Alan's and the sphere of blue energy grew around the group. Simon told all the Warriors to concentrate on strengthening the sphere. It grew stronger, more solid and brighter. *I wonder if the other Warriors can see it as clearly as I?*

When Simon felt that the area was secure, he explained the first purpose of the night's ritual was to teach everyone how to create bolts of magical energy. "As you will see later, we may need to learn magical defense...and warfare." The Warriors looked at each other, puzzled over Simon's comment. A barrage of whispers began, but Simon quashed it by knocking the heel of his wand against the floor with a loud rap. Immediately he had the group's attention.

Simon gave instructions for the generation of magical energy through secret techniques of breath and visualization. Then, demonstrating the method, he showed how magical energy could be sent out from the palms of the hands.

He had the Warriors practice generating the energy. Several of the Warriors who worked with Simon for a year or more were quickly able to do quite well. Others needed much more work. *I knew most of the Warriors would be able to do it. After all, our rituals are all based on creating and controlling magical energy. This is just another way of using that energy. But if thing get bad, will the have developed enough for what might come?*

Simon brought out some cardboard cutouts and everyone had fun trying to knock them over with magical energy. Simon was able to blast them over. One figure actually exploded into powder and fibers. Other Warriors could tip the figures over or move them around. Some, including Allenda, were not able to make them move at all.

Simon explained how they could imbue the energy with the powers of the magical elements of Earth, Air, Water and Fire. After a half-hour of practice Simon ended the work. All of the Warriors had exhibited some degree of success. Even Allenda, much to her surprise, had been able to push one of the cardboard targets a few feet across the floor. When it moved she burst into spontaneous giggling. Simon explained that laughter was one of the ways the body expended excess magical energy.

Alan, too, had been able to make one of the targets jump. But then, since he knew he could do it, he became bored and was unable to concentrate in order to direct the force anymore. A few people quickly showed the ability to blast the targets into shreds. Simon advised the Warriors to spend at least 30 minutes practicing the techniques each day. "They may come in handy sooner than you think."

Simon gathered the remaining targets and let the Warriors settle back in their chairs. Then he revealed the second reason for the gathering that night. To surprised gasps he told of the attack on himself and Allenda. The Warriors were held rapt as he wove the story. He paused when he finished and chatter swam around the circle. Simon struck the heel of his wand against the floor, the loud rap again grabbing the attention of those assembled. "The other purpose of tonight's ritual," he continued, "is to find out who attacked us and why. We will use the *Ritual of the Pythia* to answer these questions."

A simple grey folding chair with a thinly padded vinyl seat was set up to the east of the central, double cubic altar. Angelica Firestone—Soror Ad Astra—saluted and came forward. Angelica was barely twenty-one, but for the most part she still acted and talked like she was seventeen. She had short hair, dyed jet black, and liked to use pale make-up except for the black she used to heavily outline her eyes and the dark red for her lips. When Angelica was younger she had wanted to be a ballet dancer. But her legs grew more slowly than the rest of her and she had to settle for being a gymnast.

She never made the top rank of gymnasts, however. Although her torso was trim and muscular, it was too long. Still, she made an elegant picture of youth and had left many broken hearts in her wake. Until she found the Warriors her only purpose in life was partying The spirituality and order brought into her life by Simon's group had changed her. Still, she had a tattoo permanently placed high on the inside of her right thigh a few months ago. It was a red rose with an ornate dagger through it, dripping one drop of blood. "I don't know why I designed it. It just came to me like that," she would explain as she showed it to just about anyone who asked to see it.

Angelica stood in front of the chair, again saluted and said her ritual lines to the group: "I, Ad Astra, am Pythia to the Warriors. Tonight I use my ability to guide us all. May I see truth and speak truth. So mote it be."

As Angelica sat in the chair, the group responded to her, repeating "So mote it be." She was a natural channeler, and Simon had worked with her for many hours so she could put her abilities under her own control rather than under the control of external entities or externalized manifestations of her own subconscious.

The man who worked the incense came forward after placing a large quantity of incense on the coal. He positioned the censer so that Soror A.A.—Sister to the Stars—had the smoke slither to her face. She closed her eyes and Simon began a quiet and relaxing hypnotic induction. When her head nodded forward he asked her several times about the source of the attack. She made no response, something which worried Simon. Her clairvoyance and ability to obtain information like this had been proven in ritual time after time. Yet this time she didn't even move. She sank deeper into her chair and Simon realized that she was also sinking even deeper into the hypnotic trance. This had never happened before.

Something was wrong. Terribly wrong.

Calmly, Simon tried to wake her. He gave the appearance he knew what he was doing and understood what was occurring, but inwardly he feared he was rapidly losing control of the situation.

Finally, Angelica's head slowly started to move. With her eyes closed she started to talk. "Too late!...Hah hah hah ha!...Far too far along to stop now...Too late. Too late. No escape...All will bow...I like this one. This one will be used...I, Barra Edinnazu, am here. I, Barra Edinnazu, will be there...Hah hah hah ha!...Soon I will be again...I await. I am. I sleep. I am awake...This one will be used...Hah hah hah ha!"

The laughter peppering the strange speech was ghastly; inhuman. Some of the assembled members started to titter. This ritual had been performed many times before, but such a response never occurred.

Suddenly, Angelica jerked to her feet. "Gerastophoalalah peofenakaro teodeklarano!" Angelica was beginning to speak in tongues. Simon rose and spoke her magical name, "Ad Astra..." intending to bring her out of the trance.

"Oh-ee-pay Tay-ah-ah Pay-doh-kay! Barra Edinnazu. *Barra Edinnazu!*" she said. Simon took a step back, his mouth agape, eyes wide in surprise. The first part of Angelica's speech was in *Enochian*, a rare magical language with which, Simon knew, Angelica was totally unfamiliar. The latter part sounded familiar, but Simon couldn't place it.

Angelica burst out in perspiration and her robe stuck to her body. Alan was surprised to see that her petite, boyish figure was now full and voluptuous. He thought she must have kept her figure hidden behind baggy clothes, but then remembered she usually wore close fitting garb. She opened her eyes and leered at Simon. He realized it was no longer Angelica's consciousness within that body. Someone—*something*—had taken over her mind. He called out to her again but she laughed, stood up and started to spin around the circle.

She threw back the hood of her robe. Gasps filled the room as she revealed long, wavy, blonde hair. It was slick with perspiration, and as she swung her head drops flew off and rained on those sitting in the circle. Several people rose to stop her but she laughed and pushed them back to their chairs.

She spun on one foot like a ballet dancer in front of Alan. She stopped for a second, made a brushing motion as if being bothered by an invisible fly or gnat, and looked at him. He thought he had never seen eyes with more sensuality. "Poor Alan!" came the low, breathy voice from her throat. "So needing in love from mommy." His face colored. He felt humiliated. "So needing in love from a woman, from Barra Edinnazu!" She danced away and Alan's face fell to his chest. He felt the heat in his head, chest and face which told him that in a second he would begin to cry.

"Oh Alan…" her strange, deep voice oozed with lust as she returned to taunt him. "Is this what you want?" She grabbed her robe at the neck and pulled with both hands. The robe tore down the center revealing a voluptuous, naked, firm body. Alan was both shocked and excited by her aggressiveness, his earlier embarrassment now forgotten.

She parted and licked her lips as if getting ready to kiss him. Instead, she lunged toward him and clawed at his crotch. "Must have! Must love!" she yelled over and over. She reached under his robe until she found his penis. Alan jerked back with the touch, knocking his chair over backwards. They tumbled to the floor, like two cats fighting with one another. By the time members of the order finally got to them she had ducked her head under his robe and had his penis in her mouth, bobbing her head and making intense sucking sounds. Alan's face was a total confusion of lust, surprise and fear. Two men grabbed her and started to pull her from her feast. She bit down hard, drawing blood. Alan screamed in pain. Angelica came away laughing, a small trickle of blood running down the side of her mouth. Alan curled into a fetal ball and moaned while rolling on the floor, his face contorted in agony.

The two strong men held her while she laughed and wiped most of Alan's blood from her chin. Once again she brushed away a pesky, invisible insect. She looked at Simon and said, "You're next!" and laughed some more. The laugh ran through several octaves, as if numerous entities were fighting for control in her body. Suddenly, a swirling, icy wind flew around the room, the unearthly laughter following it along. Members jumped as the ball of air sped around the circle a few inches above the floor. A high-pitched squeal made everyone cover their ears. Then the wind stopped and where it had been a bolt of electricity shot across the room, made a small hole in a window and left the house, traveling into the night. The silence in the room was welcome, but seemed almost out of place.

"Look at Angelica!" someone shouted. The young woman's body had stiffened as if rigor mortis had set in. Her face twisted in the shadows, her muscles pulled by a sadistic animator. Those who could see well in the candlelight were sure they saw her hips shrink and breasts recede until she once again had a petite figure. Her hair withdrew into her scalp and darkened into the unnatural black color she usually wore. She blinked her eyes and looked around, imploring. Simon saw her eyes and knew that Angelica's soul had returned home.

Her eyes rolled back in their sockets and she went limp. The two men holding her laid her gently to the floor and Simon pulled her torn robe to cover her. Blood started to ooze, then poured from her mouth, nose and ears. Crimson tears flowed from her eyes and more dripped from her nose and ears. In seconds what was left of her robe and body were covered with glistening gore. A pool of scarlet formed on the floor as she hemorrhaged. Her feet started to kick wildly and several men held her down. The smell of the blood—warm and tart—quickly filled the room. It was too much for Allenda. She started to scream, "Somebody do something," repeating over and over, and crying hysterically.

Simon stood up and knocked loudly on the altar with his wand. It drew everyone's attention to him. "By the power vested in me I declare this temple banished and closed." He then knocked on the altar with his wand four times, then three times and then four times. He rarely used the *Closing by Wand,* but in an emergency such as this it was necessary. "George," he called to one of the members, "call the paramedics." For a second George just sat there, aghast at the bloody scene. Simon woke him from his torpor with a louder voice, "Call the paramedics—now!"

* * * * *

By the time the paramedics arrived the bleeding had stopped. Although she should have been weak from the loss of blood, Angelica said she felt fine. The paramedics said hemorrhaging like that was serious but frequently looked much worse than it actually was. Simon, however, insisted she go with the paramedics to the hospital. He called a friend of his, a doctor on staff at Washington Hospital, the hospital in nearby Culver City where she would be admitted, and made sure she would be kept there at least two days for observation.

By the time the paramedics left, most of the people who had been in the temple had also departed. Simon went into his den, a large room with three heavy leather chairs. Allenda went to talk with him only to discover the door to the den closed. She waited patiently until it opened from the inside. Then she silently entered, crossing paths with Alan who was leaving. Alan's head hung toward the ground, and when he looked up she could see a hangdog look on his face. He lowered his head again and quickly left the house.

Allenda looked around the den. Its walls, like the walls of many of the rooms in Simon's home, were covered with books. He sat in his favorite easy chair. It had a rocking mechanism, and he gently rocked back and forth, his eyes closed and his fingertips touching in front of his chest. He was deep in thought over tonight's events.

"I've failed you again, haven't I." Even with his eyes closed Simon recognized Allenda's voice. He slowly opened his eyes to look at her. Her body language—head down, shoulders slumped—read, "Daddy, I know I've been a bad little girl."

"You know I'd never lie to you, Alli, and I won't start now. The truth is I'm both disappointed in your failure and elated in your realization of your failure."

"E...Elated?" she asked, incredulous at his response.

"Alli, the beginning of wisdom is the realization of ignorance. A person cannot truly learn until he or she knows something is lacking. You've become aware of shortcomings in your personal and magical development. I think you don't like some things you see in yourself and would like to overcome them. So now you know the direction to head and where you need to go to get beyond those shortcomings. It's a great beginning."

"But how will I find the strength to be what you want..." Simon glared at her with anger in his eyes. "I mean," she changed her question, "how will I find the strength I need?"

Satisfied with her change, his expression changed and he responded. "In a sense, it will find you. That strength is an inner strength. You will not find it outside of yourself. And yet, you may need some exterior motivation—a kick in the butt, so to speak—to help you find that strength."

Allenda straightened up. She couldn't believe Simon not only wasn't mad at her for falling apart during the ritual, but he also saw something good in it. She kissed Simon on the forehead and started to leave. Simon stopped her, speaking to her back.

"Alli, you know you're good at it, and right now I think it's the only way to find out what's going on." A chill went down Allenda's back. She knew what he was going to ask and did not like it a bit. "We need to do the *Rite of the Sparrowhawk...*" Allenda's shoulders drooped. "And we'll need some help. Please call Eris. I want both of you here for the ritual, day after tomorrow. To work at the hour when the magical forces for this will be at their peak we'll need to start at 9:38 P.M.

Allenda didn't like performing this ritual. But if she was going to do it, she knew damn well she didn't need additional help with it, especially help from Eris. She turned and faced Simon, intending to speak her mind. Simon's eyes were hidden under furrowed brows. He was furious. "Somebody or something hurt Angelica," he said. "*Nobody* hurts my people. Angelica trusted me. I assumed this would not be a difficult session. I was wrong and she suffered. Alli, we're going to resolve this in two days. This is never going to happen to any of my students again, *never!*"

Allenda was shocked. She had never seen Simon angry, let alone furious. She had been going to try to simply escape and not let Simon see her tears—she did not want to do the ritual with Eris—but instead she mumbled "Okay." A barrage of emotions flooded her and she realized she didn't know what she wanted to do. Finally, she just quietly left.

* * * * *

Later That Night

"WHY DIDN'T YOU TELL ME what would happen, Mother?"

"Would it have made a difference, my son?"

"Of course it would." Simon stamped an angry circle in the sand. The Moon had already set and he could feel his feet more than he could see them. He did not want to yell at Mother and needed to calm himself before responding. "I could have been more careful, I could have performed more banishings, set up more..."

"It would not have done any good, my Son. The forces in play here are far more than you can even guess."

"Then tell me what's happening, Mother! Help me. I have to know."

Simon was answered by silence. "Mother," he said quietly, "one of my students—one of your daughters—was hurt. It must not get worse. Tell me what is happening so at least I can be prepared."

Again, there was only silence. "Why can't you help me? Talk to me. Tell me what I need to know."

As the waves flowed in and out he heard a long sigh. *"I told you, my son, that your participation in this has only just begun. I have been fighting for a long time."* There was a long pause and Simon realized her usually robust voice seemed weak, tired and fragile. *"I have almost lost."*

"What?" Simon was aghast. "I thought you were..."

"...all powerful? No, my son, I am not. My strength is as the Earth itself, but if you lose the battle which is to come everything will be lost. Even my personality will be no more."

Stunned, Simon said nothing. Death loomed around him and he could see no way to avoid it. When he looked up his eyes glistened with tears. "I have fought many magical battles. I know what losses feel like. I know the elation of victory. The one thing I am sure of, Mother, is that the Warriors do not yet have the training. They are not ready for any strong magical battle. To take them into battle would turn them into cannon fodder. They will all die."

"There is more at stake here than you can possibly realize. If one or more die, it will be a small price for the lives and safety of so many others. You are willing to die for the Light. Do not underestimate my children whom I allow you to teach. And do not underestimate what they can do when they need to."

"There has been too much death in my life, Mother. I want no more. Can't I get out of this?"

The sound of the waves was all he could hear. Simon's shoulders slumped as he knew he must accept what was to come. "What can I do, Mother. What can I do?"

"Be a warrior, my son. Be a warrior."

* * * * *

It had been Allenda's habit to go to the Denny's restaurant on Santa Monica Boulevard and have a cheeseburger and fries after rituals. Tonight was no different. But when the food came she didn't feel like eating. Instead, she simply stared at it. Her mind was racing. *Who—or what—has been attacking us? Why were we being attacked?* Her mind ran through all of the books she had read, but she could think of no answer to the puzzle. Why had Simon let me see him so angry? *I know he is just a man and must have been angered in the past, but I never saw him that way before.*

As she considered the events of the night she lost track of the time. In the middle of her musings she looked at her plate. All she had done was push the food around. The fries were all over the table, leaving greasy snail trails from the paper-lined basket in which they had been served. It looked grotesque to her and very unappetizing. Allenda just left everything where it was, put a ten-dollar bill on the table and left.

* * * * *

It was ten-thirty in the morning when Allenda called Eris. Eris sounded sleepy and Allenda had a feeling she might have wakened her. *Good!* thought Allenda.

"Eris, this is Alli. Simon told me to call you. He wants you to join him tomorrow night to perform the Rite of the Sparrowhawk. Be there so you can start the rite at 9:38."

"So," Eris yawned like a stretching cat, "Simon *needs* me." She knew Allenda had possessive feelings about Simon and her teasing would get Alli's goat. She didn't know why she did it, but she liked the angry, little-girl reactions she got when she teased Allenda by flaunting her own open sexuality.

"Actually, he needs *us*," Allenda responded, not hiding her jealousy very well.

"Simon, Alli and me. Oh this will be fun," cooed the awakening woman.

"No, it will be a ritual. Rituals should be enjoyed, but they all should have your utmost effort put into them. When it comes to the practice of rituals there should be no difference between this ritual and any of the other ones we do."

"Right." Eris dragged out the word so even though it sounded like she was agreeing with Allenda, she was actually mocking her. Eris paused until the silence became awkward. Then she laughed. "Well, we'll see about that, Alli. By the way, you might like to know I've looked forward to working this ritual with you. And Alli, I promise to give it my 'utmost effort'." Eris laughed again. Her laugh dripped with sarcasm because she knew of Allenda's timidity when it came to this type of ritual.

"Goodbye, Eris," said Allenda, hanging up the phone, not waiting for a response. She realized her cheeks were flushed.

Damn her. Damn her for insulting me. Damn her for knowing me. And damn me for being so closed to life. She threw herself onto her bed and cried for awhile. *Okay, it's a new experience. From now on I'm going to welcome new challenges and experiences. And Eris is not going to get the best of me again with anything she does or says. Starting today, Allenda Henley is a new woman.*

Allenda went into the bathroom and washed her face. She began to reapply her usual layers of makeup when she began to cry again. This time it was a different type of crying, with enormous sobs coming from deep inside her, releasing long-held pains, disappointments and angers. *This isn't going to be as easy as I thought.*

Then she started to laugh.

Chapter Four

Fourth Night; Fifth Morning

HE KNEW ALL THE NAMES his group, the *Barony*, had for him: Baron Blood, Baron Cock, Baron Gore, Baron Lust, Baron Fire, Baron Sex, Baron Fury, Baron Tongue, Baron Pain, Baron All Night, Baron de Sade and Baron Nine Inch. They came up with new ones all the time as a result of their fear and awe of him. He learned of them quickly even though to his face, they only called him "The Baron." He told people his Christian name was Baron and he simply wanted to be known by his first name. That was untrue, of course, but they seemed to accept it.

The chair where he sat was huge and solid, heavily padded and covered in black velvet. It had a back that rose two feet above the Baron's head. The Baron was six-foot-four and weighed close to three hundred-thirty pounds. He had wide shoulders and stocky legs. He wasn't fat, he was just big, like a football lineman. His exercise regime made him enormously strong. He would be good competition for any power lifter. In contradiction to his bulk, he had sharp facial features that gave him a handsome but cruel look. His eyes were deep set under bushy brows, and although he had perfect, twenty–twenty vision, he wore a black patch over his left eye. In the center of the patch was a small, diamond-shaped ruby.

For many years it bothered him that he didn't look like British rock star David Bowie—thin, ethereal, almost feminine. When he finally took the time to consider why it upset him, he realized the media had implied the skinny British rock star look was what women wanted—and the Baron wanted women, lots of women.

He learned, however, that a large number of women did not like the scrawny look. Many women wanted—even preferred—a powerful man. His bulk had never prevented him from finding women who wanted to have sex with him. Indeed, many told him they liked the feeling of his size on them…and in them. They liked the feeling of being totally possessed, of having their entire body rocked with each of his powerful thrusts, something a small-bodied man could never do.

It wasn't just his size that made women want him, it was his power. His years of magical practice enabled him to establish a persona of a secret, hidden power. His walk, his talk, his very presence exuded power, but it was a power that was cold and cynical.

Many tried to win him over only to fall under his control. It wasn't that he had magical powers over others, it was that they gave their power—their free will and autonomy—to him. They wanted, needed, to be a small part of a greater power. They saw that greater power in him and he did nothing to stop their belief. He simply used what he was given and took what he could, not caring about the result.

If anything, the Baron was ostentatious. His followers supported him nicely, allowing him his worldly pleasures. The Baron liked the finest foods, wines and drugs. He liked clothes, but one couldn't easily find the latest fashions in his size. He had several tailors who kept his measurements on file. As a result, he always wore the newest styles which, although proper and in fashion, didn't always look good on his large, craggy figure.

Sometimes he still felt pangs of wanting to look like the media's idea man, but then he became involved in something and the pangs would pass. Usually, the "something" he got involved with was either sex or magic. Or both. Tonight it was sex and planning for the ultimate ritual of his magical career. It was after two in the morning as he looked over the large, high-ceilinged room from the comfort of his throne. This was both his public magical den and private orgy room. The room was filled with large cushions. Men and women in various states of undress and copulating postures sprawled everywhere. Many were asleep from exhaustion as the orgy began at seven that evening. He recognized three women, asleep in a puppy pile, who he already used that night.

The Baron was interrupted in his thoughts by a woman standing in front of him. She was young and tall. Her large breasts, out of proportion to her small, flat stomach, heaved as she breathed. *Do I know this woman?* She was covered by a thin glow of perspiration. A long, sheer, unbuttoned blouse stuck to her in various places and revealed far more than it hid. Her pale red hair was darkened by sweat. It was evident from the totally wanton look in her eyes that her passion had been stirred but left unfulfilled.

He nodded slightly, giving her permission to approach. Nostrils flaring, mouth open in arousal, she looked at his face as she neared, then ducked her head under his striped, multicolored robe—called the orgy robe by his followers. He soon felt the soothing warmth of her mouth on him. He sank back a bit in his chair, giving her easier access to him. She threw the bottom of the robe over his waist so he could watch her work. Soon, she needed both hands and her mouth to encompass him. Her eyes grew large as saucers when she saw what she had created.

As she worked on him, the Baron thought about why he must complete the ritual he was in the midst of creating. *There was no "New World Order." Countries "liberated" from spirit-stifling totalitarianism now suffered from internecine battles over territory, religion, or power. There was no great world-wide peace. Wars raged around the globe. In many countries crime was rampant. The husks of drug abusers littered streets and prisons. Suicide was pandemic because people looked at the future and saw there was no future, only a bleak, dark sunset leading to poverty, disease and death. The world would soon be overpopulated, over-polluted and overtaxed. My grand ritual will resolve all of this. No more war, crime, poverty. The resurrection to come will make everyone forget the resurrection of the gentle rabbi.*

As the woman continued to work on him, the Baron went into a semi-trance, visualizing every step of the preparation and ritual that would occur. He saw how everything he had done for the past three years had led to this moment. *I will continue to search everywhere, from the lowest dives on the physical plane to invading the highest realms of the astral, from the camps of mine enemies to the depths of dreams in order to manifest this magical opus.* He carried this into the future, looking at each step that would occur today, tomorrow, and all the way up to the inevitable conclusion. *The stronger I visualize what will happen the more I am sure it will happen. This is the way of magic. Aum.*

Sensing she had lost his attention, the woman released him from her mouth, turned so that her back was to him, and sat on him, impaling herself with a gasp—she had never felt such size within her. She reached behind, grabbed his hands and brought them to her breasts. She pressed his hands, encouraging him to squeeze harder as she moved up and down.

Even the intense physical pleasure could not separate the Baron from his visualizations. The completed steps and those yet to be, became clearer and clearer in his mind. Suddenly, he saw the image of Simon Raven, arms akimbo, fire shooting from his chest and eyes. Simon stood between Baron and the goal of world peace and prosperity. Simon was blocking him just as he had years ago. The Baron felt his blood rise and he roared in anger. He stood, still impaling his sex partner. The woman, striving for her own release, shrieked in surprise. He turned around, trapping the woman between him and the chair. The moans which she had been emitting turned to small cries of pain as he powered into her again and again. Now she used her fingers to try and pry his powerful hands from the pain they were inflicting on her breasts.

He was oblivious to the woman's pain. All he could see before him was Simon's face. The rage rose in him like a seething fire and he exploded with a scream. He threw the woman from the chair, sat in it and stared into the distance. "This time you'll lose, Raven. This time you'll lose." There was silence in the room as the people who were awake stared at their leader. Then they quickly turned away and returned to what they had been doing before the Baron exploded in anger. The Barony was used to their leader's sudden outbursts and the painful result if you paid too close attention to them.

The woman he had just abused moaned and cried softly on the floor, crawling to get away from the Baron. Her breasts were covered with forming bruises and bloody traces from fingernails which had bit into tender flesh. Her buttocks, too, was sore from the pounding. A slight trickle of blood came from between her legs, where he had ravaged her.

The Baron ignored her.

* * * * *

Fifth Day

FOR THE PAST TWO DAYS Paul investigated a simple murder that was the result of a lover's quarrel. A jilted suitor came forward and confessed to the crime. *They should all be so simple.* Paul sighed. He knew this occult case wasn't going to be that way. It was after three-thirty in the afternoon when Paul parked his police assigned Ford near The Magic Box, the shop owned by the Fullons. As usual, traffic out to the Valley on the 101 freeway was terrible. With the cost-cutting measures in the department he wasn't allowed to turn on the air conditioner, so he had sat in bumper-to-bumper, smelling the exhaust and smog while trying to ignore his own sweat. *I perspire like anyone else, yet people have always told me my perspi-*

ration doesn't smell. I wonder why that is? Natural lack of odor? The copious amounts of aluminum-laced antiperspirant I use? Paul laughed out loud at the flowery language—he usually called deodorants "pit-stop." *I don't know, but I'm glad for it.* Yet today he could smell himself. The air was brown from being unclean. News reports already talked about thousands of hospitalizations and hundreds of deaths due to the killer smog. Authorities claimed they were doing everything in their power to stop it. Yeah. Right.

But there was more than just smog in the air. Mixed with the unusual humidity it seemed like everything smelled as if coated with an arcane evil. Paul gave up wondering about the cause of his odor when he took the freeway exit.

Actually, Paul drove past *The Magic Box* twice. He thought it was going to be a grandiose edifice, so he didn't look too closely as he drove down Ventura Boulevard. Another reason he missed the address both times, was that his attention was drawn to the majesty of the nearby mountains—the bright swatches of colors, deep shadows and tremendous feeling of size projected through the sickly, yellow-brown air.

The Magic Box was a small building that looked octagonal from the front. The outside was painted glossy black, on top of which were various symbols in white, silver and gold. It reminded Paul of some of L.A.'s unique kitsch architecture from more than half-a-century earlier. As he walked to the store he saw the paint was old and flaking. A feeling of decay, demoralization and death hung over *The Magic Box.* Paul was reminded of a bug wrapped in a spider's web and held for later consumption. *Maybe I'm on to something here and this case can be closed quickly.* He reached into his pocket and brought out a couple of Tums, popped them into his mouth, crunched them into a paste, then swallowed. *Close this case quickly? Fat chance.*

An electric eye triggered an annoyingly brittle-sounding buzzer as he entered the world of the Fullons. The room he entered was dark, dusty and dirty. He didn't like the feel of it. There were bookshelves on the wall, but the books for sale appeared used, shop worn and beat up. He looked at a few and saw nothing different from those at the *Bodhi Tree*. He did notice, however, that the prices of the books all had stickers over them with higher prices marked by hand on the small, white rectangles.

There were a few glass display cases filled with overpriced, cheaply-made rings and necklaces, wands and daggers, statues and games and other occult bric-a-brac. *Maybe I* am *close.*When his eyes finally adjusted to the dim light, his heart jumped. Painted on each of four of the walls was a large symbol. Although similar, each symbol was obviously different from the others. They looked like the curves and lines which had been painted on the thighs of the murder victims. As Paul fumbled in his pocket to get a copy of the blood-drawn shapes to compare with those on the walls, he heard the shuffling of feet. Angus Fullon entered through a sixties-style hippie bead curtain that hung over a doorway near the back of the shop.

Angus was a huge man. He was just over six feet tall and weighed close to five hundred pounds, maybe more. All of his weight was fat, too. Paul thought that the poor guy probably never did an exercise in his life. Angus breathed heavily and loudly through his mouth. The exertion of walking from the back room to the front had caused him to break out in beads of sweat across his forehead.

Angus took out a handkerchief and wiped his face while looking Paul over. "Can I help you?" asked Angus. Not recognizing the customer, Angus spoke with boredom in his voice.

"Yes," replied Paul. In discussing the case with his commanding officer, Captain Minelli, they decided that if Paul wanted to, he could try another tact. From books his superior read they created a scenario for Paul to try, if and when he thought it appropriate. Paul put it into play now. "You see, six months ago I had a heart attack. I was dead for seven minutes. Obviously, the doctors were able to revive me. But the experience..."

"Did you experience the feeling of going through a tunnel toward a light and being greeted by an angelic being?" asked the interested Angus.

"You know about it?" asked Paul with feigned shock and excitement. Angus smiled and nodded. "Well, that experience changed me," Paul continued. "I quit my job because it seemed so unimportant. Now I want to, *I must*, explore the greater reality.

"I tried some forms of meditation, but it wasn't enough. As I read books I knew I needed to be more active, and that meant the ability to change the greater world and my personal world. Somebody told me I was talking about magic, so here I am."

One of the things Angus prided himself on was his skill as a salesman. He sensed a killing, one that would pay cash. "You picked the right place. I've spent the last twenty years of my life teaching magic. Before that I was a computer programmer for the government. We created a series of books especially designed for people such as yourself, people who want to avoid the traps and errors of *all* the other books and learn real magic."

Angus looked under the counter and made some shuffling sounds, but didn't find what he was looking for. "Honey," he called out, "Have you seen any copies of *How to...?*"

"They're out there," came a high-pitched female voice from the back, followed by the slight clicking sound of shoes on a hard floor. A tall but thin woman came though the bead curtain. She was not as tall as Angus and was his exact opposite.

At first Paul thought she looked elegant. Now, seeing her more clearly, he thought she was cadaverous, reminding Paul of pictures showing the victims of Hitler's concentration camps. Paul swallowed and wondered how they ever became a couple. She, like Angus, did not appear very healthy and had to quickly sit down. The exertion of the short distance she walked obviously exhausted her.

She pointed to a wooden stool with a pile of photocopies on it. "Look over on the stool, dear."

Angus saw what he was looking for, thanked the woman, and took the top set of photocopies off the stool. He handed it to Paul. The cheaply bound "book" had a color photocopy for a cover. On the cover was a picture of Angus and the woman in ceremonial garb. The manuscript was titled, *How to Make Magic*, and subtitled, *The Ultimate Beginner's Guide to White Magic*. The photocopied pages were printed on only one side ofeach page, and had obviously been created on a poor quality typewriter. The authors were listed as the Reverend Doctor Angus Fullon and the Reverend Doctor Lisa Fullon. Both had a list of letters after their names, showing their alleged credentials. Paul recognized none of the supposed degrees. The book had one hundred ninety-four pages including eleven pages in the back, consisting of advertisements for other books by the Fullons. The price of *How to Make Magic* was forty-nine dollars and ninety-five cents.

"Listen," said Paul. "I'm not so sure I can learn from a book. Do you have classes or know somebody who teaches magic? I'll pay for it, of course."

Lisa Fullon looked at Angus, who returned the glance. Paul didn't know if they were merely hungry for his money or sizing him up to see if they would be willing to teach him. Finally, Angus said, "We do teach magic to a few people on a limited basis. Come in the back and let me show you where we work."

Angus led Paul through the bead curtain. They were followed by Lisa. The trio went through a short hallway. The door to a bathroom was open on one side of the hall. It looked as if that room had not been cleaned in some time. On the other side of the hall was a doorway marked with poorly drawn letters, "PRIVATE, DO NOT ENTER." Angus remarked that this was the door to his and his wife's living quarters. At the end of the hallway was a room just slightly smaller than the entire shop. It was not crowded with books and occult *frou-frou*, however, so it seemed much larger. The ceiling was high, and the walls were painted black. Florescent fixtures with black light bulbs illuminated the room with a purplish glow. For a second,

Paul thought he had stepped back into a "head shop" from the psychedelic sixties. The overpowering scent of a cheap incense made him want to cough.

"This is our Sanctuary of the Power of Justice," intoned Angus, majestically.

"Why 'Justice'?" asked Paul.

"Twenty years ago I was a partner with another person who claimed to be a magician. He lied about me, and cheated me out of a great deal of money. He has done the same to many others since then. I want the truth to come out and justice to prevail. My wife and I started this Sanctuary of the Power of Justice for just that purpose. Some day I will be successful."

Paul thought Angus Fullon gave new meaning to the terms fixated, anal and obsessed. He decided to get out as quickly as possible. "When I was…dead…I was shown a symbol by an angelic figure. After I came back I started to draw it everywhere." Paul pulled the paper with the symbol from the murders from his pocket and gave it to Angus. "Can you tell me what it is?"

Angus looked at the paper and Paul immediately saw the look in Angus' eyes showed no recognition. "There are many symbols used in magic," said Angus, "and this one can be powerful as your personal symbol. In the classes we teach, you will learn how to make many symbols and how to use any of them. You will learn the mysteries of astral travel, talismans, the Kabalah and much more. You will learn…"

Paul listened to Angus talk, but realized this was just crap. When Angus finished his pitch Paul said, "I'm game. When does the first class begin?"

"One week from next Monday," replied Angus.

"Good, I'll be there." Paul left the room and called out as he went through the bead curtain, "See you then. Goodbye."

Angus and Lisa stayed in the Sanctuary until they heard the buzzer followed by the sound of the door opening and closing, indicating Paul had left. The two looked at each other. Angus felt sad. He knew many people believed fat or sickly people were dumb. Neither he nor his wife were stupid. They knew Paul would not return. Although Angus enjoyed the thrill of closing a sale, he and his wife didn't really need Paul's money—Angus' investments over the years had made them rich—but they didn't like their visitor's attitude. "Let's go out to the front and I'll rub your shoulders," Angus said to his wife. As they walked down the hall Angus wondered if Paul was sent by Damon, his foe for the past two decades. He decided no and started thinking about what spells he could do to finally teach Damon a well-deserved lesson.

Damon had long since left the practice of magic and was now the owner of a fan and air conditioner shop in Claremont, a small city on the far-eastern edge of Los Angeles county, near Big Bear mountain. Claremont's claim to fame was its high-quality, small colleges. Damon was unaware of Angus' machinations against him. He hadn't thought about the Fullons since they fought out a lawsuit fifteen years ago. Now all he worried about was getting the compressor he was working on fixed and how he was going to dodge the laws regarding the release of freon into the atmosphere so he could recharge older air conditioning compressors. *Hell, people like to be cool.*

* * * * *

It was after five when Paul parked in the red zone in front of the Hollywood house painted entirely indigo blue. Paul had read up on "Dr. Orlac." His birth name was Hans Stringmeier. He had never been convicted of a crime or even arrested, although he was accused of many foul, illegal and immoral deeds. Stringmeier had worked in a barrage of odd jobs, from carnival barker to gourmet chef, from photographer to tabloid reporter. He also spent some time working as a projectionist at a silent movie theater on Fairfax Boulevard where he learned to love the old films

Closed since the owner was murdered. Hmm. Well, with a location in Hollywood, it figures. Stringmeier legally changed his name to "Dr. Valdemar Orlac," a name based on characters from old horror movies.

Along the way he met the dregs of humanity and learned that when Barnum said there was a sucker born every minute, he was being an optimist. He spent five years in the army's "black operations" division, also called "black-ops" or "psy-ops." This was the section using psychology and terror to help defeat enemies. Now, as Dr. Orlac, he developed a philosophy based on Nietzsche, Bentham, Darwin and the life of a carny. This he mixed with some superficial occultism including rituals culled from old movies and books. He made a living off of this by writing books and selling memberships in his Temple. In order to offend as many bourgeois, middle-class people as possible, Orlac called this money-making hodgepodge "Satanism."

According to what Paul read, House Indigo, as it was popularly known, had originally served as a school for movie children. Young actors and actresses lived there, went to school there and learned everything from English to dance, from math to singing. Supposedly, Mickey, Judy, Cagney and several of the Our Gang kids had lived there. Besides over thirty rooms there was also a pool and a small amphitheater.

Paul chewed on some more Tums and walked up the spotless walk to the front door. He was struck by the ordinariness of the house. True, it was large and indigo, but other than that it was just another house on a Hollywood side street.

Yet, there was something odd about the whole thing. Maybe it was just the idea of Satanism. Like many people, Paul had been brought up a Christian and the very notion of Satanism made his skin crawl. There was something...something *evil*...that surrounded the entire idea. Orlac may not have committed any crimes, but just the concept of Satanism made Paul think of tales of Black Masses and human sacrifices.

He shivered at the door, wondering what he would see beyond the portal. *Perhaps his evil reputation was Orlac's own idea. He has no powers. I know he doesn't even believe in an entity known as Satan. Is his choice of calling his philosophy "Satanism" just an attempt to intimidate?*

Paul brought his thoughts back to the matter at hand. At the door there was a button above a speaker. He took another antacid, rang the bell and waited for a response. He looked up and saw a sign painted in dripping, blood-red letters: "Abandon all hope, ye who enter here." Paul didn't know if the reference to Dante was a joke or if Orlac was serious. He decided to be more direct rather than giving an undercover story.

"Hagln. Cnah doshumth inkfryu?" The voice, with its incomprehensible words, peeped out from the intercom's cheap speaker.

"I'm sorry," replied Paul, wondering what language the voice had spoken. "I didn't understand what you said."

"Hello. Can I do something for you?" the voice repeated.

"I'm Lieutenant Paul Christian with the Hollywood police department and I'd like to ask you some questions." There was silence, then the door quietly swung open. "Are you Dr. Orlac?" Paul asked.

The man standing in front of him was short and strongly built. Black, deep-set eyes glared at Paul from beneath heavy, dark eyebrows and a forehead tracked with deep, horizontal lines. He had short hair, also black, and wore jeans and a loose, flowing shirt. "No, my name is del Florio, Miguel del Florio," he answered. " I'm Dr. Orlac's assistant. How can I help you?"

"I'd like to ask Dr. Orlac some questions," Paul said, displaying his badge.

"Well, Miguel, don't let the Lieutenant stand out there, invite him in." The voice came from behind del Florio. "Please come in, sir. I am Dr. Orlac."

This man was different from del Florio in appearance. Tall and lean, he had a shaven head and odd, pointed eyebrows. He wore neatly pressed trousers, a patterned silk shirt open at the neck and a tailored jacket. Unlike del Florio's glare, this man's triangular face had a quick smile. Yet there was something disconcerting about his white-toothed grin. Something distasteful and hidden.

"Thank you, Dr. Orlac. As I told Mr. del Florio, my name is Christian and I am a detective with the Hollywood police." Both del Florio and Orlac had grimaced at the sounding of his name, but Paul ignored it. "The reason I'm here is because there have been some murders with occult overtones and I..."

"Damn you!" shouted del Florio, his dark features taking on a reddish hue. "Damn you! Sure, a murder takes place, some idiot finds a scribble or a scratch and claims it has to do with the occult, and the first thing anybody does is blame it on us Satanists. We're easy targets. We do nothing and still you accuse us of all sorts of inhuman crimes. Maybe we *should* go out and..."

Orlac's expression, a gentle smile Paul thought might hide a great deal of emotion, did not change during del Florio's outburst. He placed his hand on del Florio's shoulder and quietly called him by name, "Miguel..." Del Florio paled and stopped in mid-sentence. He looked from one of the men to the other, then turned and walked away. "Please excuse Miguel," Orlac said. "He's young and quick to anger. Let me show you my home. I have nothing to hide. Later you may ask any questions you like."

As they traveled through the house, Orlac opened the door to every room they passed, from broom closet to master bedroom. Although Paul did not comment on it, he realized that as they moved, Orlac took control of the conversation with a quick monologue.

"Lieutenant, I know you must have a file on me as thick as your arm. I'm sure you read it before driving here."

Paul smiled in acknowledgement.

"You know, then, that I have never been arrested or convicted of any crime," Orlac continued. "It's interesting. I have been accused of many rather nasty, not to say illegal, actions, but my accusers are always from another religion. They try to use the law to root out my 'heresy' although they have no proof I've committed any crime. Miguel del Florio lost his job with a large computer firm not because he did a poor job but because coworkers complained that he was a Satanist. The stress they put on him, along with the loss of finances, ruined his marriage. I hope you can at least understand his anger at those who falsely accuse us of crimes. He's suing his previous employer now. I hope you can see why he was so upset. He's a fine person, a hard-working member of the Temple Of Satan, the TOS, and has become my second-in-command."

They turned a corner and came to a section of a wall that that was unpainted. "What happened here?" Paul asked.

"Ah, that's the mystery wall. It is said this house is haunted. I've never seen any spooks, but we do have this one, odd, phenomenon. Do you see the list of names written on the wall?"

Paul peered at the unpainted area until he could just make out where some names had been printed with a pencil. He nodded that he could see the names.

"The names are supposedly those of children who died in this house. I have tried to erase them and paint over them, but they keep coming back. I even removed the section of wood the names are written on and put in a new piece of wood. The names appeared on the new piece. I have now given up and simply let their names stay."

Paul tilted his head and slightly smiled at the obviously bogus story.

Orlac smiled, then laughed. "Okay," Orlac said, "*you* get rid of the names."

A can of black spray paint was near the area and Paul went over to it, picked it up and shook it as he returned to the spot. He held up the can and his host signalled him to go ahead.

"That's why we keep that can of paint there," Orlac told him. Paul sprayed over the names several times until they were covered with paint. "Now, Lieutenant, while we wait for the paint to dry, ask your questions."

"Have you ever seen this symbol?" Paul asked, pulling the paper out of his pocket.

Orlac took the paper. "It looks familiar," he said, cocking his head to look at it from different angles. "Perhaps it's from one of the *Keys of Solomon* or the *Armadel?* It could be from the *Black Pullet* or even *Abramelin.* Frankly, I don't know. We at the TOS have our own systems and books."

"Do you know anybody who would commit ritual sacrifices?"

Orlac sighed and looked down at the oriental carpet on the floor. "Look," he said, "people who are atheists or members of churches, mosques or synagogues commit murders. People who never graduate from high school and people who hold multiple degrees commit murders. Today my group, the Temple Of Satan, is almost completely run through the mails. Could somebody who is a member be a murderer? Possibly, but Hollywood and L.A. police keep an eye on us as do the FBI, the ICC, the Postmaster General and probably INTERPOL and the CIA! If any of our members commits a crime associated with the occult they are immediately expelled from the Temple.

"But to directly answer your question, the only person or groups I know of that commit ritual sacrifices are governments. They call it war. They call it execution. They call it abortion. They also create environments that stifle individual creativity so for all intents and purposes they create societies of the living dead."

Paul's eyes narrowed. "I don't have time for word games and philosophy. Do you or do you not know anyone capable of performing a ritual human sacrifice?"

Orlac shook his head and laughed. "Okay, Lieutenant. No philosophy. No word games. How about psychology? How about the good Germans who were turned into torturers during World War II? How about the medical doctors who, instead of healing and saving lives became sadists in the concentration camps? How about people who turn into riotous mobs? How about the Spanish Inquisition? How about the games at the Roman

Coliseum? 'We who are about to die salute you, Caesar!' The crowds may watch as we turn into animals and kill each other.

"So, lieutenant, you ask if I know anybody who *could* perform a human sacrifice? Yes, I do. Everybody. Anybody. Even you carry a gun, don't you? But do I personally know anybody, Satanist or otherwise, who *would* perform such a sacrifice? Not that I am aware of."

Paul looked at Orlac for some time. He detested word games and people who tried to hide the obvious behind language. Paul no longer saw Orlac as being intimidating. He was only a suspect, one who thought he was clever. Finally he calmed himself enough to ask the next question. "Dr. Orlac, I hope you understand I have to ask you the following question. Where were you over the past three days?"

Orlac smiled, but his face looked like a sneer. *Why am I even wasting my time with this lowbrow simpleton?* "I'm afraid you'll have to look elsewhere for suspects, Lieutenant. Miguel and I just got back this morning from two weeks in Germany. We can produce our passports and airline ticket stubs if you so desire."

"No, that won't be..." Paul stopped in mid-sentence. He looked at the area of the wall he sprayed with black paint. As the paint dried it faded in color. The penciled names reappeared. Paul looked at Orlac then back at the wall. Orlac laughed at the puzzled look on Paul's face. "Uh...no, that won't be necessary at this time," Paul finished. *I can check it through official sources.*

Orlac continued to show off his house. In one set of rooms there were tens of thousands of dollars in computers, printers and mailing equipment. People were using them, and Paul noticed there was a variety of letterheads and return addresses. *Lots of mail order outfits have numerous names and addresses. There's nothing wrong with that. Still, I may have to make a more in-depth check on Orlac and del Florio later.*

By the time Paul and Orlac worked their way back to the front door, the main room had a dozen people beside del Florio. Orlac's eyes' narrowed. *Damn! I didn't want the police to know about these others.* "Uh, we're having a closed meeting tonight. Uh, if you like you can come back to one of our public black ma…, er, rituals."

"I may do that in the future," Paul said as he left without saying goodbye. Paul walked to his car across the neatly tailored lawn and thought about the strange ending to their meeting. At the sidewalk he turned and stared at the house which now looked imposing to him and actually felt hostile. *Hmm. When Orlac saw the people his voice suddenly became disturbed and nervous, just the opposite of what it had been. There's more to what Orlac is doing than just some weird Satanic ritual. I'll have to find out what. And how does it apply to this case?* Does *it apply to this case? Is it just my imagination? There's no direct line in this case to Orlac, at least not yet, but if I don't get some more leads I think I'll check on him some more.* He sat in his car, shook his head, belched quietly and popped two more Tums.

Chapter Five

Fifth Day, Late Afternoon

Simon slumped in his chair and drummed the fingers of his right hand on the chair's wooden arm. He knew he needed to rest from the ritual of last night and to prepare for the exertion of tomorrow night's ritual with Alli and Eris, but it was hard to do nothing, so hard.

After he arose this morning he performed his daily rituals. He also restrengthened his protective magical wards and set up some special "surprises" for any physical invaders. Then he exercised, showered and dressed. He tried reading some kabalistic theory but couldn't concentrate. He tried to read some Anne Rice, but quickly became bored and put it aside. He tried the TV, but on 50 cable channels all he could find was game shows, soap operas, infomercials and sitcom reruns that were bad the first time they were on. He flipped the remote control several times just to see what he might land on.

Simon ended up with an infomercial on cooking with an overpriced, low-quality, Chinese wok and realized that he was hungry. He went to the kitchen, pulled his own wok out of a cabinet and cooked up a light lunch of barely sauteed fresh vegetables and sprouts with fried tofu and white rice. He set the table and served himself. Before eating he performed an old, traditional, Rosicrucian blessing over the food. The brief, Latin phrases brought his mind back to focusing on the nature of God and his own, small part in the life of our universe.

Simon, as was his practice, ate slowly. He let himself savor the flavor and texture of each bite of the vegetables and soybean curd. He made a point of concentrating on the food and nothing else, both a practice of mind control and, he thought, good health. When he was finished he immediately washed the dishes.

But that was hours ago and now he was doing nothing but waiting, waiting. This was not his style and he was having a hard time dealing with it. *For as long as I can remember I have had...trouble...with patience.* Simon examined his feelings and emotions and tried to trace his impatience back to its source. But he could not concentrate and was unable to complete the exercise. Damn! he cursed, frustrated at the futility of the work.

Simon rose and paced the floor. *Okay, let's look at what's really bothering me. Who might have attacked us and had enough power to do so? It must be...* But there was no answer. Simon could think of no one who might want to attack him. Besides, few people could have marshaled the amount of magical power that was demonstrated against him, Alli, Angelica and the Warriors. Those who did had no reason to attack him. *Or did they?*

Am I taking people away from other groups for the Warriors of the Light? Is somebody mad at me for that? Simon purposely tried to keep a low profile over the past few years. He had written a few articles for magazines and taught some classes, and of course there were the Warriors themselves, but that was about it. In fact, few of the Warriors had been members of other groups previous to their membership in the Warriors of the Light. This could not be the motive for the attack.

Could it be somebody in the Warriors had offended another group? That was unlikely. They were too busy studying and practicing the techniques

Simon taught them. For the most part, the members of the Warriors of the Light did not have the training to magically attack anyone. *I don't think any of the Warriors could have offended somebody else.*

Could it have been something I had written? His articles, printed in magazines like *Gnosis, Fate, New Age Journal, NewWitch* and *Green Egg* had been general in nature. He had attacked occult frauds in one article, *but a fraud wouldn't have the power to make the two attacks on us.* He had also attacked the recent move by Satanists to become part of the occult mainstream.

Simon stopped his nervous pacing. *Could it be? Was it that simple?* Simon quickly ran scenario after scenario over in his head. *This is too obvious. I have to check this lead out in person.*

He went to his car which he kept parked under the carport next to his home. It was the immaculate, '56 Thunderbird hardtop convertible he had driven for years. Simon started the car and felt the familiar rumble that throbbed under him. He left the top on and used the air conditioning to cool the passenger compartment on this unusually hot, terribly smoggy and muggy late afternoon.

Simon drove down his long driveway and took Inglewood to Venice Boulevard, then headed east. He turned up La Cienega and got caught up in the heavy, late rush hour traffic to Hollywood. It was a little after six when Simon finally pulled up in front of House Indigo. As he got out of his car he watched a Ford, which had been parked illegally in a red zone, pull away from the curb. *Where's a cop when you need one?*

Simon walked up to the door and rang the bell. After a few moments passed the intercom speaker squawked with static and went silent. A few more moments passed and the speaker came alive again. "…se the…" came a voice through the cheap speaker.

"What?" asked Simon.

"I said, 'who's there?' " came the distorted voice.

"This is Simon Raven. I'm here to see Orlac."

"Do you have an appointment?"

"Just tell him that Simon is here."

There was a long silence, then the door swung open. Simon's jaw dropped when he saw the dark man who had opened the door. "Miguel?" he said in surprise. "For God's sake, Miguel, what are you doing here?"

"I don't have anything to say to you, Simon."

Simon was puzzled. "Why are you acting this way, Miguel? We've been friends for, what, seven years now? I've recommended your book on the Norse Elder Eddas to hundreds, maybe thousands of people. It's brilliant."

"Yeah, but what did it get me? Nothing. I spent years researching it and the publisher does nothing to advertise it. I get almost no royalties.

"After it came out, someone where I worked found a copy and brought it to the attention of my boss. I was fired. For six months I couldn't get work. Then Elizabeth left me..."

Simon's mouth dropped in shock. "You're wife? I'm so sorry, Miguel."

"But you haven't heard the rest of the story. Tell me, Simon, have you read any of my more recent books?"

Simon looked at the ground, sheepishly. "I'm sorry, Miguel, but I haven't. There's only so much one person can study and master, and the Norse traditions have not been one of my major interests."

"Well, Simon, you should look at them. You see, four years ago, after my wife left me, I decided to study Satanism from a strictly theoretical viewpoint. Much to my surprise I discovered that in Satanism there is power, Simon, real power. I spent a year studying with Dr. Orlac. I got a new job at twice what I was earning just months later. And women? I have so many now I have to keep an appointment book for just the ones I *want* to see.

"Simon, I was so elated with my discovery of the power in Satanism that I wanted to share it with everyone. I've included Dr. Orlac's Satanic theories and philosophies in my recent books. In my writings I've had to call it part of traditional, ancient, Norse religion because a lot of people don't like the name 'Satanism.' Most of them don't know what real Satanism is."

Simon looked in shock at his old friend. *How could he so misuse his power as a writer?*

"Do you want proof of how powerful Satanism is, Simon? Well, sales of my recent books have been up and we've begun our infiltration of…"

"Simon," interrupted Orlac with a loud voice. "How good of you to visit. We seem very popular with unexpected guests this evening. Miguel, would you get us some drinks?" Del Florio turned to say something, but he looked at Orlac, bowed his head in submission and simply walked away.

Simon looked at Orlac and tried to sense what was deep in the Satanist's mind. "How were you able to turn Miguel del Florio into your flunky?" Simon finally asked.

Orlac laughed, but to Simon the laugh seemed tense and practiced rather than real. Orlac's smile, likewise, seemed fake, almost a sneer that merely approached being a smile. "Si-mon," the Satanist said, stretching out the syllables in mock surprise. "Miguel is not my 'flunky.' He's worked hard and is my second-in-command. As a result of our work together we've been able to merge the Norse traditions with Satanism. But enough of that. What brings you here?"

"The Warriors and I have been attacked twice over the past few days…"

"And you're looking for help from us Satanists?" Orlac finished Simon's sentence. Mock surprise again filled his tone of voice. "Considering what you've written about us I think that's highly unlikly, Simon."

"No, Valdemar," Simon said, both surprised and impressed at Orlac's audacity. "I wanted to find out…uh…I wanted to find out if you were responsible."

"Me?"

Again Simon detected contrived fakery in the outrage of Orlac's voice.

It reminded him of the Muppet Miss Piggy's *"Moi?"* protestation of wrongdoing when she and everyone else knew she was guilty.

Orlac put his hand on Simon's shoulder, making Simon cringe. "Simon, old friend, I assure you that I…"

Simon shrugged off Orlac's hand and stared into Orlac's eyes. "Don't play games, Valdemar. You know very well that we are not friends."

"Iced tea, anyone?" Miguel del Florio interrupted what was about to become an anger-filled argument. Orlac took a large glass and sat down.

Simon took nothing, but also sat. "Look, I'm sorry, Valdemar. I'm a guest in your home and I've behaved rudely…"

"True," replied Orlac, "but it's also true that we're not friends. As I said, I read what you wrote about me, my followers and other Satanists in *Magical Blend* magazine several years ago. I was not…amused." Orlac took a big swallow of the chilled tea and continued. "But did you notice, Simon, that I didn't try to refute your anti-Satanist arguments, even though I could have exposed your miserable illogic?"

Simon bristled at the insult, but before he could speak Orlac continued.

"No, Simon, I have other fish to fry and frankly I'm not interested in wasting my time by doing anything so mundane as attacking you."

"I didn't say I thought you did it, I said I thought you might be responsible. Do you think that some of the people in this mail-order Temple Of Satan of yours might have done it?"

Orlac, infuriated, pinched his lips together so he wouldn't explode. Then he took another drink, calmed himself and set the glass down. "You should try some of Miguel's iced tea, Simon. It's really quite good."

Simon made no move toward the tray of iced tea which del Florio had placed on a table before leaving the room.

Orlac shrugged, then continued. "Simon, I don't know anybody who might have done this to you and yours, but I have a suspicion. There is a group of fundamentalist Christians who are using a form of magic they call 'God's Work' in order to attack magical groups such as the Temple Of Satan. They might even attack your Warriors of the Light. I think they could be the ones who have worked spells against you."

Simon looked skeptically at Orlac. *It was far more than "spells" that were worked against us.* "I haven't heard anything about this group before," Simon said, "and I try to keep up on anti-occult groups. What can you tell me about them? What proof do you have of this?"

"I have it on good authority from a variety of people. Simon, you know there are Christians all over the country who are against anything occult. They already consider you to be a Satanist." He leaned forward and peered into Simon's eyes. "Simon, the Temple Of Satan has many good people. We should all stand together against our common, anti-occult enemy."

I don't want anything to do with Satanists. What is Orlac trying to do? He can't really think that I or any of the Warriors of the Light would join him. "I have to disagree with you, Valdemar. The vast majority of Christians aren't against the Warriors and other positive occult groups. The loud, anti-occult Christians who have a hold on the media right now are just a tiny minority of the Christian faith, led by demagogues who're trying to get followers, money and power." Now Simon fired his main salvo. "I have nothing against Christ, Christians or Christianity in general, although I do resent the few who have small, closed minds. Besides, even the Temple Of Satan is basically a Christian organization."

"What?" shouted Orlac, standing in anger, his hands knotting into fists.

"Sure. Your theology is all Christian, or rather, anti-Christian. Some look at the various spiritual entities of Christianity as types of spiritual beings, even gods. You just follow a different deity in the Christian pantheon. Your rituals are anti-the Holy Spirit and anti-Jesus. If you were not Christian, why even bother? Satan is only a part of Christian belief."

Orlac turned away from Simon so the guest would not see his host seething in rage, his face taking on a reddish hue from the rush of angry blood.

Simon let a small smile cross his lips.

Orlac felt the rage roil in him like a boiling Witch's brew. He was orphaned as a child and sent from one foster home to another. He thought with anger about the Christian organization that ran the foster parent program and how all of the devout Christian families abused him and other children, mentally, physically, emotionally, spiritually and sexually. He felt the pain of the beatings he received and how nobody believed him when he described the sexual abuse at the hands of his "good Christian" foster father. By the time he ran away from home at fifteen he had learned to despise everything Christian. *And now Simon accuses me of being a Christian. How dare he!*

Orlac took a deep breath and brought his mind back to the present and his guest. *He's trying to get my goat. I won't let him. I have a need for him and I'm not going to let this opportunity get away.* He turned back to Simon as if nothing had happened. "Come, now, Simon. We both know that Satan is also part of Jewish belief..."

"I'm sorry, Valdemar, but that's incorrect. In the Old Testament he is always called "The Satan" and functions the same way as what we would call a devil's advocate. Even in the book of Job, 'The Satan' does nothing against God-fearing Job. He just encourages God to see what Job would do if his circumstances changed for the worse. Satan as the source of evil is a Christian concept, not a Jewish one."

Simon has control of this conversation. I have to regain control now. "Okay, Simon. I don't want to argue with you. So go ahead, think what you will about me and the TOS. But you must admit that there are those who are against anything occult, true?"

"True," replied Simon.

"Then we should join forces and work together."

Something funny is going on here. I've insulted him here and attacked him in writing yet he continues to try to unite us. Why? Simon looked at Orlac for a long time, as if puzzling over what to do. "There are those who see any occultist as evil, Valdemar, and there is strength in numbers. Supposing I were to agree to a common front. You would have the support of myself and the Warriors and we would have the support of the Temple Of Satan. That's a very small army."

Orlac smiled. *At least now I've got his interest.* "Come with me, Simon. There are some things I'd like to show you."

Orlac led Simon toward the back of the house. "It all started with Miguel. He came to me wanting power. He found it in Satanism. As a result, he introduced Satanism into his magical group, the Hammer of Thor. They don't know they have become a front for the Temple Of Satan, but that's exactly what has happened.

"Simon, it then became clear to me what I should do—my experience in black-ops should have made it obvious—but I only became aware of it slowly. There's no need to overpower people when you can subvert them. No, Simon, I have no desire to attack you or the Warriors. I'd much rather have you join us."

Orlac opened the door to a large room. Inside, around several tables, were people whom Simon recognized. They were members of several local, national and even international magical groups. Miguel del Florio had people from several Norse-oriented groups around his table. There were also members of groups involved with Golden Dawn style magic, Crowley style magic, Chaos magic, SACRED and even numerous Witches and Pagans. Simon's mouth dropped open when he recognized Jerry Gross, an initiate of the Warriors of the Light.

"All of these people are at work turning their occult orders into groups that will stand united against anti-occult forces. They will also promulgate Satanic philosophy in those groups. Soon, most of the occult community will be under my indirect control. Together we'll be able to gain freedom for all of our groups."

Simon shook his head. "I don't think so. I know many of these people and the groups they belong to. They're all non-violent. You implied there'd be an army to defend occult practitioners. I still don't see such an army."

"Come," said Orlac, leading Simon from the room. "I'll show you." They walked slowly down the hall. "Miguel and I recently came back from Germany. There we made contact with, well, how should I put it…"

"Just give it to me straight, Valdemar."

"Okay." He paused in front of a door and looked Simon in the eye. "We need an army. I connected with several fighting groups in Germany. They are commonly known as skinheads. Neo-Nazis."

Before Simon could say anything Orlac opened the door. On the far wall of this new room was a large picture of Adolf Hitler. Above it was a red, white and black flag. Displayed in the center of the banner was a large swastika.

There were several young men in the room, all with short hair or shaved heads and wearing armbands bearing a swastika. When they saw Orlac they rose and saluted him with a raised hand. *"Seig Heil!"* they shouted in unison. Simon couldn't believe this was actually happening.

"Sit!" ordered Orlac. "Identify your commands." As a group they resumed their seats. Then, one by one they rose and gave the names of neo-Nazi groups in the U.S. like the Aryan Brotherhood, Norse Power, White Pride and others. Orlac turned to Simon. "Each group is small," explained Orlac, "with only a handful to maybe a hundred active members. Normally they are ineffectual and fight among themselves. But under my command they are united. They are a small army, but they are my army."

Orlac turned to the skinheads and ordered, "Rise!" The group again rose and saluted as Orlac and Simon left the room. "We're now financing almost every Nazi and skinhead group in the country. There are a few members of the Temple Of Satan who have contributed a great deal of money to this cause."

"Orlac, you know these kids better than I do, but I know a bit about psychology. Your 'army' is filled with anger and rage. They'll switch to some new fad or sell you out the first time somebody puts pressure on them."

"I don't think so, Simon. You see, before they can join us they must give us full information on their families including names, addresses and phone numbers. We also have parties and get pictures of them in, uh, compromising positions. We threaten that should any of these soldiers try to reveal our plans or leave our organization we would use the information to embarrass or humiliate them. We also imply we might do bodily harm to a relative." He paused and looked at Simon, whose face was knit in shock. Orlac quickly added, "We'd never do anything, of course. The threat alone is usually enough to keep them in thrall."

Simon hid his feelings as best he could. *I've got to find out more about what Orlac is doing.* "Valdemar, just having groups under your control isn't enough—as part of psy-ops you should know that. You need to be able to communicate with everyone quickly and accurately."

Orlac pursed his lips and nodded. "You surprise me, Simon. I didn't realize that you'd be so aware of military theory and tactics. Follow me." Orlac led the way to another room. It was the computer room he had shown Lieutenant Christian earlier that afternoon.

"This is our communications and data center. We have full desktop publishing capabilities and mailing facilities for printing and mailing agit-prop. For faster communication we have FAX machines, automated calling machines and high-speed cable modems. Of course we have our own internet web site. People use their computers and modems all over the world to log onto the Night Shadow web site on the internet. This is also where we store all of our data on disk and tape."

Orlac led Simon back to the main room where the glasses of iced tea still stood, dripping wet rings around their bases. They sat again, and this time Simon drank some of the now-diluted tea. They drank in silence while Simon considered what he was going to say. "Suppose I join you, Valdemar. What's in it for me? After all, I lead a group of my own. Why do I need to become your flunky?"

Orlac laughed. " 'Better to rule in hell than serve in heaven,' eh?"

Simon laughed, too, at what he thought was an out-of-place reference.

Orlac stared at Simon, looking directly and intently into his eyes. "You still miss the point, Simon. I don't want to become the head of the Warriors of the Light. I just want us all to work together, to become a sort of union. Together we can overpower those who would deny people like you and me and Miguel their freedom, their civil rights."

"So what would I have to do?"

"Nothing much. Simply support the Temple Of Satan's actions and include our philosophy and teachings in with what you do with the Warriors. I know you're familiar with what I teach. For example, convince them that mysticism, the reaching of higher levels of consciousness and merging with divine powers, is meaningless—there are no higher powers. It is a waste of time. Point out that Christians are attacking them and they should, therefore, revere Christ's foe, Satan, and His policy of libertinage. Is that asking too much for the freedom and power we can achieve if we work together?"

Simon rose and pursed his lips. "Instead of simply turning you down, I find myself thinking I need some time to consider your proposition. I'll let you know in a few days, okay?" Without waiting for an answer he rose and headed for the door. "Thanks for the hospitality. I'll see myself out."

Del Florio re-entered the room as Simon was leaving. "Come again, Simon," said Orlac. "We can talk more." When the door was closed the smile he had worn almost continuously for hours left Orlac's face. For months he had wanted to try to bring Simon over to his side. Simon's surprise visit to House Indigo had given him the opportunity to do just that.

"Why did you tell him everything?" del Florio asked.

Orlac continued to look at the door. "I showed him some of what we were doing to try and win him over, Miguel. When that didn't work I tried to impress him with our size and strength." Orlac knew he had failed. He didn't believe for a second Simon Raven would come over to his side. "Miguel…I think we have a problem. He'll do something to try to stop us. I can't let that happen. Nobody must be allowed to stop our new world order.

"Have him followed, Miguel. Pick one of those young Nazi idiots. Tell him to follow Simon Raven. And when the opportunity arises, Simon Raven is to be terminated with extreme prejudice.

Orlac's eyes narrowed as he stared into the distance. His mouth curled into a hate-filled sneer. "I want Simon Raven dead."

* * * * *

It was after eight-thirty as Simon drove home. *I'll rot in hell before joining racists, Nazis and Satanists.* As he drove on the streets back to his home he formulated a plan of action in his mind. Lights seemed to flash as he drove past them, his consciousness both on his driving and on setting up what he was going to do. *This is something which has to be done tonight, before Orlac can prevent my actions.*

Then something else struck him. *Orlac may be a bastard, but at least he was up front about it. Maybe he's an honest bastard. That means he didn't attack us. Who did? I'm back where I started.* For awhile Simon tried to figure out who had attacked him. Soon he gave up and started mulling over what, if anything, he should do about Orlac's Temple Of Satan. He was so wrapped up in his plan of action for tonight he didn't see the truck that followed him.

Miguel del Florio came into the room where the racists were planning strategies. When del Florio asked for a volunteer for an important mission the entire group stood, wanting the opportunity to serve. Del Florio looked around and pointed to a member of the New Nazi Youth, Mark

Johnson. They left the room and del Florio gave him his assignment.

Mark easily followed Simon's T-Bird. His beat-up Chevy truck was camouflaged in the street traffic. He watched as Simon pulled into the almost hidden driveway that led to his house. Mark parked his truck around the corner at the bottom of the hill and walked up to the long driveway which Simon had entered. The five-inch-long barrel of the Walther P38, a Nazi relic in perfect condition, felt cold against his leg.

Mark hugged the bushes at the side of the driveway as he quietly neared Simon's house. As he moved he felt an odd "hollowness," a feeling of emptiness, sorrow and fear. He became filled with a nameless dread. With each step his fears seemed to increase. Mark's pulse raced as every sound, every breeze, filled him with terror. *Calm yourself. Don't hyperventilate.*

A new feeling came upon him. His body was suddenly invaded by biting, stinging insects. He kept brushing his hair, face and arms, trying to get them off. He slapped and rubbed them all over. Mark's eyes widened as he felt them crawling up the inside of his pants. *I will not scream. I will not cry out!* The insects moved slowly up his pants toward his genitals. Mark felt faint. *Concentrate, damn it. Concentrate!* His fingers clawed desperately at his belt buckle and zipper. He ripped off his pants and brushed his legs. Nothing was there.

The neo-Nazi shook out his pants, just to be sure, before he put them back on. *They seem heavy, as if I had rolls of quarters in all the pockets.* As he started again down the driveway the sensation of weight surrounded him, as if with each step a thousand pounds was thrown upon his shoulders. By the time he was halfway down the driveway his feet weighed a ton each and he could barely move them. A noise, like people humming, rang in his ears, getting louder with each step. With each step he was filled with greater and greater fear and terror. He wanted to run away and scream, but he kept moving on. It was hard to breathe and he had to fight for each breath. Still, he struggled forward. *I won't let Miguel down!* By the time he moved far enough down the driveway to see Simon's house he was covered with sweat from the exertion. He was bent over from the weight, and each step was a tortuous, pain-filled exercise in what might prove to be futile. *I'll never make it...*

Mark tumbled to the ground. He gasped for breath, but he knew it was over. He was going to die where he lay. And then the feeling of dread and the pressure against him suddenly vanished. The humming voices were gone. He lay on his back and rested for a few moments, then he rose and followed the bushes to a point where they were closest to the house. *I have to complete this for the NNY and Miguel and Dr. Orlac.*

As he caught his breath and regained his strength he thought about what had led him to this point. He had been the youngest of seven children. When he was five his father moved the family to a small town to work at an aircraft factory. Within one year the federal government came to the factory and demanded more minorities be hired. As a result, his father was laid off. There was little work available and his family was quickly on welfare. His father turned to alcohol and started blaming the "damn niggers and kikes" for all of their problems. He started to beat Mark's mother as well as Mark and the other kids who were still at home. Mark pursed his lips as he felt each stroke of his fathers large, black belt hit him on his butt and thighs. *I will be strong! Whatever doesn't kill me makes me stronger. No one will ever whip me again.* Six months after his father had first beaten him, the man, drunk and depressed, abandoned his family and his pain when he drove his car into the side of a mountain. The young Nazi grimaced, but did not know whether it was from the pain of the remembered beatings or the pain from the loss of his father.

Mark's family struggled by. Because they had little money they had little food, and the lack of nutrition meant Mark was small for his age. He became the butt of every bully in school. He grew up filled with anger at the cause of it all, the "damn niggers and kikes." *I will be strong! No one will ever whip me again.*

He dropped out of school as soon as he could and talked his way into a job as a mechanic. Finally he had enough money to eat well. He also purchased weights and exercised for hours every day. He needed to be strong to fight the "damn niggers and kikes."

Mark thought about how he had gotten involved with the NNY. At rock concerts, up in the mosh pit near the band he would jump around and slam into other people. It was only at these times, when he was releasing his anger and rage, he felt good. At one concert he met Wolf who had a swastika tattooed on his arm. *I remember thinking that Wolf must have had balls of steel to wear such a tat.* They talked for awhile. When they met the next week in the mosh pit they planned to get together apart from the concerts. They became friends, and Wolf told him why he wore the Nazi symbol. As Mark heard the racist philosophy and propaganda he became convinced; a true believer. Soon he became a member of the NNY, the New Nazi Youth.

He thought about how he quickly rose through the ranks. *My attacks on Niggers, Gooks and Kikes are still legendary in the NNY. When Dr. Orlac offered to finance us we jumped at the chance. With his money I'll be able to get my revenge on the subhumans who had ruined my family and killed my father, the "damn niggers and kikes." And I know just where to start!*

Mark brought his attention back to the task at hand. *I will complete my assignment.* He was looking for the safest path to the house when he heard…*it.* At first *it* sounded like nothing more than a rustle in the bushes. *Just a squirrel or field mouse.* The rustling sound came closer and closer to Mark. *Odd, I thought that wild animals tend to stay away from people.* And then the animal's rustling stopped. Silence was everywhere. It crept over him as if a cloak had been tossed over his head. He realized he was again gasping for breath. Something was near, something terrible, something foul.

Mark felt it behind him. It was dark and big—no, huge!—like a giant black bear. The creature made an odd sound, low pitched and yet a squeal at the same time. It shook Mark from his toes to his forehead. When he felt the thing's hot breath on the back of his neck the Nazi youth bolted in terror. He ran across the yard toward the driveway. Another dark shape, a giant black shadow, lumbered out of the bushes and blocked his way. The infernal squealing doubled in intensity. Then the eyes came.

Every way he turned there were huge shapes with dozens of ugly, feral eyes. The shapes stank of burning sulfur. Mark ran one direction, then another, but an ugly, dark behemoth was always in front of him. He thought the squealing they made would destroy his hearing or drive him out of his mind. As he ran, trying to dodge the shapes but never succeeding, he didn't really care whether deafness or madness was his fate, just as long as it ended.

Inexorably, inevitably, the shapes closed in around him. The circle Mark ran in got smaller and smaller. Soon he was surrounded by unspeakable monsters. There was no way out. Panting, exhausted, half-crazy from the noise, Mark fell to the ground and covered his head and ears. "Help me! Help me! *For the love of God, somebody help me!*" he shrieked.

* * * * *

When Mark had first tested Simon's wards at the edge of the driveway, Simon immediately became aware someone was coming, unbidden, onto his property. He moved to a spot in his home where he could get a good view of the driveway. He was frankly surprised at the strength of the young man who forced his way through the newly reinforced magical wards.

Simon released the wards and quickly cast the *Spell of the Shadow*. Mark fled from the shadows in terror, but he could never escape. The shadows were manifestations of his own, darker self, the part of himself he feared the most. And there is no way to escape from who we are. Simon watched until Mark was a small puddle of emotions near the door of his home, crying out to God for help. He quietly walked out to the broken man.

"Look at your past and what you have accomplished by yourself." Mark, tears of terror and fear staining his face, looked up at Simon. The shapes were gone, as was their mind-numbing squeal. The mage held out his hand to Mark who took it and rose from the ground.

"I was going to…"

Simon held up his free hand and interrupted. "Nobody ever said this world was fair or easy. You raised yourself up from poverty through your own strength."

Mark looked at him, awestruck. *How could he know so much about my life?*

"But you've wasted so much strength on hate. Think of what you could have accomplished if you had put your strengths toward what you could do rather than what you thought you were prevented from doing."

Mark was confused. "I don't know, Mr. Raven. I was going to…"

Simon turned and walked away. "Good night and good luck. You are free to go. The shadows will bother you no more tonight." Simon stopped and turned suddenly, the dim light casting weird shadows across his face. He stared at the young man. "Come again without an invitation and they will never leave you alone. No matter where you run, no matter where you hide, they will follow you and haunt your every waking and sleeping hour. Again, good night."

Mark watched Simon as he turned and walked toward the door of his home. *I have to complete my mission!* He reached under his belt with his right hand and pulled out the pistol. With his left hand he pulled back the slide which dropped the nine-millimeter cartridge into the firing chamber while the hammer moved back with an audible "click-ik." Carefully he sighted it on the back of the man walking away. Then he supported his right wrist with his left hand and moved up the sights until he had a clear head shot. One squeeze and the task would be accomplished. He could return in victory.

Simon did not look back. The sound of the bullet being chambered told him all he needed to know. He could feel his heart start to race and his breathing quicken. *No time for a ritual.* Instead, Simon visualized something Mark was unused to—pure, unconditional love. He quickly let it grow and mix with psychic energy, then directed it in waves toward the young man.

Mark's hands started to shake. Simon sensed the change in Mark, but knew that something else would be needed to end this. He paused under the light outside the door to his home. He didn't look back. He said, "God be with you, son," in a voice just loud enough for the young man to hear.

Mark looked at his shaking hands. He closed his eyes and took a deep breath to try and steady them. He exhaled and opened his eyes. He looked through the sights of his now-steady hands, aimed at the man in the light, and started to gently squeeze the trigger. *Its a perfect shot.* That was when Mark became aware of a new feeling. He sensed the love.

Years of anger and rage flooded him and exploded. The love rushed in to fill years of emptiness. Too controlled to cry, too restrained to understand the emotions he was feeling, Mark did the only thing which seemed to make sense. He slowly lowered his arms until the gun was pointed toward the ground, carefully decocked the hammer and walked slowly down the driveway, away from the house.

When Simon heard the hammer being gently closed he knew it was over. He took a deep breath of relief, exhaled slowly and opened the door to his house. "God be with you, son," he quietly repeated, and went inside.

Mark walked down the hill to his truck and drove to his apartment. He packed his belongings and drove off. No one ever found out where he went.

Chapter Six

Fifth Night

AGAIN INSIDE HIS HOME, Simon's feet fell in a steady march as he started up the circular stairs to his magic room. His mouth was set in determination; his face a mask of fury. *Orlac will pay for this. His reign of terror will not even have a chance to begin. In one of his books he recommends "returning evil for evil." What he is going to get in return for his attacks and attempted murder will...*

Simon flung open the door to his magic room, spread his arms and declared, "Friends, I am here!" He went into the dark room and lit a few candles, then quickly changed from his regular clothes into a simple, over-the-head cloak, a magical robe. It was the same as the one worn by the Warriors when Angelica had been attacked. Tonight he worked as a magician, not as a leader of a group of mystics.

Simon's presence in the room was so powerful he did not need to perform an opening ritual. He clapped his hands and the atmosphere changed—the room and its non-physical inhabitants waited for what was about to happen. The temperature dropped and a scent of frankincense filled the air, although no air conditioner or cooler was activated, no censer was lit. From the depths of the darkness it seemed as if friendly eyes watched Simon as he worked. Except for Simon, the room was empty, but the space was also filled with life.

Suddenly, Simon laughed. He knew what he was going to do. "I don't think you will enjoy your dreams tonight, Valdemar. I don't think you will like them at all!" He peered around the circle and smiled. "Welcome one and all. Tonight we make magic! Tonight we strike for humanity and the Light of the Divine." He spread his arms in welcome. "Let us begin."

* * * * *

"No, don't!" cried the woman.

"Stop prattling, Salome. Just deal with it," said Orlac. He was kneeling in the bed behind the young woman. Another woman, already exhausted from sex with him, was asleep in the bed. Orlac grabbed Salome by the shoulder with one hand and pulled his member from her vagina with the other.

"No!" she cried again. Orlac ignored her and concentrated on his assault of the tight ring of muscles at her anus. "Agh!" she cried out, as Orlac forced himself deeper. Soon he was pummeling her, ignoring her cries and tears and blood.

Orlac felt the pressure build in a mounting swirl of ecstasy until he exploded within Salome. He held her against him as he pulsed his fluids into her bowels. When he was finished he got up and went to bathroom. He ignored Salome's tiny cries.

He cleaned himself off and came back to bed. After sex with both of the women he was tired. Orlac got into bed between the women, who were now both asleep, and closed his eyes. He counted slowly backwards from one hundred and allowed himself to drift into the arms of Morpheus. This was a technique he had practiced for years. It always helped him fall asleep quickly. He rarely got to fifty. Tonight he was asleep by seventy-four.

It was dark. Valdemar saw a light ahead and somehow knew he had to walk toward it. He started toward the distant glimmer. After a time his eyes became used to the darkness and he was able to see his surroundings. He was in a long tunnel or hallway. *Funny, no matter how far I walk I don't seem to be getting closer to the light.* And then the ground trembled.

It was as if some gigantic creature stepped behind him. There was a huge "whomp" and the ground shook briefly. Valdemar's pulse raced. *What was that?*

Once again the ground shook from the weight of what must have been a terrible creature. The temperature sank until it was so cold he could see his breath. The ground shook again and a shiver went down his back, stopping him in his tracks. Orlac looked behind him and saw nothing, but he knew the creature was coming. He started to hurry toward the light.

Again and again the ground rocked. Orlac started to jog. Still, the creature got closer to him although he got no closer to the light. The creature's steps landed more quickly. Valdemar could suddenly feel the hot, putrid breath of the creature on his neck. It stank of burning sulfur and death. Orlac ran as fast as he could toward the light, driven by sheer terror.

No matter how fast he ran the light never got closer. He pumped his arms wildly, but couldn't move any closer to the light. His breath, at first, came in pants and then changed to wheezes. Still, the light never got closer and the creature's breath seemed to grow in fiery intensity. Then the floor changed.

At first Orlac thought his feet were merely tired from the running. When he looked down, however, he saw the floor was sticking to his feet. Each step became harder and harder to make until he couldn't move at all. He pulled at his legs to free them from the gummy surface, but the goo, like powerful, greedy hands, reached out and pulled his feet back to their places.

I can't try to run any more! Orlac bent forward and leaned on his knees, wheezing loudly. Suddenly he noticed all he could hear was his speeding heart and raspy breath. It was quiet in the darkness that surrounded him. *Is it over? Is this madness finally over?* The hiss of demon-breath sounded behind him and Orlac's eyes spread wide in surprise and fear. He slowly turned. At first he saw nothing in the dark. Then the large, snake-like eyes opened just inches in front of his own. They flashed with hatred. And hunger.

Orlac's scream rose from the depths of his soul into a high-pitched shriek of terror. He tried to step back but the floor rose up like a thing alive and surrounded his feet to his ankles with a thick, foul-smelling paste. The creature's mouth opened. Five feet wide and filled with multiple rows of shining white spears, the tips of its trifurcated tongue danced in the dim light as a sticky, translucent slime trailed from its teeth. A blood-curdling hiss came from what passed as its vocal cords as the creature moved forward. Two massive fangs unfurled, dripping poison.

Orlac screamed again as the creature moved in for the kill. All he could see was fangs and row after row of shiny teeth; some serrated for cutting, some razor sharp for ripping and tearing and some flat for grinding. Terror seeped through every pore as Orlac knew his painful death was inevitable. His third scream came from a deep part of his being, a part Orlac didn't even believe existed—until now. It continued as the sharp teeth closed around him. The creature's breath was overwhelming. Points dug into his flesh and pain ripped through him as the creature started to enjoy the results of its victory.

And then he was falling. At first Orlac was relieved to have made his escape. *I feel like Alice.* After a few minutes, however, his lack of control brought back the fear; brought back the terror. He spun around and flailed his arms in a useless attempt to slow himself. The wind pressure increased until, like a dog with its head out the window of a speeding car, he could barely catch his breath. Each inhalation was excruciating. *Let me die now, before the pain gets worse; before I feel the pain at the bottom of this crevasse!* The fall seemed to last for hours. Finally, he hit bottom.

Surprisingly, the landing had not hurt. Exhausted, he simply lay where he fell until he could catch his breath. When he felt he was sufficiently recovered, Orlac rose to his feet and looked around.

He was in a large room, the walls hidden in the dark. There was one light on a small table near a figure in a chair. The figure had its back to Orlac.

"Come closer," the figure said in a raspy voice. Orlac walked near the table and chair. "Do you know who I am?" the figure asked.

"No."

The figure laughed until it choked and coughed something into its hand which it wiped on the arm of the chair. "No, I suppose you don't know who I am." It slowly turned around.

The face of the man in the chair made Orlac grimace in horror. It was filled with diseased pock marks and pulsing open sores. Its toothless mouth was incapable of any emotion and the eyes were an aged, sickly yellow. "I am Satan."

Orlac's mouth opened in surprise. Then he laughed out loud. "You're nothing but my imagination. I don't believe in you. Hah! I don't believe you exist."

"But you believe in magic, don't you?"

"Yes…"

"Well, *you* might not believe in me but those who follow you or read your books believe in me. Their beliefs have created me this way."

"Then they've done a terrible job. Look at you. You're old, powerless, a weakling. You're just the opposite of what my Satan would look like."

"Oh? Would you prefer me to look like this?" He waved his arms and his face changed to a smooth reddish hue with high cheekbones. Goat horns rose from Satan's forehead. His chest and arms, also red, were massive and strong. From his solar plexus down, his body changed into a serpent, its winding, rattle-tipped tail bobbing languidly in the air.

"Please," said Orlac, "isn't that a bit gauche?"

"Not really. This is how those who fear me think of me. Of course, you don't fear me. You merely use my name."

"Why did you say my followers created you in that ugly form?"

Satan laughed. His eyes narrowed as he stared at the guest. "Deny me as you may, I do exist. I am hidden just below the surface of your heart and the hearts of your followers. I am a reflection both of what they want and what they are. I am the reality of what you are. This is the way they think I look." Instantly he changed into a duplicate of Orlac. Valdemar snorted. "Yes. It's the way you present yourself," Satan said. "But this is the way you and I really look." Slowly Satan changed back into the hideous creature, powerless and horrific, as he had originally revealed himself to Orlac.

Orlac refused to accept Satan's claim. "No! I am not that way."

Satan laughed through his toothless mouth. "Your hatred of others and your quest for power merely masks your self-hatred and lack of power over yourself. You're right, though. If I really reflected your heart and soul you would look like this." The face began to change again. The skin filled with pustules that dripped a glowing, greenish ichor. The eyes, now blind, dried in their sockets and rolled down the cheeks, hanging from wriggling stalks. The lips dried and curled back from the gums in a hideous grin. It was helpless and horrible and useless, yet it cackled in glee at Orlac's horror at seeing his inner self.

"No! No! It's not true. No!" Orlac threw his arms over his eyes and fell to the floor. When he stopped yelling he was surrounded with silence. He looked around and was in a comfortable room. Against the wall was a heavily-padded chair. A tall drink sat on a small table next to it. Orlac struggled up and fell into the chair. He took a sip of the mint julep and felt the cold and alcohol calm and revive him. He put the drink down, closed his eyes and allowed himself to sink into the comfortable chair.

Orlac opened his eyes when he heard the odd sound, something like a mixture between bending metal and a sticky, wet, viscous substance. In front of him was a chrome, bullet-shaped thing that moved with life. It was about three feet tall and eight inches wide, tapering to a rounded point. The tip of the bullet came up and the point "looked" into Valdemar's eyes, one at a time. then it moved down and tried to enter one of Orlac's nostrils. As it moved up the passage Orlac screamed in pain. The bullet quickly retreated.

Orlac tried to rise from his seat, but the comfortable chair had now become a prison and held him so he couldn't move. Metal bands sprung from the upholstery and surrounded his wrists and ankles. Trapped, Orlac could do nothing but watch as the bullet approached him again. This time it went for his mouth.

Before he could scream or gag it had forced its way between his teeth and slid down his throat. Orlac's body writhed in pain and he bit down. The chrome bullet's surface gave way to his bite and it squirmed in reverse out of his body, retreating to its original form in front of him.

Valdemar coughed and gasped for air, his body dripping in sweat from the pain. He sank back in the chair. Exhausted, his ability to resist was gone. He just shook his head, refusing to accept what was going to happen as the bullet approached again.

This time the bullet went between his legs. "No!" Orlac said weakly, as he heard the material of his pants tear and felt the cool metal skin of the invader slide between his buttocks. When it entered him Orlac's eyes bulged and he screamed at the burning pain. His body shook back and forth as the invader slid through his intestines, bulging his stomach obscenely. His body jerked like a helpless marionette. His only hope was a prayer for death to come soon. Very soon.

* * * * *

Simon came down from his ritual room. He had changed back into his street clothes. In his kitchen he made some Lemon Zinger tea. As he drank it his face once again took on its set image. There was still more work to do, the work Simon had planned on his way home from House Indigo.

When the tea was finished Simon rose and went to his main library on the third floor of the turret. He sat down at the extended keyboard attached to one of the four Macintosh computers in the house. *I was such a fool to believe Orlac. Of course he was the one who attacked us. His magical attacks failed so he tried to murder me.* Simon turned the computer on and waited for the main screen to come up. He requested access to a particular folder on the 280 gigabyte hard disk. The folder was simply named "private." Instead of the folder opening, however, a message appeared on the screen:

ACCESS DENIED TO UNAUTHORIZED PERSONNEL.
PLEASE ENTER PASSWORD.

He typed in his password, a long line of random letters, symbols and numbers which only he knew. The message on the screen changed to read:

ACCESS GRANTED.

In the folder were a variety of programs he obtained some time ago from a friend, Katerina, who was a computer cracker. He remembered how contemptuously she had glared at him when he said, "So you're a hacker.

"I am *not* a hacker. Hackers simply examine code and find ways into programs. I am a cracker. I do what hackers only dream of doing. I finish what a hacker starts. I can send in computer viruses, trojan horses, or spyware without an enduser even knowing I was there. From a continent away I can trash a $5,000 computer and make it worthless in minutes. Hmmph! Hacker, indeed."

Simon's attention came back to the folder where there were secret access codes to a wide selection of private internet web pages as well as special programs—viruses, trojan horses, and other malware—designed to do damage to other computers. They were compressed, "zipped," to save space on the hard drive. Simon unzipped them and thought about what he was going to do. *I hoped never to need these. Now I hope they're advanced enough to get by any protection Orlac may have.*

Simon used a Motorola cable modem to acess the internet and open Orlac's Night Shadow web site. He logged on using one of Katerina's programs, *Kracker*, to break through the minimum protection provided by Orlac's firewall. In the next five minutes Simon uploaded two viruses and a trojan horse. *Okay, do your work!*

Simon turned to another part of his plan. He drafted a letter to all of the occult groups who had members at the meeting he observed in House Indigo. He explained how Orlac was attempting to subvert their authority and take over their groups from within. He e-mailed copies to the orders, then made copies on his laser printer and placed them in envelopes to duplicate his e-mail.

Simon also wrote a letter to the police department and a friend in the FBI. He described in detail how Orlac was financing the skinhead and racist movement in the U.S. and listed his international links with the German neo-Nazis. He then wrote an open letter to every occult magazine and newsletter he could think of, describing what Orlac was doing:

AN OPEN LETTER TO THE OCCULT COMMUNITY

For over 1,000 years, we in the occult community have had to suffer under the claim we were all Satanists. Much of the work of those of us who are able to be more public has been countering this false notion. The facts are simple: although some Satanists are occultists, they are a tiny minority and few occultists want anything to do with them.

Over the past decade attacks on the occult community by a tiny number of vocal Christian sects have increased. The

Satanists, as represented by Dr. Valdemar Orlac and his Temple Of Satan, have proposed that Satanists and other occultists should unite as a force against a common foe. Some in the occult community, swayed by the seeming logic of his arguments, have agreed. Most of us, not wanting anything to do with Satanists, have ignored his call or refused to participate. The vast majority of occultists want nothing to do with Satanists.

Earlier tonight I met with Dr. Orlac and was shocked by two revelations. First, he has recruited members of various magical groups (even my own) and is training them in order to subvert those groups. I urge every occult group to interview all members and discover their relationship, if any, with the TOS. Understand that their goal is to indoctrinate the members of your group into accepting the tenets of Orlac's Satanism. This will give Orlac indirect but *de facto* control of your group. You should act accordingly.

The second revelation is that the TOS is financially supporting racists, neo-Nazis including neo-Nazi skinheads and various white supremacist organizations in order to have a functioning army that will fight, and if necessary kill, to promote the agenda of the TOS. To support the TOS in any way is to support hatred, racism and the eventual undermining of your authority within your group.

Finally, I regret to report that Miguel del Florio, whose books have aided so many in their studies of Norse traditions, admitted to me tonight that his recent books include TOS philosophy and techniques under the false guise of "tradition" and magical groups which follow his teachings are simply fronts for the Temple Of Satan. I was also informed he is now second-in-command to Dr. Orlac in the TOS. In the past I

urged seekers of northern European mystical traditions to use his books as resources and consider joining one of his groups. I hereby rescind my recommendations of any of his books and will no longer support any of his groups.

I urge all occultists to take the actions they deem appropriate.

Fraternally,
Simon Raven,
Warriors of the Light of God

After he signed each of the open letters he placed them in size ten envelopes, sealed and addressed them.

Finally he brought up a file and filled in the blanks using a calligraphic type font. The document stated Jerry Gross was permanently expelled from the Warriors of the Light for subversion and working at cross purposes to the Order. He addressed a copy to Jerry and kept another for the Order's archives. After putting stamps on each of the envelopes, over eighty of them, he went to his car and drove to the post office.

* * * * *

It was after midnight when Miguel del Florio ran into Orlac's bedroom. Orlac was still in bed with two young women who, exhausted from his assault on them, remained asleep. Orlac, lost in his induced nightmare, was writhing between them. His body buckled and moved as if something was inside of him, trying to get out.

"Dr. Orlac. You're having a nightmare. Wake up."

"Eh? Eh?" Orlac was covered with perspiration, his breath came in gasps and his eyes were filled with horror. He finally realized he was awake and saw del Florio in front of him. He took a deep breath to calm himself. "What is it? What do you want, Miguel?"

"Please, Dr. Orlac, come quick. There's something on the computers you have to see."

"What?"

"Just come. Please."

Orlac got up and put on a smoking jacket, then hurriedly followed del Florio to the computer room. On the way del Florio raved. "He must have loaded it through the web page. I knew we should have stayed away from that damned ActiveX crap! It came on all the screens at the same time. We don't know how to stop it."

They arrived in the computer room. All of the monitors were flashing a series of brilliant, swirling colors. At the end of the series of colors the screens turned white and a repeating message wrapped around the screens appeared on the monitors:

YOU TRIED TO KILL SIMON RAVEN AND FAILED.
FIRST YOU SAW YOURSELF IN YOUR DREAMS.
NOW YOU WILL BE TERMINATED.

YOU TRIED TO KILL SIMON RAVEN AND FAILED.
FIRST YOU SAW YOURSELF IN YOUR DREAMS.
NOW YOU WILL BE TERMINATED.

YOU TRIED TO KILL SIMON RAVEN AND FAILED.
FIRST YOU SAW YOURSELF IN YOUR DREAMS.
NOW YOU WILL BE TERMINATED.

YOU TRIED TO KILL SIMON RAVEN AND FAILED.
FIRST YOU SAW YOURSELF IN YOUR DREAMS.
NOW YOU WILL BE TERMINATED.

Then the original patterns in psychedelic colors came back on the screens, followed again by the written message.

"Get that off the screens," said Orlac, a cold intensity in his voice.

"We can't. We don't know how," wailed del Florio.

"Fools! Just turn off the computers and reboot them."

One of the computer operators protested. "If we do that and he loaded something else it…"

"Just turn off the computers and restart them," Orlac thundered, fire and anger flashing in his eyes. He was used to being instantly obeyed.

The computer operators paused and looked at one another. Then, dutifully, all of the computers were shut down. After five minutes they were restarted. The boot-up seemed to be taking a long time. "Why is it taking so long to start up the computers?" asked Orlac.

"I tried to tell you," said a computer operator. "If he loaded a virus it might take effect on reboot. Look at the usage lights on the hard drives. They're constantly lit. He's erasing everything!"

Orlac sat down in a chair, stunned. All of their records and data were lost. All of their contacts and information, all of their dossiers and inside information—it was all wiped off the computers. In a single move Orlac's attempt to take over the occult and neo-Nazi movements had been set back by months or years. All of the information would have to be re-entered and filed—if they could even find the original, handwritten, hard data.

Finally, normal welcome screens appeared on each of the monitors with the standard look of the Microsoft Windows Vista Operating System. In seconds the room was filled with the sound of keyboards being attacked as the operators searched all of the hard disks and file servers. There was nothing. No records, no fonts, no art, no files, no data…

*Unless…*Orlac looked up. "Don't we have back-ups for all our information?"

Miguel's eyes lit up. "Yes, of course we have a tape back-up on DAT," said del Florio.

"Well load it! Load it!" cried Orlac. A computer operator went over to a tiny, thick-walled safe and removed a small tape. "Don't we have multiple copies?" Orlac asked.

"We did, but somebody left them on a stereo speaker. We only found out about it yesterday. They're all totally corrupted from the speaker's magnetic field. Except for this tape they're all completely useless. This tape, however, has everything up until two A.M. yesterday when we made the back up."

"Well, load it," repeated Orlac. *We're saved! Raven thinks he's so smart. Of course we have a tape back-up.* Orlac watched as the tape was placed in its playback device and a reload of all data from the tape to the computer memory began. *Wait a second. Raven would figure we had a back-up.* "No! Stop! Don't load the tape."

"Sorry, Dr. Orlac, but if we cancel now we'll corrupt this tape, too. Don't worry, though. The loading is going fine."

It took forty minutes for the tape to load. The computers were rebooted. Everything went normally, and Orlac took a deep breath and relaxed.

Then, the monitors went dark. This was followed by a barrage of colors and exploding fractal images. The colors spun into a whirlpool and vanished in the center of the screens. A message came up on the monitors:

THANKS! I FEEL BETTER NOW.
I ALSO WIPED CLEAN THE BACK-UPS.

THANKS! I FEEL BETTER NOW.
I ALSO WIPED CLEAN THE BACK-UPS.

THANKS! I FEEL BETTER NOW.
I ALSO WIPED CLEAN THE BACK-UPS.

THANKS! I FEEL BETTER NOW.

I ALSO WIPED CLEAN THE BACK-UPS.

As they watched, the round figure from the old Pacman video game appeared at the upper left-hand corner of the monitor screens. It worked its way back and forth across the monitors, making its famous beep-uh beep-uh sound until it ate the written message. Then the figure looked out of the monitor and the computer made a burping noise. This was followed by Pacman spinning around while the computer sounded the famous Pacman wee-wee-wee end-of-play sound. Finally, Pacman dropped to the bottom of the screen. A message came on each computer monitor in small type:

"Bang. Bang. You are terminated."

Then the monitors slowly faded to black. Every scrap of RAM and hard drive storage space, every bit and byte, had been wiped clean from the entire system.

Hollywood is known around the world for its uniqueness and strangeness. Tourists look for weird things to happen in tinseltown. Most never see anything. Tonight, however, was different. Orlac's cry of rage could be heard for blocks around House Indigo. The locals—either sleeping or engaged in hot tubs, sex, parties or watching TV—simply ignored it. It was just another night in Hollyweird.

* * * * *

Simon put the letters in the mailbox that stood guard in front of the post office on Grand View Blvd. He hopped back into his car and drove south on Grand View to Washington Place. He turned west and drove to the end of Washington where he parked. Washington ends at the beach.

He walked north on the boardwalk past Venice Pier. He was tired, but there was a smile on his face. Simon walked out to within feet of the moving waters. "Mother," he called, "I've rid the world of the great evil we talked about. Is it over now, or is there some minor result of what Orlac did that I must clean up?"

There was a long silence. All Simon could hear was the lap of the waves on the sand at his feet. The smile slowly fell from his face. "Mother? Can you hear me?"

Silence.

I don't understand. It's over. I defeated Orlac. Mother should respond right away. She should be feeling better. "What's wrong, Mother?"

Silence.

Simon kicked at the sand. He couldn't understand what was wrong. *The evil was ended. Orlac was defeated. Why isn't Mother speaking?*

Stillness. Silence. Simon sat on the sand, awaiting…something. After awhile he heard an odd sound, like sobbing mixed with laughter. Finally, Mother spoke.

"My son, you have done a great good tonight. But the evil you defeated is small compared to what will confront you. I am sorry, but if you think you have won the battle that confronts me, you, and the entire world, then you are mistaken."

Simon's mouth fell open in surprise and shock. "What?"

"I have to laugh at your pride in thinking it was over. I have to cry for the lives that will be lost in the battles which are to come."

"But how can this be? Orlac was trying to take over the occult community. He attacked me and the Warriors. He…"

"He was unimportant in the overall picture. Yes, he was evil. But evil is always coming up anew. It must be confronted on a daily basis. The petty evil of Valdemar Orlac was only a minor challenge compared with what is to come.

"Simon, the evil you defeated today had nothing to do with the attacks on you and the Warriors. There is so much more, but I am so weak, so weak from fighting it. My energy, my life force, is almost gone. I can say nothing more. Besides, you wouldn't believe me if I did."

Simon pursed his lips and slammed his right fist into his open left hand. This had been a long day. He had accomplished much, but in the end he had finished nothing. He felt his exhaustion. Disappointment filled him. "Will this all never end?"

"Oh yes, my son, it will end. That was never in doubt." For a moment there was silence, as if Mother was using up the last of her energy to finish her thoughts. Then, she added in the quietest voice he had ever heard, *"The real question, the only question that matters, is how it will end."*

Chapter Seven

Earlier, the Fifth Night

"Hellooo," answered the voice, dripping with honey, "this is Sylvia.

It was after 8:00 P.M., and Paul, back at the police station, wanted to at least make contact with another one of the people on his list. He tried some of the other numbers, but either there were no answers or he left messages on the inevitable answering machines. Sylvia Scorsi, however, was in. "Ms. Scorsi, my name is Paul Christian. I'm interested in learning magic and I saw your flyer at the *Bodhi Tree*."

"Yeeeessss. I'm sure we can help you. We have a cla-ass (she put it into two syllables) starting tomorrow. It meets once a week for the next moooonnnnth. Shall I signnn you uuup? The entire course is on-ly five hundred and fifty dollars."

"Actually, I was thinking of something more private. Something faster."

"Yeeesss. I'm sure we can help you. We provide per-sonal training at only one hundred and fifty dollars per hour af-ter you are initiated."

"Initiated? Into what?"

"Into our spir-it-u-al society, The Ssssociety of the Mercurial Star, the S.M.S., of course. If you're in a hurrr-ry we can initiate you tomorrow night."

"Well, I do have another appointment tomorrow so I don't know…"

"Yeeeesss. Well that's no problem because we can perform a proxy initiaaaation…"

"A proxy initiation?"

"Yeeesss. We'll initiaaaate another person in lieu of you actually beeee-ing there. It's only two-hundred and twenty-five dollars. Do you waant to put that on your Vi-sa or Maaas-tercaaa-ard?"

The oiliness and sugar in Sylvia Scorsi's voice made Paul want to laugh. Her greediness made him want to gag. *Did people really fall for this sort of hucksterism? How could there be people with any money left who were interested in the occult with people like Scorsi around? Sure the occult was flakey, but people like her would give any group or organization a bad name.*

He decided to cut to the chase. "I'm specifically looking for information on the *Grimoire of Armadel.* Can you help me with this?"

"Yeeeesss. We can help you with anything magical. Do you nee-eed a spell or ritual worked for you? Do you nee-eed us to end a curse? If you can't come out here we can mail or faaax you a list of our services along with the charrr-ges for them."

"Listen, is there someone I can talk to about this book?"

"Yeeessss. For advi-ice we have set up a special phone number."

"Great! Let me have it." When he called the number she gave him, a 900 number at $9.95 per minute, it was answered by a man with an effeminate voice and vocal pattern. Paul knew many gay men, most of whom had no physical appearance or vocal pattern that would hint at their sexual identities. He remembered how he was surprised in college when two of his friends admitted to him they were a gay couple. Through talking with them he started to be more open about accepting people who were different from him. He came to appreciate individuals for how they treated others rather than his own inherited prejudice.

One day while they were walking to class, Reuben, one of the gay couple, turned to Paul and said, "Want to see something funny? Watch what happens when we talk 'butch.'" Just like that, Reuben and his lover changed their voices and voice patterns to imitate the archetype of the swishy gay voice. As they walked, people from all sides did double takes and stared at them. Finally, Paul, Reuben and Charlie, Reuben's lover, couldn't take it and fell to a nearby patch of grass, laughing at people's reaction to them until their sides hurt.

"Is anyone there? Hello?" The butch voice brought him back from his college reveries.

"Yes. Who am I talking to?"

"I am called…Sandalphon." Then he quickly ran through a canned disclaimer: "Youareovereighteenandyoudorealizethatthiscallwillcostyouninetyfiveaminutedon'tyou? Andyoudoacceptheseconditions, right?"

"Uh, sure. Yes," answered Paul, coming back to the point at hand.

"Good. How can I help you?"

"I called Ms. Scorsi and she gave me this number. I have some questions about the *Grimoire of Armadel.* Can you help me with this?"

"I can help you with anything. Why are you interested in that book?"

"Well, I had a dream where I saw a symbol," he said, creating a new lie. "A friend told me it was from that book. What can you tell me about it?"

"My friend, why does it matter? What do you really want in life? A symbol can't bring that to you."

"Yeah, but how could I use the symbol?"

"You could use it as a talisman. We can send you a book on how to make and use talismans. It's only $39.95 plus shipping and handling. Do you have a credit card?"

"Uh, I think I need personal advice. Do you S.M.S. people work a lot with the book?"

"We know all about that book, but we choose not to work with it…"

"Do you have any members who work with it regularly?"

"Oh no. No, no, no. Not at all. They all work only with the books we sell."

Paul was feeling frustrated. Here was another dead end. "Do you know of any people doing magic from that book?"

"No, we stay to ourselves unless some organization wants to pay us to come and lecture to them."

"Then why the hell did you say you could help me with anything?" Paul asked angrily. "I asked a question about the occult and you don't have a clue…"

"Oh, but we can help you. When you become a member of the S.M.S. we can help you with any project, with any plan. All you have to do is stay a member."

"And how much does that cost?"

"My friend, how can one place a value on success? All we ask is a donation of one-third of all you receive. Why don't you come down and be initiated. Then we can…"

Paul hung up the phone angrily. He had wasted the past seven minutes at seven bucks a minute. He didn't want to give them a penny and they had extracted half a c-note from him. Paul felt his bile flowing and started swallowing Tums whole.

He spent the next hour writing up what he had experienced and sent a copy of the file to the bunco squad. He didn't know if Sylvia Scorsi, "Sandalphon" and company were doing anything illegal, but if he was getting ripped off so were others.

* * * * *

Paul's phone rang at 9:17 P.M. He picked up the phone and heard a roar from the receiver. He held the handset away from his head and realized there was a wild party going on at the other end of the line. Finally, he was able to make out a single voice. "Hello?...Hello?...I'm calling for Lieutenant Paul Christian....Is he there?"

Paul brought the handset closer to his head. "This is Lieutenant Christian," he replied.

"Good. This is Jim Dodge of the Templars. I just got back into town and we're having a party. Sorry for the noise. I'm returning your call. What can I do for you?"

"I'd like to ask you some questions."

"I'm sorry, but I can't hear you. Could you speak up?"

Paul cleared his throat and spoke louder into the phone. "I said, I have some questions about the occult I need answered as soon as possible."

"*No problemo!* But doing this over the phone is impossible. I have to stay here—the party's in my honor—but you're welcome to come over. We can find a quiet room to talk in."

"There's going to be a quiet room there?" Paul asked, doubtfully.

"Well, a relatively quiet room."

"I'll be there in fifteen minutes." Paul hung up the phone and sighed. He wanted to stay in his office at the police station during the rest of his shift so he could go to the site of any murder as fast as possible. Instead, he got back into his assigned Ford and drove to a large house on Beverly Glen.

He had studied a dossier on the Templars. They were a semi-personality cult, following the teachings of the Crowley guy. Over the past few years several of the members were busted on drug charges, but the drugs were always in small quantities and for personal use. There was no evidence they were dealers. Also, the drugs they were busted for—marijuana, LSD and peyote—were all non-addictive. These were drugs that produced hallucinations, although Paul figured the Templars referred to what they experienced as visions. *Hmm, they might use those drugs as part of their rituals like some American Indian tribes do.* A few members were busted for illegal weapons, but when he checked into the charges he saw the "weapons" were ceremonial paraphernalia—ritual daggers and such. The only exception to this was the discovery of a small cache of black powder, but it turned out this was owned by a person who had a fireworks license. The only law being broken was for poor storage of a legal explosive.

All in all some individual members were more interested in stretching the law for their own enjoyment—they'd probably call it mystical enlightenment—rather than breaking the law for money or power.

The houses in this area were kept up well, with the exception of the Templar's house. The house looked good enough, but the yard was a dirt pit with a few scraggly weeds and no lawn. It looked hard and dry, as if it hadn't been cared for in years.

Paul walked to the door over a crack-covered cement path. As he neared the front door the noise of the party became louder. He took three Tums and crunched them in his mouth. While he chewed he looked at his Casio watch. It was 9:40 P.M.

The house was a 1930's structure, typical for this area in West Hollywood. There was one step up to the wide porch. Painted around the door was an elongated woman, her hands touching the ground on one side of the door and the toes of her outstretched feet touching the ground on the other side. She was naked, but her body was filled with stars. *Looks Egyptian*, Paul thought. He pushed the white button on the right side of the door which rang the bell. When there was no response he rang it again.

The door swung open and the party noise poured out. A young woman with long, straight, brown hair wearing a body suit and a short skirt opened the door without looking at who was on the other side. She was laughing as if she just heard an amazingly funny joke.

When she saw Paul she forced herself to stop. "Do what thou wilt shall be the whole of the law!" she said, then muffled some giggles.

"Huh?" Paul was bewildered by the strange greeting.

"Can I help you?" asked the woman.

"Yes. I'm here to see Jim Dodge.

"Oh sure. C'mon in."

The large main room was packed with a wide assortment of people. Dress ranged from business suits to black leather, from skin-hugging black spandex to what looked like rubber. Jewelry was mostly silver rather than gold, and there was plenty of it in evidence. The woman led him to an average-looking man: five-eight, short hair, average build with a growing paunch. He wore Dockers and an Izod knit shirt with its now out-of-fashion crocodile. *Or is it an alligator?*

"You must be Lieutenant Christian. Come on," said the man over the loud crowd. "Let's go into another room."

He led Paul to a bedroom, and when the door was closed the sounds of the party were muffled. "I'm Jim Dodge. How can I help you?"

Paul pulled his badge from his pocket and flashed it. "Here's my badge for identification," Paul said. "I'm investigating some recent murders which have occult overtones and…"

Ford sighed and sat on the bed. "You know, Lieutenant, I just came back from San Francisco. Members of a lodge of the Templars up north were accused of child abuse. I'm a lawyer and I not only won the case, but got a large settlement from the city as a result of the false accusations against us. That money is now in the Templars' coffers and will help pay for any defense in a lawsuit. That's why we're celebrating.

"But it was a long case and I'm tired. Now if you've come to accuse us of…"

"No, Mr. Dodge, you misunderstand. You and the Templars are not accused of anything. I was wondering if you could give us some help…"

The door burst open. A woman and man were in a heavy embrace, kissing passionately, their hands a whirl of action. His hands were pressing her breasts through the cotton material of her blue blouse. She had her hand inside his fly, fondling him. "Excuse us," said Dodge, loudly.

The couple broke their kiss but didn't move their hands. They looked at Dodge without embarrassment. "Sorry," said the man.

"Come on!" demanded the woman. They left, closing the door behind them.

"I apologize for the exuberance of the party. Back to the matter at hand. I'll be glad to assist you in your investigation in any way I can, as long as you agree to write a letter on Hollywood P. D. paper saying that I gave you assistance."

Leave it to a damn lawyer to try and get something out of helping someone. "Well, if you give me anything that can help me I'll be glad to write a letter stating that. So tell me what you can about this." He pulled from his pocket the now beat-up paper with the odd symbol copied from the legs of the victims.

Dodge took the paper and turned it around several times. "It looks like something from the *Grimoire of Armadel* to me. Or maybe it's from the *Lesser Key of Solomon?* I don't know. We Templars don't really work with that sort of standard stuff. We create our own symbols. They tend to look nothing like that. You can ask some of the other Templars about it if you like, but I think you'll get the same answer."

"No, that won't be necessary at this time." Paul pulled some Tums out and crunched them. "Don't you have some sort of lodge room? I'd like to see it if I could."

"You did already," answered Dodge. "The main room is also our Lodge room. We just decorate it for rituals. We perform a weekly *Mass of the Eucharist*. Although it's generally a private affair you would be welcome to attend, if that is your True Will."

Harmless partyers. The drugs they use are recreational. They party among themselves. When it comes to these murders there's nothing suspicious here. "Thanks. Maybe some other time. "Oh, one last thing. Can you tell me the meaning of a Tarot card, the Tower?"

"The Lightning Struck Tower? Why do you ask?"

"I'm just checking out what some people told me," Paul lied.

Jim looked at Paul for some time. *He's obviously a dilettante. Let's see, how should I explain it…*"I call it the card of revolution. Old things are destroyed so new things can come forth."

Paul was puzzled. "That sounds a lot like the Death card."

Jim was surprised Paul knew even a little about the Tarot. "No, there's a big difference. With the Death card, things fade away in their appropriate time. It is inevitable and expected. The Tower shows the inevitable change has been delayed. The result is a revolution instead of an evolution. The Death card indicates the old gives way and peaceably accepts death in order to experience rebirth. With the Tower, the old fights change tooth and nail until it is destroyed. In the long run, the Lightning Struck Tower is as positive as the Death card. In the short term it's a disaster.

"For example, if a society needs to evolve but the leaders won't allow it, a revolution follows. The end results of evolution and revolution will be similar, but the destruction that comes with revolution can be terrifying. The card signifies major changes which are terrible at the time they occur. Does that help?"

Paul went to the door and turned to look at Jim. "I don't know, Mr. Dodge," he said, as he opened the door, "I don't know."

Paul worked his way through the party and out to his car. He stood by the driver's door and looked at the street lights. They seemed to have an ugly, brownish tinge, a result of their light shining through the dirty air. Normally, the orange-brown smog would dissipate by this time as the cooler night temperatures ended the inversion layer that locked the smog into the Los Angeles basin. But the temperature remained hot and his lungs burned from the oppressive humidity and smog. He crunched a Tums. *What's being destroyed? More importantly, what's going to come out of it?*

* * * * *

Back in his office, Paul leaned back in his chair and pushed the heels of his shoes off so that they hung from his toes as he rested his feet on the desk. He wiggled his toes and his feet felt better being unconstrained. He chewed a couple of Tums and took a long slurp of his coffee—decaf with two sugars and lots of milk.

Paul closed his eyes and went over the case. Edison had said that genius was one per cent inspiration and ninety-nine per cent perspiration. Paul thought police work was the same. Still, that one per cent was important. He started to quietly hum the opening strains to Beethoven's *Ode to Joy*, the last movement of Ludwig van's ninth symphony. The people at the station knew not to bother him when he was humming that music.

Paul thought there was more going on in this case than had come to light. Until he got more to go on there was little he could do except continue hunting for information. Worse, there would be more killings. *Damn! Didn't anyone know what was going on?* They had an occult expert on the force, but he was on vacation until tomorrow. *Why are the parts missing from the bodies? Usually, when some whacko hacks off a body part the cut is sloppy. Flesh is torn and ripped, not neatly sliced. And why different body parts? FBI profiles indicate a person who commits such murders usually has a fixation on a particular body part and makes a fetish out of it. He keeps taking the same parts with each murder.*

Paul spent the night running the case over and over in his mind. There just wasn't enough information. It frustrated him. He didn't want to see anyone else die.

"Sir? Lieutenant Christian? Your shift's over. It's time for you to go home."

Paul opened his eyes to look into the clean face of a young female officer dressed in a black uniform. She couldn't have been over twenty-three. Her short-cropped hair and almond-shaped brown eyes reminded him of his sister.

Paul rubbed his face, felt the growing stubble, and then rubbed the grit out of his eyes. "No murders last night, uh Klendennon?" he asked, getting her name from the tag above her badge.

"There were two, sir. One on Highland during a robbery and one on Argyle, a family dispute."

"No missing body parts?"

"Sir?" questioned Sara Klendennon.

She was unfamiliar with his case. Luckily, they had been able to keep most of the details of the case, including the missing body parts, out of the papers and even away from most of the police department. Information on this case was made available only on a need-to-know basis. The fewer people who knew about it, the better. Paul wanted no copy-cat killings or false confessions as the result of some accidentally-released information. "Nothing, Klendennon. Nothing at all. Forget I said anything. I was just joking."

"Yes sir."

Paul wedged his feet back into his shoes, grateful there had been no murder in his case this night. He rolled his neck, easing out the cricks, and made his way to his old Chevy Impala. *Maybe the occult crap was nothing but a guise. Maybe it was just a crazy killer out to...Hell, I don't know any more. Well, Lieutenant Christian, I guess we go back to more footwork, the ninety-nine percent perspiration, when we get back on shift. Still, if it is some pattern, why was it broken? Why was there no murder tonight?*

Unfortunately, the pattern had not been broken. The body simply hadn't been found.

Yet.

* * * * *

Earlier

Three Mercedes stretch limos slithered down the Santa Monica Freeway, moving together like a snake across open desert sands. In unison they exited on La Brea, driving north to Sunset Boulevard.

This was actually a roundabout way to get to their destination, but the passenger in the rear limo enjoyed this scenic route. At Sunset they turned west. The shaded glass drew little attention from the street people, but the *touristas* turned, pointed and stared. They wondered if the darkened vehicles contained diplomats, rock stars, billionaires or movie stars. A few street hookers flashed their wares, hoping they could turn a big trick. The limos silently ignored it all and proceeded directly to their destination.

Soon they came to the curve that marked the real beginning of the Strip. The shell of Tower Records, Ned Terner's (originally Turner's) Liquor, the Whiskey (née Whiskey a go go), the Viper club, the Roxy, and finally, the Rainbow.

It was here the limos double parked. The driver of the first limo, dressed in grays and wearing a short-brimmed cap, raced around the front of his vehicle to open the back door on the curb side. Two men stepped out. They were dressed totally in black, including black turtle neck shirts and silk jackets. One had curly, collar-length, light brown hair. The other had straight, blond hair that was cut short to make him look like Steve McQueen. Both had the chiseled features of models. They straightened their clothes, and as they buttoned their jackets the edges of washboard stomach muscles could be seen under their shirts.

The driver of the second limo, dressed identically to the first, made a similar move to open the door for the passengers of his vehicle. Two women stepped out. They, too, were dressed in black, including grey eye shadow, although their lips were slashes of crimson. One, a blonde, had short-cropped hair brushed forward forming a cap to her head and a frame to her face. The black spandex leotard revealed more of her voluptuous figure than it hid. A wrap-around skirt barely reached her mid-thigh. The second woman was a bottle blonde with a perm and the big hair which was returning as the current fashion. Skinnier than the other, she wore a cat suit that covered her from head to toe yet, like her companion, left nothing to the imagination. Both wore simple, sterling silver earrings, shaped like pentagrams, in their left ears.

The scene was now attracting the usually jaded attention of even the regulars waiting to get into both the Rainbow and the more exclusive Over the Rainbow, a second club above the first. This was especially true as the magnificent four made no move to get out of the street. Instead, they waited for their drivers to regain their mounts and allow all three limos to move forward so the trailing vehicle was now in front of the doorway. Once again, the three vehicles stopped as one. The passengers of the first two limos formed two couples and stood to either side of the car door as the third driver scuttled around his car. Much heavier than the other two drivers, he made an odd appearance against the Jane Fondaed perfection of the couples-in-black as he puffed and moved like a crab until he could finally open the door for his passenger. The couples-in-black ignored the man-crab.

The physical perfection of the couples-in-black prevented the people on the street from noticing that the four *el perfectos* were actually rather short. This changed immediately as the passenger of the third limo came into view. His six-foot-four height unfurled from the vehicle and towered over the people around him. He said to the driver, "I'll beep you when we're ready."

The Baron walked to the stairs that led to Over the Rainbow without acknowledging the couples-in-black. They waited for him to pass and then followed behind. Unlike the elegant washboards of the two men, the Baron was built like a rock; a huge, solid piece of granite. Rather than wear a turtle neck he had chosen an elegant silk shirt, calming the sharpness of his rocky angles and drawing attention to itself because of its bright red color. He wore no tie, but a long white scarf surrounded his neck. He also wore a black suit, only his was far more tailored than those of the men who followed him. Although the night was mild, he wore an overcoat.

Raoul Dante was the doorman at the top of the stairs leading into Over the Rainbow. At least that was the name which Robby D'angelico thought would get him into the movies. Three hours of workouts with free weights each day had earned him this job. Selecting who could go in and out of the club was the only power he had in Hollywood. His entire movie career consisted of an undistinguished and uncredited appearance in one porno film. "Hey," he would explain, "if it was good enough for Stallone, it's good enough for me."

When Raoul saw the Baron and his entourage he ran down the stairs to greet them, pushing those waiting in line on the stairs to the side. "Hello, Baron. It's good to see you again. Glad you could make it. Here, let me take your coat."

He ushered the five up the wide stairs and opened the door to the club. Loud music flowed out into the night from within and the group entered. Raoul ignored the man on the stairs who yelled, "Hey, we were here first!" Didn't he know that Raoul had the power?

When Raoul took the Baron's overcoat and gave it to the owner's latest bimbo who worked as the coat check girl, he revealed the red carnation pinned to the Baron's left jacket lapel. Its color matched the ruby in the black patch over his left eye.

Raoul led them to a booth. The Baron sat at one end and the couples-in-black slid around to fill up the space. The music, which moved in unlikely patterns from Bowie to Bono, from the Kinks to Lords of Acid, was deafening. By the time a waitress squirmed through the crowd to their booth, only the Baron remained. The rest had gone off—on assignment. The Baron ordered a dry martini, shaken not stirred.

Who did this guy think he was, freakin' James Bond? But instead of saying her thoughts, she merely replied, "Yes, sir." As she did, she looked into his eye and felt like she was being pulled into a deep pool of mystery and passion. "I'll get it...uh...right away...uh...I'll...uh...yes." She tore herself free from his gaze and vanished into the crowd, gasping for breath.

Behind her the Baron gave a slight smile.

It was the short-haired blonde in the spandex who came back to the table first. With her was another woman. The woman was obviously drunk or stoned. She wore a loose, low-cut blouse and no bra. Her right nipple, tiny and pink, kept popping in and out of view over the top hem of her shirt. She was pretty in a hard way, and the tilt of her head indicated an attitude. The Baron looked her over from hair to heel. There was nothing here, so he shook his head slightly and ignored them. He closed his uncovered eye. When he opened it the two women had been replaced by the waitress with the martini. He reached into his coat and pulled out a wallet filled with crisp bills. He gave the woman a twenty.

She began to count out change, but he waved her away. "Thank you!" she said, smiling broadly.

For the next several hours the couples-in-black, one at a time, brought women for the Baron's approval. All were striking, yet none really caught his attention. The Baron looked at his Rolex President. It was one-thirty. He still had not found the right woman. When he looked up his male follower with the shoulder-length brown hair stood in front of him with a young woman. She was tall and slender. He was surprised to see one of her eyes was pale blue and the other an intense green, but quickly realized she was wearing a colored contact lens. She wore a green leotard with a blue mini, the colors matching her eyes. He looked down her body past a tiny waist and skinny, boyish hips. *Nothing there,* he thought.

Then he saw her feet. They were magnificently formed with elegant, long toes. The toenails, visible though the open tips of high-heeled shoes, were perfectly rounded and daubed with red. The arch of both feet formed curves of such grace he was reminded of the cathedral ceilings he had seen in his younger days in France. The gentle jut of the ankle bone made him think of terms like purity and perfection. These were not just feet, they were *the* feet—feet truly fit for a goddess. Tonight, she would be the one, but only if she would freely give of herself. *A sacrifice was meaningless if taken. It was only of value if it was given.*

Cindy deGrasse was looking for excitement. She had been in

Hollywood for over a year, trying to become an actress. Most of the time she worked as a secretary for a temp agency. So far, all she had gotten was a non-speaking walk-on in a crowd scene. Two nights ago she broke up with her boyfriend and kicked the freeloader out of her apartment. She thought going to Over the Rainbow might provide the excitement she sought to cheer herself up.

She had finally been allowed in the door at around a quarter-to-one, ordered an Apple Martini, and looked around to see if there was anyone in the club who she knew. Suddenly, she felt a presence behind her. She turned to face a pretty boy, his perfect features dressed in black. They talked. They danced. After several fast numbers, a slower song was played. He pulled her to him and their bodies danced a passionate *pas de deux*. He felt hard. Everywhere. She smacking her lips. *I know who I'll be going home with tonight!*

He looked deeply into her eyes and she felt sure he was going to kiss her. Instead he surprised her by saying, "Cindy, there's someone here I'd like you to meet." He took her to the Baron.

The Baron smiled and bade her to sit down. He ordered her another Apple Martini.

She looked into his eye and and suddenly felt weak. *I feel like I'm a little girl next to him. I feel like they used to say in cartoons, "I am in his power." But I feel safe, too, like the way I always felt safe when I was around my father.* Cindy had never been attracted to big men before, but there was something about this man's power that drew her to him. They talked about nothing and everything. She was entranced by him.

He reached into the pocket on the side of his jacket and when he pulled out his hand, palm up, she saw the artificial nail which had been glued to the nail of his pinky. In the cup of the nail was a fine, white powder. "It's for you, if you like," he said.

She cupped his large hand in both of hers and bent her head. She inhaled the powder deeply, quickly getting the familiar jolt and rush of energy that shivered through her body. This time, however, it was far more intense than usual. She shivered again and opened her eyes wide. *Whoa, that's powerful white.* Then slowly, sensually, she licked his palm from the middle finger to the wrist.

"There's more at my home. We can all party there. If you wish, you may come." Without waiting for her approval he rose. He reached into his pocket and pressed the beeper to signal the drivers. The Baron put his arm gently around Cindy—he wanted to make sure that she could refuse to go further at any time—and started walking to the door. The couples-in-black deserted the people they were with without giving a word of explanation. They lined up behind the Baron, who had by now retrieved his overcoat, and they all went down the stairs. The three limos waited directly in front of them, their doors open like gaping mouths. Cindy went with the Baron while the others entered the vehicles they arrived in.

The Baron waited to get into the limo. He turned toward the Rainbow and calmly held his right hand out, palm up. A reddish sphere of energy appeared on his palm and he blew on it gently. It spread out, like a fine dust, covering everyone and everything in sight. The Baron knew it would also go through the walls and into the club. He smiled slightly. No one would remember that he or the people he had brought spent any time with, or left with Ms. Cindy deGrasse.

By the time Cindy was in the Baron's limo she felt very sleepy. *Had there been a sedative in the drugs?*

The Baron, entered the limo shortly after she made herself comfortable in the elongated vehicle. She closed her eyes for a second and when she opened them the Baron was talking softly to her. "Come on, Cindy. The party's just beginning. If you prefer, though, I'll have my driver take you home."

She blinked awake. Somehow, time had stopped and now the limo was parked in front of the Baron's Venice mansion. Taking the Baron's hand, she exited the vheicle and walked to the house, entering through the large front door. There, with the couples-in-black, they were joined by at least a dozen more people in a huge room that was dimly lit. On a table were bottles of mid-priced wine, beer and harder liquors. The Baron sat in his large chair and Cindy sat in a smaller chair next to him. Drinks were brought to them and for the next hour her glass was constantly filled. The Baron entertained her with delightful conversation. The background music was loud, but not so loud as to take away from their talk.

Cinddy became aware that the lights had dimmed even further and the music slowed. Couples were dancing and kissing and feeling each other. *The temperature in the room has become uncomfortably warm,* she thought.

The Baron left for a few moments, and when he returned he said, "Look, Cindy." In his hands was what appeared to be a miniature pirate's chest, about a foot wide, five inches deep and eight inches tall. It was covered with decorative leather strips held on by antique-looking brass tacks. He opened it and her eyes widened. It was filled with white powder, at least half a kilo.

A mirror was brought out and lines were made. People struggled to get their straws on the mirror. Laughing, the Baron started making lines on the linoleum floor. "Cindy," he asked, "are you sure you don't want to go home?" They laughed and Cindy was soon on the floor with the rest of them. Bodies brushed against hers to get the powder. *No wonder the Baron's so popular,* she thought. Like sharks in a feeding frenzy the bodies went after the lines of the drug.

It slowly dawned on Cindy that not all the bodies were after the cocaine. Hands and lips found themselves on her legs and thighs, her arms and shoulders. At first they added a pleasant tickle to the drug's effect. Then she felt lips on *that* spot on the back of her neck. When hands reached into her leotard and played with her breasts it was too much. She was lost.

It was all a haze. Hands, lips and other body parts were all over her, caressing, caressing, as her clothes were removed. She was sure someone asked her if she wanted them to stop. *Is he crazy?* She grabbed the man who asked her, kissed him hard and explored his teeth with her tongue and crotch with her hand. Her tongue tingled from some cocaine on his lips.

Cindy lost track of time. She had no idea how many men or women she played with, how many fingers, organs or devices had entered her. She looked at herself and saw she was covered with sweat, sperm and lubricating juices. She reveled in it. Laughing, she rubbed the fluids into her skin. *It's right for me to be here. I want—need—more!*

She felt her arms and legs being held. She writhed in pleasure as she heard the strange, foreign words being chanted. *What is the meaning of those words? What does "Barra Edinnazu" mean? They're chanting it over and over. And what is that smell? Incense?* Suddenly, for the umpteenth time that night, her body arched in release. She moaned and a red flush came to her naked breasts. Cindy felt the quiver of a penis ejaculating within her. She moaned again and opened her eyes. They grew wide as she saw several people now dressed in black, hooded robes. Helpless because she was held in place, all she could do was watch in terror.

The Baron, also now in a black robe, towered above her. From within the folds of the robe he withdrew an ornate knife that glittered in the candlelight. He held it up in the air with both hands, as if making an offering. He chanted, mumbled and cried out foreign words Cindy didn't understand, although he again repeated that odd phrase, "Barra Edinnazu." Finally he nodded and the person who was holding Cindy's head pulled her hair to force her chin back cruelly, revealing the long, white taper of her neck. To Cindy, the Baron's eye seemed to glow with unholy desires as he waved the knife in a fluid motion above her. Then, before she could move or resist, he brought the blade down across her neck in a single, smooth motion.

She tried to scream but a hand came down across her mouth and stopped her. The actual feel of the razor-sharp knife didn't hurt. She struggled briefly as the life flowed from her neck. Her thoughts went back to the one part she had played in a movie. It was the only thing she would be known for. *I'm feeling so cold, so very cold.* Her eyes opened weakly. *Who will water my plants?* Her last sensation was of the partyers licking her blood with a passion superior to their attack on the cocaine. It seemed they were taking more than her blood, they were drawing from her the very energy of her body. They were taking her soul. She had wanted excitement and had found it in her first—and last—starring role.

The sun would rise shortly, and the Baron hurried to finish his work. When he was through he told Thom, the one with the blond hair who accompanied him to Over the Rainbow, to dump the body quickly. "Only this time hide it a little better. We don't want the police to think we are being too easy on them."

* * * * *

Sixth Day

Paul Christian was summoned out of his sleep to see the body. It was after ten in the morning when he arrived at the site on Cahuenga. She had been hidden under some bushes instead of being left out in the open as in the past. *Hmm…A change of M. O.* He looked at her sadly. She had been beautiful—tall and slender with shoulder-length brown hair and wearing a green leotard and a blue miniskirt. Her eyes were blue, but in one was a green-tinted contact lens. She had the same ghastly blue pallor as the previous bodies. *It almost seems like something more than blood had flowed from the gash in her neck.* He could also detect the faint odor of incense.

Her feet had been severed from the legs just above her ankles. The searched for two hours, but no sign of the feet was found. Paul knew they wouldn't find them here.

Paul turned from the body, kicked a rock in the street, sighed, and looked up at the sun. It was odd how brown the sun looked to him. *The smog seems to be getting worse every day. I wonder how many more people will end up in the hospital because of it?*

Paul didn't need to read the reports to know what would be in them. He took the pack of Tums from his pocket and popped one in his mouth, thought about it, and took two more. He asked the officer from forensics for the name of the card that had been placed in her. He knew one would be there without even examining the body.

The officer, unaware of the previous cases, looked at Paul in surprise. *How could he know that a card had been found in the victim's vagina?*

"It's The Lovers," he said to Paul. "The Lovers."

Chapter Eight

Sixth Evening

The evening started on a bad note. Paul had been called into the office of Captain Minelli, the head of detectives and Paul's immediate supervisor. "The news guys have more of it," Minelli had said calmly. "It'll be on the internet in an hour, the TV tonight, and in the headlines tomorrow."

Paul's mind raced. The locals citizens tended to ignore gangs killing each other off, yawned when domestic quarrels ended in death and merely tisked at the drive-by shootings of innocents. But add in some occult weirdness and they go crazy. "Where is our protection?" they cry. "Who will save us from the Satanists?"

"How much of it do they have?" Paul asked.

"Some. Not the card or the symbol or that the missing body parts are different with each victim, but the occult crap, drained blood, missing body parts and the serial connection." He pivoted the seat of his chair so his back was to Paul. He leaned back in his chair, showing Paul a growing bald spot, and tapped the tips of the fingers and thumb of his right hand against those of his left. "Paul," he asked slowly, "do you have *anything* which isn't in your reports, anything at all? Guesses? Clues? Hints? You know..."

"No, sir. It's all there."

Minelli rose from his leather-covered chair behind a beaten desk. "Hmm," he mumbled, beginning to pace the back of the room. He put his hands behind him, slapping the back of the right against the palm of the left with a gentle, fleshy thwap.

Oh-oh, Paul thought, *here it comes. He's goig to say "As you know, the Chief of the Hollywood police department is elected..."*

"As you know, Paul," Minelli began, "the Chief of the Hollywood police department is elected."

"The election is only harumph months away."

"The election is only four-and-a-half months away."

"The Chief needs to keep the voters happy so they'll re-elect him."

"The Chief needs to keep the voters happy so they'll re-elect him."

"Weird cases like this make the voters unhappy."

"Weird cases like this make the voters unhappy."

"When the Chief is unhappy he makes me unhappy."

"When the Chief is unhappy he makes me unhappy."

"When I'm unhappy, heads roll."

"When I'm unhappy, heads roll."

For the next hour Paul listened, yessed and uh-huhed everything Minelli said. Both he and Minelli knew Paul would ignore it, but they went through the act anyway. Minelli gave Paul every tired suggestion and all the advice from every class and detective book around. He fumed at Paul, yelled, cajoled and left him with an ultimatum: an arrest in ten days or Paul would spend the rest of his career on the police force collecting quarters from parking meters.

It was just after 5:00 p.m. when Paul gingerly sat on the hard wooden chair in his office. He had wondered if he would fit after the way Minelli had chewed him a new butt. Paul pretended to shuffle papers at his desk. *Sometimes police work sucked, especially when politics enters.* He knew how laws were bent to make arrests and how lies were told to get convictions. Like almost every other cop he knew, when he first joined the force he had wanted to get the bad guys off the street. But he had seen how some cops lied to get those bad guys, only to discover the guy in jail was innocent. Then, rather than lose a job and put the city at the losing end of a lawsuit, they would grab the real bad guy for something else and let Mr. Innocent rot.

Or rather than put the wrong person in prison they could just ruin lives. Paul thought about the preschool case by the beach a few years ago. The whole thing started with wild accusations from a drunk who died of cirrhosis during the trial. It was mishandled by the police, the psychologists, everyone except the first prosecutor who had sense enough to leave the case when she realized there was no evidence and no way they could ever get a conviction. She saw the videotapes of how the psychologists coerced the children into telling stories of Satanism, sacrifice and abuse. Now the lives of those kids and their parents would be shaken for years, perhaps for as long as they lived. And those teachers, who never did anything but care for children, would never be able to care for children again. All because a few public officials wanted some convictions of Satanists to hold up to the newspapers so they could get re-elected.

He hated it. He couldn't abide it. He let everyone know it. That was one reason why he was still only a lieutenant after so many years on the force.

Paul knew Minelli wanted a head—the real bad guy or just someone who would do. Solving the crime wasn't as important as getting re-elected and keeping jobs. *Being a cop isn't enough. I also have to think like a damn politician. C.Y.A. has become the rule: If something bad happens blame it on someone else, anyone else, just so long as it doesn't rub off on you. Cover Your Ass.*

Paul pursed his lips and yanked at the wide, center drawer of his desk.

As usual, it stuck and made screeching noises as he wiggled it left and right to get it out. He rarely used this drawer, and Paul shuffled through the messy papers that lined it until he found the one he was looking for. Just two lines. Simple. Straightforward. It was unsigned and undated.

> This is to inform you that as of today I, Paul Christian, am resigning from the Hollywood police force.

He looked at it for a long time as it lay in the drawer. He picked it up, held it in his hands and sighed. *I've saved so little over the years. If I quit now I'll lose most of my pension. All I have to do is give Minelli a name, a body, just somebody convictable. In a few years I'll be able to retire in comfort. It would be so easy…*

How simple it would be to give Minelli a name. As he considered it, he felt his stomach twist and turn. He knew it wasn't from his ulcer. *Hell, why does just thinking about this make me feel guilty?*

Paul put the paper down. *Every arrest I ever made was of someone I truly thought had committed a crime.* Sometimes he was wrong. When such a case was solved Paul would personally go to the person he arrested in error and explain why he had done it, apologize and ask for the person's understanding. As a result, not one of his arrestees ever sued for false arrest. *All I'd have to do is make one bust of a throwaway person who really didn't commit the crime. I'd keep my job and my pension. I'd be able to survive in retirement.*

Paul picked up his resignation and read it over again. The typed letters on the page blurred in his vision. *What would the other cops think of me? Hah! Did I ever care about that? What would life be like on just Social Security, even if it lasts 'till I die? I could retire in style in a few more years. All it'll take is to throw an innocent, mentally ill transient with no family into prison. No one would care. Minelli and the Chief would be happy.*

Paul drummed the fingers of his right hand on the desk. *No, damn it! I'd care. The knowledge would haunt me every day for the rest of my life. Not only would the wrong guy be locked up, but the real perp would be free. It would rot in my gut like a…*

His mind set, Paul grimaced, reached into his jacket pocket and pulled out a Cross pen. He looked at its sleek metal surface and remembered how it was given to him by the mother of a young girl who had been killed. He had found the murderer. The mother gave it to him when the killer was convicted. She felt her daughter could now rest in peace as justice had been fulfilled. He twisted the barrel and the point appeared from the hollow tip. As Paul watched, the bright, florescent light glinted off a dent on the barrel of the pen. He gently rubbed a finger tip over the dented area and remembered how it became dented when he fell chasing a punk who held up a liquor store on Little Santa Monica Boulevard. He always wished he had caught that kid. The boy was only thirteen. He was killed two months later when he tried to rob another liquor store. The dent reminded him of his failures, and each one was painful.

He moved to sign and date the paper in front of him, but stopped. *I've got ten days, ten days to stop a murderer.* Paul repeatedly tapped the end of the pen against his lower lip. *Aww crap*! He twisted the barrel of the pen and the point disappeared within the barrel, then he put the pen back in his pocket. He placed the resignation back into the top center drawer and wriggled it noisily closed. From the top side drawer he removed the pad of paper where he had been keeping careful notes about this case. He thumbed through the pad to figure out what he should do next. *If I've only got ten more days to work, I'll damn well make each day count.*

* * * * *

At 5:48 P.M. Paul received a call from Greg Timmons. Timmons was the staff occult expert. Back from his vacation, he had time to see Paul now.

Paul walked over to Timmons' office, knocked on the door and was invited in. The office was awash in posters with occult signs and symbols. In the back was a large cross, beneath which were the words I am the way, the truth and the light. *Oh-oh…*

He looked at Timmons as the officer got up to shake Paul's hand. Timmons was quite slender, a gangly plank of wood. Above his oblong face was greyish hair that was somewhere between a flattop and wild. His bulging, black eyes seemed to shift between paranoia and craziness.

"I have a message you wanted to see me, Paul. When I read about the occult sacrifices I knew why you called and I knew I had to help you. There you go."

"Uh, tell me, Timmons, how did you get interested in all of this? What made you become an expert?"

"I first became interested when my pastor gave a sermon about the international, world-wide conspiracy of occultists and communists who are out to destroy Christianity. Later I took a course on the occult and learned everything I could."

"Who taught the course?"

"His name is LaMont. He publishes the best newsletter for the police on the occult. It's called *File 14.* Here's a copy. There you go." He handed a couple of poorly typed and photocopied pages to Paul.

Paul looked at it and read a few scurrilous passages filled with innuendo and ill logic. "How many weeks was the course you took on the occult?"

"Well," Timmons said defensively, "it was more of a seminar. It, uh, it took six hours."

I think this may be a wild goose chase. "What experience do you actually have with occult cases? I haven't seen or heard of any of your work."

"I've been called in to consult on many cases, but I was only a part of those investigations. On my own I've reopened some cases and discovered amazing links. So there you go."

"Which cases are those?"

"Manson, Ramirez, the Black Dahlia, Oswald, Ed Gein, Jack Ruby, Son of Sam, Kevin Bianchi, Zodiac…"

A very wild goose chase. "Did you find any new hard evidence in those cases?"

"Well, yes and no. You see, all of those cases have incredible cover-ups by superior officers. Evidence is missing even though they claim it was never collected and never existed. But I know better! There are incredible circumstantial links between those cases that point to an international conspiracy of murders done in the name of Satan in order to overthrow Christian society. They commit sacrifices all the time, about fifty thousand per year just in the U.S."

Paul gulped. "Uh…fifty thousand? Don't you think that might be a little high? The FBI estimates less than half that number of people are murdered in the U.S. each year."

"Of course they do! Don't you see? They're part of the conspiracy. They know what's going on. There you go."

"Well, what happens to the bodies?"

"They have several ways of dealing with the bodies. They bury them far out in wooded areas or they have portable crematoriums."

This is getting a little too wacked out. "Look, Timmons, can you give me some information on the case I'm working on? There are some things about the case which we haven't revealed to the public. For example, Tarot cards are found with the bodies and…"

"Do you see? Only Satanists use Tarot cards. There you go. This is obviously the work of a generational Satanic cult. They've probably committed lots of murders that you aren't aware of."

"The victims are missing body parts, too."

"Well, there you go. See, these Satanists have been sacrificing people for years. The victims you've found are missing parts because they were going to reveal the secrets of the cult. That's their typical way of punishing those who would break their blood oaths to the cult."

Paul stared at Timmons for a moment. *How deep a hole will he dig for himself?* "What do you think should be done?" he asked.

"There's only one thing we can do. We must get back to the true teachings of our Lord and Savior, Jesus the Christ. Only He can bring us back to the path of righteousness. All other paths are false. When we catch the perpetrators we have to share the Good News that Jesus has died for their sins."

"What if the person is from a Jewish, Islamic, Buddhist, Hindu or other religious tradition? Once they're caught and convicted shouldn't we approach them in a way that is familiar to them?"

Timmons' eyes looked at Paul with a lack of understanding. "But Paul, all of those are false religions. Only traditional, orthodox Christianity worships the true God. Hinduism and Buddhism are nothing but fronts for Satanism. Judaism was superceded by the new covenant of Jesus Christ and Muhammad was a false prophet. We have to rid the world of…"

"Timmons," Paul interrupted, disgusted with the religious monologue, "some of this isn't quite clear to me. You know, the Mafia had blood oaths yet their syndicate had people break away and testify against them. Same with the Ku Klux Klan. We even infiltrated them. But when it comes to Satanists, nothing. Why is that? And also, how can you make such pronouncements without even examining the physical evidence?"

Timmons stood, the muscles of his neck tensed and his fingers were white against the desk where he gripped it. "Wha…what are you trying to do?" he sputtered. "Now I understand." He pointed an accusing finger at Paul. "You're in on it, aren't you? There you go! You're here to defame me. So tell me, Lieutenant Christian, how long have you been a part of this Satanic cult? Did they make you take your surname in order to put others off the track? How many people have you sacrificed? Who's putting you up to this?"

Paul stood, his mouth open in surprise and shock at these wild accusations. He said nothing, but turned and walked to the door.

"Oh, yeah. There you go. I know you now. I'll be keeping my eye on you. I'll break open your cult and prosecute every one of you Satanists."

Paul walked out the door. As he started to close it he looked back with pity at the enraged officer. "I think you should visit a psychiatrist."

"Oh right. There you go. I visit a shrink and anything I say is suspect. I know their game. Do you think I haven't visited psychiatrists before? Besides, psychiatry is nothing but a front for Satanism. I know. I've investigated. I've done the research. I've…"

Paul closed the door without waiting for the rest of Timmons' diatribe and walked back to his office.

* * * * *

Sixth Night

Paul sat in his chair, sipping decaf with two spoons of sugar and lots of milk. *I think Timmons is more interested in rooting out heresy than solving crimes.* Paul looked at the issue of *File 14* Timmons had given him. *They should call it* File 13. *That's where it belongs.* Paul had read the newsletter. It was filled with paranoia and dogma disguised as police material. He tossed in in the trash, sighed, and took another sip of coffee. *I'm going to have to report Timmons and the garbage he's spreading.* Paul hated the thought of turning in another officer. He took a large jar of Tums out of the bottom drawer of his desk, opened it and used a mouthful of coffee to swallow several chalky pills.

Paul made some more phone calls. He finally reached Alexander Gardner. Alex was upset and fired away at him over the phone. "Paul, I heard about the murders on the radio. Why didn't you tell me about the other killings? I've spent hours and hours going through books and all of my research is useless because you didn't give me the full information. Look. I don't mind helping you, in fact I'm glad to be able to do so. But I don't like wasting my time!"

"I'm sorry, Alex." Paul sighed and let his shoulders droop. He felt thoroughly lost on this case. He didn't know much about the occult. He solved other so-called occult crimes simply through good detective work: following up on clues, interviewing witnesses, following leads and checking finger prints. On those cases he didn't need to know about the occult. This case was different. "You know I don't know much about this occult stuff. I didn't mean to mislead you." Paul fumbled with his notes. "But even you said that the murder was, uh, oh yes, quote, a crime which may be repeated in the future, unquote. I've been kind of busy dealing with it."

"Yes, well, I guess I understand," replied the calming professor. "Did all of the murders have the same card and symbol? Were they all missing their breasts?"

"No, they had the same symbol but different cards. Different body parts were missing from each one of the…"

"*Different body parts?* Are you sure?"

"Of course I'm sure."

Alexander's voice changed in quality. "Look, Paul, I'm not an occult practitioner. I'm just a teacher and a student of the occult. This puts a new light on the subject. If you want to stop this you will need to fight fire with fire. Do you understand, Paul? Find a magician who will help you."

"What do you think's going to happen, Alex?"

"Paul, I think somebody is…that is to say, they might be… No, I don't want to mislead you. I want to make sure I'm right on this." He paused for a second and then he repeated himself. "Paul, get a magician. Make sure he knows his stuff."

"Well, who do you suggest, Alex?"

"I'm sorry, Paul, but I can't help you there. As I told you before, I don't keep track of groups or individuals. But Paul…"

"Yeah?"

"Get a magician. Do it now. Do it today. I'll call when I know more.

God bless us all."

The telephone connection clicked off in Paul's ear. He sighed and leaned back in his chair, considering what Alex said. The air conditioning in the building had failed. Again. A few fans helped to circulate the air, but it was still oppressively humid and the air hung like a heavy weight, making it hard to breathe. The smog burned with each breath, causing his chest to hurt. It smelled bad, too. No, it smelled awful.

Paul thought about Alexander's voice. At first he couldn't place the change he had heard in it. Then he knew. It was something in Alex's voice he had never heard before in all of the years they had known each other.

Fear.

* * * * *

Paul looked through his note pad and a card dropped out. It was the one that Donna Fortuna had given him. *Fate?* He called the number several times and finally reached her at 6:36 P.M. He reminded her of their meeting and revealed his full identity. He talked about the case with her, although he revealed little other than what the media already knew, and asked if he could talk with her about it. She agreed, and invited him over that night.

He drove through the traffic and darkening sky to her Hollywood Hills home. After college and the navy just before Viet Nam, he moved to the most famous city in America, Hollywood, California. Back then it had been beautiful. Paul was a young officer walking a Hollywood beat. It was the early days of the hippies, and he thought they were wonderful. T*hey were friendly to the cops and we laughed with them. We took the kids to the free clinic on Sunset and about the only trouble we had was with the drug pushers and trying to tell if some of the "hippie chicks" were giving it away or selling it and trying to keep them from being hurt by the polyester sleaze.* In those days a cop could always trust a guy with long hair or a girl in hippie garb.

Then came Manson. The bad guys started to look like the good guys. The good guys moved from acid and grass to speed and heroin and became bad guys to support their habits. Viet Nam exploded and the police were called in to enforce the politics. Cops became pigs. Police did a job instead of protecting and serving.

Paul frowned as he remembered the changes. He thought of how instead of receiving thanks he was spit on; how people looked at cops with disgust or anger instead of respect. He remembered how the streets got dirty and the people got poorer. Families fell apart and gangs replaced them. First it was the Crips and the Bloods. Later more gangs came, and the gangbangers killed each other off as if life was nothing more than a video game. Parts of Hollywood had turned to pure crap. At times fighting the beast seemed useless. He remembered his disappointment and sadness the first time he looked in the eyes of a child and saw neither trust nor respect, only fear.

Still, every once in a while he saved the good guys and caught the bad guys. He even got his fifteen minutes of Warholian fame for solving some crimes. Sometimes it was worth it.

His assigned Ford had a pitted windshield, and the low-lying sun greedily exploded in each chip and scratch. His view was either blurring brightness or dimming daylight. Both ways made it difficult to see.

Donna Fortuna's house had no driveway, so he found a spot on the tree-lined street that fronted her home. As he walked across the gravel path that led to her front door he noticed that in front of her inconspicuous wood and stucco ranch house was a large, bizarrely-shaped tree. At a height of about eight feet above the ground it had a huge, thick branch that ran horizontally for four feet.

"It's the hanging tree," said a quiet, mellow voice.

"Excuse me?" said Paul, looking for the source of the voice.

"It's the hanging tree," said Donna Fortuna, stepping out from her front door. She walked across the octagonal red bricks set into the ground leading to the tree. She ducked under a branch and came up next to Paul. She looked at the tree and gently stroked its large trunk. "Can you sense it?" she asked. "Can you sense the lives taken here? From the mid-1800s until 1912 this was the official hanging tree for forty miles in each direction. Nobody knows how many people were sentenced to death by the courts and died from ropes that dangled over the horizontal branch. When I bought this house I was told Billy the Kid died on it, but of course that was untrue. He was shot by Pat Garrett on July fifteenth in 1881. And he was shot in Fort Sumner, New Mexico, not California.

"Supposedly, a rare, magical herb known as the mandrake—no relation to the usual roots that pass for mandrakes—grows under the spot where a murderer is hanged. I dug under that branch many times, but I never found one. I guess the story of the mandrake is a myth, archetypal or just plain false." She paused dramatically as an enigmatic smile crossed her face. "Or maybe they had all been dug up before I got to them." She started walking to the door and said, "Let's go inside."

Paul followed Donna through the door of her home. It opened into a huge living room with an open-beam ceiling. The floor was a rich parquet which shone from frequent polishings but squeaked from weak joists in several places. They went through it into a much smaller dining nook/kitchen. Here it was warm and friendly. The yellow refrigerator had a few dents in it and was covered with goofy magnets. Paul saw one of the Pillsbury Dough Boy and smiled.

Donna laughed. "I honestly don't know how I got all of those. Somebody gave me one at a party I went to and I guess I was too effusively thankful. Anyway, it became a trend. Friends found ones they liked and gave them to me. At birthday parties I'm inundated with them. Look."

Donna went over to the sink, opened the cabinet under it and pulled out a large box. She brought it back to the table in the dining nook. She reached in and pulled out a long line of magnets sticking to one another.

When one line stopped, looking like the political map of a gerrymandered state, she reached in and pulled out another bunch. Laughing, she asked, "Do you need any magnets? I can't get rid of them! They stick to my metal trash cans." They both laughed and as she put them back under the sink.

She offered Paul some coffee. He said, "Yes," to some decaf and watched as she put freshly roasted beans into a grinder and waited for the little machine's ratcheting roar to smooth out. Then she put the grindings into the glass cylinder of a French-press coffee maker and poured in boiling water which she had heated in a teapot. Donna let the beans and water brew for a few minutes, then pushed a stainless steel plunger to the bottom of the pot, separating the sopping, ground beans from the coffee. She poured two cups and gave him one, but quickly grabbed it back when she noticed the chip on the cup she had proffered. She gave him her cup instead.

After years of living the life of a bachelor he liked this. He felt relaxed and comfortable. He had forgotten how much he enjoyed a woman's company. It wasn't just the sex, it was the companionship, the being around one another. After his wife divorced him—what was it now, ten, no eleven years ago—he had resigned himself to living alone. *Perhaps I should look to change that.* He added two scoops of sugar and lots of milk to his cup.

As they settled down at the table he realized he had seen no occult symbols anywhere around the house. "Ms. Fortuna, most occultists I've seen have occult stuff all over. I don't see anything here. Are you really a magician?"

Donna laughed and told him to call her by her Donna. "What exactly do you think a magician is, Paul?"

He immediately bristled at not being called "Lieutenant Christian," but something in her voice made it sound right. He considered her question for a moment, then realized he didn't have a clue. "I don't know," he said honestly. "I guess somebody with lots of occult stuff who is constantly trying to, uh...what do you call it, invoke...uh...strange beasties?"

At this they both laughed. "Paul, most people—even many budding occultists whom I've met—have a weird idea as to what being a magician is. Many think the more books you have, the more occult bric-a-brac—I call 'em dust catchers—on your shelves, the better a magician you are. That simply isn't true.

I have a friend named Emmy who is not an occultist, but she has an… uh… unique vision for interior decoration. An acquaintance who visited her place and mine at different times found Emmy's home to have far more of an occult ambiance than my place."

"Does that bother you?"

"On the contrary. People who require a big show of occult objects, unless they're also collectors, are rarely very good at performing real magic. They're too busy putting on the show which they think is a part of magic, probably as a result of reading too many cheap novels and seeing too many stupid movies. They're egotists, not magicians. They don't want to spiritually evolve, they want to do spells and curses, invocations and evocations, rituals and levitations."

"Isn't that what real magic is all about?"

"No."

"Well now I *am* confused," said Paul. "What does a real magician do?"

She considered her answer for a moment, then asked Paul a question: "Would you bring an active bomb to nursery school?"

"Don't be ridiculous."

"And yet, there are people, nursery school level beginners, who spend hours invoking and evoking spirits and demons and entities without immediately banishing them. These people have nothing but trouble in their lives, as if a bomb had gone off. They blame it on everything *other* than the magic. In a sense, they don't believe that magic works. Otherwise, they would be far more careful with what they do.

"A real magician is *capable* of doing those things, and doing them well. He or she will perform them, when necessary, to improve his or her life or the lives of others. All that 'stuff' they show in movies is only a tiny aspect of real magic."

"Okay, then, Donna. You tell me. What is real magic?"

"Magic—real magic—is the highest form of spirituality. As a result of years of practicing various physical and mental techniques, a magician can develop a direct link to God. It's called, rather ungrammatically, the Knowledge and Conversation of your Holy Guardian Angel. It takes many years of study and practice to achieve this goal. Some spend many years and never achieve it."

Donna caught the look on Paul's face and laughed gaily. "I know what you're thinking, but don't assume we're all crazy and have inflated egos. Part of the training is learning how to avoid exactly that. We don't go around preaching. Our relationship with the Divine is very personal and helps us to fulfill our individual lives. We don't try to convince others of our personal vision. Nor do we tell people to sell their belongings and move to the middle of nowhere. We all have free choice. We want to change and improve our lives. We have no right to change the lives of others. It's sort of like the prime directive on *Star Trek*: learn, study, evolve but don't force your will on others. They have the right to evolve as they will.

"Part of the mythology of real western magic is the story of Christian Rosencruz. He is the mythical founder who gave his name to Rosicrucianism. He told his followers to wear the clothes of the society they lived and act like the people around them. They were to claim no powers except the ability to heal, and for that they were to charge nothing. Well, I'm a nurse and I do help people heal. The fact is I charge far less than most nurses. Unfortunately I do have to charge as I can't live without making some money. I may be a magician, but I can't live on nothing." She smiled and her eyes twinkled. "At least not yet."

"What about magical powers?"

"They exist," she said, matter-of-factly.

Her simple response stunned Paul. Her conversation was so logical, philosophical and reasonable he thought she would tell him magic powers were a hoax or hypnotism.

She took a sip of coffee and continued, "In India magic powers are called *siddhis.* It is believed that if you practice meditation and yoga for a long enough period you will develop these powers. Perhaps the most famous example of this is the power of levitation—they call it flying—practiced by the Maharishi's followers. It's described in full in the ancient book known as the *Aphorisms of Patanjali.*

"But the Indian mystics were very wise. They knew the true goal of yoga and meditation was to become enlightened, to join the higher self and God in unity with the universe and appreciate all as one. They said the *siddhis* got in the way of achieving enlightenment. People got caught up in producing magical phenomena and ceased their striving to become enlightened. Likewise, in the West, there are people who develop powers on their way to the Knowledge and Conversation of their Holy Guardian Angel. We refer to it as the K and C. Some stop there and never achieve the K and C. Others go on to achieve the K and C, but also more fully develop their magical powers. Some are blinded by the light. Others thrive in it."

Paul looked at this strange woman while sipping his coffee. *Is she real? Is she pulling my leg?* "Donna," he said, "I don't know what to believe anymore. I'm too much of a skeptic to accept magic, but this case has people who do believe in it. You're obviously sane and rational yet you believe in it. All I know is that something weird and evil is going on. I need people who know about magic. More than that, I may need someone who can *do* magic. Is that person you, Donna? Are you a real magician? Do you do magic? Do you teach magic in your group, what did you say it was called, the Silver Sunrise? If you can't help me, is there someone in your group who can?"

Donna smiled broadly, rose, and went over to the counter where the coffee pot stood. She picked it up, came back to the table and asked, Refill?"

Paul nodded.

She refilled hs cup and her own, sat down and placed the pot on the table. She took a long drink, then held the chipped cup between her hands and stared into the deep blackness.

Paul added milk and sugar to his cup and wondered if she had gone into a trance.

"No, Paul, I'm not in a trance."

His jaw dropped in surprise. "How? How did you know…"

"I've been involved with the study *and practice* of magic for a long time. As I said, on the way to the K and C people develop magic powers.

"But I'm not the one you want, Paul. The Silver *Moon*rise is not *my* group. It's an international organization, democratically run, that is over two centuries old. Our only goal is to help people who are on the same spiritual path. Sometimes it's fun to show off, but my goal now is to reach and extend any periods of the K and C I can achieve. That is the goal of all members of our order. Those looking for excuses to… uh… zap people and cast love spells will soon find themselves bored with the Silver Moonrise. Some people come to the S.M. seeking power over others, but they quickly drift away or begin to seek *true* power—power over themselves. I could do it, but my goals for the last decade have taken me in a different direction and it might take a few days or weeks for me to get back into the… uh… aspect of magic I think you need."

"Donna, on the phone I described as much of this this case to you as I can. I've told you what I need so I can help people and stop the killings. If you can't help me can you point me in the right direction?"

Donna bit her lower lip. "The Silver Moonrise is rather insular, I'm afraid. There are people who are members of a variety of groups, but we aren't interested in that type of initiation gatherer. They leave and we don't hear from them again. I wish I could help you, but there's really nothing I would be able to do."

"You know," Paul paused for a long second, considering what to say, "it's women who are dying. If you know of someone who can help... Aren't you afraid of dying?"

Donna laughed. "Lieutenant, when you have traveled the astral planes as much as I have you learn that death is only a change, a "metaphysical inconvenience" as they once said in a movie, and not an end. My consciousness has separated from my body so many times that death will only allow me to travel further and explore more. It will be very exciting.

"Don't get me wrong, Paul. I love life and want to live as long as I can and experience all I can on this world. I do not want to die. Even so, I don't fear death, although at times I get queasy thinking about the method by which I'll die. Drowning particularly frightens me."

"Donna, uh... these killings have been far more brutal than the public knows."

"Oh." She was lost in thought for a second. "I'm sorry, but I don't know of anyone. I wish I could, but I can't help you."

Paul was disappointed, but there was nothing she could do. "Well, I want to thank you for your time...and the decaf, Donna." He rose to leave.

Donna escorted him from the kitchen past her main room to the door. She stopped him there and closed her eyes. She seemed to be a thousand miles away from where they stood. Slowly, she opened her eyes and said with a smile, "Don't worry. Someone you initially won't trust will become an ally. Have a good night." She closed the door behind him and shivered. She felt cold, but it was not from the weather. It was still hot and muggy outside. The smog that had already killed over 100 people still burned at her lungs. She peered at Paul through the miniblinds that covered the window in her front door. He had brought something with him; not directly, but it was in some way attached to him or associated with him. It was something innately evil, something whose very essence was dark and malevolent. She went into her private temple and performed protection rituals for two hours. When Donna arose the next morning she realized that it was still not spiritually clean in her home and she repeated the rituals. When she came home from work that evening she repeated them again.

What the hell did she mean? Paul crunched through the gravel on the way to his car. The humidity hit him hard as he left the air-conditioned house and he could feel himself starting to sweat. The coffee, good as it had tasted going down, was starting to sour in his stomach. He reached into his pocket but found the Tums packet empty. "Great, just great," he said aloud, as he got into his car.

The sun was down. Night had set. With the humidity, however, it did not feel cool. *At least I won't be blinded by the sunlight on the way back to the station.*

The radio in his car squawked once and went dead. He cursed, then pulled into a convenience store and bought some antacids. He took two and finished the drive. The bright moon, a shining, yellow-brown crescent, reflected off the pits in the windshield, making driving difficult.

When he arrived at the station he saw the note on his desk. Another body had been found. The victim's legs, from the hips to the ankles, were gone.

* * * * *

Paul drove directly to the site where the body had been discovered. The area was still encircled with yellow warning tape. A small crowd had gathered, but was being held behind the tape that marked the police line.

Voices from reporters and the lights of TV cameras exploded into the night. "Is this another in the series of killings? Do you have any suspects? Are there lots of Satanic covens around? Do you keep them under observation? Have they committed other murders? Why haven't you arrested them?"

Paul ignored both the questions and the questioners as he ducked under the tape and moved to where the body lay. He was getting used to the ghastly blue appearance of the corpses by now, but this one was different. The legs had been sliced off with surgical precision. As before, there was no blood. Her feet lay near the body, cut off just above the anklebones. They reminded him of a pair of old shoes, discarded because they were no longer in fashion. *Have I really become that jaded?*

There were no thighs. *Had the killer placed the symbol elsewhere?* He looked more closely at the corpse. Nothing on the arms or front of the torso. Nothing on the face or behind the ears. Nothing on the feet. He had two officers turn the body over. There was nothing on the corpse's back.

Paul stepped back a few paces to get a wider view of the site. He almost tripped over a fist-sized rock. He looked down and noticed the rock was out of place. Neither it nor the rocks lying next to it should have been there. He looked at the arc of rocks to which it had belonged and gasped when he realized what it was.

The rocks formed the symbol that previously was found on the victim's thigh. Only this symbol was five feet across instead of four inches and made of rocks instead of painted in the victim's blood.

How had the killers had enough time to do all of this? There must have been more than one to pull this off. He ordered all the rocks collected and dusted for fingerprints, although he suspected this would be another dead end and they would be clean.

As he went back to his car, he was again assaulted by voices from the media. He turned to them and said, "As soon as we have completed our investigation we will let you know."

They continued to barraged him with questions and he figured he better give them something to get them off his back. "There are indications these killings may have some occult overtones. We are investigating this. Currently we don't know if we are dealing with one or more persons. We also don't know if the occult overtones are real or an attempt to try and lead us away from the truth. We'll let you know when there is more."

He got to his car, thinking his statement was so wide open the press people would all be running to find occult experts to interview. Suddenly he remembered there was one thing he hadn't checked. He went back across the police line, ignoring the stream of questions from the media who hadn't left as he'd hoped. *Why won't they just leave me alone to do my job?*

A forensics officer was bending over the body when he got there. Paul asked if a card had been found in the victim. The officer picked up a small plastic baggy from the ground and handed it to him. Inside was a card which was folded in half. He forced it open within the bag and laughed at the irony. The card showed a woman pouring fluid from one pitcher into another. The card's name was Temperance.

* * * * *

When the report on the latest killing came in hours later he learned he had been correct. No fingerprints were found on any of the rocks. The report described the rocks, saying that they seemed to have been wiped clean of all fingerprints. It also said each stone had a daub of blood on it. It probably was applied with a cotton swab. The blood belonged to the victim.

As he looked over the report, he felt the hair on the back of his neck stand on end. The police station began to roll and gently shake. He had been through earthquakes before and this one seemed like it was too small to do any damage, so he continued looking at the report to see if there was anything he missed. After ten seconds he started to look around. Everything was still shaking. Paul moved to the doorway. Still the shaking continued. A pencil rolled off a desk and bounced loudly against the floor. The shaking continued.

Paul suddenly felt small and helpless. The earth was moving for miles around. He was nothing but a tiny fly trying to live in the face of this massive power. He gasped for air and his lungs burned as they filled with smog.

The building seemed to ride the wave like a surfer on his board. But there was something more. He felt like the quake was caused by something oozing, undulating under the earth, something evil, looking for an opening to escape to the surface. *Ridiculous. That's just my imagination.* Finally, the rumbling sound ceased and the earth calmed from her shaking. The following morning the news would only say that the quake was a mere two-point-seven on the Richter scale, but it went on for over forty seconds.

When it finally stopped and everyone in the station had calmed down, Paul noticed Blackie, the cat which the station had adopted—or rather, the cat had adopted the station—was acting weird. He was hopping and jumping like kittens sometimes do, but Blackie was at least seven years old. The black and grey hair that ran across Blackie's back stood on end as if he was in a field of static electricity. He hissed at everyone. Somebody set out a bowl of food, but the cat ignored it, something Blackie normally would never do.

Blackie came up to Paul and rubbed against his leg. This was a tradition between them, and Paul reached down to scratch Blackie between the ears. Blackie screeched and lashed out with the claws of his right forepaw, slashing the back of Paul's hand. Paul yelped and jumped to his feet, the slender gashes starting to glisten with red. The cat ran out of the building like he had been hit by lightning. Paul went to the first aid cabinet to get some antiseptic and bandages for hia bleeding hand.

Blackie was never seen again.

Chapter Nine

Earlier, the Sixth Night

It was ten minutes after nine when Allenda used the ram's head knocker to signal she had arrived at Simon's house. She waited, apprehensive over the Rite of the Sparrowhawk in which she would soon participate. She paced the front porch waiting for someone to answer the door.

The lot Simon's house was built on, cut from a hill, was only a few miles from the ocean. Even on the hottest days there was almost always an ocean breeze. Zephyrs would waft down the hillside and cool the southern California heat. When Simon moved into the house after the turret had been built, one of the first things he did was add central air conditioning. That proved to have been a waste of thousands of dollars as he almost never used it—all he had to do was open some windows to get a cool breeze from the sea.

Tonight, however, there was no breeze. It was cool, but with the unusually high humidity, it felt stifling. The strange weather pattern that caused the humidity also trapped smog in the area, burning Allenda's lungs and giving the moon an ugly, reddish-orange patina. *There's blood on the moon.*

Where did I hear that before? Was it a movie title? What did it mean? Maybe it's an omen.

The door finally opened. Eris was standing there. For some reason Allenda was relieved to see her already in her ritual robes rather than her usual sexy clothes. "'lo, Eris."

"Hello, Alli. You can change in the robing room. Simon is getting the magic room ready. I'll come and get you in few minutes."

They walked together toward the turret. Allenda looked over at Eris as they walked. She saw the robed woman's breasts sway gently and freely beneath her robe. Eris wore no underwear.

From somewhere Allenda felt a cool breeze. "I guess Simon is getting his money out of the air conditioning tonight," she said, laughing.

Eris smiled slightly, but did not laugh. "I'll be back soon," she repeated.

Allenda went into the women's robing room outside of the lodge room. *Eris' already has her mind focused on the ritual.* The only sound she heard was the decrescendo of Eris' retreating steps. Soon it was silent and she felt keenly aware of being alone. The silence itself seemed to be alive. She cleared her mind and tried to focus on the forthcoming ritual. *Time to get ready.*

First she took off her clothes and put on the black robe she brought in her over-sized purse. She told herself she was going to perform this ritual properly and the robe she brought was one she purchased months ago, but hadn't the nerve to wear, even in her private rituals. It was of a thinner material, verging on the transparent, and it clung to her figure.

When she put it on she was surprised at the fit. It was looser than she had remembered. She moved over to the full-length mirror. *Simon did know women liked to make sure they would look good, even in a darkened lodge room.* She was thankful for the looking glass. Allenda focused on the reflection of her face. She took out a make-up kit from her purse and clicked it open. With a sable-haired brush she increased the blush to her cheekbones and gave a bit of color to her forehead. She lengthened her lashes, outlined her eyes and shaded them with three neatly blending colors of reddish-brown hues that, she knew, would cause the candles' illumination to highlight her hazel eyes.

Allenda leaned over and brushed her hair forward letting it reach for the ground. Without changing position she fumbled in her purse until she found a pump of hair spray. She treated her hair with it and waited a few moments. Then she rose, throwing her hair back and brushing it lightly. She looked in the mirror and gazed intently at the appearance of her mane. "Big hair," she giggled. She had never done her hair in that fashion before, but she thought it looked good.

Finally, she looked in her purse for the special plastic bottle she purchased at Hot Topic in the Galleria earlier that day. Inside was a colorless, odorless, cinnamon-flavored gel with bits of sparkle suspended in it. She plopped some onto her palms, then lifted her robe and smeared it over her chest and breasts. She shivered slightly. The goo was cold! Then she dropped the top of her robe and oozed some onto her neck, shoulders and arms. She ended by putting a few drops over her cheek bones and eye shadow.

"Well, let's take a look, shall we?" she said aloud, looking again into the mirror. This time, however, she took in the overall view rather than just her face or hair. She gasped at what she saw.

All her life, Allenda thought of herself as second rate. She had always been overweight, although only slightly so for the past several years. Still, when she was younger she always tried to befriend the beautiful, popular girls. That way, when they went to dances she would be near the boys who would flock to the popular girls and maybe she could catch a leftover. Although that led to furtive kissing and groping when she was in high school, and brief encounters and one-night stands in college, she realized early in her life that in relationships she would always be second choice. Or third. Or last. She may have been smart, but she also knew she was fat and ugly. It was a pain that had riven her all her life. Sometimes, when she was alone, she would cry into her bed pillows for hours, not knowing the cause of her pain and depression. Two years of therapy hadn't ended her crying jags, but they helped her realize on a secret, inward level she hoped the tears would end the anguish of her feelings of ugliness and lack of self-worth. It never worked.

That's why she gasped when she looked into the mirror. The young woman who looked back at her was neither fat nor ugly. Sure, she had lost her appetite for the past several days and eaten little. And yes, she had run around doing lots of errands and worked out extra hard at the gym. But by her appearance in the mirror she guessed she had lost seven, maybe nine pounds. The little pockets of fat she hated were gone. *I may be egotistical for thinking it, but I look…beautiful. And sexy, very sexy.* She had never felt that way before. Now she had to admire herself. *Even Eris might be jealous of the way I look.*

Allenda continued to look at herself in the mirror. She turned to the side and arched her back. She never thought she had large breasts, but with her improved figure her breasts seemed to stand out. The air conditioned chill gave her nipples a point and the material of the robe hid nothing. Her breathing increased at the sight of herself looking so sensual, and the resultant movement of her breasts under the robe excited her even more. She wore a bra when she tried on the robe, and now, with no underwear, she noticed when she moved the material was like a gentle hand, further exciting her. She also noticed a slight bulge to her tummy and promised herself she would lose the remaining weight in a few days. *I'll make better use of that gym membership I've had for the past year.* But she was too busy looking at what she had become to let those five pounds worry her. *Look at me now!*

She spun around in glee. Allenda truly felt sexy for the first time in her life. She looked in the mirror to try and get a view of herself from all sides. This wasn't being egotistical. She just never felt or looked this way before and wanted to revel in the sensation of this moment. Allenda burst into laughter as she released emotions held within for her entire life. The emotions flowed forth and she knew she either had to laugh or cry. *I have changed! I am different! I...*A knock on the door took her from her reverie.

"Come on," said Eris' voice. "It's time to start the..." Eris opened the door and saw the new Allenda for the first time. It stopped her in mid-sentence and now it was her turn to gasp. Eris had always been the most beautiful, most sensual woman in any group. Now, the mousy, overweight Allenda was easily a challenge to her. Strangely, though, Eris felt no challenge. Instead, she felt a kinship and an admiration. She smiled as she looked at Allenda, and as she continued to look her smile widened.

"Do I look okay?" Allenda asked, knowing damn well she looked magnificent.

Eris, with no trace of anything other than admiration in her voice, said, "You look absolutely wonderful." Eris had experienced sex with many people, including women. Although sex with women had been fun and unique, her primary attraction was directed to men. For the first time in her life she was attracted to a woman. Pangs of guilt rose in her as she thought of how she had mocked and abused Allenda in the past. She cleared her mind and started to focus, once again, on tonight's ritual. "C'mon, let's go," she said, atonally.

Allenda saw Eris was waiting for her to go first. *I don't think that's right.* She came up to Eris and took her arm so they could walk together. Eris' nostrils flared. She moved a bit closer so she could feel the side of Allenda's body against her own. The curve of Allenda's breast touched her arm and Eris caught her breath as she felt a familiar dampness begin between her legs.

Allenda sensed what happened and looked, for just a second too long, into Eris' eyes. *A month ago—hell, a week ago—I would have recoiled from Eris' touch. Now it just feels warm and good. Maybe I'm changing in other ways, too.*

They ascended the stairs in silence, although Allenda caught Eris stealing glances at her. At the top of the stairs they looked at each other until the look became awkward. At exactly 9:38 P.M. they entered the magic room.

* * * * *

The room, lit only by candles, was shrouded in the multicolored smoke of heavy incenses. New glass filled most of the windows, although three had wooden boards over them awaiting repair. In the center, where the altar once resided, rested a large cotton-filled pad, a futon. Simon sat cross-legged at the center of the futon, the Place of Holy Comfort. Naked, he was lost in meditation, his lips barely moving as he repeated either a silent prayer or mantra. Allenda didn't know which.

For a few moments the women waited where they were, allowing their eyes to grow accustomed to the light. Allenda took the opportunity to look at Simon and admire his trim figure. She had performed this ritual with him before, but always kept her eyes closed. Tonight, however, she wanted to see everything. She knew her body would be erotically exciting, and she wanted to experience the excitement of her partners with all of her senses.

Both Eris and Allenda knew Simon had prepared the circle with several banishings before they arrived. They had each performed the Rite of the Sparrowhawk individually with Simon (*And,* thought Allenda, *perhaps Eris had performed it with others.*), so they both knew what was expected.

Lying on the floor over the painted circle were two daggers. Their matched, undulating black handles set off nine-inch-long silver blades, sharp on both sides, which glittered in the candlelight. The women bent over, each taking a dagger in their right hands. Keeping the tips of the daggers together, they raised them straight into the air until the blades, pointing straight up, were at Eris' arm's length and near the full extension of Allenda's arm. Eris moved to the right and Allenda to the left until they were about four feet apart, then they brought the blades down to the ground. The robed women entered the circle through the "door" they had created.

Once inside they picked up the blades and reversed their motions, meeting in the center of their doorway and bringing their united blades down to the floor. There they crossed the blades, forming a silver X, and slid them a foot toward the center of the area. The "door" was closed; the circle resealed.

Allenda sat on on one side of Simon and watched as Eris sat on the other. She adjusted her robe so that she was not sitting on the material and noticed that Eris did the same. *Let's see, the first step is to deeply relax by breathing slowly, regularly and deeply.* This had worked many times to help her open psychically, a necessity in order to perform rituals. Allenda focused on her breath. She felt the air enter and leave her lungs. Soon she sensed her breathing slowing. She could hear that Eris' breathing pattern had already slowed. Allenda allowed her shoulders to sag. Her eyes closed and her head nodded forward. She was at peace and ready to begin.

It never fails to amaze me that when my eyes are closed it doesn't stop my vision so much as open it to the greater world—the astral plane. Her vision into the astral plane allowed her to see the magical circle was totally enclosed. She felt safe and protected. To the east, she noted, was a large, heavy curtain. Past this astral curtain, she knew, was the entry to other dimensions.

Without moving, she allowed her consciousness to expand. *I can feel Eris and Simon. They're filled with love and power.* She looked with astral eyes and saw them as two glowing eggs, suffused with energy. Looking down, Allenda noticed she looked just like them. She used her will to send out from the top of her astral egg form a thin band of energy. She directed it to join the energy field in the center, the one that belonged to, that was the essence of, Simon. As she watched the union, she saw Eris had done the same. Two bands of energy came out of Simon's field and wound around the energy forms of Allenda and Eris. As soon as it wound around her, Allenda felt warm and comfortable. Her energy field grew stronger, wider and brighter.

Another band of energy extended from Eris' field. It wrapped around that of Simon and then continued over to Allenda. When it touched her egg Allenda felt friendship, warmth, love and...and lust. It reached into the deepest aspects of Allenda's self and created harmonics in her own deep emotions. The lustiness made Allenda shiver, and the visual images of the astral plane began to waver and fade, but she controlled it and the images returned.

My turn to reach out to Eris. She intended that energy band which she now sent out would enter through the top of the Eris' energy egg shape. It started out okay, but Allenda lost her control (by accident or on purpose? she later wondered) and it wound around Eris, entering at the bottom. She saw Eris' energy field vibrate at the entry of the energy through her lowest *chakra* and thought she heard a low moan. Eris' quiet moan was so erotic that Allenda felt like a voyeur, a thought which excited her. She noticed she was feeling wetness within her and began to focus on the erotic sensations. *No, not yet.* She quickly brought her attention back to the ritual in which she was involved.

The energy of the three was united. Now they needed to make it grow. Before the ritual started Allenda felt skittish about this method of raising their energy level. Now she felt comfortable with it—it was just part of the ritual. A hand touched Allenda and ran under her robe to caress the skin of her back. The hand was cool and she shivered. Leaning over, she touched Simon on his chest. It was firm and covered with a light mat of hair that enticed her fingers. She brought her hand down to the washboard below his chest and leaned over to kiss him, only to find another head already there. She moved down and licked his nipples, pushing with her head so he leaned back onto the Place of Holy Comfort. She sucked one of his nipples into her mouth and he moaned. *God, this feels good!*

Soon the robes Allenda and Eris wore were memories and merely littered the floor. Allenda, still looking though her astral eyes, saw the three eggs of energy unite and divide, unite and divide. She kissed and was kissed, touched and was touched. She felt hands caress her and a battle of tongues passionately raged in her mouth. Lips on her womanhood fluttered her open, and when a tongue tickled the bud she bucked and grabbed for those around her, caring not who it was, only that her energy would build.

They moved, they rolled, they kissed and licked. Together they explored one another, not caring who touched, who kissed, who entered where. Allenda shivered to the edge of an orgasm, and quickly directed the energy from it into their combined energy field. Together their energy grew, expanding until the sphere of their united power filled the place of safety where they writhed. Seconds passed into minutes and minutes into hours. Always they came up to orgasm, but rather than explode they merged their individual energy with the energy of the trio. Something unconscious rose up in Allenda's mind. *Was it a psychic call from Simon?*

It was time.

Allenda straddled Simon, moaning as she guided him into her. Eris mounted Simon's face, using his tongue as if it were his manhood. For a second, Allenda opened her eyes to see on the physical plane. Before her was Eris, her hair slicked with the sweat of passion, her eyelids half closed with lust. The perspiration on her face and breasts glittered in the candleglow. Although Allenda never had sex with a woman before, she reached out to cup one of Eris' breasts, the brown nipple peeking from between her fingers. She looked into Eris' eyes and saw thoughtless, mindless lust and passion. Eris caressed Allenda's breasts and suddenly squeezed—firmly but softly. At the same time, Simon thrust deeply into her. Allenda groaned and threw her arms around Eris, pulling her closer, kissing her lips, exploring the dark mysteries of Eris' mouth with her tongue. She writhed in ecstasy as the oral intrusion was returned and Simon filled her inner emptiness time after time.

They moved and moaned, loved and made magic. *We look like a massive triangle of energy. Soon, the sparrowhawk will fly.*

Simon felt bathed in the energy they were creating. Several times he jerked forward with the beginning of an orgasm, but he was always able to control his energy through slow breathing and concentrating on moving his eyes in a large, clockwise, rectangular pattern. *If I have an ejaculation I'll lose my erection and the ritual will have to stop.* His long hours of practice with Tantric techniques had showed him the difference between orgasm and ejaculation and allowed him to experience multiple orgasms without releasing his bodily fluids. He called on that ability now as their lust and love increased the psychic energy and prepared the sparrowhawk for flight.

When Simon determined that the energy had reached the maximum attainable level, he called out to his spirit animal. *Come, Adoniel! It is I, Simon, who calls you.* A sparrowhawk, about the size of a small falcon, slowly appeared before him. Behind the sparrowhawk the astral curtain parted and the large, ornate and heavy doors behind it swung open. Simon looked into the eyes of the avian and willed his consciousness into the flying animal. He closed his eyes. When he opened them he could see three energy spheres before him. Simon and Adoniel had merged. Simon *was* the sparrowhawk. He flew past the curtains and out the door.

* * * * *

In the form of Adoniel the sparrowhawk, Simon could fly through the multiverse of dimensions which for most people lies undreamed of just a quantum step outside our ordinary perception. Adoniel was a creation of Simon's mind, but as a result of frequent evocation Adoniel had developed a personality, a mind of its own. Adoniel had Simon's consciousness, but Simon thought of Adoniel as more of a partner than a creation.

Simon had flown Adoniel many times and was comfortable in that form. Adoniel had greater or lesser strength and endurance dependent upon the amount of energy Simon brought forth in the evocation. Simon usually flew Adoniel alone, but sometimes he worked with a partner. He had worked with both Alli and Eris separately, but this was the first time he worked this ritual with two aides. Even to him the result was astounding. Adoniel had never been so strong or powerful. Each stroke of wings moved him further and faster than ever.

Together they soared through the levels of existence. A brilliant kaleidoscope of colors and shapes, scents and sensations, flooded Simon in his expanded consciousness. He was here/there simultaneously. Think it and it was so, even before the thought was finished. Exhilarated in his new freedom, he found the astral breezes flying past his beak were intoxicating. His vision seemed to go to forever. He drank of the energy being tapped from the ritual like a junkie craves a drug.

Ah, the freedom of a bird. He floated like a gull with wing feathers minutely moving to take advantage of every tiny wind and breeze in order to stay aloft. He made loops and circles and power dives at speeds beyond those a jet fighter pilot could absorb without blacking out. Everything was extended as time and space converged into a whole unit and exploded in its plenitude.

Ecstasy! Ecstasy! Freedom is your name! Take my books, my home, my students, my life. Just let me fly forever through eternity! "Screet! Screet!" he cried. "I am Adoniel. I can do…"

What am I doing? I can't get lost in the sensations of this experience. Simon blinked Adoniel's eyes and found his control. The loss of control and the turning over of his consciousness to Adoniel had never happened to him before. *It must be the result of the added energy from the three-fold rite. Certainly nobody could know I'm flying the astral planes. After all, I'm not trying to attack or defend, just search. No one even knows what I am doing right now and certainly no one could have planned and launched an attack against me. There could have been no spell to make me forget I am Simon Raven.* He turned his mind to the task at hand and flew forward with purpose.

Simon/Adoniel flew in circles around the area of Simon's home, or rather, its equivalent on the astral plane. Simon looked through Adoniel's eyes for a sign of something which had attacked Angelica. Through thousands of planes and for what seemed like thousands of hours he searched, swooping down to levels near the physical world and soaring to planes so high the brightness of the pure, spiritual light that suffused them was blinding.

Nothing.

Simon/Adoniel floated on an astral wind, relaxing while trying to figure out why he couldn't find the source of the attacks. *I'm totally stumped.* Then, like a bolt, it hit him. He blinked his eyes as he realized what had happened. *Curse me for a novice! There is no time here.* He spoke to himself to convince his logical mind about the nature of time on the astral. *Time is a continuum with space, a field where we can jump from one place to another instantaneously.* He thought of the many books he had read which showed occultists had claimed this for millennia. *Scientists, at least some physicists, have been saying it since Heisenberg and the poor cat of Mr. Schrödinger which was both alive and dead at the same time.* He remembered Einstein described this when he predicted the possibility of wormholes, and it is seen in the odd behavior of subatomic particles.

Our day-to-day living indicates that time is on a straight line. Science says this is an illusion. I say it's a necessary illusion for life on the physical plane. But I'm on the astral, now.

For a moment, Simon/Adoniel could not get past the standard ideas about time. He knew he would be locked in this current location until he could alter his attitude. *On the astral plane, time, as we normally think about it, does not exist. Think about a great distance and I can be there. Think about going to a time considered to be in the past on the physical plane and I can be there.*

Simon/Adoniel closed his eyes and concentrated, then relaxed. And then it happened. In a flash, he was watching the Ritual of the Pythia which had ended so disastrously. Still, nothing was there to see.

Adoniel/Simon soared up through the planes. A quick flip turned them one hundred and eighty degrees and Simon looked through the levels they had traversed. Still nothing.

They moved back in time and then dove until they were a heartbeat from the physical. *Nothing… Nothing… Wait! There it is!*

A slender string of brownish smoke, a thread much finer than the enormous physicality of even a tiny strand of the smoke from a single stick of incense, was slowly snaking around his home's turret. He could see it grow and grow, finally shaking the building until it forced itself in, past the magical wards which Simon had not regularly enhanced. It was the attack on him and Allenda.

Simon looked dispassionately at the scene as it unfolded below him. *Strange how something which involved me so totally at the time seems so distant now.* He knew what the result would be, so he willed himself forward in earth time but to the same location. In full control of his presence on the astral, he was instantly there. Ha! he shouted triumphantly to himself. There again was the strand of dark energy, and he could easily see it. The energy wound around the building and had entered the circle which Alan failed to perfectly banish before Simon and the Warriors could reinforce it. The tip of the thread snaked up Angelica's robe. Just then, a cartoonish-looking bee—*It seems familiar, but it must be some minor astral entity*—buzzed by. He chose to ignore it.

Simon didn't need to see the rest. He knew what was going to happen. Instead, he followed the thin strand of smoke/energy. His plan was to trace it to its source. There he would find the key to the identity of the attacker.

Whoever sent the tendril of dark energy was good, very good. The tendril of energy would narrow and widen, change color and shape, all while winding through numerous planes and levels, some of which Simon never previously visited. Still, Simon/Adoniel, imbued with energy from the continuing ritual, followed it. Miles had no meaning. Time had no front and no end. Twirling and twisting through dimensions beyond thought, he followed the dark energy. At times he felt he was in the presence of angels. At other times he felt like he was in a combination of H. R. Giger's and Hieronymous Bosch's worst nightmares. Before him, always, was the stream of dark and dirty energy.

Suddenly the energy tendril rose straight up. Adoniel/Simon soared up, too, following it higher and higher. As they rose, the light which permeated these other planes seemed to dim and grow murky. Finally, the dark energy leveled off, forming a huge pool of slowly moving inky blackness, an astral Sargasso that even Adoniel's acute vision could not fully see in the dim light.

Adoniel/Simon, saving energy, floated lazily on astral breezes above the dark sea. Simon had been in the astral plane for some time and he thought it best to conserve energy. Simon/Adoniel made slow circles around the darkness, looking for a source; either to this dark sea or, hopefully, to who—or what—had attacked Angelica. They traveled for what seemed hours. Or was it days? Years? Simon couldn't understand why they hadn't found anything.

With a start, Simon/Adoniel's eyes grew big. *Was this all a ruse to kep a searcher from the true source?* He zoomed back to the tentacle of dark energy he followed to this evil sea and looked at it closely. *Fool! Fool! I've been overconfident in my abilities again.* The smoky tendril had not entered the dark pool, it only came up to it. Then it changed to a fine, almost invisible strand and went off in another direction. Whoever created this set it up as a trap so that a traveller following the dark energy could not trace it to its true source. It was a trap that would fool many. For a skilled practitioner such as Simon, however, it would only delay tracing the energy to the source. Still, it did waste his time and energy. Perhaps the source of the dark energy hoped whoever tried to trace him, her or it would simply become exhausted in the astral Sargasso and snap back to their physical body, suffering a bad case of astral whiplash. Perhaps there were more traps to come.

Adoniel/Simon followed the new trail. Once again it went through numerous worlds and universes as it changed color, size and sensation. It rose what appeared to be miles high, then went straight down, vanishing in the distance below. He started a dive to follow the path when he realized something was wrong. *Something was very wrong!*

Just as it rarely is totally silent on the physical plane, it rarely is silent in the astral worlds. Sounds, commonly described as winds, bells, voices or choirs are reported by those who visit these realms. But for some reason, the sounds around Simon/Adoniel had stopped. Rather than continue the dive he hovered in the astral winds. All he could hear was the sound of his rapid heart beat. His eyes darted nervously, looking…looking…

"Awk! Awk!" came a chilling scream from a mammoth eagle that burst through the bottom of an astral blur of color, pushing it aside like a jet fighter diving through puffy clouds. Talons extended, it came right for Simon/Adoniel.

Simon, cursing himself for falling into a trap, folded his wings. It was an unusual maneuver for a bird, and Adoniel felt uncomfortable with it. Still, it had its effect. Adoniel/Simon dropped like dead weight and the eagle's talons found empty space instead of flesh and feather.

Simon/Adoniel spread his wings and flew. The eagle was much larger and Adoniel/Simon would be no match for the attacker. Simon had only wanted to look. The eagle—or whoever sent it—wanted war. No matter how hard Simon/Adoniel soared and flew, the eagle, larger and more powerful, was there. Smaller and more maneuverable, Adoniel/Simon flew in loops and curls showing astounding aerial gymnastics. The eagle, however, didn't try to match Simon/Adoniel's grace. Instead it used its strength and power to simply keep up and wait for an opening. Sometimes it would even fly a circle around him. Taunting…taunting…

Simon/Adoniel was tiring and the eagle could sense it. The eagle's circles got smaller and smaller. With a screeching cry, the eagle closed in for the kill. Simon, instead of using his smaller size and mobility to elude the attacker, tried a different war plan—he turned and attacked! The eagle, talons extended for its own attack, was taken by surprise. Before the eagle could react to the startling attack, Adoniel/Simon was inside the talons, using his own talons and beak to claw and rend and tear.

"Awk!" The eagle screamed in pain and surprise. Adoniel/Simon, encouraged by the success of the offensive, replied with a war cry of his own, "Screet! Screet!"

But it was no contest. The eagle was surprised but barely hurt, and in seconds had the upper hand once more. Simon cried out as the eagle's claws raked the side of Simon/Adoniel. There was really only one choice—escape.

The two astral enemies flew in circles, dipping and diving, spinning and soaring through the astral worlds, the smaller always just missing being destroyed. *Destruction here means the loss of the soul and the energizing life force. This is no game. Death here means death on the physical plane.*

The battle went on for what seemed hours. Simon was exhausted. His shoulders felt like heavy weights and he knew he could not dodge his attacker much longer. Death was inevitable. Yet on and on he struggled. *I will not go gentle into that good night.* He dodged and floated and dove and continued evading the eagle. He folded his wings and made one last dive to escape. "Awk," cried the attacker, so close that its breath fluttered the feathers of Simon/Adoniel's tail.

In seconds it would be over.

Then he saw it. The door! His way home! Protected on the other side by their rituals the eagle could not enter. All he had to do was cross the portal and he would be safe. Adoniel/Simon flew as fast as possible to it. He landed mere feet from the doorway and started to scrabble toward it. But before he could cross the threshold, the eagle flew between him and his escape.

Simon/Adoniel had no more energy. He could not fight. He could not flee. For long moments the eagle and the sparrowhawk stared at each other, panting for breath. The eagle knew he had his victim. Simon/Adoniel held his head up proudly. *I'll show him what a good death looks like.* The two raptors gazed into each other's eyes. The eagle slowly moved toward Simon/Adoniel until they were so close that less then an inch separated them.

"Awk! Awk!" The eagle cried in victory. And then the eagle laughed. Not with an eagle sound, but with a deep, human, voice. It just laughed and laughed.

That laugh, it's so familiar, so very familiar. Where have I heard it before? Birds have no facial expression, but Simon could swear the eagle looked at him with contempt and hate. Then the eagle took to wing and flew away.

Simon/Adoniel watched as the eagle's massive wings drew it away through the astral plane. When he could no longer see it or sense it was there, he staggered slowly to the door. Simon thanked Adoniel for allowing them to fly together as they walked through the portal. Then he separated his consciousness from that of Adoniel and watched as Adoniel flew back into the astral worlds beyond the door. He allowed the door to close and the curtain to slide across in front of it. Simon was home.

* * * * *

Simon opened his eyes, then grasped his side with a start. He looked down and saw blood on him. His side had three deep scratches. They were four inches apart and almost a foot long. It was as if he had been attacked by a giant bird of prey.

He got up on his elbows and looked around. The candles which had lit the room were burned almost to their ends; some had burned out. As his eyes focused he saw the women. Their bodies, like his, were totally drenched in sweat. They were splayed on the futon, more as if they passed out from exhaustion than as if they merely fell asleep.

"Alli, Eris," he called gently. He repeated it several times, touching their hands until they roused from their state of sleep. Allenda, reverting to her previous patterns, quickly grabbed for her robe to cover herself while Eris simply stayed where she was and regained her strength. When the women saw the blood on Simon they insisted on taking care of him. They rose, all somewhat shakily. Eris put on her robe and Simon put on some boxer shorts which he had brought into the room. They went down to the kitchen where Eris tended to the wounds (*Quite professional,* thought Allenda. *I wonder where Eris trained?)* and Allenda made coffee.

When his wounds were bandaged to Eris' satisfaction, Simon went off and returned in a bathrobe. Allenda and Eris took turns going to the bathroom, getting into street clothes and straightening themselves up. By then the coffee was ready and they sat around the kitchen table, looking into their cups of hot, dark liquid.

It was Simon who finally broke the silence of meaningless chit-chat. "What happened here when I projected onto the astral plane?"

The women looked nervously at each other. Eris started first, "We continued uh… raising energy and sending it to you. It seemed to go on for a long time. Then…"

"…something happened," Allenda continued. "It was as if we were having the energy drained from us rather than freely giving it to you."

"Yeah, that's exactly how I felt," concurred Eris. "And that's when it happened. As the energy was sucked from me all I wanted to do was give and give. It was hypnotic. I lost control. I had an orgasm. Then another. Then another. Soon I couldn't stop. I felt my body wrench around with my orgasms, each one pulling more and more energy from me. I was helpless to stop it. Finally, I couldn't move. The sensations just went on and on, draining me until I blacked out. I don't remember anything else until you woke me."

Simon looked at Allenda.

I know he wants me to answer honestly, but...well, sure I've read all the books about sex and multiple orgasms. I've even had a few, although I prefer having just one big one. But talking about it with people I just...well...it's difficult. She looked down at her coffee and felt her body warm as she flushed. "The same thing happened to me," she said quietly without looking at either of them. *Maybe I haven't changed as much as I thought.*

The women both looked at Simon. They listened as he told of his experiences on the astral. Simon was a natural storyteller and his adventure was thrilling to the women who could visualize everything he described, especially since they were both experienced astral travellers themselves.

Simon came to the end and described how the eagle had laughed. Then he stopped in mid-sentence. "By the gods, it was Barton!"

"What?" asked Allenda, confused with this sudden transition in the story.

"I knew that laugh was familiar. It's been many years since I last heard it. But I remember it well. It was the laugh of Barton Oliver. He must be the one who is behind this." He leaned back in his chair with a smile set in his face. "You always thought you could top me, Barton, and you always liked to gloat. But I have you now because I know who you are." He sat back up and looked seriously at the women who had given him the energy necessary to let him fly. "Now all we have to do is find him, and find out why he attacked us."

* * * * *

Seventh Morning

The doctor, dressed in an immaculate, white coat, picked up the chart from outside of Angelica's room and walked through the door. It was not yet 7:00 a.m. He looked the chart over, going through the several pages, then looked at Angelica, who greeted him with an overly friendly, "Good morning, Doc. You're new here. So tell me, how am I? Am I still alive?"

The doctor smiled and placed the chart on a table. "That's what I should be asking you."

"I feel great and I'm ready to get outta here. Please let me out before the food kills me."

The doctor said nothing to this, but smiled slightly. He pulled a flashlight from its holder on the wall and used it to look into her eyes, hmming a noncommittal response to his investigation. He checked her reflexes with the traditional, small rubber mallet and prodded her ears with an otoscope. He felt under her chin and arms to make sure her lymph nodes were not enlarged. He put a cuff on her left arm and checked her blood pressure. Finally, he used the stethoscope to check her heart and lungs. Each examination was concluded with either a "hmm" or an "uh-huh." The doctor marked some things on her chart and looked through the pages again. "Well, Ms. Firestone, everything looks fine. It's time for you to get out of here so we can give this room to some sick people."

"Ex-cel-lent," said Angelica, bobbing her head and starting to hop off the bed.

"Whoa! Hold on a minute young lady. I'm afraid you can't get out that easily. Do you have anybody to pick you up?"

"Well no, but I can make some calls..."

"Your chart says you live in Venice. It so happens I live there, too. It will take about half an hour to discharge you and that's when my shift ends. I can give you a ride home."

"Could ya? That would really be great. I've imposed on my friends enough."

"It will be no problem. I'll meet you in the hallway near the main entrance after you're discharged. Please wait here 'till they come for you. There are some discharge documents you'll have to sign."

It was many minutes before a nurse with a wheelchair came for Angelica. They argued for some time before Angelica acquiesced to be wheeled to the entrance. She signed a bunch of papers, then was wheeled toward the main doors. At the end of the hall, near the entrance to the hospital, she saw the doctor who would give her a ride home and waved.

The doctor, sitting in a chair, waved back and came to meet them. "Thank you, nurse," he said with a tone of authority. "I'll take her from here." But the nurse insisted she push Angelica out of the building, which she did while the doctor walked beside them.

Angelica noted the doctor was now dressed in an immaculate suit, perfectly pressed, although it was really evening wear and not appropriate for this time of day. *Maybe he had a hot date last night, before he came on duty*. At the curb, waiting for them, was a long limousine. "Wow!" said Angelica. "A limo. This is way cool." She got out of the chair and into the back of the limo through a door being held open by an overweight chauffeur. The doctor, a burly man well over six feet tall, got in behind her and sat across from her. *He must be rich, and he's so big. I wonder if he's big all over?* She looked at him and with a voice betraying a growing personal interest asked, "By the way, what did you say your name was?"

"Uh…You can call me Doctor Baron," said the man, unconsciously rubbing the ruby in the center of the patch resting over his left eye. "Yes, call me Doctor Baron."

Chapter Ten

Seventh Day

It was well into the afternoon when Simon, relaxing after the events of the previous night by studying a copy of the real *Necronomicon* (not the spurious ones available in every bookstore), was interrupted by a phone call. His answering machine was triggered before he could get it and he decided to monitor who was calling before answering.

"Hello, Simon Raven here," said the machine. "I can't answer right now, but if you leave your name and phone number after the beep, I'll get back to you as soon as I can. Thanks for calling and be well."

The electronic pleep sounded and Simon listened to a rather gravelly man's voice. "Mr. Raven? This is Lieutenant Paul Christian with the Hollywood police department. I got your number from this flyer at the Bodhi Tree and...uh...you see I'm investigating some crimes and I thought you might be able to help. Please call me as soon as you can. My number is..."

Simon picked up the phone. "Hello, Simon Raven here. How can I help you?" he asked, trying to make it sound like he hadn't heard what Paul had said.

"Uh, yes," said Paul, surprised by the intrusion of a real person. "Uh, my name is Lieutenant Paul Christian with the Hollywood police department. I got your number from a flyer I found at the Bodhi Tree. As you've probably heard, we've had a few crimes lately with occult overtones. I was hoping you might be able to help."

"If you check with the L.A., Venice and Santa Monica police departments, Lieutenant, you'll discover they all know me and I'm always happy to help in any way I can. The occult has a bad reputation to some, and I always try to clear up anything that might further hurt that reputation as quickly as possible."

Paul, of course, already checked with those departments, as well as with several others, the F.B.I. and even the D.M.V. "Well, if you could come over here I'd like it if you could answer some questions about the occult, look at some photographs and tell me if you can see anything we non-occultists might have missed. I'm on second shift, here, so could you come over in a couple of hours? I'm doing some paperwork at the moment."

"Sure. But unless I come over right away I can't make it until much later. I have some work I have to do and a previous engagement that will keep me busy until about nine-thirty tonight. Can I come over now?"

"Well, it would be better for me if you could make it later. Would, say, ten be okay for you, or do you need more time?"

"Better make it ten-fifteen. With the traffic it may take that long."

"Thank you for your cooperation, Mr. Raven. I'll see you at ten-fifteen tonight."

* * * * *

Eris and Allenda left his home around one-thirty in the morning. Simon was totally exhausted, but his mind was going over the events that had taken place earlier so when he tried to fall asleep he couldn't. He considered doing some relaxation techniques, but decided instead to get up and work.

First, he made entries in his magical diary. He wrote down everything he could remember about his experience and what the women said of their experiences. The entry took over seventeen pages. Next, he went to his exercise room, located off of his bedroom in the main house. It had free weights and various exercise machines along three of the walls and a large mat on the floor in the center of the room. There he practiced Tai Chi Chuan to get his muscles moving and the energy flowing through him, enervating and recharging him. This he followed with some Kung Fu "forms" to strengthen and build his muscles and help him increase his poise and balance. Then he went through a selection of Qi Gong exercises to add to his psychic energy, his *Qi*. When this was completed he did thirty minutes of aerobics followed by thirty minutes of resistance training using both free weights and machines. By the time he finished it was almost eight-thirty, so he shaved, showered and made a breakfast of English muffins, sautéed tofu and scrambled eggs.

There were five stories in the turret, and a large, circular room filled each level. The bottom-most one held the ritual room and the one at the top was the magic room. The room above the ritual room was a lounge for people to sit and talk after meetings. The floor above that was Simon's main library. Its walls were book shelves and it had tables and chairs for furniture along with a high speed photocopier, four Macintosh computers, a scanner and a laser printer. There were also several cassette players, CD players, MP3 players, and record turntables, all with headphones, so people could listen to music or various recorded lectures. Numerous volumes overflowed the bookshelves of this room and found their way into other rooms of his house. Virtually every room except the bathrooms and kitchen had at least one bookcase.

The remaining level of the turret was always locked. It was Simon's personal temple. Very few people were ever invited into his temple, at least not since Paris. At nine-thirty he entered the room for his daily personal magical work. There he banished the area and cleansed his aura. The banishing was the same as he performed before, only this time he did it with renewed vigor and concentration. The cleansing of the aura consisted of visualizing psychic energy and spinning it through his aura. Known as the Ritual of the Circulation of the Body of Light, he moved the energy down the front of his body and up the back several times, then down the left side of his body and up the right. Finally, he visualized it spinning tightly around his body—like mummy wrappings or an insect's cocoon—from feet to head, only to explode outward like a water spout of energy, bringing the force back to his feet for repetition.

Next, he invoked his Holy Guardian Angel and asked for guidance, clarity of thought, energy to complete what he would need to do, and finally blessings of peace and love for all who were around him and any soul that might need it.

When he finished, he sat on the floor, crosslegged, and began deep breathing. This would set up the relaxation response necessary to reach a meditative state so he could get deeper insight into the meaning of the experiences from the previous night. He inhaled, counting one, two, three, four and held his breath for one, two, three, four. He exhaled, again counting one, two, three, four, and finally kept his breath exhaled for the same count of four. As the minutes passed he extended the length of time it took for him to complete the four-fold breath. Normally, this breathing pattern would cause both psychological and physiological changes in him, relaxing him, getting him into the altered state necessary for true meditation. Today, however, nothing worked. Try as he would the meditative state would not come. Thoughts of Barton and Paris, a mess of stew and soul vampires, kept filling his mind, disturbing him, keeping him away from what he desired. It dawned on him this might be a message from his Higher Self or his Holy Guardian Angel, so instead of fighting the memories, he let go of his resistance, remembering, remembering…

* * * * *

Paris. The summer of 1975. Simon was barely sixteen, but everyone at *L'Ecolle du Magie* was talking about him. He had been recommended for training by three respected American magicians who had long been associated with *L'Ecolle*. One could only gain entrance through recommendation, and none of the three had ever made a bad choice. Usually a candidate for entrance to *L'Ecolle* received one nomination. Two nominations was highly unusual, but it did happen. Three was unheard of and everyone wanted to know why the new student was so special.

Simon had been interested in magic for as long as he could remember. He was unusually precocious as a child. When he was six, he saw a magician on television perform an intriguing trick which he later learned was called "Soft Soap." The magician placed three stained handkerchiefs in a soapbox, turned the box over, and pulled out three clean ones—the dirty ones were supposedly cleaned by magic. Simon knew, of course, the performer must have previously hidden three clean handkerchiefs in the bottom of the box and pulled them out, leaving the stained ones in the box.

But then the conjuror did something unexpected. He tore up the box! There was no chance of the stained handkerchiefs being anywhere. Where did they go? Simon had to find out.

He remembered seeing ads for magic tricks in the comic books his mother let him read. His mother taught him phonics at three and by six he was reading way over the norm for his age. He wasn't interested in Dick, Spot and Jane. He was already into Heinlein and Norton, Batman, Superman, Spiderman and the Flash.

So he used some of the money he saved from his allowance (fifty cents per week *if* he made his bed every day and did all of his chores), and sent away to learn the secrets of magic. Instead of getting those secrets, however, all he received were catalogs from Top Hat, Kanter's, Tannen's, Chicago Magic Inc., Abracadabra and others. He was disappointed the secrets of magic weren't revealed to him. But in those catalogs, some thicker than most of the books he had read, Simon read descriptions of other tricks and illusions that caught his young attention. Some of the illusions described, which cost thousands of dollars to purchase, were entire evening shows, filled with flowers, waterfalls, handkerchiefs and beautiful assistants. As he read the descriptions, he saw them being performed, over and over, in his mind. He was hooked.

Although his mind was developed far above most boys his age, his intellect, his wisdom, his knowledge of the world had not caught up to the facts he knew—he was still just a little boy. This is why he was surprised to discover there were books explaining magic at the library. *How could they give out such wonderful secrets so that anyone could come in and discover them?*

His youth and lack of experience was also why he didn't notice the shelving error that would change his life.

After all, if people could come up with *imitations* of real magic, which took many hours, if not months or years of arduous practice to master, why couldn't real magic be accomplished through the same means? He couldn't do many of the tricks listed in the books that required sleight-of-hand because his hands and body were too small and he did not have the years of experience necessary to master the most important skill of the magician, the art of misdirection. But he could study and learn so when his body was ready, he would be able to do it. When the book, *Magick in Theory and Practice*, a book on real magic by Aleister Crowley, was on the shelves next to *E-Z Magic You Can Do*, he studied it, practiced it, and learned it. No one told him real magic didn't exist and everyone thought all he was studying was sleight-of-hand.

As a child, Simon was very much a loner. He was also far more comfortable in the company of adults than children his own age. By the time he was twelve and could perform some of the more intricate sleights, his parents were tired of his tricks. Although they feigned interest, as any good parent was expected to do, Simon (as every child is capable of) could see their exasperation and boredom with him over this. He ceased showing them what he could do and practiced all of his magics in private. No one knew that along with the cards, coins and handkerchiefs—the conjuror's art—he was also learning spells, the generation and control of psychic energy, invocations and evocations—the skills of a real wizard.

One night, two weeks after his fourteenth birthday, he was awakened by a muffled scream. His father, a pharmaceutical representative, was on the road. Simon was always told, "When your father is gone, you are the man of the family." As "man" of the house, he went to investigate.

He crept out of his room and down the hall toward his parents' room. Their door, usually closed at night, was open. Three men were in the room. One was on top of the bed, sitting on his mother, his hand over her mouth. Her eyes were wide with terror. The other two were going through drawers, as if looking for something.

Simon moved away from the door so he wouldn't be seen. He was scared, but he was also now the "man of the house." *What to do? What to do? I gotta do something, but what? What could make them leave?* The young Simon felt helpless. Then he got an idea.

He breathed into his cupped hands and formed a sphere of psychic energy. This he charged, by the force of his young will, with the nature of elemental Fire. This was a basic magical technique he had been practicing for over a year. When it was complete, he separated his hands, thus dividing the fiery energy into two balls. He breathed on both of them, adding magical energy to them until they were strong. Then he put one down and divided the other. Again he breathed energy into them and put one down. He repeated this several times, and in a few minutes had a pile of elemental fireballs.

He took one in each hand, crept to the door of his parent's room, and blew them with his mouth toward the behinds of the two men rummaging through the room. He got another fireball and did the same to the one who was on his mother.

The three men started to get antsy and yell at one another. Simon, remaining hidden, repeated his magical attack. Soon the men were arguing with each other.

Simon grew bold, grabbed some more fireballs and stood out in the open doorway. "Look! It's a kid," one of them shouted. "Get him!" The three thieves came at Simon, but he stood his ground and threw three more fireballs at them. They laughed at the way he was throwing empty air at them, but then started itching and yelling as if they were on fire. One thought he was being attacked by fire ants.

By the time they reached the door where Simon was standing, they had lost their interest in the boy or the theft. Yelling, screaming and itching, all they wanted to do was leave. Simon threw the remaining fireballs at the now fast-retreating invaders. They howled out the window they used to enter the house and ran down the street, hopping and yelling at each other.

Simon's mother, terrified as parents always seem to be when it comes to the health and safety of their children, grabbed him and held him to her. She had seen nothing, but simply thanked God the men left without hurting her or her son. He told her he used his magic on them, but she, of course, didn't believe him. Neither did the police who investigated the break-in, although they had no explanation as to why the men left without taking anything.

Simon could not understand why adults, the people whom he liked to be around, didn't believe him. *Why should I lie? Why didn't Mom see the fireballs? Why didn't they believe in magic?* He slipped into his own world, isolated from adults and children his age. But that was okay. He could study and practice on his own. He had seen the results of his practices and knew what he wanted from life. *I'm going to be a real magician!*

Simon was innately bright and had skipped grades in school so most of the kids in high school were bigger than he. As a result, although he was very talented athletically for his size and age, he really couldn't compete in sports with older and bigger boys. So instead of high school athletics he was on the debate team, in the marching band, in the acting club and in the chess club. He worked out with weights on his own and attended a martial arts school.

Like all youths, he occasionally felt the need to be popular. Simon would regale some of the older kids with slightly exaggerated versions of his magical exploits. They all laughed. Mr. Yenap, his music teacher who overheard the story, however, didn't laugh. He was a member of a secret magical order.

Simon was too young to recruit for the order, but the music teacher talked with a couple of his magical friends about the boy. A few days later Mr. Yenap asked Simon to stay after school. There Simon met Mr. Yenap's friends. For three hours they questioned him. First they got the true story of the events from the boy. They shook their heads in disbelief that a boy so young could know so much. They tested him on divination, astral travel, the creation of artificial elementals (similar to what he had sent at the burglars) and other aspects of the magical arts, both in theory and in practice.

Two days later, Mr. Yenap made an appointment to meet Simon's parents. He told them Simon was very talented and he could go to summer school, all expenses paid, in France. However, he would have to learn French before he could go. His parents thought Simon would be learning music in Paris, and although Mr. Yenap didn't deny it, he did nothing to imply their assumption might be wrong. Mr. Yenap told the boy the truth. A year-and-a-half of intensive French lessons later, Simon made his first trip to Paris.

Normally, a person would have to study for four years at *L'Ecolle* leaving only for brief spring and winter breaks. Mr. Yenap suggested it; Simon's parents would not allow it. His American endorsers, after discussing the matter, thought Simon could learn a year's material in three months time and they could drill him for the rest of the year. Therefore, special arrangements were made which allowed him to study during his summer break. This alone made him news to the other fifteen students, thirteen boys and two girls, as well as the faculty members.

His American backers underestimated their protégé. Simon was able to learn in just two months what took most of the students a year. This was no small feat. Learning in *L'Ecolle* meant not just the ability to remember facts and regurgitate them on demand, although that was a large part of it. It also meant learning techniques of magic and being able to master them. Each student might excel in one or several of the magical techniques, but none could advance until he or she mastered all of the required skills at each grade level.

Simon found it all so easy to do that everyone was amazed. Unlike most of the other students, however, he had been studying and practicing these things on his own for years. Classes at *L'Ecolle* merely gave Simon new terms and a structure under which his knowledge and abilities grew so fast that at times it amazed everyone. His fellow students would frequently challenge Simon, to see how far he could go. He would always accomplish what they asked for, and usually more—always ending with some sort of prank that got everyone laughing. By the end of his first three summer months at *L'Ecolle* he was looked up to by all the students, but his horseplay kept everyone thinking that he was still just one of the guys. The staff of *L'Ecolle du Magie* was amazed at Simon's progress, and everyone, including his American endorsers, was proud of how well he did.

His parents, however, wondered why he hadn't improved any musical skills. Mr. Yenap explained that it was a French school practicing an immersion technique for the teaching of French. They were puzzled over how they could have been so confused, but this new explanation seemed to make sense. Beside, the staff of *L'Ecolle* had sent them such praises over their son they could hardly refuse to allow him to continue the next summer.

But things changed the following year. An older boy, Barton Mordus Oliver, had become the class leader. He did this through his own talent, which was indeed excellent, but also through bullying the rest of the students. The two girls, tired of his bullying and precocious sexual advances, and three of the boys, simply dropped out, leaving him to rule in a kind of "lord of the flies" scenario. He was older, bigger and the acknowledged leader. Then Simon came for the summer.

Simon later found out the story of Barton. Like Simon, Barton was a member of the baby boom generation. Born in Chicago, his mother died giving him life and his father blamed it on the boy. For six years he was yelled at and abused. Then one day Barton's father just didn't come home.

He ended up with foster parents who ran a farm. At first it was fun, but the fun soon turned to hard work. The work made him strong, and the large quantities of bread, milk, cheese and potatoes made him large, so large that the kids at school made fun of him. While walking home from school one day, bloodied and bruised from yet another fight when some kids mocked him for his size, he vowed he would do anything to get ahead and be the top dog. But he knew he needed power.

His family was poor. They had a radio, but no TV. He only watched movies at school. At home The only entertainment was Sunday services. And entertainment it was. Wild preaching and excited singing. It thrilled the young boy's heart. He loved going to church and he had talked to the preacher about becoming a clergyman himself.

When he was twelve he attended a service that changed his life. A raving, evangelical preacher was a guest and led the service. For hours he railed on about the evils of the occult. To young Barton's mind, if the church, powerful as it was, was so frightened of the occult then the occult must be very powerful indeed. Since it was power he wanted he made a new vow: he would become the greatest occult master in history.

Barton began by studying books in the library. Then he found out about mail-order occult shops and ordered more advanced books. He studied in secret and with great intensity. Soon he was successful with minor magical experiments. Finally, he decided to publically demonstrate his new powers.

He was a high school senior by now and the most unpopular kid in school. First he used his ability to make himself sexually desirable. When the girlfriends of half the football team swarmed around him the team decided to get even. They attacked him *en masse*. He not only escaped their attack unharmed, but he caused all of the threads in the seams of their clothes to dissolve. The result was that the entire varsity football team had to run naked from the school to their homes!

Merely overcoming his foes was not enough for Barton. He needed to gloat. In this way he came to the attention of an alumnus of *L'Ecolle du Magie* and he was recommended for membership. The rectors kept him out for a year, hoping he would mature, but finally let him in the following year with the hope their training would calm him down.

Simon was saddened at what happened to the school and wondered why the staff allowed it. Still, he continued on, figuring he would get out of *L'Ecolle* as much as he could. But the need to be the single Alpha Male leader was all Barton could think of. He challenged Simon to contests of magic. Simon hadn't cared too much about it, but at the prodding of the other students, he fought magical battles with Barton. He knew he was better than Barton, but always arranged it so their battles would end in a draw. That way he would not be seen as a leader over Barton, something which Simon knew would have led to an all-out war. The fact that there was no clear-cut winner, however, infuriated Barton, as did Simon's ease at learning.

The following year, Simon's third at *L'Ecolle*, looked like it would be the same. Something, however, had happened to Barton. Although his power grew, his wisdom had not. He was more of a bully than ever. Several of the students were thinking of dropping out but stayed, waiting to see if Simon could break Barton's control.

Simon was given a partial copy of the course of study for the third year when he left the fall of the previous year. His studies and practice left him far above all of the other students. Barton went wild over this, and determined to get even. It took two months for Barton to solidify his plans.

Meals at *L'Ecolle* were a communal affair. It was here Barton would strike. There was no need to hurt Simon when he could humiliate him. That was his plan. In his spare time Barton spent two days preparing for the ultimate insult to Simon Raven.

At this time the students looked up to both Simon, for his wisdom, talent and friendship, and Barton, for his abilities and because he bullied them. Barton intended to make Simon the fool so they would all look up to only him, Barton Oliver. All day long Barton laughed, amused by his own joke, making the other students wonder what was going on.

As they sat down to dinner, Simon realized something was fishy. He could feel the magical energy soaring and sparking around the room. He put his vision slightly out of focus—a technique he learned at *L'Ecolle*—and saw the streaks of magical power. He also saw the source of the streaks. He stayed ready for anything.

The attack didn't come until the middle of the meal. All the faculty and staff were out of the room in the kitchen when the bowl of stew being eaten by a boy across the table from Simon suddenly flew off the table at the American. Prepared, Simon made a dodging move to his left and was missed by both the bowl and its contents. "*Je regret,* Simon," apologized the startled boy across from Simon, "It was not my doing."

"*Je connais,*" replied Simon, "I know."

Abruptly, another bowl from near the end of the table flew down the length of the table's oaken planks and then at Simon. Once again Simon ducked, only this time he continued eating calmly, as if nothing unusual was occurring. Two more bowls came flying at Simon and he raised his right hand. They stopped in their mad dash and gently settled down without losing a drop of their contents.

"Impossible!" shouted Barton. "The only way you could have stopped those is if you knew about this in advance. Who told you?" thundered Barton, not remembering in his anger he had told no one of the attack.

"So, the big bully reveals himself at last," said Simon. "We have been putting up with you for many months. I have met every challenge you have thrown at me and let you come out even…" Hearing this, Barton paled. He always thought Simon just barely equalled him. "Your days of bullying are at an end."

Simon, who had been preparing for such an occasion should its need arise, stood and waved his right hand in a circle above his head, gathering magical energy. When crackling power surrounded it, he pointed both of his hands toward Barton. Barton, screaming and cursing, found himself floating in the air. In his seething rage, he could not come up with any counter-spells. A bowl of stew slid down the table and up into the air. Its contents flew directly into the front of Barton's pants. This was followed by bowls and pitchers of stew, potatoes, milk and wine. Barton, except for his face and head, was a mess. A large pool of slop was under him, dripping through his clothes. The rest of the students screamed their approval and banged on the table with silverware, cups and plates as Barton sputtered, "I'll destroy you, Raven!"

The *coup de grace* came with a bowl of mashed sweet potatoes to the face, leaving an orange blob above the mess that had been Barton and his clothes. Simon waved his hands again and Barton fell to the floor, landing in the goo beneath him with a squorch.

The whole scene took barely a minute. Some of the students had blocked the doors to the kitchen so the staff couldn't get out. When they finally moved aside and allowed the staff to rush in the students were immediately confined to their dormitory rooms.

Barton, cursing and spluttering, threatened to kill Simon and everyone else. "You're dead meat, Raven. Do you hear me? Dead meat! I'll kill you if it's the last thing I do. I'll never forget this." But there was nothing he could do. Barton had been so totally humiliated, both in magic and physically, that the other students would never look up to him, or fear him, again.

That night, Simon heard a pounding on his door. Each student had a suite of two private rooms in the dormitory. One room was the living quarters and one was space for a private magical temple. Outside of Simon's door were several of the students, fear etched on their faces. From down the hall that united the suites came an uncanny cloud of mist, undulating across the floor. Occasionally eyes and maws, fangs and pincers could be seen in the haze. Simon brought the students into his room, slamming the door behind them. He herded them into his temple room. Before he closed the door to that inner sanctum he saw the fog ooze under, over and around the outer door jam.

Inside the temple the students calmed. Under Simon's directions they set up a powerful magical wall of protection. The fog slithered past the inner door, but as it neared their protective barrier it held back and would not approach. They were at an impasse.

One of the students whispered, "Mirror." Then several of the other students repeated it. Soon the desire for the mirroring spell was universal. Together they concentrated on creating an astral mirror to send the fog back where it came from. The mirror slowly formed, then sprang to a crystalline existence. The fog seemed to halt in front of the mirror. Then it slowly retreated.

There was a period of silence. Only their breaths could be heard. A sound in the distance changed into a horrifying scream of terror and pain. Again there was silence.

Seconds later, Simon's temple exploded in a fiery ball of uncontrolled magical energy. Some of the students—through lack of skill and lack of experience—had kept a link to the mirror. When the fog attacked its sender a whiplash of psychic energy had come back through the astral mirror and into those students. The energy exploded into Simon's temple and, enclosed by the protective spell, which, although it was meant to keep things out, also had the effect of keeping things in, shattered everything in it.

Simon blacked out. When he came to, he was in bed and one of the staff was looking over him. The fog, known as the *soul vampires,* was the result of a ritual Barton had attempted in order to show his superiority. The mirror ritual had been a bad choice—the energy should have been dissipated, not returned to its source. The result was the reversed attack on Barton and the backlash into Simon's temple. Simon was okay, but Barton was not. It took the staff three weeks to help Barton regain all of his soul. Most of the other students were okay, but three never fully regained their souls and were mentally slow for the rest of their lives. One student, a freshman, had no personal barriers or protections in place. The staff could not retrieve his soul. His heart beat for three more days, but he never came out of the coma. As a result, *L'Ecolle* was disbanded for three years.

Barton blamed it all on Simon. The last time Simon saw him, Barton threatened to destroy him. "Hear me, Simon Raven. Neither time nor distance shall stop me from destroying you and grinding your bones to powder."

Before he left *L'Ecolle* to go home, Simon worked a *morpheus ritual*, putting the staff and students to sleep. He went to the files and made copies of the complete course of study for the rest of the year and the final year.

After he returned home he got a surprise visit from Mr. Yenap. "We know what happened and we don't think you were responsible. We know all about Barton Oliver, but the staff at *L'Ecolle* felt that their training might direct his magical talents and change him. We also know enough about you to figure you would manage to obtain the study and training schedule for the remainder of this year and next year. If you need help, give me a call."

Simon called him many times over the next eighteen months. When he finished the course, Simon was egotistical enough to claim to be a magician and powerful enough to back up his claim, but had grown wise enough not to brag about it to anyone.

"No matter how good you are, there is always somebody better," said his Kung Fu teacher, Master Wong, back in 1974.

Simon respected his teacher greatly and took the advice to heart. From that time on he never bragged about how good he might be at anything.

Simon had not heard from Barton Oliver since that fateful day at *L'Ecolle du Magie* in Paris, France, over twenty years ago.

Until last night.

* * * * *

It was early afternoon when Simon performed the last of his daily banishings and emerged from his private Temple. He spent the rest of the day in his library. He answered mail, paid bills and thought about what Barton might be up to. *How had Barton gotten so strong? Why was he attacking now? Was the attack against me personally or against the Warriors of the Light?* There was something missing in this equation, and Simon knew this was far from over. He put it out of his mind and was relaxing, reading a book, when he received the call from Paul.

At 6:30 P.M., Simon was waiting outside of The Ivy on Robertson in West Hollywood for his semi-annual dinner with his financial advisor. When Simon's parents died in an auto crash seven years ago, Simon discovered he was the only remaining relative of the Ravenswood family in England. It turned out they had a large estate which was being taken care of by a conservator who was more interested in a cushy job than finding out to whom the estate belonged. Simon sold the inherited estate and received a sum which, if invested wisely, would keep him financially secure for life. His financial advisor, a family friend named Gordon, had seen to it, and tonight Gordon would give him a semi-annual financial report.

It was good to see Gordon. Gordon was a trusted advisor and a link to Simon's own past. He loved these dinners and wished they could happen more often. But Gordon was getting up in years and didn't want to leave his comfortable home or the office he set up in it. Gordon had moved to Palm Springs four years ago and Simon was not big on driving there, so they met when Gordon came into L.A. for other business reasons.

Simon ordered a salad. Gordon ordered chicken. The financial advisor, whose dental implants continually pained him, complained as he ate the chicken prepared *au nouvelle cuisine.* Simon smiled, long since used to Gordon's way of sharing by discussing his aches and pains. His own salad was elegant, with numerous fresh vegies and several types of lettuce complemented by a freshly-made herb vinaigrette dressing adding flavor.

When the meal was over Gordon brought out the paperwork showing the condition of Simon's finances. The initial capital investment was enough to allow Gordon to invest it very conservatively. Even so, Simon quickly saw he had earned more than enough interest to continue to live in luxury and reinvest, adding to the original capital.

In short, his finances were as good as the dinner.

* * * * *

Seventh Night

The leisurely dinner ended at nine. Simon thought it would be futile to drive all the way back to his home in West Los Angeles. *I'd just have to turn around and drive back this way for my meeting with Lieutenant Christian.* So he drove toward Hollywood.

For awhile he made his way east down Melrose. This street had once been a slum. Inexpensive, trend-setting shops moved in. That brought people with money. Landowners raised rents. The inexpensive places moved out, or became materialistic and raised their prices, and the expensive places moved in. Melrose became the Yuppie center of West Hollywood.

However, in the evening, Melrose, especially further east, became what it had been for well over a two decades, a hangout for the boys of the night, ready to sell their bodies for money, drugs or fun. Simon never had any homosexual desires. He believed in letting others behave as they would as long as it did not hurt anyone else. Still, some of the faces he saw were so young, so young. He knew sometime tonight, maybe several times, a chickenhawk would swoop in on his prey. With a promise of money or drugs or just a meal and a place to spend the night, they would take advantage of a young boy. Or perhaps a cynical, city-hardened boy was simply doing what he liked to survive. Simon was no savior to those who had no wish to be saved, however. So he simply drove on.

At Vermont he turned north and went up to Sunset Boulevard. There he made another left turn and went back in the direction he'd come. Here the boys of the night were replaced by ladies of the evening. The streetwalkers were doing little walking, however. They seemed ensconced, two or three to a corner, talking, laughing, encouraging potential customers to come over and discuss business. Some also stood in front of the few cheap motels on the Strip. He guessed that more were in the lounges of the expensive hotels and motels although they would be of a higher class and demand a higher price. Stopped at a red light, he looked over to the assemblage of prostitutes that stood on the corner nearest to him. A hooker with short, bleached-blonde hair and too much makeup advertised her wares by lifting her elastic tube top revealing grotesque scars around her nipples where her breasts had been surgically cut open so she could have them silicone enhanced. Then she crooked a finger and rapidly flicked her tongue in and out of her mouth as a signal for Simon to come over and buy what she was selling. He ignored her. He looked ahead and saw a very young woman in a tight skirt and high heels. *Some of these women could barely be given that title. They look more like girls of fifteen or sixteen. Or younger.*

Simon turned up La Brea and made his way north to Hollywood Boulevard. The street had been repaved with ground glass mixed into the tarmac. In the glare of the streetlights it made the roadway glitter beneath his tires. Simon's classic Thunderbird attracted little attention from the jaded natives as he watched the tourists stare at the stars embedded in the sidewalk's cement on the Boulevard's Walk of Fame.

Traffic was always slow at this time of night on the Boulevard, but he slowed his car even more as he passed Burt Wheeler's Hollywood Magic store next to the building that had once housed Fredrick's of Hollywood, the granddaddy of all lingerie stores. He looked at the trick shop as his car slowly lumbered by and wondered if they ever actually changed the display in the front window. He'd been going there for what, twenty-five years? Maybe longer. It still looked basically the same, with the fake guillotine, the light-bulb-that-lights-in-your-hand and the faded top hat. *Macy's this isn't. Hell, Woolworth's this isn't!*

He sped up, as traffic would allow, moving past the outdoor newsstand on Cahuenga, and the occult shop, Pan Pipes, half a block to the south. *I miss the bookstore that used to be half a block down the Boulevard. What was the name of it again? Gilbert's? I shopped there so many times, finding rare occult books at greatly exaggerated prices. Still, they found for me what no other bookstore could find. And where was Cherokee Books, also a place where I purchased numerous overpriced volumes? It, too, was gone, beaten by chain stores in malls and discount stores that made up in quantity what they lacked in profit per title. They were destroyed by stores that sold remaindered books for pennies on the original dollar and chains that made more money selling calendars with men's buns, women's boobs and cartoon cats than on any books. Buns, boobs and cats.*

Nostalgia for an earlier time? Simon laughed at the thought. *Damn! I'm starting to sound like my parents.* He recently heard a couple of people his age decrying rap music because "it had no melody and you can't understand the words." Isn't that what his parents, and the parents of his friends, had said about The Beatles, Hendrix, Cream, The Moody Blues, Yes, Janis, and so many others? *The more things change the more they do stay the same. Still, rap music is basically strong, simple rhythms with little or no melody.*

How much more elementary can popular music become? I wonder what people who listen mostly to rap will say when they criticize their kids' music in the future? I wonder what pop music will be like in the future?

As he continued east the area got seamier. It felt dirty. For the first time Simon really noticed how humid it was. L.A. was almost never humid, so this stickiness was odd. And the smog was the worst he had ever remembered. *I know when there's smog it's always worse in Hollywood at the base of the Hollywood Hills, but...* Then he realized it was not just the humidity and smog that was making him feel uncomfortable. Something else was in the air. Something evil. Something unnatural. He turned up the air conditioning in his car. It should have become easier to breathe. It did not.

The next thing he knew, cars were beeping at him five-deep. He pulled over to the side of the Boulevard and felt a cold sweat. *Something terrible has happened! I know I'm involved but I don't know how.* He smashed his hand against the dash in rage. *What is going on?* He looked up at the stars, wondering if a good horary astrology chart and interpretation would tell him something. *Things do change, and not always for the better.*

Simon continued to drive down Hollywood Boulevard. The Walk of Fame with its ersatz golden stars had long-since ceased to appear on the sidewalk. There were fewer streetlights now. The darkness hid how ugly the world-famous Boulevard had become. The hookers looked harder and older. They also looked thinner, many to the point of emaciation. He figured they were drug addicts—*Heroin? Crack? Speed? Did it matter? Why would anyone want to leave their cars to make use of the services of these "workers?" The Johns probably looked as bad as the women whose favors they purchased by the moment.*

When Simon arrived at the police station it was seven minutes after ten. He parked his car in a spot labeled "visitor" and went inside.

Chapter Eleven

Seventh Night—Late

When Simon came in and announced his appointment to the desk officer he was ushered into Paul's office. "Thank you for coming in at this hour, Mr. Raven," said the voice from behind the desk. "I'm Lieutenant Paul Christian. Please have a seat." Paul pointed to the chair on the other side of the desk and Simon sat on its hard, wooden surface. "As I mentioned to you on the phone, I'm dealing with a case which has some occult overtones. Things are not clear on this case and I feel I need to get some expert advice."

"I believe I've heard of you before, Lieutenant. Aren't you known for dealing with occult crimes?" interrupted Simon.

"Well, that may be the way some of the public sees me, but it's not true. I deal with crimes, period. I'm sure you know there are wackos around who use the occult as an excuse to commit crimes, but even the FBI admits there's no national or international conspiracy of occult criminals. I solved those so-called occult crimes using standard police methods. Knowledge of the occult had nothing to do with it from my end. If somebody commits a murder, I use fingerprints, tire tracks, eye witness testimony, international computer systems, logic and hard work to find the culprit. I gather clues, evidence and determine motive—greed, anger, politics, revenge, stupidity, ego, psychopathology, the occult or whatever—to make sure a jury will convict the person or persons who committed the crime.

"But when someone or a group of people commits a series of murders, my first goal is to stop him or them. I can determine motives later. Look, if somebody robs you, sticks a gun in your ribs and demands your money, terrorizes you and rapes your mind and soul, do you care why? Of course not. You just want that person to stop. So do I.

"People are telling me the occult is heavily involved in this case. Although I've been called the occult crime stopper, this is the first time I've really had to investigate people involved with the occult. To do that, I find I need people knowledgeable on the occult. Unfortunately, the people I've contacted so far for advice, both inside and outside of the department, and who are supposed to be occult-minded, are either fakes and frauds or not able to help me.

"This is rather awkward, Mr. Raven. I know you've helped other law enforcement agencies concerning crimes with occult overtones, and I know from the flyer I picked up at the Bodhi Tree that you've got some sort of magical group. But... uh... you see, I've been advised to look for...uh...well...uh...*Mr. Raven, are you a real magician?*"

Simon laughed and sat back in his chair. "First, call me Simon. Mr. Raven was my father's name," he joked. Then he leaned forward and looked deeply into Paul's eyes with a surprising intensity. "And second, I can't tell you if I'm a magician because I don't know what you mean by the term."

"Come on Mr. Raven, Simon, you must know what I mean. Wands. Rituals. Spells. Invocations. Candles. Incense..."

"Lieutenant, some people have a mixed-up view as to what magic really is," replied Simon, leaning back.

"You're starting to sound like Donna Fortuna."

"You've talked with Donna? She's a good woman."

"So you're telling me that magic like spells and rituals and things like that aren't regularly practiced?" asked the detective. "Are you saying you can't help me?" Paul pursed his lips in disappointment.

"As Donna probably told you," Simon replied, "the real purpose of magic is spiritual development, to reach periods of unity with God. But I disagree with Donna on one point. As far as I'm concerned real magicians try to evolve spiritually *and* develop magical powers. Donna and I have had many discussions about this and, well, we agree to disagree."

"Simon, are you a magician? Do you know the occult world? Do you do magic?"

Now it was Simon who pursed his lips. He also started to tap the thumb of his right hand against his thigh as he considered the best way to answer Paul's question in a meaningfully. "Have you ever purchased something you needed, Lieutenant?"

"Of course. Everyone has."

"Well, before you purchased it you had to realize your need. In a sense, you created it in your mind before you bought it."

"Okay…"

"That's similar to what I do. I create things on what occultists call the astral plane through trained abilities of visualization, ritual and working with a type of energy that Western science hasn't yet been able to quantify. We simply call it psychic energy. As a result of this creation, a physical manifestation of what I have created on the astral plane must occur. In other words, what I create magically comes to pass in actuality. Usually this takes some time and happens only by natural methods."

"Usually?"

"Sometimes things need to happen faster. In some cases I have been able to accomplish this. On another level, being able to generate and control psychic energy can make for startling effects. If I direct some of this energy under an object, the object will rise. If I imbue the energy with some quality, it can very quickly effect the physical world." Simon closed his eyes for a second, smiled, then opened his eyes and continued, "If this makes me a magician in your eyes, then I am a magician."

They looked at each other for some time. *I don't need this,* Paul thought. *I don't need to play these word games. Damn it, people are dying! I need someone who can just look at the evidence and say, "Oh sure, here is the reason the criminal has done this and hey, I even know who did it." I need to have the killings stopped.* Paul shifted in his chair and realized he was going to break out in a sweat. He felt as if the temperature had suddenly risen by thirty degrees and was continuing to rise. It became difficult to breathe. His mouth felt like a desert. Simon watched as Paul rose from his seat. Immediately, Paul felt cooler and better.

"As an example of what I described," Simon continued, "I could, for example, generate some psychic energy and imbue it—or as we usually say, 'charge it'—with the qualities of heat and dryness. Occultists call the mixture of those two qualities 'elemental Fire.' I could then project this at someone and make them feel hot.

"Lieutenant, why did you get up?"

"Well, I got up because I…" He looked at Simon who had just described what he had done to him. *It's not possible.* He sat down in disbelief, shaking his head. "No. I don't believe it."

"As I said, Lieutenant Christian—Paul—If this makes me a magician in your eyes, then I am a magician. But whether or not I'm a magician, I am a student of the occult. How can I help you?"

Paul sat up in his chair and glared at the man on the other side of the desk. "Wait a second. You can't change the subject so quickly. You just claimed that you did something that's impossible."

"Fine. Then the heat you felt wasn't really heat. Maybe you just imagined it, or perhaps you were hypnotized?"

Paul leaned forward and slapped the desk hard with both hands.

"Don't play games, Raven," he said angrily through clenched teeth. He did not like being made fun of, and he knew how to use his own authority to intimidate others. "If what you're claiming is true, you could be a dangerous person, a person who needs to be investigated, perhaps even incarcerated for the good of the community."

"Whoa, Lieutenant. Hold on. Time out," said Simon, making the letter T with his hands like a football player signalling the referee to get a pause in the action. "I'm sorry. I didn't mean to offend you." After an awkward silence he continued, "Look, I've grown a thick hide over the years because I frequently deal with people who only criticize and make fun of or mock what is my work, my life, my very being. I have a response, it comes out a bit too quickly at times, I'm afraid, to fight back with sarcasm and humor. Sometimes my quirky sense of humor offends people. I really do apologize."

Paul saw the reaction he wanted in Simon and moved on. "I assume you've heard about the occult murders on TV or in the papers."

"I read a bit about it in the *L.A. Times,* but figured they only had part of it right. The police wouldn't reveal all of the evidence to the papers for fear of getting false confessions and letting the real criminals know how much the police had on them. I also know that when the crimes were solved, the police and district attorney still wouldn't reveal all of it to assure a fair trial for the accused. For most people, the only news which is important is the news that happens today. Yesterday's news is nothing more than irrelevant bird cage lining. I wrote it off as something that would be forgotten in a few days.

"It's funny, though. Usually I get calls from radio stations, TV stations and newspapers requesting interviews around Halloween or when there's been a crime with occult overtones. I haven't received any such requests about this case. It seems like there's something unusual about it…" Simon leaned back in his chair, considering what he had just said, and left his sentence unfinished.

Paul got up and walked around the tiny room. He took the packet of Tums from his pocket, carefully removed one and popped it into his mouth. Then he folded the packet up and put it away. Even though the blinds on the window were closed, he stared out, as if the window opened onto a scene of great pastoral beauty. Finally, he turned and looked directly at his guest. "I always look for every clue I can find, Simon. But if I don't know what to look for I may miss something. I've been trained to see things at a crime scene that look different, out of place. I've been trained to find things other people overlook. But I haven't been trained in the occult. I've no desire to cast spells or curses. I'm not a magician."

Paul turned around a picture frame that was sitting on his desk so that the photo in it was facing Simon. "Mr. Raven, see that lady? That's my ex-wife. She's the mother of my daughter and two sons. My daughter married a boilermaker and moved to Iowa. One of my sons is in Guam. He's a computer technician with the air force. My other son is in pre-law at USC. My wife and I were divorced eleven years ago. Mr. Raven, to me that's real. My gun is real. My car is real. My bills are real. My ulcer is all too real. My reality is as old as I am. I can't just up and change now.

"But I've got a case. This case doesn't...well...it doesn't fit the mold. It deals with things I *know* aren't real, yet people keep dying." Paul went to the file cabinet on the other side of the room and took an inch-thick manila folder from the second drawer. He returned to his seat and placed the dog-eared folder in front of him.

"I want to solve these murders before there are more deaths. Will you look at the file and see if there is something I've missed?" He pushed the file toward Simon. "Naturally, I'll have to ask you to keep everything you see and hear about this confidential."

Simon thought about it for a second, wondering what this might get him into. *I already have enough problems with the attack on the Warriors.* But people were dying, not merely being attacked, so he slowly nodded his assent and started to look through the file. He went through the pictures of each murder, one at a time, grimacing at the brutal photos. He was impressed with Paul's thoroughness in record keeping. Paul had written down everything he saw, experienced and even guessed at. He had also written down the comments and ideas of others. Simon always insisted his students keep accurate records of the magic-oriented books they read, the magical rituals and exercises they practiced and even their dreams. Right now he wished he could show them this file so they could see how it should be properly done.

Paul paced the room nervously. He took a Tums to settle his stomach and then went and got two cups of coffee, putting two spoons of sugar and lots of milk in his decaf. Simon thanked him for the coffee and returned to the papers and photos in front of him. It was a half-hour later when Simon finally closed the file and pushed it back to the other side of the desk.

Paul finished the last slurp of his coffee which also washed down two more Tums. "Do you know who did it?"

"No."

"Do you know why these crimes are being committed?"

"No."

"Do you know why different body parts are missing?"

"No."

"Do you know the meaning of the symbol found on the thighs of most of the victims?"

"About that I'm not sure. It *looks* like it comes from a book called *The Grimoire of Armadel*, but if my memory is correct I don't think it's exact. It may be from a book I was looking at just this afternoon entitled the *Necronomicon.* I'll have to search my library to find out what it really means."

"Oh, that's great, just great! I was already told the symbol was from that *Armadel* book. I thought it was an important clue. Now you're telling me even that lead may be bad. Can you tell me anything about this case?" asked Paul, in exasperation.

"Yes I can. Even though you've not been trained in the occult you're right about one thing: something *is* missing. I don't know what it is, either. Still, there's something about the symbol drawn on the victims' thighs that seems familiar, but..."

They were interrupted by a buzz on Paul's intercom. Paul excused himself after being summoned out of the office. He returned moments later. His face was grim, his lips a narrow, straight line. "I want to thank you for coming, Simon. May I call on you again?" he asked, not waiting for a response. "Something has come up and I have to go."

Paul started to put on his suit coat and leave when Simon stopped him. "Paul, is it another murder?"

Paul's hand was on the door knob, his back to Simon. He nodded, not even looking at his visitor. He pounded his fist against the door and turned to look at Simon. His face was set. Simon couldn't tell if it was anger, rage, helplessness or some other emotion that had locked his face.

"Are they sure?" Simon asked.

"The symbol is on the thigh, but there's been a change of M.O. This time the Tarot card was found in the victim's mouth."

"Do you have any guess as to why the change?"

"Well, yes, Mr. Raven. You see, the head, arms and legs are there, even the breasts are there. All that's missing is her torso. Excuse me, I have to go."

Paul was halfway out the door when Simon stopped him by putting his hand on Paul's shoulder. "Paul, let me come with you. Perhaps there's something I can see there at the site that you and the photographers who took the photos in your file missed."

Paul turned his head and looked at this man. *He's a strange bird, dressed all in black and claiming to have knowledge and talents others do not.* Paul liked to work on his own. He hated the thought of having to get aid from someone else, let alone someone who was external to the force. But Paul was also a pragmatist. *Well, why not? Maybe he can help.*

"Okay, Simon, let's go." On the way out Paul stopped to pick up keys for an assigned vehicle. He looked at the number on the keys and said, "Damn!" They went to the Ford with the pitted windshield. Paul started the engine, took two more Tums, put the transmission in gear, and they were off.

* * * * *

The site where the body was discovered was on King's Road, a hill just off of Sunset Boulevard. When they got there they could see four black-and-white police cars, quartz halogens lighting up the area, and yards of yellow tape to keep out the onslaught of reporters, camera crews and locals who were awakened by the ruckus. As they left the car one of the reporters saw them.

"Hey! That's that Simon Raven guy. He's supposed to be a wizard. Mr. Raven, are you involved in this case? Are you a suspect? Is this another of the occult murder crimes? Are you being called in for advice?" he shouted.

Simon and Paul ignored the questions and ducked under the tape to reach the site. The body was that of a beautiful, young woman. The unmoved parts that remained were laid out on the ground as if her body had been whole. The breasts were laid where her chest would have been if her torso had not been missing. Her face was turned to the side and barely hidden by the short, dyed, jet-black hair.

Paul talked quietly to some of the officers who were there to catch up on the information already gathered while Simon moved back to get a better view of the entire scene. *Sometimes people get too close to something and don't see the entire picture.* He didn't know what he was looking for. Perhaps something strange or out of the ordinary. In ten minutes all he noticed were three rocks that had been turned over. They could have been moved or kicked by accident at any time in the last several hours or days. Still, they did form an arc…

Simon stepped back further, finally clambering up a small boulder to get a better view. There it was! The three stones, mixed with the natural formations of rocks and plants and a few other stones which had been moved, formed a pattern. It looked a bit like the symbol for the astrological sign of Cancer. It also looked a bit like the yin-yang symbol of the orient. Yet, it was different.

He jumped off the rock and walked quickly back to Paul, who was standing by the body. Simon started to speak, but then he saw the right thigh of the victim. On it was tattooed a red rose with an ornate dagger through it, dripping one drop of blood. "Oh no!" he cried, falling to his knees, "Oh no!" He reached for what remained of the body, as if by caressing it he could bring it back to life. Two officers grabbed him, preventing him from doing so.

"What are you doing, Simon? Have you gone crazy?"

Simon had stopped resisting the officers. His head hung down in loss and pain. *Damn, damn, damn! I tried to protect her and failed.* He asked if he could stand. Paul nodded his assent. Simon rose, brushing the dirt off his pants. He continued to stare at what was left of the young woman as he answered Paul's question. "I knew her. She was a student of mine. She was a friend." Simon's face was a mask of sadness and bitterness over his loss and his failure.

"How can you be sure?" asked Paul. "You haven't even gotten a good look at her face." An officer came up and gave Paul a folder. Paul opened it and quickly perused the contents as Simon responded.

"It's her, alright," said Simon, finally turning to face Paul. "Her name was Angelica Firestone. She was one of my students. That's her tattoo."

Paul looked up from the folder and stared at Simon. This time the detective's eyes narrowed with suspicion. *Simon must be in his late thirties or forties, maybe even in his late forties. This woman was about half his age, maybe less. What was he doing looking at a tattoo way up on her thigh?* "Stay here for a moment, Simon."

Paul walked away while Simon turned back and just looked at what had once been a woman so young and full of life. *Oh, Angelica, I am so sorry! I never meant for you to be hurt.* He didn't see Paul talk with both plainclothed and uniformed officers. When Paul came back he asked, "When was the last time you saw her?"

"Two days ago. We were doing some work and, uh, she was hurt. I had her taken to the hospital."

"Un-huh. She had been identified through her fingerprints while we were on the way here," he said, shaking the folder he was holding. "They ran her name through city records and discovered she had been taken to a hospital from your home. The report said…" Paul changed his speech pattern and spoke very slowly. "The report said that she had lost a great deal of blood."

Simon's eyes got large. He realized what was happening and did not like it a bit. "Angelica was a good friend and student. I did everything I could to protect her…"

"And yet she was rushed to the hospital with a loss of blood. The report also said her clothes, a robe, were ripped. Did this occur as part of a ritual?"

"Well, yes, but it wasn't…"

"What were you doing this morning around ten A.M.?"

"I was doing some…uh…spiritual practices."

"Do you mean magical rituals?"

"Well…yes."

"Was anyone else there?"

"No."

"So you have no witnesses. Was Angelica Firestone there?"

"I said no."

"Did you know any of the other victims of these crimes? Christy Brown, Cindy deGrasse…"

"No."

Paul, who was slightly shorter than Simon, stared into the other man's eyes. "Mr. Raven, did you ever have sexual intercourse with Angelica Firestone?"

Simon always prided himself on his honesty. "If you aren't honest and worthy of trust by other people," he would tell his students, "why should you be trusted by spirits, angels and the gods?" He saw where this was leading. He had performed the Rite of the Sparrowhawk with her once, but her youth had prevented her from controlling the enormous psychic energy released during sex. She became oriented toward the physical sensations rather than the ritual and as a result the Rite had failed. Still, he did have sex with her and knew it would make things look bad. "I think it is time for me to go," he said.

Paul nodded and two policemen grabbed Simon by his arms. "I'm sorry Simon, but there's too much circumstantial evidence here. I'm placing you under arrest for the murders of Angelica Firestone, Christy Brown, Cindy deGrasse and other Jane Does both known and unknown. You have the right to remain silent. Anything you say can and will be used against you in a court of law. You have the right to an attorney. The attorney may be with you during any questioning. Should you not be able to afford an attorney one will be appointed for you at no cost. Do you understand these rights?"

Simon looked at Paul as handcuffs were being placed on him behind his back. "Paul, you asked for my help and I offered to give it to you..."

Paul said nothing. He looked away but felt Simon's glare at his back.

"Okay, Paul," said Simon, defiantly, "I tried to help and this is what you've done to me? Fine. We'll play it your way. I have nothing to say until I speak to my lawyer."

Paul, feeling glad he now had a suspect, stood tall and played the role. He turned and told the officers holding Simon, "Take him down and book him for murder one." *God, I sound like I just stepped out of* Hawaii 5-0.

Simon didn't want to move. They dragged him to a car while he shouted behind him, "Paul! You know I didn't do it. Paul! Listen to me. It isn't going to stop!"

Lieutenant Paul Christian straightened his tie and buttoned his jacket. *Now* he would have something he could say to the papers. *Now* he had a collar to show Captain Minelli. He ignored Simon's yells because he knew he had his man. *Criminals would always do anything, say anything, to get out of having to admit to their deeds.*

Paul turned back to the body. Next to the corpse was a small, clear, plastic bag with a Tarot card inside of it. A number written on the bag identified it as evidence. He picked it up and looked at the image on the card. It showed a young man about to walk over a cliff. The name of the card was "The Fool."

* * * * *

Simon sat uncomfortably in the back seat of the police car. Silently he glared out the front windshield as he was driven to the West Hollywood police station on San Vicente, just down the street from the Whisky. The station looked like a simple, one-story building from the outside, but when he entered he learned that there were numerous levels below that visible one.

Simon was taken to a cell on the main floor where the handcuffs were removed. Also taken from him were his watch, wallet, change, appointment book, belt and shoes. He was kept there for over two hours and not allowed to make a call. Finally he was cuffed again and taken to a private room where two armed guards watched as he was told to take off his clothes. After he did so another officer, who wore a skin-tight vinyl glove, gave him a complete body search. The two guards, who had by now completely examined his clothes, snickered at Simon's humiliation. When the search was through Simon dressed and was recuffed. From there he was taken to the booking station where fingerprints were taken along with photos of his bedraggled face, front and side. He was then paraded down through several floors of the building.

Guards with drawn guns pointed the way to yet another cell. This cell had three beds and a toilet. Simon made the seventh resident of the cell. He was kept there, incommunicado, for several more hours. "Hey! I've asked three times to be allowed to make a call," Simon yelled to a guard. "I'm supposed to be allowed to make a call. Why am I not allowed to make a call?" The guard ignored him.

"Hey, white boy." Simon turned toward the voice that had called him. It belonged to a large Black man who had a top bunk to himself. His feet extended past the end of the bed. He looked at the ceiling while he spoke. "They'll let you make a call when they feel like it."

"But I have rights…"

The Black man turned to look at Simon. "Huh!" he snorted. "Now you know what it feels like to be a brother. Welcome to jail, white boy. Now shut up and go to sleep."

* * * * *

Eighth Day

At 8:40 a.m., over six hours after he was arrested and booked, a guard came to Simon's cell. Simon sat meditating in a corner, and the guard had to shake him several times to wake him from his reverie. They were finally going to allow him to use the phone.

His only lawyer was Gordon—Simon had never been in legal trouble before. He called Gordon and explained what happened. Gordon told him not to worry, he would do everything necessary.

It was noon when a guard, with a young lawyer named O'Ryan, came to Simon's cell. Simon was taken up to a discharge area where he was given back his belongings.

"How can they get away with not allowing me a phone call?" Simon asked.

"You're lucky they let you call so soon," said O'Ryan. "You're allowed a call, but the law says they can hold you for up to three days without filing arrest papers. You only get the call after you are officially arrested, and they can hold up filing the papers for a long time."

"I never heard that before."

"Welcome to the wonderful world of legal machinations, Mr. Raven."

"So how much was my bail?" asked Simon.

"You're out on your own recognizance," replied O'Ryan.

"How did you manage that?" he asked in astonishment. "They charged me with multiple murders."

"Your record was clean with no prior convictions, you helped various law enforcement agencies in the past, you had no motive, evidence was totally circumstantial and nothing could place you at the scene of any crime. You have a home and many friends in the community so you have no reason to leave. Plus, the judge and I are members of the same law frat."

Simon laughed. Then he asked, "Didn't the D.A. object?"

"Yeah. She went crazy. She wanted no bail at all. When the judge heard my argument, however, the D.A. asked for a million dollar bail."

"How did you get it down to nothing?"

"Well… it's not quite nothing. You have to wear this." A police officer brought out a bulky bracelet and locked it onto Simon's right wrist. "It's a radio sender that always shows where you are. Try to leave the area or take it off and they'll pick you up in less than five minutes."

"Wait a second," bristled Simon. "I don't want to wear this hunk of electronics."

"You want out now?" asked O'Ryan.

Simon let his body relax. He had lost this round. "Can we just go now?" he asked.

O'Ryan gave him a ride to his car at the other police station. Simon slowly drove home. The smog-filled muggy air had grown worse, and it was even more difficult to breathe than before. For awhile he felt as if his childhood asthma had returned. He was exhausted from the ordeal. When he finally got home he went to his bedroom and collapsed onto the firm, waveless waterbed without taking time to remove his clothes. When he awoke it was dark.

Eighth Night

"Forward, two, three, step. Backward, two, three, step. Move your arms, girls!"

Allenda, along with about forty other women, moved to the thump, thump, thump of the blasting music in the large room. They tried their best to follow the directions of the smiling woman instructor *with the perfect figure, damn her,* giving instructions. The woman working out immediately in front of Allenda was a curvaceous blonde with blue eyes whom everyone called "Moose." They called her this because she used to weigh over 150 pounds. With exercise, dieting and determination she brought her weight down to a svelte and sexy 108. She kept the nickname, originally used as an insult, as a sign of pride.

Moose was Allenda's "exer-buddy," for the evening. This was a term used by the athletic club for people who would work out together. Moose perspired heavily when she worked out and as she flipped her head, getting her long hair out of her eyes, Allenda got a splash of Moose's sweat in her face. Allenda, clad in metallic silver tights and a brilliant blue leotard, lost her step and almost tripped. She caught the beat and started exercising again. Allenda wiped her face with her forearm and found all she did was add her own sweat to the mixture. Soon the exercise class got busier and Allenda focused on the movements. Finally, after a slow-down period, the class ended. The music stopped, but she could still feel the thump, thump, thump of the drums and bass in her body. She knew from experience it would be a while before that faded.

Allenda and Moose sat down and patted themselves with their towels.

"Want to do some spinning?" Moose asked.

"Sure," Allenda replied, and they walked to the stationary ellipticals. They waited until two adjacent stationary bikes were free, got on and started pedaling.

For some time they rode the bikes in silence. Moose could sense something was on Allenda's mind, but didn't feel close enough to her to ask. *Maybe a general topic would be a good conversation starter.* "Did you hear," asked Moose, "that they found the serial killer? It was some occult guy."

Allenda bristled and stopped pedaling. She stared at Moose for a second, then started pedaling, quickly getting back into the rhythm. Allenda didn't want to go public with the fact that she was an occultist for fear of being considered weird, crazy or dangerous. One of the Warriors lost his job because he was too public about his occult interests. Allenda was still "in the broom closet," but she hated it when people who knew little of the subject started talking about it. "How do you know that it was some 'occult guy'?" she asked.

"Oh, the guy they busted is famous. His name is Simon something-or-other."

Allenda's foot slipped off a pedal in shock. She almost fell off the bike. Allenda re-established her pedaling rhythm again and asked, "Simon? Do you mean Simon Raven?"

"Yeah, that's it. Mr. Oogah-Boogah from West L. A. I'm sure glad they found out who did it. I was getting worried about going out at night."

"But how do you know he did it?" Allenda asked. "Isn't he supposed to be innocent until proven guilty?"

"C'mon, Alli. Wake up and smell the Frappuccino. The cops wouldn't have busted him unless he did it. They know what they're doing. Besides, those idiots let him go."

"He's free?"

"Yeah. They just let him go. When I heard about it I couldn't believe it. They didn't even make him pay any bail. I think it's just another example of how the legal system in America doesn't care about women, letting a serial killer of women like that go. I'm going to write a letter of complaint to the *Los Angeles Times*."

Allenda coasted to a halt on her bike. "Listen, Moose, I gotta get going. See you in two days, okay?"

"Yep. Take it easy, girlfriend," she said.

Allenda took a quick shower, dried herself and dressed. With her exercise gear stuffed in a large purse slung over her shoulder, she got in her Mazda Miata and drove to Simon's house.

* * * * *

Alan Crawford was a mess. He belched as he slowly munched on a twinkie, then dug out some of the white goo from the center of the piece in his hand and savored its texture and flavor on his tongue.

He sat in a leather recliner, only getting up to get some food or go to the bathroom, for the past four days. After the debacle at the ritual Simon had called him into his den for a private, closed-door conference.

"Why are you a Warrior of the Light?" Simon asked.

"Uh, to achieve knowledge of, and conversation with, my Higher Self, my Holy Guardian Angel," Alan replied.

"No, that is a reason for anyone to become a Warrior. What is *your* reason?"

Alan, feeling uncomfortable, bowed his head. "I'm not sure what answer you're looking for, Simon. The Warriors are the only thing that has ever given meaning to my life. It's part of me."

"I know, Alan. But being part of the Warriors is not helping you the way it should. You learn something and then forget it. I saw what happened earlier. You learned you could work with magical energy and then, bored, you could do nothing further with it. You know the Lesser Banishing Ritual of the Pentagram. I remember how impressed I was when

I first saw you perform it. Tonight you did a very poor job of it."

Alan looked up, his face a picture of disappointment and shock. "Do you mean I'm responsible for what happened to Angelica?"

"No, Alan. Whoever is in charge of a ritual is responsible for whatever happens during the ritual. *I'm* responsible for what happened earlier. But if you hadn't done such a bad job, perhaps, just perhaps, I might have not have had to pay attention to the banishings and would have detected the invading force before anything took place.

"But that is not why I called you here. Quite simply, you're not advancing. You're fighting the changes being a member of the Warriors should bring to you. I don't know if being a member of the Warriors remains beneficial to you and the Order.

"As of tonight I am changing your status in the Order to 'provisional.' I want to see something from you within two weeks..."

"What do you want to see?"

"That, Alan, is up to you. It should be some sort of change. Either you should begin to put what you've learned into practice in your life or you should give us your resignation."

"But how can I prove to you I'm doing what you ask? How can I show you..."

"Thank you, Alan. If you do not hear from us within two weeks I will expect to hear from you. Good night." Simon leaned back and closed his eyes.

Knowing he was dismissed, Alan left the room and drove home. He turned on the TV and veged out on the sofa for the past four days.

I can't even think of what I'd do without the Warriors! I'm starting to get my life in order. Can't Simon see that? He took another bite of twinkie.

A comedian was on TV. The set was an old Zenith, and somethng in the set was failing. The colors looked pastel and horizontal lines moved continuously up the screen, like a personal barber pole. The audience for the comedian, enhanced, of course, with a prerecorded laugh track, was roaring at his jokes.

"And what is the deal with twinkies?" the comedian asked. "They got a shelf life of 117 years! And what in God's name is that white crap in the center of them? Does anybody know? I mean, a thousand years from now philosophers will still be asking, 'What is the meaning of life and what is that stuff in twinkies?' And what's really weird is that we eat that stuff!"

Alan looked at the twinkie in his hand. *Is that what Simon was talking about? If the intelligence of my Higher Self tells me to do something, shouldn't I do it? If I don't, I'm not putting the teachings of the Order to work.*

Alan thought back to a book he once read. There were two sentences he always remembered, although he wasn't positive about their meaning, "Magic isn't something you do. Magic is something you are." *Is that what this is all about? I have consistently tried to learn magic as something to do, but I have never been a magical person.*

Alan looked down at his fat belly. *My God, how could I have done this to myself?* He threw down the remains of the twinkie. It landed in an open pizza box which held the remains of a day-old pie. He rose, quickly cleaned up the food wrappers and boxes, and placed them all into the trash.

Is that it, Simon? Do you want me to be magical instead of just doing magic? He held his right palm up, and following the instructions Simon had given, created a ball of energy. He directed it at the power switch on the TV. The sound and picture vanished, leaving only a small dot of light in the center of the picture tube.

It is my will to do the bidding of my Higher Self! He looked over at the NordicTrack cross-country skiing machine which had been gathering dust in the corner. Alan dragged it to the center of the room and got onto it. He started to laugh as his heartbeat moved up into the aerobic range. His laugh left him and his face set with determination. *Resign from the Warriors? Never!*

* * * * *

When Simon arose he was famished. He busied himself by preparing some *Grillers*—imitation beef-patties for vegetarians. He always enjoyed their almost-hamburger taste. By the time he sat down to eat, his fury over the events of the last twenty-four hours returned and he merely gazed at the food. *During my entire adult life I have helped people and advised law enforcement agencies. Now, with the murder of poor Angelica I'm accused primarily because I knew her. How could they do it? Why wouldn't they listen to me? What were they…*

Simon's anger was interrupted by the sound of the ram's head knocker. For a second, Simon looked at the *griller* sandwich in his hands, trying to decide if he should take a bite or answer the door. Finally he tossed the pseudo-burger sandwich onto the plate where it promptly split open and bounced onto the table, spreading ketchup onto the glass tabletop. He sighed, looked at the mess and laughed. What else could he do? The knocker sounded again and Simon rose to get the door.

When he opened the small panel in the door, he was greeted by Allenda's smiling face. Without saying anything he closed the panel and opened the door.

Allenda breezed in. "New jewelry, Simon?" she asked, pointing to the radio transmitter on his wrist.

Simon looked at her for a second, surprised she would be that open and joking. Not that he minded, but she was never that outgoing before. Somehow, she was changing. "Cute, cute," he said, obviously feigning anger at her remark.

They went into the living room. Allenda sat on the overstuffed sofa while Simon sat in a firm, leather chair.

"How did you get them to let you out without bail?" she asked.

"Basically, their case was impossibly weak. The little evidence they had was all circumstantial and proved nothing. I also agreed to wear this radio sender so they'll always know where I am," he said, holding up his wrist. "And the judge and my lawyer were frat buddies."

Allenda laughed. "How do you get yourself into such messes? First the attack on us, then Angelica, then the attack on you on the astral and now this. Why is it all happening now?"

Simon, who had been looking at the floor, suddenly looked up. He thought that the murders, including the murder of Angelica, were separate from the attacks on him and the Warriors. *Had Allenda picked up on something he hadn't realized? Were the murders and the attacks somehow connected?*

"Alli," he asked, "do you have your cards with you?"

"Sure. I always keep them with me." She reached into her purse and pulled out a multi-colored Tarot deck.

"I'd like a reading. Let's go into the kitchen and I'll put on some coffee."

Simon went to the refrigerator, pulled out a bag of ground coffee beans and put them and some water into the Braun coffee maker. Allenda sat at the table and shuffled the cards repeatedly. Simon sat in a chair and she asked what his question was. "I'd rather not say," he answered. "Just focus on important trends in my life."

He left the table and got two cups and saucers. He waited for the coffee machine to finish hissing and poured. He brought them to the table and Allenda stopped shuffling, reached into her purse and pulled out a packet of Splenda. *She's really changing. She looks different, too. Trimmer, more fit.*

She took a sip of coffee. *Ah, Irish Cream.* Allenda shuffled the cards one more time and looked Simon in the eyes. "Here we go." She put a card face down on the table and said, "This is what's on your mind." She flipped the card over. It was the Knight of Wands, reversed. It showed a picture of a winged warrior riding a black horse with a tail and mane of fire. "There is someone on your mind who is evil-minded, cruel and brutal," she said. "Was it the cop who busted you?"

No, it was Barton. Aloud he gave no response, but asked her to continue.

"This next card is something related to the current trend that happened some time ago." The card she flipped showed four hands holding eight swords around a fifth hand holding a single sword. "Hmm. The Nine of Swords. The cards tell me you went through a period of oppression and someone showed you cruelty and malice through the use of subtlety and craftiness."

She flipped over the next card. "This has to do with more recent events that effect the current trend." The card showed a man sitting on a simple throne with a ram by his side. "The Emperor. You've been in a war fighting someone's ambition.

"The next card shows what you must do to win this situation." The card showed a tower struck by lightning. People were falling off the tower's parapet. Her voice slowed as she interpreted the meaning of the card. "Uh...The Tower means there's nothing you can really do because you are trying to fight events which are beyond your control. This last card reveals the final outcome of the current trend." She lifted it from the top of the deck.

Simon grabbed her wrist before she could turn it over. He looked her in the eyes and took the card out of her hand.

He knew what it was going to be without looking at it. The hair on the back of his neck stood on end. He turned it over and placed it next to the other cards. It showed two hands, each holding two almost upright swords. A third hand held an upright sword in the center, giving the impression it had been thrust swiftly between the other two. The petals of a rose in the center of the image were slashed and falling. Simon just looked at the Five of Swords.

"It means defeat," said Allenda, almost in a whisper. "It means defeat."

* * * * *

They finished their coffee in silence. "Alli, did you hear about the most recent murder?"

"Of course."

"Do you know who the victim was?"

"Well, no. I didn't pay that much attention. Does it really…"

Simon stood up quickly and walked to a table. He rested his hands on it for a moment. Then he turned and looked at Allenda. His face was a mass of emotions Allenda could not decipher. "It was Angelica, damn it, Angelica. It was Angelica."

Shocked, Allenda opened her mouth to say something. But there was nothing to say. She hadn't been close to Angelica, but as a sister of the Warriors she felt the loss. They worked together many times in ritual, and for a few minutes she thought of Angelica's quick smile, easy laugh and fabulous ability as a seeress. Allenda made up an excuse to leave.

Simon went back to the leather chair and sat down sideways with his feet over one of the arms. *Defeat. Defeat. So far we survived two attacks but lost Angelica. Defeat, but for who? For who?*

* * * * *

Allenda walked slowly, sadly to her car. She stopped at the door, dropped her keys and bent to retrieve them. She held them tightly in her hand. She remembered Simon's anger over the magical attack on Angelica and understood his feelings. *Defeat? By everything holy I vow the only ones to suffer defeat in the end shall be whoever attacked us and killed Angelica. So mote it be!*

She unlocked the door to her car, got in and started the engine. She pushed the accelerator to the floor causing the wheels to spin and the engine to flood and splutter to a stop.

Allenda looked at the dashboard for a long moment. "Defeat?" she called to the universe, "I've just begun to fight you. Whether you are a single person or the very legions of hell, I will fight you to my dying breath; and I'm not going to die easy. Nobody hurts my friends, nobody. Whoever you are, be warned—I no longer need a protector; neither my father nor Simon. I will defeat you by any means necessary. So do your damnedest.

"I'll be ready."

* * * * *

"Mother. I now know who our real enemy is…"

"No, my son, you know nothing."

"What? How can you say that? I've found out who attacked me and the Warriors…"

"You have only discovered what is on the surface. Have you forgotten Angelica?"

Simon reddened. "You have no reason to think that, Mother. I will never forget her. But you told me loved ones will die…"

"Yes, that is so. But you have become too involved to see the danger. The source of the evil dictated her death and its method. Stopping one person will not stop the evil."

"How do I find the evil, Mother? What should I do?"

"Continue on your path, my son. Look for the source, not the manifestation; you must destroy the root—if you merely pluck the weed it will regrow and further poison your garden."

"Mother, the cards foretold defeat. Is that defeat ours or someone else's? Will we be the ones to win or will we be the ones who are defeated?"

"The evil is getting stronger, my son. Can you not smell it in the air? Can you not feel the way the very earth rebels at its touch? If you are defeated then all is lost."

"But will we win?

"Mother?

"Mother?"

Chapter Twelve

Ninth Day

Elaine Renault was a New Ager. She lived in the upstairs of a creaky, cobweb-filled house in Sacramento. The upstairs had its own entry and she thought it might have been a servant's quarters when the house was built decades ago. The house was just a mile or so from where an elderly woman had murdered some of her boarders for their Social Security checks. Elaine always thought the story sounded like something out of *Arsenic and Old Lace.*

Elaine looked at herself in the mirror, set her thin lips and sighed. At forty-one, even the make-up no longer brought back the beauty of fifteen or twenty years ago, a beauty which had allowed her to live as the mistress of some wealthy men. Still, when she brushed back her reddish-gold hair, now kept that color with the help of Lady Clairol, and when the single bathroom light hit her just right she could see what she once was. *One day I'll have enough money for a full face lift.*

She looked down at her body and felt frustrated. Her once elegant size four figure had bulged into a size ten. And her breasts! Somehow her genes betrayed her and in less than a year during her late thirties her bosom had grown from nice, firm B-cups to enormous double-Ds. Once, while walking down the street soon after the change, someone driving by had shouted, "Hey, look at those melons!" Elaine spent two minutes looking for a fruit stand, hoping for some nice honeydews until she realized what the driver meant.

Not that Elaine was stupid or slow—to the contrary, she was highly intelligent. Unfortunately, she would get her mind into a single focus and it became almost impossible to change her. Elaine lived alone, but was happy with that. She had been married four times and had several lovers and live-in boyfriends. But over the years, as her appearance changed, so had her addictions.

Elaine had been very fat as a child. She suffered through years of insults and snickering by other children as she grew up in Los Angeles. At seventeen she finally couldn't take any more of the slurs—even though they were now mostly whispered behind her back—and became bulimic. Eventually she became anemic and ended up in a hospital. She finally learned how to balance her eating habits and turned to exercise to keep her weight down.

After she recovered from bulimia (vomiting had always disgusted her anyway), Elaine never went to further therapy. The brief therapy for bulimia focused on that one disorder. As a result, she never acknowledged her addictive personality, nor did she get treatment for it. She quickly fell into her next addiction—drugs, including cocaine and speed. After she broke her addiction to drugs she told everyone she was free from any addictions. In reality, her life was a series of them, including food, bulimia, drugs, sex, religion, work and exercise.

Currently her addictions were to the New Age and her enormous ego. She was always right (just ask her) and anything that got in the way of her particular path was suspicious and dangerous. Her paranoia—a side effect of her previous drug addictions—still ate at her.

When she was in a cycle of using drugs or exercising she was filled with energy and had a lust for life. That once-dynamic lifestyle had decayed into work, New Age studies, and her two cats, The Rat and Julius Caesar. She had a small coterie of friends, all of whom were also involved in the New Age. But unlike Elaine they had lives outside of work and their New Age interests. Elaine could not understand why they weren't as dedicated as she.

Throughout her life, Elaine had blown off her relationships. Now she thought she was incapable of loving, no longer even knowing what love is. Since she no longer was looking for a man, a partner for her life, she referred to herself as "the eternal virgin." She had not had a boyfriend in several years. She had not had sex in well over a year. When she tried to have intercourse with an old lover it was painful. As a result of her lack of regular sex, the skin inside of her vagina actually started to adhere to itself, almost as if it wanted to seal itself up. Her lover tried to break through the vaginal adhesions, and although it was painful for her, she encouraged him to thrust harder with his penis. He saw the agony on her face and finally gave up.

Because of her asexuality and self-righteousness, those who knew her called her "the ice queen," but not to her face. They also laughed at her because of it. However, since they were her "friends" they only laughed at her behind her back. After all these years people still laughed at her.

Unlike most occultists, Elaine did not think the New Age was merely a superficial form of occultism or that the followers of the New Age, as well as the entire movement, lacked heart, soul and depth. She didn't care that many of her co-workers thought the New Age was just an excuse to over-price useless garbage by wholesalers and stick fat profits in the pockets of conscienceless retailers. "Call it 'New Age' and jack the price up by two hundred per cent," they said. Elaine couldn't care less about that.

Elaine had three aspects to her New Age interests: study, rituals and what she called, "stuff." The stuff consisted of everything from crystals to candle holders, from cutesy pewter statues to incense braziers and was everywhere in her home, filling her small quarters until it looked like a maiden aunt's house. All it lacked to complete that picture was noisy, plastic slipcovers on the furniture and the smell of burned garlic in the background. Elaine would frequently spend hours moving and readjusting all the stuff so it looked fresh and balanced.

Her rituals were taken from all sorts of books, some historic, some recent inventions and fantasy. Her knowledge was neither wide nor deep, although she liked to think it was both. Sometimes her rituals were imaginings she thought had some mystical effect. The only effect they had was their ability to take up time.

She could never figure out why, although she was happy being alone, she still felt lonely. The rituals did not end her loneliness, although she did rituals for that purpose almost every day. Nor did they end her general lack of finances. The fact that she was always buying more books and stuff rather than paying bills or saving for her lift didn't help, either. As a result of her purchasing useless extravagances she found that every few months either the gas or electricity or phone was turned off for lack of payment.

Still, she spent hours every day performing her rituals in private. They kept her from having to be around other people and possibly chancing the passion of love only to end, as her other relationships had, in the pain of separation.

The third aspect of her New Age interests was study, and to this end she bought books. Lots of books. Used books, new books, it didn't matter, as long as they were even remotely related to the New Age. Almost any topic could be included in her definition of the New Age: philosophy, psychology, mysticism, magic, theology, astrology, numerology, Eastern philosophy and religion, Tarot, Western religion, positive thinking, comparative religious studies and books on ancient cultures and their philosophies (which were frequently channeled or invented by contemporary New Age writers). Which is why she was humming as she got dressed. It was five in the morning and she was going down to all of the New Age stores in L.A. and San Diego. The run would take three days, and she was taking the time off, unpaid, from her work as a data entry expert so she would not lose vacation time. She would be staying at two nice hotels. The rooms were booked and she had packed the night before.

Elaine picked up her suitcase and checked for the fourth time to make sure the vacation feeders and waterers, which she placed on the porch outside the back door for her cats, were filled. Julius and The Rat were already munching on the food as she petted them goodbye, explaining to them she would be back in a couple of days. They ate, paying no attention to her.

She walked five blocks to the light rail system. She timed it perfectly and boarded the streetcar which just arrived. It took her to the Amtrak station. There she boarded the Coast Starlight, the train that would take her to L.A. Since it was an express run and not a local, it only made three stops: San Jose, San Luis Obispo, and Santa Barbara.

Elaine, wearing jeans, a sweatshirt and tennies, settled back into the thick comfort of the heavily padded seat. *Why couldn't they make airplane seats this comfortable*? She had been doing rituals late the night before, and the thick seat reminded her body of how tired she was. Soon, the gentle clackety-clackety sounds and slight rocking motion of the train put her to sleep.

Elaine rarely remembered her dreams. Sometimes she doubted if she did dream, even though every book she read on the subject of dreams said we all dreamt every night. In fact, we probably have several dreams each night. But the dream she had on the train would stick with her when she awoke.

It began with her walking down a dark corridor. The ceiling was very high, and torches, which were a good thirty feet above the ground—*How did they ever get lit?*—barely allowed her to see her way. On and on she traveled for what seemed like hours, or was it days? Finally, there was a door in sight at the end of the corridor. When she opened the door she was flooded with bright light, blinding her with its brilliance. She quickly covered her eyes until they could adjust.

When she could lower her dream-hand from her eyes, she was shocked to see naked bodies. Men and women were writhing, sweating, copulating. Moans filled the air and made her feel weak Try as she might, Elaine could not turn away from the scene in front of her: it was both enticing and frightening. The bodies moved and touched and caressed and united with a passion she had not felt in many years. Then, as if a director had made a signal, they all stared at her.

"Come on, Elaine," they started to urge, signaling for her to join them. "Come with us. Our bodies yearn to touch you. Our mouths long to taste you..." They waved her over, wanting her to join them.

Elaine felt her knees wobble. She felt herself perspiring and remembered the wonderful releases she had experienced during sex. *No, no, no! This no longer interests me.*

Elaine slid along the wall of the room, feeling her way, her back tracing a path against the hard wall. All the while she looked at the twosomes, threesomes and moresomes ecstatically enjoying themselves. The sex they were having looked sensual, gentle and erotic; animalistic, energetic and dirty. She desperately wanted to join and she desperately wanted to stay away. Elaine was saved from having to make a decision by the feel of a doorknob under her fingers. She opened the door and backed through it.

When she closed the door the sounds of people enjoying themselves were shut out. Relieved, she closed her eyes and leaned her back against the door while she tried to catch her breath. That type of sex, that type of passion was part of her past. It was no longer part of her life.

The door was cool against her back and helped calm her down. She focused her eyes on the area she was in. The new room was also dimly lit. She could make out that the room was a magical temple. *Now this is more like it!* The room's ceiling was pure crystal. A light came from beyond it and was diffused through it, providing the room with its dim light. The walls were solid mahogany, rich and warm and filled with centuries of incense. Pew-like benches lined the walls. Halfway down each side of the room, in front of the benches, were lecterns.

It was the middle of the the room that drew her attention. Two pillars, one black, one white, both of marble, reached to the ceiling. Between them was a massive, black chair; *No, it was a throne.* In front of the throne was an altar. It was about four feet high and a two feet wide on each side. At the top corners of the altar were protrusions that reminded her of horns.

The altar was black. As she walked toward it, and then slowly around it, she could see visions floating in each of its sides. In one side she saw herself, beautiful, popular, younger, having a wonderful time going dancing with friends. She felt the joy and spontaneity of those days. Then she frowned. *The naturalness, the pleasure, the excitement—it's all gone now, gone from my life. What happened to me? How did I lose it?*

She moved to the second side of the altar and looked at it. In its depths she saw herself making love. Elaine stared at this scene for some time, remembering the feeling of a man's mouth on her breast and the sensation of having her womanhood filled. She wondered what had happened to the passion she used to experience. Tears filled her eyes at the loss. Elaine was suddenly filled with a longing for love. *Now I know why I've felt so empty. Without love, nothing I've done has mattered at all.*

She continued around the altar and on the third side saw herself as a queen with servants and followers around her. She reveled in the feeling of power the vision gave her, but suddenly realized the queen was cold, egotistical and very lonely. A shiver of recognition slithered up her spine. *That's not me; it's not! I can't be like that.*

She quickly moved to the side where the throne was and sat in the large chair. *In* the side of the altar facing her she saw visions of the universe. Stars and galaxies, nebulæ and quasars, black holes and novæ. The three dimensional quality of the vision seemed to draw her in so she could become part of the panoply in front of her. She felt it pulling, pulling…

Tentatively, Elaine leaned forward and reached out with her left hand. To her amazement and horror her hand sank *into* the side of the altar. It continued to pull her inside itself. As she was about to fall in, a dark, rich voice tore her away from what was happening and allowed her to free her hand.

"It's beautiful, isn't it?" said the voice.

She quickly got up from the chair and turned to see the source of the intruding words. It was a big man, well over six feet tall, as stocky and as powerful as a bull. He stood a few feet away, dressed in an immaculate suit. He had an eye patch over his left eye. It had a ruby in its center. She could sense the physical and spiritual power glimmering around him.

"I can show you how to find that beauty within you, Elaine," he said.

"How do you know my name?"

"I know many things about you, Elaine. I know you are lonely and long to find a partner, although you hide it from your friends. I know you long to be touched. I know you want to transcend this world of pain."

Elaine started to cry softly. *How could he know my inner secrets so well?*

He stepped closer until she could almost feel his breath. She looked into his face and the piercing look from his eye seemed to go through her. His left arm went around her waist and drew her to him. She limply went along. His right hand grabbed a fist of her hair and pulled her head back. She could do nothing. She basked in his power. She gloried in it. She craved it and devoured it.

The hand on her head softened its grip and he stroked her hair, sending little shivers of pleasure up and down her spine. "I can give you more pleasure than you have ever known. I can lead you to transcendence. I can give you everything you want. *Remember me. Look for me.* I can give you what you need. Volcanos will thunder, mountains will flatten and the universe will tremble at our passion. *Remember me. Look for me.*"

His right hand tightened to a fist around her hair and he pulled her face toward his, lifting her to her toes. The kiss began lightly, tenderly, but soon moved to depth and passion. She threw her arms around him. She had never been with a man that stocky before and the strength of his size thrilled her. Elaine clung to him as their tongues began to explore each other's mouths. His left hand, with maddening slowness, moved up her side to her breast, squeezing and caressing. The action made her squirm, and for the first time in months she could sense her fluids were beginning to moisten her most feminine spot. She pushed her body into his, wanting to become one with him. She moaned and writhed, wanting more, the hand on her breast thrilling her, thrilling her, thrilling...

"What the hell do you think you're doing?" a voice shouted.

Elaine awoke with a start, only to find her sense of smell assaulted by an ungodly reek. She blinked her eyes and realized some transient had his hand on her breast. She shrieked and slapped the bum hard across the face. The man fell back and Elaine was on him, pounding away with her fists. "I'll kill you, you sonofabitch, I'll kill you!" Elaine screamed in a very un-New Age fashion. The man did the best he could to protect himself from her blows, but her storm of punches broke a vessel in his nose and the blood started to run. The porter, whose yell had brought Elaine from her slumber, watched the man get his due, then pulled her off.

The man, with long, bedraggled hair and a scraggly beard, now covered in blood, scrambled up and ran—into the arms of another porter.

"Don't worry, ma'am. We'll take good care of him," said the first porter. "He'll be in jail at the next stop."

Elaine couldn't stop her shaking. She went to the tiny excuse for a women's restroom to tidy up her clothes and put on a fresh coat of make-up. A spot of blood had landed on her Guess? jeans, but it was hard to see it unless you were looking for it. She tried to reapply her make-up, but it was no good. She was shaking too much. She put down the lid on the toilet and sat on it. She closed her eyes and consciously changed her breathing pattern—slower, slower. Soon she felt relaxed. She opened her eyes and was shocked to see to see in the mirror the image of the tall stocky man with the eye patch.

He spoke to her, saying, "*Remember me. Look for me.*" Her breathing sped up as she was reminded of the passion she had felt. That passion, long contained, grew from inside her and finally exploded as she sucked a deep breath of air and felt the blood rush to her breasts and harden her nipples. She shivered and moaned through her orgasm, then looked at the floor panting from the rush of energy. She finally looked up and once again saw the image in the mirror.

"*Remember me. Look for me.*" The image faded.

Elaine waited until her breathing returned to normal, got up and went back to her seat. She didn't fix her make-up.

* * * * *

The train finally arrived at L.A.'s downtown Union Station, and Elaine went through the usual rigmarole to get her rental car, a red Toyota Corolla. From there she drove to the Holiday Inn on Sunset. Rock stars frequented that hotel, although she had never seen any, so she stayed there, hoping she would meet one. Sure, the chance of meeting a star was just an unfulfilled fantasy from twenty years ago, but there was always a chance.

Her room was on the eighth floor. There she unpacked her clothes and took a relaxing bath. When she finished she got dressed, ate a late lunch and went New Age shopping.

Her first stop was in the Valley at Zandria VII. The tinkly New Age music in the background soothed her as she walked along the aisles of books and products. The prices on all of the crystals and gems had dropped. New Agers weren't interested in them too much any more, so she got a bagful. She also found a rare first edition of *UFO… Contact From the Pleiades*. She put the stuff in the trunk of her car and drove west toward PCH, the Pacific Coast Highway. She loved the drive and she loved watching the people and stores along Ventura Boulevard. A new bookstore had opened in what had been a motion picture theater. They claimed to have one million books at discounted prices. She stopped in and went to the New Age section, but all they had were the usual titles and remainders.

She continued down Ventura to Topanga Canyon, then took that turn-filled road to the ocean. There is a traffic light where PCH meets Topanga. As she waited at the light she turned off the air conditioner and rolled down the windows. *Too bad I didn't get a convertible.* On every other trip that had been her standard procedure. Weather in the Valley was hot and smoggy, but it cooled and became clear near the beach. Elaine turned south on PCH and expected to enjoy the fresh, negative ion-filled ocean breeze. But there was no breeze. Even with the car moving, the air hung like a wet rag, making her feel hot and uncomfortable. The smog was so heavy her lungs hurt as if she were inhaling razor blades with each breath. The oppressive humidity reminded her of a brief stay in St. Paul in the summer of 1984. As she drove she realized the stench in the air wasn't smog, or at least wasn't just smog. There was something else, something that made her want to look over her shoulder in fear, as if someone, or some *thing*, was following her. She took a breath and tried to let the emotion pass through her. When the third traffic light stopped her, she began to feel a rivulet of perspiration drip down her back. She rolled up the windows and turned the air conditioner back on, thankful for its blasting cool and ability to filter the air a bit.

PCH winds through a tunnel and ends in Santa Monica, although it restarts further south. Santa Monica was Elaine's goal, however, because here she would find Aleph Books. "Aleph," she had discovered, was the first letter in the Hebrew alphabet and was pronounced "ah-lef," however most of the people who hung around the shop called it "ai-lef." Aleph had high ceilings with fans to circulate the air. The walls were covered with books, and the shelves in the middle were filled with the usual New Age stuff. She looked around and found nothing of real interest. Aleph Books was the store where she purchased her incense. It was the best she ever found. She bought a wide assortment: sandalwood, frangipani, musk, amber, strawberry, myrrh and others. It cost her thirty dollars. The bag of incenses joined the crystals and book from Zandria VII in the trunk of her car.

From there she drove back to West Hollywood and the Bodhi Tree. She spent well over an hour and $137.46 on older books from the used book annex. She trudged them to the trunk of her car and then went into the main building where the new books were located. Here she purchased more books, some silver jewelry, a Tibetan "Singing Bowl" made of crushed quartz crystal and two painted plaster statues, one of the Hindu goddess Kali and one of the Hindu god Ganesha. The plaster for the small statues had been made from mud taken from the sacred Ganges river itself—or so she was told.

From there she returned to the hotel. Tomorrow she would take all this stuff to a mailing store that would pack it, insure it for her, and send it to her home up in "Sack-a-tomatoes," as she liked to call it. She took a quick shower and dried off. It was just after eight when she left her room for the restaurant on the top floor of the hotel.

* * * * *

Ninth Night

The chicken Marsala warmed and filled her, or was it the Cabernet? In any event, Elaine felt calm and relaxed, and decided to go to the lounge in the next room and people watch. She sat at the bar and ordered a White Russian. When it arrived she took a sip through the tiny, green, plastic straw. The thick fluid seemed to expand from her throat as it went slowly down to her belly.

Elaine enjoyed watching people. She saw the poseurs trying their one-upmanship on each other, and the attempted pick-ups, both the successes and the failures. She stirred her drink with her index finger, tinkling the ice cubes, and licked the liquid that clung to her finger when she removed it from the glass. It made her feel wonderfully decadent, and she wondered if it was related to the large man of her dreams. *How did I come up with him, anyway?*

Typically, she felt superior to those around her at the bar, although she wouldn't admit it. Elaine had also tried to bury most of her emotions. The altar in her dream revealed to her that she still had deep feelings—love, lust, loneliness. *I wonder if the barflys feel the loneliness I feel?*

As if that emotion were a magnet, a man sat down next to her. She couldn't believe her eyes. He wore a green polyester leisure suit. He had no tie and his shirt was unbuttoned half-way down to the beginning bulge of a growing waistline. He had five, no *six* gold chains around his neck. *What time warp had he come through? Didn't he know disco was dead?*

"Hey honey," he said, staring at Elaine's large breasts, "lemme buy you a drink." It was still fairly early in the evening but his speech was slurred and his breath stank of alcohol.

"Got one," she answered brusquely, trying not to engage him in any further conversation. She looked away from him and sipped on her drink.

"But honey, I can get you a bigger one, eh? You know what I mean, don't ya honey?"

Elaine put down her drink and glared at the disco drop-out. "First, if you want to talk to me you can look at my face instead of my tits. Second, I am not your 'honey.' Third, I don't want a drink from you. Fourth, get lost."

"Oh, but honey, honey, honey. We can have a good time together."

Wouldn't he quit? She pivoted away from him on her barstool and looked right at the chest of a large man wearing an immaculate black suit with a red rose in the lapel. She gasped.

The man rose and looked at Mr. Goldchains. "She has been looking for me tonight. You, sir, may leave walking or on your back. Which is it to be?"

Goldchains rubbed his tongue in his cheek, thinking and looking at the football-player sized man. He turned and left, muttering "stupid, frigid bitch" under his breath.

Elaine couldn't believe what was happening. She looked up at the face of her savior. He wore an eye patch with a small red ruby in the center. Her mouth gaped open. "Do you remember me, *ma cher* Elaine?" he asked.

Elaine's mind was awhirl. *This is impossible, impossible.* In her heart, Elaine was a skeptic. She wanted to believe in magic, in fairies and elves, in wizards and dragons. She had gotten glimpses of unusual things that she called "spirits" from time to time, but that could have been her imagination. *People don't come to you in your dreams and then appear in your life later on.* She wanted to believe, but on a deep, inward level she feared, no, she knew, that there was no real magic.

"Elaine, do you remember me?" he repeated.

She looked at him, still not believing any of this. "Yes…" she said dazedly.

"Did you look for me?"

He had said in the dream, "Remember me. Look for me." She continued to look at him and felt his eye look into her soul. "It was a dream…" *This is all so confusing.*

"No, Elaine," he said, looking deeply into her eyes, "it was meant to be. That is why I looked for you. We have lived many lifetimes together, Elaine, and now we can move on to another level of being, transcending the reality of the mundane in our passion. Do you remember the stars, Elaine?"

The stars. The stars. Why can't I concentrate? Wait a second. Now I remember. There were stars in the altar. They tried to draw me into another world. "Yes," she said dreamily, almost as if hypnotized, "they…they were in the altar."

"We can go there again, you and I. The universe can be our home. We can do anything. Go anywhere. The passion you have felt in the past is nothing compared to what I can give you. Come if you wish."

He didn't touch her. He paid for their drinks and picked up his overcoat which was neatly sprawled over a barstool. She simply followed.

Waiting in front of the hotel was a long, black limousine. The chauffeur opened the door and Elaine got in, followed by the man in black. The car started off, rumbling gently down Sunset. Quiet music filled the passenger compartment. She could not believe the luxury and wealth of this man. Power was everywhere. It seduced her. She looked at him and said, "I don't even know your name."

"Call me Baron."

* * * * *

The Rat and Julius Caesar survived for three days on the food and water Elaine Renault had left them. They were ignored by the police who searched her apartment. The cats stayed around for two more days, yowling and crying, scratching at the door. They caught and ate some bugs but couldn't understand why their mistress hadn't returned to feed them.

The next day they left. The Rat found a new home a few blocks away. It was with a family where they had a young girl who liked to play with him. They called him "Garfield." He didn't care what they called him as long as they fed him regularly and gave him a warm spot to sleep.

Julius Caesar wasn't as lucky. A woman with four cats found him eating at one of their bowls. She let him eat and was nice to him, but she could not afford to keep him. She took him to the Society for the Prevention of Cruelty to Animals. They kept him in a cage for a week. A couple of times some people came and looked at him. A little girl looked at him and said, "No! I don't wanna old cat. I wanna baby kitty."

At the end of the week a woman took him to a room where a man in white poked him with a needle. Julius jerked with the sharp stab and looked at the people around him. *Why did they poke me? Why couldn't they just feed me and let me run free like my mistress did? Why am I feeling so shaky and sleepy?*

Julius Caesar took two quivering steps. He arched his back and fell over. He looked up at the people and the room, took a breath of cool, air-conditioned air, closed his eyes and was gone.

* * * * *

Tenth Morning

It was 6:50 A.M. when Simon was awakened by the tweep-tweep of the electronic "bell" on his telephone. "Yes?" he asked, rubbing the sleep from his eyes.

"Simon?"

"Yes…"

"This is Paul. Lieutenant Christian. We're dropping all charges."

Simon was relieved but instantly knew what would have caused Paul's change in attitude. He sat up in bed and said, "Tell me about it."

"He struck again last night." Paul paused for a moment. "Look, Simon, I'm really sorry. I needed something for my boss and for the press. You made a great suspect. The evidence indicated it could have been you."

"It was all circumstantial…"

"Okay, Okay." There was another pause and Simon heard some crunching as Paul took some Tums. "Look, Simon. I'm back to square one. We found another body in Hollywood and our tracking shows you were in West L.A. Come in and we'll remove the transmitter. And Simon," Paul paused again, this time very awkwardly, "uh…will you still help us on this case?"

Simon sat there for a moment, flabbergasted. Then he laughed at Paul's audacity. He admired that, but thought, *I'll be damned if I let Paul rule me.* "You cuffed me, did a cavity search I'm still sore from, locked me up, ran me ragged and put me through indignities that go beyond any insult, not to mention my legal fees," Simon raged. "I could easily sue the city for false arrest and you, the one person responsible for it all, you have the *cojones* to ask for help? Are you crazy or just stupid?"

Normally Paul would have fired back at Simon for the insult. He started to, but instead, he paused and took a deep breath. "Simon, will you help us?"

Simon said nothing for a long time. Then he asked, "Have you been up all night with this case?"

After a pause and a slow, audible sigh, Paul said, quietly, "Yeah."

Simon took a deep breath and decided what he would do. "I'm still tired from what you and your storm troopers did to me. I'm going back to sleep now. I'll come in at 7:00 P.M. to have my bracelet removed. If an apology appears on the evening news I'll help. If it doesn't, I'll file the papers for a false arrest suit. I'll see you then." Without waiting for a response Simon hung up the phone.

He lay back down to return to sleep. Now, however, there was a smile on his face: *I'll help Lieutenant Christian and the police, but it will be on my terms, not theirs.*

* * * * *

"There was another killing in the so-called occult serial murders last night. As a result of this new crime the police said they have dropped all charges against their previous suspect, the well-known occult expert Mr. Simon Raven. A police spokesperson said that the arrest of Mr. Raven was a terrible mistake and offered their sincere apologies to him. He said that only a mistake had caused Mr. Raven's arrest. The Hollywood Police Department and numerous other law enforcement agencies have the utmost regard and respect for him. Mr. Raven has helped many law enforcement agencies in the past, and they were actually hoping they could call on him for advice in this case. We have been unable to contact Mr. Raven for his comments."

Simon, who had been leaning back on the sofa sipping some spring water while listening to the T.V., smiled. He turned his attention back to the book in front of him, the *Necronomicon*. He turned the page and was confronted with an exact duplicate of the symbol he had seen in the photos at Paul's office. Simon's mouth dropped open as he read the caption:

"Thee Signe of thee demmonness Barra Edinnazu who was olde before thee rule of thee gods of Sumer."

Barton and this Barra Edinnazu must be related to all of the murders as well as the attacks on me and the Warriors. How are they connected? And how can I prove it to Paul?

* * * * *

Tenth Night

When he arrived at the police station Paul already had a visitor, so Simon had to wait outside Paul's office. While he waited an officer removed his radio transmitter bracelet and Simon rubbed his wrist where it had chafed his skin. The visitor in Paul's office was none other than Bob Jorgenson. Bob was an evangelical minister with a radio program. He made a living specializing in Satanism and Satanic cults. He tried to imply that the police around the country agreed with him, but, save for an occasional individual officer, none did. Law enforcement agencies quickly saw he was not objective in his understanding of crime because he came from a particularly narrow viewpoint. This viewpoint was one which he and those with a similar theology wanted to identify as Christianity per se, even though they made up only a small percentage of Christians across the U.S. and around the world. With him was an entourage of three followers along with Father John Reilly, a priest at St. Peter's Cathedral on Franklin Boulevard in Hollywood.

Bob was playing a tape for Paul. In it, a young boy, perhaps fifteen, was screaming his lungs out. Bob's voice commanded a spirit or demon named, "Hokey" (*God,* thought Paul, *didn't this guy see how he was being made a fool of by some kids?*) to leave the boy's body. There was a long pause as the boy made some sort of vomitous body noises, followed by an even louder scream.

Bob looked at Paul and asked, "After hearing that-uh, how can you deny-uh, the reality of de-mon possession-uh?"

"Look. I'm sorry, but all I heard on that tape was you manipulating some kid over the phone. You sound good at it. But I don't see any proof of demon possession."

Bob was furious. "You didn't hear everything-uh. He talked about events that took place ten years ago. There is no way-uh, the boy could have known that information-uh, unless it came from an e-vil spirit-uh."

"What type of information?"

"It involved an exorcism that I-uh, was involved with back then-uh. The person we exorcised eventually committed suicide-uh."

Paul perked up at this. "Really? Where did this happen?" *If this man had been involved in manipulating some kid who committed suicide… well… there was no statute of limitations in a case like that.*

Bob realized what was happening and responded, "It was in South-uh, Carolina."

"So let me get this straight. You're an expert in Satanism because kids call you on the phone and you manipulate them. You know, it could be these kids are manifesting this behavior because of family or psychological problems. Your 'exorcisms,' after a fashion, are a treatment for these kids. Where did you get your psychotherapeutic training?"

"I-uh, was trained by the word of God-uh."

"So you have no training acceptable to the general psychotherapeutic community."

Bob tried to change the subject back to where he was in charge. He was used to manipulating people and Paul wasn't falling for it. "Lieutenant

Christian-uh. The reason I am here is because I have had several people call into my show-uh, and admit that they are the ones who are committing the murders-uh. The people who are doing the killings are a generational Satanic cult-uh. They are doing this for Satan-uh. They are…"

Paul interrupted him. "Okay," he said, pulling a pad of paper and a pencil from his desk, "now we're getting somewhere. What are their names and addresses?"

"Well-uh, they were on the phone-uh." He was stammering now and not affecting a type of accent. "They-uh didn't give-uh their addresses."

Paul looked at Bob for a long moment, bounced the eraser end of the pencil against the desk several times, then slowly put away the pad and pencil. "Thank you for coming, Mr. Jorgenson. If we can use your help we'll call you."

Bob sputtered in indignation. He had never been dismissed so cavalierly. "I warn you, Lieutenant, I am doing the Lord's work-uh. If you resist me-uh, then you are leading yourself down the path to hell-uh. There are people who are going to kill again for Satan-uh. There are thousands of them in Hollywood alone-uh."

"Right. Fine," said Paul, getting up and opening the door. "I have another appointment right now, and like I said, I'll call if I need you."

Bob rose and his entourage followed. "Look-uh," he said, pointing at Simon. "There is one of the nation's leading Satanists." Simon, incredulous and gape-mouthed, said nothing.

"Good day, Mr. Jorgenson," said Paul curtly. Then, in a more friendly voice, he welcomed his next visitor. "Come in, Simon."

As the group left, Father John held back. Paul, an old friend, shook his head as he looked at the Catholic priest. "I'm sorry," said Father John. "I was told to do this by some of the members of my congregation who are worried about the killings. If there is anything I can do to help, if any of the victim's relatives need some counseling, let me know. You know I'll always be there. I'll be glad to help in any way I can."

As he passed Simon, Father John shook his hand. Simon and Father John had worked together many times. From their knowledge of psychology and the occult, and with a focus of caring and love, they had helped several disturbed youngsters who thought they were possessed or were convinced by others they were possessed. Simon and Father John would find contradictions in the young people's stories which would lead to a child admitting he or she really had little or nothing to do with the occult. Usually the behavior was a response to family problems or difficulties at school or with friends. Simon did not proselytize and Father John was thankful for his help. "I apologize for their rude behavior, my friend," said Father John, "We may not be on the same path, but God works in mysterious ways."

"It's okay, Father. You know you can call on me at any time for any assistance I can offer. God bless you and keep you."

"And you, too, my son. You too."

Simon closed Paul's door behind him as he entered. Paul had retaken his seat. "What was that about?"

"Don't ask," said Paul, shaking his head and laughing. "Don't ask."

"You said there was another murder…"

"Yeah. Her name was Elaine Renault. Ever heard of her?"

Simon tilted his head and glared at Paul. "Are we going to go through this again?"

Paul paused, drummed his fingers on the desk top and decided to get this all out in the open. "Look, I said I'm sorry to you, personally and publicly. You are not a suspect. In fact, of all the people wandering around L.A. you are probably the only person who *isn't* a suspect. We knew where you were at the time of the crime.

"Now I repeat, did you know her?"

Simon looked at a picture of the dead woman. Her face was a sad, ghastly blue. "I've never seen her before," he said, handing the photo back to Paul. "Do you know anything about her?"

"She was from Sacramento. The local police force is investigating up there. We should have information on her tomorrow."

"What were the signs that make you think this was another of the killings?"

"The body drained of fluids. The odd blue color. The smell of incense in her hair and clothes. The same symbol on her thigh, drawn from her own blood. A Tarot card in her vagina, and missing body parts."

"What was missing?"

"Her left arm and both hands."

"Isn't that a change? Wasn't the right hand and arm already taken?"

"Yes."

"Could this be a copycat killing?"

"We don't think so. There are too many similarities, items which have not been released to the media. No one could have duplicated all the signs of this killer or killers. We just don't think it's a copycat."

"Paul, I want the killer as much as you do; probably more. It was my friend, my student who was killed." Simon chose not to say anything about the conversations he had with Mother. *Besides, he wouldn't believe me, anyway.* "When I was at the site of Angelica's body I saw something that wasn't mentioned in any of the previous reports. I don't know what it means yet, but if it's repeated at the other crime scenes it may mean something."

Paul was surprised. *Could I and every investigator on the force have missed something? Everyone at the station had already taken a turn looking through the photos.* He started to hand the ever-growing file to Simon. As Simon took it he asked, "By the way, what was the Tarot card this time?"

"It was the Five of Swords. Do you know what that means?"

Simon took the file but stared at Paul as he thought of the final card in the reading Allenda had given him. *Defeat. But for who?* All he said was, "Yes I do, Paul. Yes I do."

Chapter Thirteen

Tenth Night

Paul watched as Simon examined each photo carefully. Paul had already been over them many times. He had peered at them through a magnifying glass and a jeweler's loupe until his vision got blurry. He had blow-up upon blow-up of them made until he could barely make out an image through the enlarged grain. Once, Paul went to sleep thinking maybe he was in a dream about an Antonioni film and would wake up to find everything normal. *Hell, maybe I* am *in an Antonioni film.*

But as Paul watched, Simon did something no one, including Paul, had done before. He took several of the photos from the same scene and laid them together on the desk. Several times he needed more room and laid them on the floor. The patterns he formed from the pictures looked like a photo mapping survey of Mars, with their rectangles of different proportions and lighting. Simon would frequently stand up and look at this assemblage from above, only to move one photo slightly and stare at them from a distance again.

When Simon finished looking at each set of photos of separate scenes, he started comparing sets. Paul, meanwhile had brought them coffee. He filled his decaf with two spoons of sugar and plenty of milk. Simon continued examining the groups of photos. Paul already felt impotent in this case. Now he also felt uncomfortable just watching, so he went out for a breath of air.

The night air was thick and seemed tinted with an ugly color. *God, this is the worst I've seen the air in L.A.* No stars were visible through the haze and brightness of the city lights. Those lights ruined any real astronomical value Griffith Park Observatory might have had. Now it was just a tourist trap and a place where old movie buffs could go to remember James Dean's knife fight in *Rebel Without a Cause*. The Moon, nearing its fullness, was a luminous orange, a pastel gift of reflected sunlight and the smog-filled night.

The air, which Paul hoped would be fresh outside, was as stale as that in the police station. It wasn't just smog, it was also thick with humidity. "Sultry," it would have been called in the Big Easy. Here it was unusual and uncomfortable. It also seemed to him that the humidity—which had hovered over the city for what, ten days now?—was getting worse each day. It was as if something was coming. It was as if some *thing* was coming.

Paul was not religious. He respected religious people and he believed in God, but he just didn't like the trappings that went with it and the stories you had to believe in any religion. People changing into pillars of salt? Talking to a snake? A boat that carried two of every living creature? Being swallowed by a whale and living? A dying God who comes back to life? A single God who was also three persons? The world resting on the backs of elephants and turtles? Gods who came down from Olympus for sex? Killing entire cultures because God told them to? He just couldn't bring himself to believe it. Perhaps it was his lack. *What was it someone had called me? A deist?* He believed in a supreme deity, he just didn't "have religion."

Paul did believe in people. He believed people are imperfect, and sometimes they do things so horrendous they deserve to be called "evil."

Nero and the Coliseum. Pope Innocent and the Children's Crusade. Hitler and the Holocaust. Stalin and the mass murders of enemies. He did not believe there was evil in Nature, although some acts by animals seemed cruel.

And yet, he could almost say there was evil in the air. It felt bad. It smelled bad, even worse than the usual smog. It made him look over his shoulder to see what was coming after him, only to find nothing, or at least nothing tangible.

Paul aimlessly kicked at the blacktop and punted a small copper disk, which he hadn't seen, a couple of yards. It clacketed across the tarmac, drawing his attention. He went over to it and discovered it was a penny. He bent down to picked it up. *I guess this is my lucky…*

Earthquake!

The ground began to roll under him. It didn't shake like a typical San Andreas fault temblor. Rather, it rolled, forming a series of waves as if someone had taken a huge sheet of earth and lifted it up and down quickly so that waves moved across it. For a second Paul felt as if something, something evil, was traveling *through* the earth. His breath came in spasms and he fell against a car parked in the lot where he had been standing. *Was this the "big one" everyone was expecting?*

And then it was gone. Paul held onto the car, catching his breath. *Something terrible has happened.* He staggered slightly as he tried to get back to the station, but quickly regained his land legs and made his way inside. "Whew, did you feel that one?" an anonymous voice asked. He looked around, amazed to see that to everyone else this had been nothing more than a common shaker. Barely more than three on Mr. Richter's scale.

Maybe I'm being affected by this case a lot more than I think. Paul said nothing and went to his office.

Simon was sitting on the floor in a corner, his bent knees at his chest and his head on his knees. Without moving he asked, "Did you feel it?"

"It was just another quake."

Simon raised his head and looked at him. "Did you feel *it?*"

Paul paused. "Look, it was just a quake. I don't believe in this mumbo-jumbo. I don't..." He paused again, sat in his chair and then uttered one word. "Yes."

Simon slammed his fist into the wall. "Something is happening here, something terrible, and I don't know what it is. We're all involved but I don't know how. I feel so damn helpless."

"Simon, the only thing I care about is solving this case. I'm a detective. It's my job. It's what I do. I'm not worried about bigger meanings. I don't care if these murders are being committed for some weird, occult reason. I just want to find the perpetrator and get him off the street. I just want the killings to stop."

Simon rose. "The killings are only a part of this. You and I are missing the big picture." Simon looked at Paul for a long moment. "I don't know what that big picture is and that's what's frustrating."

He dusted off the seat of his pants, twisted his face into an "oh well," expression, and came up to Paul's desk. "In the meantime, let me show you some big pictures."

He took from the file a photo which had been taken at the scene where Angelica's body was found. In it were the three rocks which were out of place. "Paul, tell me about these rocks."

Paul glared at Simon. *Of course we had seen the moved rocks and inspected them. Did he think that the police were stupid?* Expressionless, he said in a bored, sing-song tone, "The rocks had been recently moved. We inspected them closely for signs of body fluids such as blood and sweat, fabric and fingerprints. They were totally clean."

Simon smiled at the officer's self-righteous attitude. "That's it? Nothing else?"

Paul continued his sing-song, "We've taken scrapings that are going to the lab. We may turn up some DNA patterns..."

Simon laughed. "Yes, I figured you would inspect them closely, but did you inspect them *distantly?*"

"Huh?"

"Watch." Simon laid the picture down on the floor and took the rest of the group of photos and laid them out around it. Although there were large gaps, the scene where the body was found took shape. When he was finished, Simon said excitedly, "Do you see it?"

Paul looked at each photo and looked at Simon with a puzzle in his face. "Don't look at the individual photos," said Simon, "look at the entire scene."

Paul looked again. Top, bottom, sides, corners. He saw the curve of the three rocks and saw how it seemed to match a curve of broken bushes. Several feet away it matched the natural curve of a flower bed. "Wait a second," Paul said in astonishment. "There's a figure here, a shape none of us saw before. What is it?"

"Yes!" shouted Simon, triumphantly. He glared at Paul. "That's what I was trying to tell you about when you had me carted off." Simon showed how objects that were moved or in their native positions formed a large circle around the scene. Attached to the opposite sides on the inside of the large circle were two smaller circles.

Paul was excited. Here was a new clue. "What about the other scenes?"

Simon picked up the photos and then laid down another set. This time he didn't even have to point out the figure to Paul. The detective could see it himself. Murder by murder they looked at the photos. Each one showed the same symbol created out of the natural scenery mixed with moved objects—rocks, plants, old bottles, even a trash can.

"Okay, Simon, Congratulations. You've seen something that none of the rest of us have seen. Now comes the big question: What does it mean?"

Simon gave Paul a rather helpless look and sat down. "I don't know. I wish I did. Let me show you what I do know. Do you have some paper?" Paul sat in his chair and pulled a legal pad of blue-lined, pale yellow paper from a drawer in his desk. He handed it to Simon, who also took a pencil that was lying on the desk. First he drew an ancient oriental version of what might be the symbol:

"This is the famous yin-yang symbol. It is technically known as the central part of the symbol known as a *pa-kua*. It represents perfect balance in nature."

"That could mean the killer or killers is trying to balance out something," said Paul. But that didn't satisfy him because there were no real links between the victims.

"The other version comes from astrology. It looks like this," Simon continued, as he drew another design on the page.

"It represents the sign of Cancer. Cancers are born in late June through mid-July. Cancers are emotional people. On the negative side they can be tenacious, brooding, overly cautious and manipulative."

Paul thought about it. "I don't believe in astrology, but maybe it has something to do with the killer's birthday. Maybe the victims were all Cancers."

"Angelica was a Libra, so that ends that possibility. But if you notice, the signs that the killer or killers left don't really match either the sign for Cancer or the *pa-kua*."

Paul got up and looked at the sets of photos which were still on the ground. "You're right," he said. "Both of the symbols you showed me are different from the symbol left at the crime sites. These photographs appear to show a circle with two smaller circles added as an afterthought, not as part of the original symbol. It's like the letter O with two smaller Os or a zero with two smaller zeros." He moved around the photos and said, "Or perhaps the two smaller circles unite with the larger one. They could be a lower case version of the letter G. Ogg? Ggo? Gog? Wait, isn't that from the Bible?"

"Yes, it's the name of one of the nations led by Satan against the kingdom of God at the battle of Armageddon."

"Well, if the killer is somebody using the occult, could he be saying that he is making the final battle? Is he trying to kill everyone off, one at a time?"

"Even if he was," mused Simon, "that wouldn't get us any further. If somebody is leaving a signature in the form of a symbol it would probably have a more obvious meaning than that. I'd like to think there is more; I just can't see it."

"Okay, maybe they're numbers. 000? Maybe the smaller numbers are linked to the outer circle making them sixes or nines. Could it be 909? That was a Beatle's song. Hmm. Manson liked the Beatles," Paul mused. "Maybe this is a leftover crazy from the Manson family."

Paul sat in his chair and spoke into the intercom. "I want a listing of the current whereabouts of all members and associates of the Manson family who are not in jail. Bring them to me…" Simon stopped him by putting his hand on Paul's and shaking his head. "Hold on a second," Paul said into the intercom.

"It's not the Manson family," said Simon. "They were a bunch of crazies who followed a crazed leader. Their ersatz occultism just gave them a rationale for their crimes. They brutalized their victims, slashing them to pieces and spreading blood all over. These cases are the opposite. They are being committed by someone, or a group, that is well-prepared and has the entire method practiced and thought out. He, she or they are the opposite of the Manson family."

Paul had been excited, but he saw quickly that Simon was correct. He spoke into his intercom, "Never mind on that request, thank you." He went back to the idea of the numbers and talked out loud. "Okay, it's not 909. It could be 099, 990, 906, 609, 660, 066, 606, 690…"

Simon, who had been listening from his chair and going over every mystical and astrological meaning of the symbol he could think of, looked at Paul wide-eyed. "Did you say 606? How could I have missed it? Oh, he thought he was so clever. But we've got him now. This ties it all together.

"Paul, the murderer's name is Oliver. Barton Mordus Oliver."

* * * * *

"I'm sorry if I seem dense, but what does the number 606 have to do with this Oliver, and how do you know that it's him?"

"Many years ago, he and I studied magic at a secret school in Paris, France. While at the school everyone was required to choose for himself or herself a magical name and number. The magical name represents our highest spiritual goals. The number would in some meaningful way, perhaps numerologically, also represent those goals. Barton wanted a number that would emphasize his strength and power. The true secret of magic is that it gives you power over yourself. He thought it meant power over others. He was a bully, caused at least one death at the school and was responsible for causing the school to close down.

"He had a great deal of trouble choosing a name—I never learned what his magical name was. He also had trouble picking a number. Finally, he decided to choose a number not to represent his highest aspirations and goals, but to simply identify himself—his lower, physical self, not his higher, spiritual self—with magic and power.

"His name, Barton Mordus Oliver is composed of three words, each of six letters. This would give him the number 666. But Barton was not interested in pretending to be the Devil by usurping the number given to Satan in the Bible. He wanted more power than Satan. So he took the initial of his last name, O, and from its shape changed it to a zero. This he inserted in the middle of his number to show that he, Oliver, is at the center of everything. The number Barton Mordus Oliver chose to represent himself was 606, the same number that has appeared secretly at all of the sites where the bodies in this case have been found."

Paul drummed the fingers of his right hand on his desk for several moments. "Simon, put yourself in my place. I need evidence to make an arrest, even if it is only circumstantial evidence. I can't arrest someone because you're claiming he chose a number years ago and the number might be present at crime sites. That symbol might mean other things, too. You just gave me two other symbols it looked like and either of those could have a bearing in showing…"

"No," interrupted Simon, "it's Barton. I know it. You see… ah… Barton has attacked me at least two times in the last ten days."

Paul sat up straight, almost jumping out of his chair. "What? Where did he do this? When? What exactly did he do? Why didn't you report this before?"

"How could I report a magical attack? He didn't leave a calling card or physical evidence. I was attacked by spirit entities. When I traced the source of the attack on the astral plane I was attacked again. When he could have killed me, he just let me go, laughing at me. I think now that he may have been responsible for the magical attack on Angelica which sent her to the hospital before she was killed. There was also someone—*something*—else involved. It called itself Barra Edinnazu' I'm not sure of what that means." *I'm not going to talk about goddesses and demonesses to Paul the skeptic.*

"So you claim he's attacked you magically and may have magically attacked Angelica Firestone before her murder. Do you have any physical evidence of this?"

Simon felt his side, still sore from the deep scratches which the astral Eagle had inflicted. He realized there was no proof as to where they came from, so he just shook his head. "No," he replied, quietly.

Paul got up, walked once around the room and sat in his chair. "You claim you've been attacked by this guy but have no proof. You claim his number was at the crime scenes, although it could be something else. That's awfully flimsy evidence, Simon. Even you can see that."

"I'm not the detective, Paul. You are. Here's a lead. Shouldn't you at least check it out?"

Paul thought about it for a moment while he drummed the fingers of his right hand on the desk. *It's such a weak lead. Still, I haven't come up with anything better.* "Where does Oliver live?"

There was a long pause. Simon sighed and admitted, "I don't know. I haven't heard from him since I was last in France, and that was a long time ago."

Paul slumped into his chair and just stared at Simon. "He might not be in the area. He might not be in the state. *He might not even be in the country!* Simon, for all you know he might even be dead."

Simon winced. "Paul, it's him. I know it. He's close by."

Paul reached into his pocket and took out a couple of Tums. He put them in his mouth and crunched them. "Assuming it is him, Simon, what is the link between the murders and the attacks on you?"

Simon leaned back in his chair. "Barton's no fool. We may think him mad for these murders, but I have no doubt he has a reason, and that reason has to do with magic. Back at the school in France I was always able to defeat his schemes. He vowed to destroy me. Since I defeated him many times before, he may want to attack me now so I won't be able to stop his plan, whatever that may be. That plan is the cause of the murders."

"Why wouldn't he wait until he accomplishes his plan to attack you? Why now?"

Simon got up and paced the room. From the back of the room he looked at Paul. "Don't you feel it? Don't you sense it? There's something… *evil*… in the air. L.A. doesn't get this humid. But the humidity is thick in the air, a foul moisture that smells bad and makes me feel worse. Sure, we have smog, but it hasn't been this bad in 30 years. And the quakes we've had recently have been unlike any other quakes I've ever felt. It's as if the very Earth knew something terrible was coming and shook in fear.

"Paul, the murders are just the start. Barton thinks I'm the only one who can stop him. We have to do exactly that."

Paul ran his tongue between his upper teeth and lip. He, too, sensed the weirdness of the humidity and killer smog, the wrongness of the quakes. He knew something was happening. "Okay, Simon. We'll look for Barton Oliver and pick him up for questioning. Is there anything else you can add?"

Simon shook his head slightly. *You know who did it. What else do you need?*

"Okay, then. Thanks for your help."

Simon nodded and started to leave. Paul stopped him. "One more thing, Simon. Cops aren't as dumb—I'm not as dumb—as you may think. I have no doubt you'll be attempting to do things in your own way in this matter. I have no way of stopping you on the astral plane, whatever that is. But do me a favor, will you? Keep in touch? Let me know what's happening?"

"Sure, sure." Simon opened the door of the office.

"What *are* you going to do, Simon?"

"Just two things. Find Barton and stop him."

Simon went to his car. It was almost midnight. He gagged on the foul air, so thick it was with humidity and smog. And now the air was also filled with a horrible stink. The news reports would blame the smell on the red tide, microscopic organisms that prevented oxygen from getting into the ocean waters. This killed fish whose decomposing bodies created the smell. Simon knew, however, there was another cause.

He started the motor on his car and turned the air conditioning on high. It blew his face and hair. He was grateful for the cool wind, dehumidification, and partial filtering of the air. Soon he was refreshed and started back home.

I will *find you Barton. And then I'll stop you. You once vowed to destroy me. But if I have to, I* will *destroy you. This I vow.*

* * * * *

Paul checked on Barton Oliver's D.M.V. records, arrest records, I.R.S. records, Social Security records, F.B.I. records, Interpol records and with the feds for information on his passport. By the time the information arrived his shift was over. It only took five minutes for him to look them over. No one had any information on Barton Mordus Oliver. There was no proof he even existed.

"Great. Now I'm hunting a ghost, too."

* * * * *

Tenth Night, Earlier

Eris looked at herself in the mirror. She usually favored loose, flowing clothes that would reveal what they seemed to hide. Not tonight. Tonight she wore a metallic red minidress with black leggings. The dress was so skin-tight it looked as if it would explode if she moved or even breathed. But it was made of spandex and simply stretched as needed. She wore a choker of American Indian design. It was made of three horizontal rows of long, wooden beads. From the center descended more rows of beads. At the bottom was a large crystal which hung at the top of, and drew attention to, her décolletage. Delicate silver rings made circles through her ear lobes. Her long hair was held up by a series of bobby pins which would allow her hair to come out, little by little, as the night wore on.

For a final fillip she tried an old vaudeville trick. From a pack of gum she took the thin aluminum paper and cut two small triangles. She placed one on each upper eyelid, her make-up holding them in place. *They looked cool that way.* Then she took a flashlight, which she brought with her for the purpose, flicked it on and shined the light on her face from above. One by one she blinked her eyes. It looked as if lightning was flashing from her stare. This would look great in the bright lights of the rave she was going to.

This was her first rave. She had heard about them for some time. Promoters would find an abandoned warehouse, hook it up with power, lights and an amazing sound system. Then they would have a dance which featured "Acid House" music, sort of like disco but with an aggressive, bad, nasty attitude.

A real rave was technically illegal, of course. The promoters didn't pay to use the building or get the proper permits. In order to go you had to get an invitation. A friend had given her a phone number. When she called it she discovered a recording which told her to go to a telephone booth in Encino. She went there and saw a long line of people, mostly kids ten or fifteen years younger than she. There was a boy in a chair handing out flyers. She got one which announced the place where she could get tickets for the rave. They would only be available after 10:00 P.M. on the night of the rave at a location in Long Beach, on the other side of L.A. county. The tickets were thirty-five dollars. *A lot of money for a dance.*

But after getting dressed, that's where she headed in her '68 Corvette. The car, painted metallic silver ("camo gray," she called it), was in perfect condition. It attracted so much attention, especially from the police, that she could never accelerate out of second gear unless the roads were totally empty.

The place to get tickets was on Broadway. The address was of a house, and when she arrived she saw a long line of people in front of it. She waited in the line and attracted appreciative stares from some of the men and boys, to the dismay of their girlfriends. She purchased her ticket and received with it a map of directions to the site of the rave. It was in Desert Hot Springs, a good two hours away.

She had heard about raves and knew this frequently happened. To prepare for it she took a nap during the afternoon. Besides, she hadn't had a nice drive in her 'vette for some time.

Eris took the Long Beach Freeway to the Santa Monica Freeway and headed east. The Alpine CD player she had installed unleashed the album *Lust* by The Lords of Acid. The one hundred-twenty or so beats-per-minute created a pounding in her groin and she wriggled in the worn, leather seat. When the disc was over, she played *Jesus Built My Hot Rod* by Ministry. Then she played The Lords of Acid again. It was in the middle of its third play when she lined up behind the cars waiting to park in a dirt field. Ten minutes later she entered the door.

The lights and music were astounding. Strobes, lasers and moving colored lights filled the room. Projected against one wall was an old water, oil and food coloring light show from the psychedelic concerts of the '60s. On other walls were projections of films, everything from campy Japanese horror films to low-budget pornos. The center of the warehouse had been transformed into a huge dance floor drenched in moving and colored lights. Everywhere you looked there was movement and color. Upstairs were smaller dance floors along with "Smart Bars" where you could get drinks filled with vitamins, amino acids, caffeine, guarana and other natural products made to keep you awake and open the mind. There were people openly selling herbal versions of drugs that provided five cents of herbs for fifteen dollars. In the shadows were people selling the real thing: LSD, Adam, Special K, X and hits of laughing gas. *You can get anything you want, at Alice's restaurant.*

Most incredible was the sound system. Eris had been to many concerts, and nothing short of the sound systems used at huge outdoor music festivals compared to what was here. Enormous cabinets, each one a massive six feet tall, lined an entire wall. These were the sub-woofers which reproduced only the lowest sounds. The constant thump-thump-thump of the bass and drums came rolling from these and shook the entire building and bodies within. Other speakers were on top of these and still more were hung from the rafters.

The rave was not a place to talk of things or even discuss the music. It was about living now, before thinking about having a career, before assuming responsibilities. It was about experiencing life viscerally, with the feelings, emotions and senses before having to face the real world.

Eris looked at the scene for a moment, her heart soaring with the music's swells. *We are one, this rave and me. My very essence is in harmony with this place. This is my true environment.* She let out a "whoop" and danced to the center of the floor.

Thump, thump, thump, thump. You didn't need a partner to dance at the rave. People danced just to dance. It was an explosion of energy, allowing people to express what they were usually told they had to suppress. Males and females danced opposite her for a while, and then moved on. Thump, thump, thump, thump.

Part of her hair had come down, covering her neck. It left her feeling warm, so she went upstairs to the Smart Bar to cool off. She ordered a "think drink" for three dollars and in a few moments the herbs and fruit juices left her feeling recharged. Thump, thump, thump, thump. She went back down to the dance floor.

Had this been a legal dance, the fire department would have closed it down. More and more bodies packed in. With the limited exits in this building, if there was a fire few would survive. Thump, thump, thump, thump. No one cared. If that happened it would be seconds from now, the future. All that counted here was now. This moment. Thump, thump, thump, thump.

Because of all the bodies the temperature in the building rose. Thump, thump, thump, thump. People were crammed in so tightly there was barely room to move. Thump, thump, thump, thump. Her hair had become completely undone, and the smell of sweat, perfume and cologne filled the air. Thump, thump, thump, thump. It all intoxicated her. People rubbed up against one another. Groups surged together rather than dancing individually or in pairs. Thump, thump, thump, thump. She didn't care; no one cared. All that mattered was now. Thump, thump, thump, thump.

After an hour or so of dancing on the main floor she was covered with a light sheen of sweat and again felt thirsty. She worked her way toward the stairs leading to one of the Smart Bars. This time it was far more crowded and she tripped over something. She fell into a group of people in front of her who then helped her regain her footing. Eris looked behind her to see what she stumbled over and saw two young people having sex on the floor. A circle formed around them to give them space. The couple moved and the circle clapped to the beat. Thump, thump, thump, thump.

She wanted to look away, but she couldn't. This was immediate. This was now. This was magnetic. Thump, thump, thump, thump. Watching the entwined lovers aroused her. Her body swayed to the music, having the effect of rubbing against someone behind her. It didn't matter who, she just needed to touch. *Touch. Touch. Touch. Touch. Now. Now. Now. Now.* Thump, thump, thump, thump.

As she watched and moved she felt a hand on her hip. It slowly moved up to her breast. She didn't care. She didn't mind. She didn't resist. It felt good. Thump, thump, thump, thump. The hand peeled down the top of her dress, revealing her breasts. There was an audible sucking in of breaths around her. She knew she was hot. She knew she looked good. She liked the attention. Thump, thump, thump, thump.

Eris broke away from the hands gently squeezing her naked breasts and began dancing around the couple on the floor. Thump, thump, thump, thump. It was as if she was joining in with their sexuality without touching them. She spun around, rubbing up against the edge of the circle. Thump, thump, thump, thump. Hands felt her and lips caressed her. But there was no romance, no jealousy, no need for it. There was just now and pleasure and erotic bliss. Thump, thump, thump, thump.

Soon the couple on the floor stopped their gyrations. They lay there, oblivious to the crowd. Eris pulled her top back up and made her way to the Smart Bar. She asked for an "energy shake" and a glass of ice water. She took the cold water, and with a little scream threw it in her own face, cooling her and wetting her some more. Then she took a long swallow from her shake. Thump, thump, thump, thump.

She turned away from the bar and noticed a semicircle near the wall. She moved closer and saw another couple having sex. The woman's back was against the wall with her legs crossed tightly behind her partner's back. His pants were on the floor and he pounded into her with each beat of the music. Thump, thump, thump, thump. Eris watched and licked her lips. Then she took another drink from the styrofoam cup she held. The woman's face—*Woman? She looked barely sixteen*—was thrown back in pleasure, her mouth open, gasping for breath. The boy continued his passionate thrusting, driving her against the wall again and again and again. Thump, thump, thump, thump.

The crowd anticipated the fulfillment and inched closer. Eris thought she could hear the young woman's cries of passion above the din. The bodies of the voyeurs pressed closer, as if by being near they could join in the climax. Eris joined with the crowd and could feel the heartbeats of the people around her. Thump, thump, thump, thump. The crowd started to sway and people held out arms to steady one another. Soon there were hands on her again, feeling, touching, caressing, moving. Thump, thump, thump, thump.

The young woman opened her eyes wide, but saw nothing. Her mouth widened to scream, but there was no sound. She crushed her partner's head to her breasts and jerked violently as he patiently continued. Thump,

thump, thump, thump. Finally, her motions became so exaggerated her partner lost his balance and they fell to the floor. Still they continued. Thump, thump, thump, thump. The woman pushed him away and fell into a fetal position, spasming occasionally. Eris could just see her lips mouth the words, "Don't touch me," over and over as a result of post-orgasmic hypersensitivity. Thump, thump, thump, thump.

The young man rested on the floor for a minute and then got up. His glazed and trance-like expression indicated to Eris he was heavily drugged. A gasp came from several of the women who had watched the scene. With his pants still at his ankles he presented large evidence he had not yet had his release. Thump, thump, thump, thump. He looked through the watchers as if asking for help. Another woman shrugged free from the hands caressing her and fell to her knees, taking him into her mouth. Now it was his turn to throw back his head in ecstacy. Thump, thump, thump, thump.

Eris enjoyed watching, but after a time it became boring. She preferred participating in physical activity. Sex, sports, exercise, dance, anything physical was what she liked. As exciting as the man and woman were to see, she had to move. She backed out of the crowd, preparing to go back to the main floor and dance.

She still watched as she backed up, though, until she ran into a solid pillar. At least she thought it was a pillar until it started to move. This unexpected movement made her jump. She quickly turned to face the "pillar." It was a huge man, tall and stocky. He wore a patch over his left eye with a small ruby in the center. For a long moment they looked at each other. Thump, thump, thump, thump. He moved his face nearer to hers and looked at her deeply. Thump, thump, thump, thump. He put his left arm around her waist and drew her to him. Thump, thump, thump, thump.

She gasped. She could feel he was erect and he was huge. He seemed to pulse with the beat of the music. Thump, thump, thump, thump. He picked up her legs and she held on to his hips with them as he placed her on one of the stools at the Smart Bar. He grabbed her hair with his hand and kissed her hard. Under the intoxication of the rave she did the only thing she could do. Respond. Thump, thump, thump, thump. She felt his hand go under her skirt to clear a path through the material. Thump, thump, thump, thump. *Wait! I wasn't expecting this. I don't want this.* Thump, thump, thump, thump.

He waved his hand in front of her. Red energy sparked at the tips of his fingers then shot out and covered her head and mind with a web of energy. This web carried a message, a message of power. She looked at his face. Entranced, now she could only see a man with power. That was what she wanted and needed. Here. Thump, thump, thump, thump. Now. Thump, thump, thump, thump. Her eyes got big and she gasped as he entered her. At first he moved slowly, allowing her to expand and fully lubricate so she could take all of him. And then he pounded. Thump, thump, thump, thump. Thump, thump, thump, thump.

Time seemed to stop. No one else was there. All she had was her own body and sensations, the need to be filled, the need to build the tension, the need to explode in ecstasy. There were words but they were meaningless hums and clicks. All that mattered was her feelings, her emotions, her now. Her passion built with each pulse of the music and thrust of the man within her. Thump, thump, thump, thump. The last thing she remembered was feeling a bolt of lightning explode from her body as she screamed at the top of her lungs. Then everything went black.

Eris had no idea how much time had passed when she came back to her senses. He was gone. The remainder of his passion was already drying over her torn leggings. *Well, enough of this for one night!* She worked her way down to the main floor and toward the door. Thump, thump, thump, thump. Outside, the desert air had become surprisingly muggy. *Must have expanded out here from L.A.* She got into her Corvette and started the long drive home. It was nearing 4:00 A.M., and it would be light before she arrived. She put a CD into the player, a Mozart string quartet. Later,

Debussy.

For the entire trip home, however, all she could think about was the man with the eye patch. *What was it he said? Oh, yeah. Now I remember. He said, "Remember me. Find me."*

She had no intention of trying to find someone she had had casual sex with at a dance. Especially one with such lines. "You have the face of a goddess," he had told her. *Ridiculous!*

Still...she mused, remembering the feelings of him filling her again and again and again...

* * * * *

When the Baron returned home he turned on all the lights, waking the fifteen or so sleepers who, after coupling during the night, had fallen asleep in the orgy room. "Awake! Awake, members of my Barony!" he called, rousing the tired revelers, followers and sycophants. "I have found her! Soon we will have everything for *Her* return. Bathed in blood, resurrected through magic, She will purify this sick world and make it well once again. And with Her power we shall rule fairly and with justice in Her name. Hail Barra Edinnazu!"

The group, excited by their leader's emotion, caught his energy. Soon they were dancing about shouting the name, "Barra Edinnazu! Barra Edinnazu!" It was as if merely saying it would give it power.

The Baron grabbed two women who had ignored the dance and were pleasuring each other. He forcefully violated one, then the other. When he was through he snarled at them. "Either participate or leave. There is no in between. Rule with us on Earth or serve with everyone else." Then he went to bed and to sleep.

When the Baron came out of his bedroom one of the women had left. The other, Tina Drabeck, somehow instantly had been transformed from a hanger-on to his most devoted follower. Trying to please him, she walked around all day repeating "Barra Edinnazu."

Tina walked for hours. Finally, she fell over, exhausted. But she kept repeating the words, "Barra Edinnazu. Barra Edinnazu." She wasn't even sure what it meant.

The Baron stared out into the distance from his throne. People looked at him and wondered where he was looking. The Baron was looking at what he knew was going to happen. He visualized everything. He knew that soon, Barra Edinnazu would be here. Soon.

Very soon.

Chapter Fourteen

Eleventh Day

Simon poured a snifter of Courvoisier cognac and settled back into his comfortable chair. He had been sitting in the chair all day, but now he relaxed into it. Each sip of the thick, sweet liquor sent waves of warmth from his mouth through his stomach. Then it expanded out to his sides and throughout his body.

In front of him was a table now piled with books and scraps of paper, all filled with scribbled phone numbers, names and information. He had spent the entire day trying to find the location of Barton.

Simon had called all over the world looking for him—from *L'Ecolle du Magie* in France to Atlantis and Skoob in London; From Pan Pipes in Hollywood to A.C.E. in Ohio; from Isis in Denver, to Circle in Wisconsin; from DragonSpace in Canada to Bell, Book and Candle in Las Vegas and the Bodhi Tree in L.A.—nobody knew where Barton was. He called even more remote contacts in Norway, Kamchatka, Ponape, Kawai, Germany, Mexico, Brazil, Egypt, Syria, Israel, Tierra del Fuego, Zimbabwe, Sri Lanka and South Africa. According to everyone who had ever heard of Barton he was either missing or dead.

As Simon relaxed he marveled at how tired he felt. He had done nothing physical. All he had done was make dozens of phone calls and talk to old friends. He took another sip of the cognac and allowed his head to loll back.

Thoomb! Thoomb!

Interrupted in his rest by the door knocker (*I'm going to have to install a bell, a gentle, peaceful bell*), he lifted his head and exhaled, his short rest now ended. Simon rose and walked to the door. He opened it without looking at who might be there. Allenda walked in.

"I've decided, Simon." Her eyes were keen and her jaw set. "I want to help get justice for Angelica's death. How do we catch the murderer?"

Simon went back to his chair and slumped into it. He took a long breath and let it out slowly. "First we have to find him. I've spent the whole day looking for him, Alli." He waved toward the assortment of papers on the table in front of him, an indication of his day's work. "I've called everyone I know and lots of people I don't know. I'm sure that the killer is either Barton Oliver or someone who is connected with him. He's responsible for the death of Angelica. He's also deeply involved with the serial killings the media is calling the occult murders.

"I can't find him," he said as he sat up and slammed his fist onto the table in frustration. "Worse, I know he's planning something far more terrible, something evil, something…Damn! I don't know what it is. And even if we were to stop him the results of the magic he has done might continue. I don't know stop him. I don't even know where to begin."

"Simon, I've spent the last four days agonizing over this. It would be real easy just to turn away. It would be real easy to let this be someone else's problem. But I can't do it. I'm not the Alli who had to depend on others anymore. Finding this Barton guy is something I have to do. Isn't there something we could try to find him? Couldn't we perform the Rite of the Sparrowhawk again?"

"Barton is too smart for that. He knows it was me when I went out as Adoniel, and even an amateur would set up blocks to stop me from trying again. I can't find him on the physical plane and I can't search for him on the astral. Frankly, I'm stuck." He leaned back in the chair and let his eyes close.

Allenda had thought a great deal about recent events. *Simon and I've been attacked. Angelica was attacked and later murdered. Simon was attacked on the astral. Women are being killed.*

Now Simon admitted he could not search for the murderer by going out on the astral plane again. *I can't do anything by myself.* Allenda started to pace the room nervously. *I've always pictured myself as just an aide, an assistant, and not the person who took the leading role. But if we wait until tomorrow another murder might take place. I can simply leave. I can simply turn away and forget the attacks on me and my friends. I can forget the murders. I can forget Angelica. I can…*

Like hell I can!

She stopped pacing and stood in front of Simon, squared her shoulders, took a deep breath and quietly said, "I could look."

Simon sat up straight and opened his eyes in surprise. "Excuse me?" he asked.

"I said, I could look. Barton wouldn't have wards against me on the astral."

Simon looked at her. *Was this the insecure woman of just a few weeks ago?* Since he had founded the Warriors of the Light, Allenda had become one of his leading students when it came to matters of theory. But her practical work was still lacking. The bottom line was he had spent over twenty-five years at this and she was still just a beginner.

"Thanks for the offer," he said as he again leaned back into the chair, "but it would be too dangerous. Anybody who went out after Barton on the astral plane with as much energy behind him or her as we used last time would easily be detected."

"Isn't there something else we could do?"

Her persistence impressed him. "I don't know. I'm very tired and my thinking isn't up to par."

"Simon, someone else might die if we don't act. Can't you think of anything? Isn't there some disguise I could use? Couldn't we use less energy?"

Simon tilted his had at a slight angle, his eyes looking out at nothing. Then came the realization. "Of course! We could…" He looked at Allenda. "No, it would be to dangerous."

She moved a straight-backed chair next to him and sat on it. She looked him in the eyes. "Look at me Simon, look at me. I've changed. I'm willing to take the risk."

"You don't know what this would involve. If you knew you'd be scared to death."

"I'm ready, Simon. I'm not scared."

"If you're not scared, you're not ready. Real self-confidence does not come from lack of fear but from facing fear and not letting it control you. Real bravery is not risking your life, but doing what you have to do, whether it's dangerous or not. You're not ready yet."

Allenda paused and thought about what he had said. "You may be right, Simon. All I can say is, do we have any choice? You and I were attacked. Angelica was killed. More deaths may come and all for some unknown reason. Everything in me is telling me not to do this, Simon. But I have to do it. Please let me help. I have to help. How do we start?"

Simon finished the cognac. He stared at the glass as he felt the last of the dark fluid run down his throat. "There is a way which might work. Rather than using energy and power we can use just a tiny amount of energy and stealth. Barton would be tuned into the pattern of my aura, so it wouldn't work with me. That's why I didn't bring it up before.

You, on the other hand, might be able to succeed. But it will be very dangerous. You would be on the astral with no security, little energy and you could not use any powerful magic. *Anything* on the astral could cause you problems. Barton would be only one of many threats."

"I've been on the astral plane before, Simon. I know there can be dangers. But it can't be as dangerous as you say," she said, filled with false bravado.

"But it is. Minor entities, both intelligent and otherwise, elementals, spirits, thought forms, just about anything out there will be stronger and more capable than you. Anybody who knows how to control the astral plane through visualization or even by accident could destroy you. I won't be able to offer you much help. You would be almost totally on your own."

Allenda thought about it and pursed her lips. Her breath came in short stabs. *Everything in me tells me to run. I don't need to do this. But damn it! I just don't have any choice.* She rose and walked a few steps away. With her back toward him she said, "It's unfair, Simon. I know I am free to do anything, but my path seems to stretch in a single line in front of me. I have total free choice, yet I have no choice but to do what's right." She turned and looked at him intently. "I have to do this."

Simon looked at her in surprise. "Having to make hard choices forces a person to change. You've developed spiritually faster than I've realized. It usually takes far longer for people studying magic to see that as much as we have the free will to choose our path, it chooses us. Every magician reaches a point, sometimes several points, where he or she realizes that they can do anything and may want to go in another direction. A few, like you, discover they must do what is right. They go on to become powerful, mature magicians."

Normally Allenda would have been filled with pride from a compliment given by Simon. This time, however, she felt shaky. *I feel like I'm being forced into something I don't want.* Then she realized exactly what it was. In the past she had always been taken care of by others—her father, various boyfriends and even Simon. Now, for the first time in her life she truly felt responsible—responsible to Simon, to Angelica, to the other Warriors, to other women who might be killed, but mostly to herself. It was scary, but it had to be done. *Is this really bravery? I don't feel very brave. I don't even want to do it.* She licked her lips which were suddenly dry. "I… I still want to do it," she told Simon.

No you don't, but the killings have to stop. He rubbed his chin and realized he hadn't shaved. He rubbed his closed eyes with his thumb and middle finger, an unconscious action he often made when he was deep in thought. Finally he took away his hand, raised his head and looked her in the eyes. "Look, I have to make another call in about an hour," he said. "I'll also need some rest if this is going to work. If you really want to do this, come back at nine tonight."

* * * * *

Simon called Paul's office at 7:09 P.M. "I'm sorry, Paul. I've checked with all my contacts on every continent. Nobody knows where Barton is. Those people who knew him said he either vanished or is dead. I can't find him, but I know he's here, Paul. I just know it."

Paul figured Simon would get no information. "I couldn't get anything either. I called all the recent contacts I made in the local occult world—White, the Fullons, Alexander Gardner, Sylvia Scorsi and several others. They knew nothing. The police department occult expert knew nothing. Our intelligence department has no records of him. The D.M.V. shows he doesn't have a driver's license and doesn't own a car. The F.B.I. has no record of him, nor does the I.R.S., the C.I.A. or Interpol. Are you sure he's the one?"

"He's the one, Paul."

"Hmmph. Well, I have one other person to check with out in Venice. Uh, Simon, are you going to do any, uh,'stuff to try and find him?"

Simon gave no answer. The silence quickly became uncomfortable. "Uh huh," said Paul trying to break the quiet. "Well, if you turn up anything, let me know? In fact, call me tomorrow whether you come up with anything or not. Okay?"

"As soon as I find out something I'll let you know,' Simon said, his tired voice not masking his disappointment at his own lack of success.

Paul immediately checked out a car. "Not that damn Ford, again!" Paul shouted. "When are you clowns going to replace that pitted front window?" Getting no response, Paul merely sighed, got into the car resignedly, started the vehicle and drove out of the parking lot. He drove to the Santa Monica Freeway and entered it, going west to Lincoln Boulevard. He traveled south on Lincoln to Venice Boulevard and headed west toward the beach.

Paul always loved Venice, and at one time had considered living there. But the crime became bad in parts and other places became too trendy and expensive. Sometimes the sections of poverty and trendiness were separated by mere feet.

He thought about how Venice, California, had been modeled after Venice, Italy. The canals and bridges had been designed by a man named Abbot Kinney early in the 1900s as sort of a tourist trap, part of an entire amusement area. Kinney even imported gondolas and gondoliers from Italy. The nickname of the sports teams at Venice High School was the Gondoliers. Curiously, Venic High was actually east of Lincoln, putting it technically in West Los Angeles rather than in Venice. Evetually, a law was passed to officially make the school a part of Venice.

Every once in a while Paul would read how the L.A. County Board of Supervisors would vote to dredge the canals and clean up the area, but there would never be enough money and the efforts were half-hearted at best. Finally, though, they were rebuilt to look as good as the originals, maybe better. Now the waters and wildlife had returned and new sidewalks urged walks around the canals. Small, decrepit, old houses were torn down and replaced with beautiful, sometimes amazingly avant-garde new ones.

I wonder how long it will last? He had seen the uninspired efforts to clean it up before. They all failed. Paul wondered why they couldn't just do a good job on it. *Well, that was L.A. for you. If it doesn't bring in sales tax money like the malls north of Venice in Santa Monica, or have high property tax rates like the condos south of Venice in Marina del Rey, nobody cares. Even though Venice was near the beach, as a city it had neither malls nor high tax returns for the government to spend. Nobody really cared.*

Paul turned up Pacific Avenue and drove to the house at number 117, the address he had been given by the Baron's secretary over the phone. The house was next to an old but small Catholic church which had been abandoned and boarded up. He parked on the street and walked to the large mansion. As he walked past the church he noticed that even the name on it, St. Lucy's, was hard to see. He wondered if there were rats in the church as they can surge in population in abandoned buildings. If so, did the Baron had problems with them?

Paul was greeted at the door by a beautiful, very slender young woman with long, dark hair, a straight nose and brown eyes. Her face was free of any make-up. She didn't need any. She was wearing a robe that covered her from head to toe. The material, however, clung to her figure, adding a mysterious aura of sensuality to her. The perfume she wore was erotic, musky, intoxicating; so much so he barely noticed the house as she led him into a large room. *She moves so gracefully. I wonder if she's a dancer or an athlete?*

She introduced herself as Beth. The room which she led him into usually functioned as the magic den and orgy room. Today it had been arranged so it was simply a large room to greet guests. In the center was the Baron's large chair. Facing it was another, smaller chair. A glass-topped table rested between them. Beth asked him to sit in the chair and pointed to the smaller one, telling him the Baron would be there in a few moments. She offered coffee or tea. At first he was tongue-tied from the sub-surface eroticism she exuded, but as he sat he requested decaf with two spoons of sugar and lots of milk. She smiled at him briefly and left.

Paul looked around the room, but there was nothing to see—no occult paraphernalia was showing. *Maybe this guy was just like Donna and he wouldn't be able to help. Hell, nobody else seemed to be able to help, so why should this guy?*

The Baron knew how to manipulate people. Keeping somebody waiting was one way to show your power over that person. He was doing nothing, but he waited for ten minutes after Paul was seated so when he entered he would already be in a position of power. *My magical opus will soon be finished and this foul world will be saved from itself. Nothing, NOTHING, must prevent it from reaching its conclusion.* He closed his eyes and saw a world that was unpolluted and free of crime. He saw children laughing and playing in a park. He saw an elderly couple walking down the street at night, hand in hand, not fearing for their safety or property. All this would come when he was finished with his magical work.

Suddenly, as if by itself, the view changed. He saw himself on a throne, wearing a crown with others bowing to him and making obeisance, giving him money and various gifts. *No! No! I want to help the world. I want to make this place a true Garden of Eden. Yes, I will rule for Barra Edinnazu. Yes I will have power, but I don't want anything for myself. It's not true. It's not true!* He blinked his eyes and came back to his normal consciousness. He felt his pulse racing and a wave of dizziness quickly swept through him. Sweat had broken out on his forehead. He quickly calmed himself. Then he looked around to see if anyone had seen him panic, but nobody was in the room. He took a handkerchief from his jacket pocket and wiped his brow, then he folded the cloth neatly and placed it back into his pocket. *Time to make my entrance.*

Paul was surprised at the Baron's appearance when the man finally entered. He was used to occultists who were thin, wimpy types or rather fat. The Baron, tall and burly, came from a side door. He wore an elegant, pin-stripped, blue suit and was followed by two women dressed in black robes. "Good evening, Lieutenant Christian. Please call me Baron." He sat in the throne/chair and the two woman stood behind and to either side of him. "I'm sorry I'm late, but I just got back from some errands. I'm throwing a party tonight for my students. I'm sure you already know we call our group the "Barony." So let's get down to business. You said on the phone you had some questions for me regarding these terrible murders that have been taking place way off in Hollywood. How can I help you?"

But before he could answer a silver service was brought in with decaf for Paul and herb tea for the Baron. "Ah, good," said the Baron. "Let's have something to drink first, shall we?" Beth poured some coffee for Paul. He thanked her, took a long swallow, and put the cup and saucer back on the glass table. She took a long time fussing with the Baron's tea and Paul took some more drinks of his coffee. The Baron finally took a sip of tea. He smiled at beth who took the tray and left the room. "Now, Lieutenant, how can I help you with these crimes out in Hollywood?"

Paul looked at the ruby in the patch over the Baron's left eye. For a second he felt confused. *Why am I here?* Then he remembered. "We know you're involved in the occult. Do you have any idea why these murders are being committed?"

The Baron blinked as if puzzled by Paul's question. "I'm sorry, but I really haven't been following the news very closely. The occult is probably not really involved and somebody is merely using it as a ruse to mislead you. However, if the occult truly is involved in this case, I imagine that, as usual, it's just some sociopath using the occult to cover up his crazed, homicidal activities. I hope you catch him soon. This person gives all occultists a bad name."

Yes, that makes...sense. It seemed to Paul his entire thinking process was slowing down. He looked again at the eye and patch of the Baron and stopped drinking his coffee in mid sip. He felt lost, as if falling down, down, down, into Alice's rabbit hole.

"Uhhhh..." Paul struggled to think of what to ask. *Oh yes, now I remember.* "Have you ever seen either of these symbols before?" He pulled a piece of paper out of his pocket, unfolded it, and handed it to the Baron.

"Hmmm. Yes, I think this one is from the *Grimoire of Armadel*, isn't it?" He pointed to the symbol that had been found on the thighs of the murder victims. "I have never seen the other one, although it looks like the oriental *pa-kua* or the astrological sign of Cancer," he said, handing the paper back to Paul.

Paul took the paper, and as he watched it while he refolded it, his mind began to clear. "The first symbol, I am told, looks like it comes from the *Grimoire…*" He looked up at the Baron's face and once again his mind clouded. He struggled to regain his train of thought. "…But…uh… we think it may actually come from another book, the *Nec…* [*What was it?*] *Nec…ro* [*Damn it, why can't I think straight?*] *Necro…nim…*"

"Do you mean the *Necronomicon?*"

"Yeah, that's the name of the book."

"Sorry. That book is a forgery. It was invented during a drunken stupor in the back of an occult shop in New York City."

"I was told that there was a real one."

"Well," replied the Baron, his expression unchanging, "if there is a real version of it, one that H.P. Lovecraft borrowed to start a whole series of fictional stories, then it is exceedingly rare. I've never seen one and my library has over ten thousand books and manuscripts on the occult."

Paul looked at the Baron and felt puzzled. "There was something else…something I was going to…going to…uh…ask you," his voice faded to a murmur as he finished his coffee.

"Lieutenant? Lieutenant Christian? Are you okay? You haven't said anything for the last ten minutes."

"Excuse me?" Paul blinked himself back to awareness. "I… I'm sorry. I had some more questions but I can't think of them. I'm not thinking well at the moment. I'd better be going."

"Well," said the Baron as he unfurled his body and stood up, "come again or give me a call if I can be of help. Lady Beth will show you the way out."

The woman who had been his escort had silently returned. Paul got up and turned to follow her. As he did his mind cleared a bit. "Oh yes, I remember, now. Baron, have you ever heard of a man name Oliver? Barton Mordus Oliver?"

The Baron, who was also leaving the room, stopped in his tracks. He slowly turned and looked at Paul. "Yes, I've heard of him. In fact I knew him many years ago in France. He was an adequate magician at best."

"Do you, uh, do you know where he is?" Paul hoped for a lead.

"I'm sorry to disappoint you, Lieutenant. He died just before I moved here."

Paul's face fell and his shoulders slumped. Another lead was gone. "Are you positive?" he asked.

"I'm afraid so. I was at the funeral and saw the body."

No further words were exchanged. Paul followed his guide to the front door and left the house. It seemed the further he got from the Baron the clearer his mind became. He stood by his car for a moment. The thickness of the air made him think that the humidity had actually increased. Again. He could feel sweat start to break out all over his body. *The hell with the rules, I'm using the air conditioning!* He unlocked the car and started the engine. He slid the knobs and turned on the air conditioning full blast. The engine stalled. "Damn!" he cursed aloud, and restarted the engine. The air came out of the vents warm, cool and then cold. Paul leaned back and closed his eyes, letting the refreshing breeze cool him off and sharpen his mind.

He heard an odd noise and opened his eyes just as a cloud of whitish vapor came from the AC vents. This was followed by warm air. The air conditioner's compressor, due to lack of use, had failed. He cursed again, rolled down the window and drove off.

The Baron looked silently through miniblinds which he had parted with his fingers. He watched Paul drive away. When he turned around, his face was lost in thought. *That detective was close. Too close! It's been many years since I used my birth name. How could this cop have discovered it?*

The Baron moved away from the window and rubbed his chin. *He must be in touch with Raven. Raven would remember me. Nobody else would. But I beat Raven on the astral plane, beat him and laughed at him. Raven couldn't know where I live and couldn't know what I'm doing. He's too smart to come after me again on the astral, but I was a fool to gloat and let him go free. I should have killed him on the astral when I had the chance.*

The Baron walked to his throne/chair and sat in it. "Bring Tina," he ordered one of the two women who stood behind his throne. She left silently. When she returned with Tina she saw the Baron's pants were neatly folded and laid to one side. He was kissing the other follower whose robe was lying discarded on the floor. One of his hands was squeezing the woman's breast with cruel force while the other had fingers in her vagina and anus. She squirmed in passion and pain.

The two women who entered quietly removed their robes and knelt at his feet. They took turns licking, caressing and sucking his maleness. At first their actions were light, slow and gentle. Their activities quickly changed to firm, fast and rough.

The woman the Baron had been kissing shuddered to a climax and went limp from the pleasure and the pain. She fell, whimpering, next to the throne. The Baron grabbed the hair of the women who were still working on him and forced them to work harder, faster.

He thought about the lesson he had learned long ago. *A single, focused thought, held through orgasm, comes to pass. Hah! Most people couldn't hold a single, focused thought, let alone hold it through an orgasm.* Through his specialized magical training, however, he had developed the ability to do so. As the women worked on him he centered his thoughts and emotions for this sex magic on one idea: *nothing can stop my grand, magical ritual. Nothing. Nothing. Nothing. Nothing.*

When he was finished he pushed the two women aside and headed for the shower. "I think the grey silk suit with the light-pink pastel shirt would be right for tonight. Prepare this room for the party."

The three women scattered to take their own showers and ease their bruises. Two men, also dressed in plain, black robes, came in. They picked up the clothes which would be sent to be washed or to the cleaner, depending upon the material they were made of. The men mopped the floor and rearranged the room for the party that would be held tonight. They smiled in their work, knowing something special would happen after the party. Another man laid out the Baron's desired clothes on his custom-built, bigger-than-king-size bed. *Ritual tonight!* He smiled as he lined up the clothes in the exact manner the Baron liked to see them. *Ritual tonight!*

He could almost taste the blood.

* * * * *

Eleventh Night

Simon took a brief nap. He arose at 7:56 p.m. and took a quick shower to freshen up and then dressed. From there he went to his main library and directly to the third volume of the massive, twenty-three-volume *History of Magic* by Yitzhack Himelhoch. *If any source could tell me about this Barra Edinnazu, it would be Himelhoch.*

He turned the pages, scanning for the name. Finally, after going from location to location, cross-reference to cross-reference, he found what he was looking for. Simon read the complete, two-page entry which began on page 319 of volume 17. When he finished reading the entry he just kept staring at the words on the page. He closed the book and held it for a few moments. Then he slowly put it away. *Even Barton couldn't be crazy enough to try this.*

It was 9:00 P.M. sharp when Allenda knocked on Simon's door. They went into the kitchen and he presented her with some herbal tea, a blend which she had not tasted before. "It will help relax you for what is to come," he explained as she drank.

"Rather than simply send you out on the astral with no safety, I think there is another way we can do this. Instead of astral projection, where your consciousness travels to the astral plane, we can use mental projection which sends just your senses, in a contrived body, out onto the astral. With mental projection you bilocate. Your consciousness can be both here and on the astral plane. I will be able to communicate with you and give you a small amount of help."

"I've never done that before, Simon."

"I know. Like I said, the tea you're drinking will help you to relax. I'll hypnotize you so that I can guide you. I'll always be there for you."

She looked at Simon and wondered if there was any romantic meaning to his comment. But she knew there wasn't and realized his statement had no hidden meaning by the emotions showing on his face. She was his student and friend, nothing more. "What's first?" she asked.

"We'll go to the magic room, banish the area and put you into a trance. Then you'll create a totally unobtrusive astral form and transfer your senses to it. I thought the appearance a common bee would work well. Then I'll guide you on your trip."

They went up to the magic room and purified the area with several rituals, including the Lesser and Supreme Pentagram banishings and the Hexagram banishings. For calmness they performed the Rose Cross ritual. When they were ready, Allenda sat in a deep, comfortable chair. Simon sat in a smaller chair facing hers so he could look at her. He held her right hand while he began a progressive relaxation hypnotic induction.

"You are at the top of a huge escalator," he said in a soothing voice. "Rather than steps, there is a large chair with your name on it. You sit in it and it feels like you always belonged there. At the side of the escalator is a sign that reads 100. Slowly, almost imperceptibly, the escalator starts down. In your chair you feel safe, protected and comfortable. A new sign can be seen in the distance. This one reads 99. With each lower number you are going deeper and deeper into that beautiful relaxed state of deep hypnosis."

For twenty minutes he talked to her, leading her, until she was in a deep trance. He took a small pin out of his pocket which he had brought for this purpose. He had sterilized it in alcohol and kept it wrapped in cotton. He jabbed her a few times in the arm. She did not wince, make a sound or bleed. He was sure she was in a deep hypnotic trance.

"I want you to do whatever I tell you. Do you understand?"

"Yes."

"I want you to visualize in front of you a small bee, a friendly bee. Tell me when you have done this."

Allenda, having practiced doing visualizations for years,easily created the image. Cute and chubby, the bee was more like a cartoon than an actual worker drone. "Done," she said.

"Good. Very good. Now I want you to will your senses to become one with the bee. Keep your consciousness here, but let your senses replace the senses of the bee. Your human eyes see through the eyes of the bee. Your human ears hear through the ears of the bee. Do not see and hear *like* the bee, see and hear *through* the bee. Do you understand?"

"Yes."

"Good. Tell me when you have done this."

Allenda willed her senses to join with the bee. It took some time, but eventually she had that feeling of *separateness* she knew from experience. She opened her bee-eyes and could see through them. *What a strange, unique feeling, being a bee.* She was small and many of her senses and emotions were different. She tested her wings and found she could easily repeat the zigging flight she had seen so many bees do.

She felt exhilarated in this new form. All she wanted to do was fly and be a bee. It was intoxicating, thrilling. *I like being here. Wait a second. Why am I here? Oh yes, I have work to do.* She focused on the mission ahead of her. "Okay," she said.

"Excellent. Now remember there is no such thing as linear time on the astral plane. Do you understand?"

"Yes."

"Good. Now use the power of your mind and will your bee-self back to the time of the attack on Angelica. Tell me when you see it and what was going on."

Allenda simply felt she should be at the time of the attack and the bee was there. She could see Angelica functioning as the Pythia. "I see it."

"Excellent." Simon remembered what he had seen when, as Adoniel, he had traveled to this time. "Now look for a small, thin, brown cord that seems attached to Angelica. Tell me when you see it."

Allenda buzzed in close to Angelica as she stood in front of Alan. Although Angelica couldn't see her, she was somehow able to sense the Allenda/bee and brushed her away. The movement was physical, but it had an effect on the astral plane and Allenda had to dodge the blow. The bee dipped and soared up, a movement copied in a distorted way by Allenda's physical body.

"Are you okay?" asked a worried Simon.

Allenda panted for a few seconds as a result of the sudden exertion. Taking control once again she calmed her breathing. "I'm okay."

The Allenda/bee didn't see an energy trail yet. She zoomed around the scene again. Now two men were holding Angelica and she buzzed in for a second time. Once again Angelica brushed away the astral bother. This time Allenda/bee went tumbling. Allenda, however, was prepared and not surprised by the sudden movements. When she finally straightened her flight she was looking right at Angelica. And then… there it was! There was the small wisp of energy flowing up the remains of Angelica's robe.

"See it."

"Excellent, very good. Now slowly follow the stream of brown energy until you come to a pool of energy. Tell me when this happens."

Allenda followed the wispy, dark energy, buzzing through strange worlds and dimensions, always keeping an eye on the thin energy strand. Suddenly, it divided into three beams. She came to a rest at their juncture. "Divides into three," she said.

"Excellent," he encouraged, although he was surprised Barton had gone to the trouble to hide his tracks. *Surely he knows his preparation for me prevents me from coming after him on the astral. Something else must be going on here.* Simon was worried, but with Allenda in the relaxed state he couldn't let on. His worry could have an exaggerated effect on her and ruin everything. "Take the right-hand stream of energy and tell me what happens."

Allenda followed the right-hand energy path. It shot straight up in ever-increasing spirals. Then it took a long dive, deeper and deeper. It spread out until it was so dispersed it formed a mist. "It's become a mist," she reported, hovering before it.

"Good. It's good that you see that." Simon smiled. He remembered when Barton sent him on a wild goose chase like this many years ago at *L'ecolle.* The mist would get more and more ethereal and eventually fade to nothing. Hours could be wasted studying the mist and nothing would come of it. It was a trap.

"There is no reason to investigate any further. Use your mind to will yourself back to the junction of where the energy beam divided into three. Tell me when you're there."

She willed herself back to the spot and was instantly at that location. "I'm there."

"Excellent. Now follow the left-most path. Tell me when you come to the pool of energy." He did not need to have her check the center way. He had taken that path when Barton tried to fool him years ago. That path, too, led to a trap—a monstrous dragon Simon astrally ran from. Simon did not think Barton would change his design. Egomaniacs like Barton thought they were always right. *I'm sure Barton would not see a need for change.* Simon did not want Allenda, who only recently became competent as a traveller to the astral planes, to meet such a beast.

Allenda buzzed down the left stream of energy. Up and down in simple loops all the way to complex spirals. At one point there was a pattern that looked like something from the mind of M.C. Escher. After going round and round a couple times she simply willed herself to be beyond it. She was now on a straight line to a bright light.

The light was blocking her path. She could not go through or around it. "Bright light blocking path,"she said.

"What color?"

"Golden yellow."

It's a solar shield. "Say, 'I come in the power of Yood-Heh-Vahv-Heh Ehl-oh-ah Vah-dah-aht. Let me pass.' Then tell me what happens."

A bee, of course, cannot talk. Instead she said the words in her bee-mind and directed the thoughts—just as she had learned to direct psychic energy—toward the light. The Hebrew words formed the name of God associated with the Sun. The words had their effect. Like a mirror struck by a stone, the light shattered into numerous solid pieces. Then the shards dissolved as if they were salt mixing with water. In a second she was beyond the blockage. Ahead she saw the large pool.

"Through," she told Simon. "See pool."

"Excellent. Now don't be fooled. The energy does not enter the pool. It goes near it and then away from it. Look closely and tell me when you see where it goes."

Allenda buzzed around the perimeter of the pool until she could finally see the thin, tendril-like flow of energy. "Found it."

"Excellent. Now follow it to its source and tell me what you find."

Allenda circled around, following the energy beam. Up and down in circles, squares, tetrahedrons and other shapes. The beam changed into a vertical line that went so far she could not see the end. She followed it up. And up. And up. Several times she paused for a rest. *How long have I been traveling? Has it been hours? Days? Oh yeah, time has no meaning here.* On she went.

Finally she came to a leveling off. On and on she buzzed. And then the path of the energy dropped straight down. It went so far it vanished in the distance below her. Allenda relaxed and allowed herself to slowly drop next to the energy beam. Down and down they went.

Wack! She collided with something hard. She staggered and her physical body moved in the chair. Simon needed to keep her in the hypnotic state. If she popped out of hypnosis before discovering the source of the energy their hours of work would be undone. "Everything is fine," he said. "Relax, let go. Take a deep breath, and as you exhale feel yourself going deeper and deeper into the wonderful state of hypnosis." He waited for her to respond and saw her body again sink into the chair. "Tell me what happened."

Allenda took a deep breath and let herself relax further into the hypnotic state. "Hit something hard. Funny lines on it."

"That's okay. Fly up and get a better look at it from a distance. Tell me what you see."

Allenda buzzed up until she could see the entire image. It looked like a shield made of silver. On it was a square divided into smaller squares, each with a number in them. She described it to Simon.

It sounds like a lunar shield. Could it really be this simple? "Allenda, say 'In the name of Shadai El Chai, let me pass.' Then tell me what happens."

Allenda tried it. There was no change. "Nothing," she reported.

Hmmm. Perhaps it was formed from a Pagan perspective. "Okay. Say, 'In the name of Diana and all the goddesses of the Moon, let me pass.' Then tell me what you see."

Allenda followed Simon's advice. At first nothing happened. Then a small door in the center of the silver shield started to open and close. It looked like a portcullis, the grate-like gate with spikes at the bottom found on castles. Such a gate would be lowered in case of attack. The holes between the bars of the gate were covered with a thin screen so she could not fly between them. The gate was moving up and down so quickly that it was almost hard to see. She reported all this to Simon.

"Good," he said with a positive tone in his voice. Inwardly, Simon was in agony. *I should tell her how dangerous this is. She can't will herself beyond the gate as whatever is there is unknown and could be even more dangerous than the gate itself. If she's trampled by the points of the falling gate it will kill the bee and could destroy her mind here on the physical plane. I should call her back. I'll… Damn it! I know she wants to discover the truth as much as I do.* Simon quietly sighed and said nothing about the danger. Instead he told her how to get through. "Watch the rhythm of the gate as it goes up and down. Stay close to where the gate hits a surface at the bottom of its cycle. Time your flight so that the gate is just starting up as you reach it. Tell me if you understand and tell me when you're through."

Allenda smiled inwardly. *I'm more advanced than I realized, maybe more advanced than Simon realizes.* She knew what the tension in his voice meant. She knew her death here could destroy her on the physical plane. *Still, I have to do this.* "I understand," was all she said.

Allenda/bee watched the gate for some time. Soon she could sense its rhythm. *I'll only get one pass at this.* She waited, watching, watching. Then she started her flight.

Just as the gate started to rise she buzzed forward. She flew as fast as she could. The gate came down, clanging in front of her. Still she soared on, flying directly at the closed gate. A fraction of a second before she hit it the gate rose—she was through!

Ahead of her, unseen from before, was another rising and falling gate! She couldn't stop her flight in time and was about to crash right into it. There was only one chance: hope that the two gates worked in tandem. On she soared, even faster than before. The second gate was up as she reached it, but coming down. She beat her wings desperately, but saw she was losing the race. *If this is my fate, then let me die well.*

Time seemed to stretch out as she flew with a strength she did not know she had. *I can't let Simon and the Warriors down. Fly! Fly!* Her head was past the gate but she could sense the breeze from the falling tips of the spikes on the bottom of the second portcullis against her. *It's over*. She felt the gate crash into her back—and slide off her stinger. Her momentum had carried her through the gate! She rolled forward and caught her breath. She was through!

Allenda/bee panted for some moments, regaining her breath. When her breathing relaxed she looked around and could see the energy stream ahead of her. She didn't want to alarm Simon, so "through," was all she said. She also realized for the first time she was far more in control of the situation than she would have been in a normal state of hypnosis. *Simon is only guiding me. He's no longer in control of me on this plane. I don't have to follow his instructions.*

"Good," said Simon. "Now continue to follow the brownish energy. Tell me what you see."

Allenda followed the energy beam. Soon she could see the physical world, but it was hazy, almost as if it were a dream. The energy went into a church. She flew around until she could make out the faded sign in the front. "I see it going into a church. The name of the church is St. Lucy's."

"Good. Now find a street sign and tell me what street it's on."

The Allenda/bee flew down the street until she found the sign. "Pacific."

"Good. Now find an address near the church and tell me what it is."

The house next to the church showed a number. "117," she told Simon.

"Excellent. You've done a tremendous job. Now follow the energy back the way you came or simply will yourself to be back here."

"No."

"What?" Simon couldn't believe what he heard. People under hypnosis were not supposed to resist commands unless they went totally against the ethics of the person who was hypnotized. This was all wrong, but to force her out of such a deep, hypnotic state quickly could be dangerous.

"I'm going to come into the present and look in the church. I have to see what's going on."

"Alli. Don't do it. It's too dangerous. They'll detect you. I want you to let me bring you out of this hypnotic state now. Do you hear me? Alli? Allenda? Do you hear me?"

Chapter Fifteen

Earlier, the Eleventh Afternoon

Eris toweled herself off and looked at her image in the mirror. Her stomach was still flat and her breasts still stood out firmly. She rubbed the towel over the water drops on her breasts and the friction made her nipples stand out. *My legs are too short but they still look good.* She looked again in the mirror and liked what she saw. *Not bad for an old bitch.* She was proud of her body, her magic and her mind.

Her mind helped her become well-to-do. She learned astrology when she was a child and discovered she had a knack for predicting what the stock market would do. As a result, she had been able to predict the electronics boom, the medicals boom and especially the dot com boom and crash. She took some of the small amounts of money she earned as a secretary and invested in the market. Her initial small investments grew to large investments. Her large investments became enormous. For the past five years she moved from high-risk, high-yield investments to secure, low risk, moderate-to-low yield blue chips and munis. She would be able to live very extravagantly off just the interest for the rest of her life.

Eris was a free spirit. She did not want to follow other people's rules. Being financially independent allowed her to do this. She could wear what she wanted, get up and go to sleep when she wanted, do what she wanted, think what she wanted and bed whom she wanted.

And Eris loved sex. She thought of herself as a sort of sexual missionary. She had taught many men of all ages how to make love instead of just have sex. She frequently stood up for the liberation of sexuality. She wanted to free it from what she saw as the moronic moralisms left over from thousands of years of religious power structures. Eris had a deep belief in God, but she simply could not accept that God would be as against the free expression and enjoyment of sexuality as some would try to force others to believe.

Because Eris had plenty of money and liked sex, many people thought she was a rich man's mistress or a high-priced call girl. It was fun to let people think that, but actually Eris would never accept money for sex. She hated that sexuality had been perverted into a way to sell everything from movies to motorcycle handlebars, from carpet to shaving cream. Sex, to her, was a beautiful gift from God. *How can we have the audacity to even think of selling such a wonderful gift?*

She turned ninety degrees and again looked at her figure in the mirror, this time getting a side angle. "Thanks, Mom and Dad, for the genes," she said out loud. For a second her face turned cold. *It was the only thing you gave me before you both deserted me. But enough of that! That was years ago.* She ran her hands down her sides, liking the sensations. Her hands moved across her flat stomach toward the juncture of her legs and she felt that wonderful tingle of arousal. *No, I'll wait 'till later.*

Eris wrapped the bath sheet around her, pinned up her hair, and started to apply her make-up. Her skin showed tiny laugh lines around the eyes. Otherwise her face was still line-free. Using a ground apricot-pit scrub gave it a bloom of youth. She needed only a bit of powder to prevent shine.

Today she applied dark maroon to her lips followed by a protective gloss. On her eyes she added mascara and subtle liner. Above this she added two colors to the lids. She reached for a cotton swab to blend the colors, discovered she was out of them and used a fingertip instead.

From her closet she pulled out clothes to wear—a loose blouse, a wraparound skirt that was two sizes too small so it was open at the side, panty hose, cotton socks and Reeboks. *Hmm. To bra or not to bra, that is the question.* Finally she took a black, push-up demi so her décolletage would garner stares. *Hell, I look good. Why not flaunt it?*

She hopped in her 'vette and headed for Dutton's in the Valley. They had just received a rare edition of Agrippa's *Three Books of Occult Philosophy.* She had asked them to do a book search for it and the three-volume set just arrived from a small shop in England. Dutton's called her yesterday and left a message on her machine saying that the books were in. She wanted to pick the set up before they put it on their shelves and someone else purchased the volumes.

Rather than the freeway, she decided to take the streets. She stopped off in Hollywood across the street from the Farmer's Market tourist trap and went into a K-Mart to get some Q-Tips. She zipped through the store, ignoring the stares her figure and revealing clothes garnered, and went downstairs to the sundries. She grabbed a box of swabs that had three hundred pieces. As she pulled them off the rack a deep voice said, "If you look at the prices you'll find the one hundred-ninety piece boxes are on sale for less than half the price of the three hundred count ones. Why not get two of them? You'll get more for your money."

Eris turned and saw an immaculate, burly man with a patch over his left eye. "It's you!" she said, surprised to see him.

"So you *do* remember me. I don't think we were formally introduced at the rave, Eris. Please call me Baron."

I don't remember telling him my name, but things were pretty wild that night. "What are you doing here?" she asked.

"Actually, I live in Venice. But I had some business in this area and came in here to purchase some supplies. I'm having a large party tonight. Would you like to come?"

Eris thought about it for a second, then said, "Sure. Maybe. What's the party for?"

"A friend of mine is being born," he told her.

She looked at him, puzzled over the wording of his answer, but let it pass. "If I decide to come, where's your place? And what should I wear?"

The Baron gave her a card. "Here's the address. As for dress, well, I have a *thing*—an obsession, you might say—about dressing formally. However, that's just me. What you're wearing is fine. Be there around nine?"

"Yeah, well, maybe I'll see you there."

"Johnson," he called, "bring the cart." A man dressed in a chauffeur's uniform pushed a loaded shopping cart up behind him and the Baron added three boxes of paper cups to the sundries stacked haphazardly in the cart.

Eris watched the large, muscular man as he walked away, followed by the cart and driver. The Baron looked back at her and smiled. She thought for a second that a beam of reddish psychic energy came out of his eye and bathed her body in it's glow. *I must be imagining things. I don't think...* Suddenly, her entire body trembled. She gasped for air and grabbed onto a display for support as she felt wave after wave of lust travel up and down her spine. She threw her head back and uttered a low, keening moan. "Ooooh," she loudly cried as orgasms racked her body.

When she came back to her senses and caught her breath she was lying on the floor and there were several people around her. A bright-faced teen wearing a K-Mart badge asked if she were okay. "I think so," she said, as she slowly moved her body and made sure everything felt normal. "Can I have a hand up?" With help from the employee she got back to her feet. "Yeah, I'm okay," she said.

"Well, you gotta check in with the store manager," said the teen.

The manager did nothing more than have her sign papers so she would not hold the store responsible for her fall. She paid no attention to the papers, but thought about the feelings the Baron had caused in her. *Nobody had ever done* that *to me before. Who is he?*

As she checked out with her swabs she remembered the Baron's comment that he was hosting the party because, "A friend of mine is being born." *He must have meant that a friend of his is having a baby.*

I think.

* * * * *

Eris drove to the bookstore and picked up the three books they had found for her. *One hundred-fifty dollars for these three, slim volumes? What a rip.* She also bought a first edition of Crowley's *Blue Equinox* and an early printing of Scot's *The Discoverie of Witchcraft.* Both were at prices below those listed in the used book catalogs she received from all over the world, so she considered the total for all of her purchases to be fair, although no bargain.

She drove down the Ventura Freeway to the Topanga Canyon off ramp. She took the curvy road through the canyon. Half-way through she stopped at the Old Post Office. It had once been an actual postal office but the large, squat building was now the site of a grocery store, a bar, a vegetarian restaurant and a few other small businesses. She went into the bar and had two tap beers. They frosted the mugs here and that seemed to make the beer colder, crisper and tastier.

When she left the bar the sky was darkening. The road ahead was still convoluted with tricky turns, and rather than start off slightly inebriated, she went over two doors to the vegetarian restaurant. As she entered she saw lots of sandals, long hair and tie-dyed clothes. The scent of patchouli—she always called it "dirt perfume"—filled her nostrils. *Ah, the sixties are alive in Topanga Canyon.*

Eris had a small salad filled with crisp, shredded vegetables. It was doused with a bland, yogurt-based dressing, but still edible. For her main course she had a vegie-burger made from grains and ground vegetables. It was heavily seasoned and had an enjoyable kick to it with a sort of barbeque-teriyaki flavor. As usual, she ate her meal slowly. She finished with a cup of strong coffee.

When she left the restaurant it was black out. Topanga Canyon Boulevard had few lights, but her 'vette had great brakes and a good suspension, so she sped through the turns. "*Remember me. Find me,*" he had said to her. *How had they just happened to run into each other? Was it Kismet? Fate? There was something about him, something powerful, something attractive. And he certainly has a powerful effect on my body.*

Eris laughed out loud. *And he is big—all over.* She laughed some more, but when she stopped laughing a smile remained on her face. *The books all talk about how the size of a man isn't really important. "It's not the size of the wand that counts, it's the magic that's in it."* She laughed, unsure if that statement was really true.

Her mind wandered as she easily made the turns in her car. Eris had received great pleasure from men of all sizes. She distinctly remembered one man who was very small. She had been disappointed the first time she saw him and thought his size was a handicap. *I'll just give him some mercy sex.* She discovered, however, he was an excellent lover. *He certainly learned how to overcome his "handicap." In fact, he'd overcome his handicap with me several times! Still, there was something about that feeling of being totally filled…*

That's it. I'm gonna go to Baron's party tonight.

Eris finished the drive, ending near the Malibu Beach Colony, home to famous movie stars and more private, wealthy people. She continued down PCH until she came out in Santa Monica. Aleph Books was still open, so she stopped in to see if anything new was there. There were some recent spiritual, philosophical and New Age books, but nothing magical. She hated leaving stores without buying anything, so she purchased a small package of amber incense.

When Eris arrived home she threw her packages on her bed. She washed her face and applied some fresh, more intense and dramatic make-up. *After all, it* was *a party!* She took a sweater and started to leave when she remembered how sexy Allenda had looked. *Baron said this was going to be a large party so I doubt if he'll mind an additional guest, especially one who looks like Allenda.* She went over to the phone and called her.

"You guessed it, I'm not home," answered Allenda's machine. "Leave your name and number with my robo-recorder after the beep and I'll get back to you when I can."

"Hi, Alli. This is Eris. Say, I'm going over to a big party at the house of a guy named Baron. If you want to, come on over. His card says that he lives in Venice at 117 Pacific Avenue, next to the old St. Lucy's church. It's 9:30 P.M. now, and the party started a half hour ago, so come on over when you can. Dress to impress! I hope to see you there. Love ya."

Eris hung up the phone and had second thoughts about her shoes. She changed first into pumps, then into high heels, and finally into boots. She stayed with her last choice. She got into her car and headed to the address on the card. *A party with the Big Baron. This should be fun. And maybe Alli will show up, too.* When Eris arrived at the large, well-lit house, she could hear music from within. *I wonder what interesting things will happen tonight?*

Hollywood
The Eleventh Night

Paul had no idea how he had managed to drive back to the Hollywood police station. He remembered he had questioned the Baron and that the Baron had freely answered his questions, but couldn't shed any light on the case. Paul found himself sitting at his desk, looking at papers and photos but seeing nothing.

At 2:00 A.M. he was disturbed by an officer. "Sir? Lieutenant Christian?"

Paul looked at the officer. He saw nothing.

The officer, seeing the glazed look in Paul's eyes, asked, "Sir, are you okay?"

"I'm fine. Fine. I think I will go home now," he said, his voice a monotone.

Paul got up and started to leave. He didn't move the marker on the magnetic chart which showed whether he was in or out. He didn't sign out. He moved with a stilted, automaton-like gait.

As he walked, it started.

The earth began to shake. Slowly, slowly. Paul moved as if he was in synchronization with the shaking. It had no effect on his movements. The rolling tremors grew worse. The walls of the station started to develop cracks and deep groans from bending lumber and pipes filled the air. People started yelling and running. Paul was oblivious to it all as he left the building.

He walked into the parking lot. Power lines were down and broken; sparks flew into the night, filling the sky like embers around a bonfire. Just down the street a screech of brakes was followed by a crash and the sound of twisting metal as a bus crashed into a small car. Screams of fear, pain and terror were everywhere.

The ground continued to shake. Paul continued to ignore the disaster forming around him as he moved in unison with the pulsing ground.

He got in his car and started to drive home. He drove around the accidents and fallen trees and power lines. He ignored the screams and bloody, pain-filled people as well as those who poured out into the streets to avoid falling structures. Some people ran and pounded on his car, begging for help, but he just slsowly drove on as if nothing was happening. A large palm tree toppled over, smashing into the trunk of his car. He didn't stop.

He didn't even notice. He just drove home.

The quake was not the most powerful to ever hit Southern California. It barely made 5.9 on the Richter scale. But unlike any other quake it lasted for over ten minutes. It began in Hollywood and traveled in an agonizingly slow path to the coast. From there it continued southwest toward Santa Catalina, fading to nothing before it arrived at Wrigley's isle. Many people in the quake zone described the experience as if something was moving *through* the earth. A few described it as something evil. This, of course, was ignored by the media and, of course, was discounted by the U.S. Geological Survey teams sent to the area. A few claimed it was an attack from the Russians who were using a secret weapon while others said it was our own government testing a weapon called HARRP which was based on UFO technology. On his radio show, Bob Jorgenson said it was a sign of the apocalypse which, of course, had been predicted by the Bible.

Before the quake even finished, a new, even more terrible stench filled the L.A. basin, a smell like dead fish mixed with rotten eggs. Scientists from Cal Tech came on TV and radio and claimed it was a mixture of methane gas released by the earthquake from hidden pockets in the earth and fish dying from the shock of the temblor. That stink, mixed with the bite of the killer smog and the heaviness of the air from the odd humidity caused breathing problems for thousands of people, especially young children, the elderly, and others with lung diseases such as emphysema or allergies. This complicated the job of the city's hospitals which were already overwhelmed trying to take care of over 4,000 seriously injured quake victims.

The quake cut a swathe of damage three miles wide across Los Angeles. The strength of the shaker was later described as a "scientific conundrum" because it sharply faded in intensity outside of the three-mile wide strip. As a result, damage was not as bad as initially feared. Even so, the Governor declared Los Angeles a disaster area and called in the National Guard to patrol the area after looting set in. Areas were set aside where martial law was to be enforced.

Television commentators later reported as a curious "factoid," that rats and mice seemed to be fleeing from L.A. They put the blame for this on the long tremor and called it a "good side" to the quake. What they did not say was that cats and dogs were fleeing L.A., too. When their owners tried to stop them the pets turned and attacked, leading to a large number of animal bites and scratches.

Paul didn't remember any of the events of his drive home. It was as if the car drove home by itself and he was just a passenger. He actively dodged all of the damage and the people seeking safety in the streets, but it made no impression on his mind. had driven home as if nothing had happened. He went to his bed, pulled the covers up and fell asleep without getting out of his clothes. He did not dream.

* * * * *

Earlier, the Eleventh Night

Eris knocked on the door. When she entered, the party was in full swing. The Baron's house was huge, and there was a large room with a full bar, fancy lighting and blaring music. About fifty people were there, talking, laughing, dancing, trying to pick each other up, eating, drinking and all the things people do at big parties. Everyone was having a great time, and the friendliness was contagious. Soon, Eris had met a dozen people. She danced some fast numbers with several of them. The Baron was nowhere to be seen.

Eris was used to being the center of attention at any gathering. Her beauty and sensuality always drew others to her. This was especially true when she met new people or came into an unfamiliar group. Since she did not know any of the people at this party it would have been normal for this reaction to happen here. It did not. She looked around and noticed that all the partyers were beautiful. Nobody was fat or too thin. Everybody had classic good looks with high cheekbones, elegant figures; clear, shiny eyes and perfect, white teeth.

Something odd is going on here. No group of people this size is so perfect. Where did all… Just then, before she could wonder more about the people, the Baron entered.

The Baron wore an elegant grey silk suit with a light-pink pastel shirt. The grateful crowd applauded their host for the fine party. He smiled and waved and returned cheek-kisses with several of the women. He finally drew close to Eris.

"Are you enjoying my little party, Eris?" he asked.

"It's great, Baron! You can really throw a wingding."

"Tell me, do you think…" the rest of his words were lost in the noise of the crowd.

"I'm sorry, I couldn't hear you over the noise."

He spoke louder. "Do you think that we…"

"I'm sorry," she shouted over the music and the talk, "but I still can't hear you." She pointed to her ears and shook her head.

He leaned over to her ear. "Let's go into the next room where we can talk." She nodded her assent. She wanted to find out more about this mystery man.

He led her down a hall and into a large room; a library with books lining the walls. When he shut the door she felt a change in air pressure and the sound outside almost vanished. "Wow! It sure gets quiet in here," she commented.

"Yes it does," he agreed. "When the door is closed this room is hermetically sealed. It is also temperature and humidity controlled. Some of the books in here are worth thousands of dollars. I made the investment in this room to protect them."

"What about a fire?"

He pointed to sprinklers overhead. "Halogen gas extinguishers will flood this room if a fire starts in here. That type of extinguisher does not harm the books. The walls of this room are fireproof brick with an iron lining. This room will not burn."

Impressive. She started walking around the room and was stunned when she saw that one of the titles was *The Picatrix.* "How did you get this book?" she asked, pointing to it. "I've been looking for a copy for years and didn't think there were any English translations."

"I have an interest in rare occult books. This one is a translation into English from the German. It was made for me and has never been published. An original German copy is in that locked bookcase," he said, pointing to a wall.

"Are you *the* Baron who advertises on flyers for his occult group, the Barony?"

"Then you've heard of me..."

"Yes, but I didn't know you had such a wealth of books."

"You may come over whenever you like to read them. This house runs 24 hours a day thanks to many of my devoted followers."

"If you have a group, you must have a temple, too. Is it here? Would it be asking too much to see it? I have an interest in the occult, too."

"Yes, I could tell by your knowledge of the *Picatrix.*" He walked close to her and she could feel his essence, his power. "The temple is in an underground vault directly beneath us," he continued. "I'll be glad to take you there... later.

"But first, I have a question for you." He stared at her and she felt her breath quicken. "Are you always so free with your body as the other night, or was it just the effect of the music, the beat and the other couples?"

"I... I'm responsible for everything and anything I do." She took a step back. "I do just what I want. Nothing more. Nothing less. I'll try just about anything once..." she smiled seductively at her host, "...more if I like it."

"And did you like it?" he asked, taking a drink from the glass he had brought with him. She smiled enigmatically, but did not respond with words. "Well, then, let me ask a different question. What won't you try?"

"Pain."

"Indeed?" He walked to a wall and looked at some of his books. Then he dramatically turned toward her. "Haven't you ever been scratched by someone when making love?"

"Of course."

"Did it feel bad? Did it hurt?"

"Of course it did."

"Really?"

Eris thought about it. "Well, maybe not at the time."

He moved close to her again. "When the human body is sexually stimulated it releases endorphins, chemicals as powerful as heroin, which mask pain. By stimulating the physical body so you can feel sensations beyond the blockages of endorphins you can reach an entirely new level of ecstasy, a level few people ever know, ever reach, ever experience…"

He was standing next to her. His presence, his personality, were like a strong, sweet perfume, overpowering and intoxicating. She stepped back and walked to the other side of the room, pretending she saw a book there that interested her when all she really wanted to do was catch her breath. She pulled out a book, it was a first English edition of Levi's *Transcendental Magic,* and looked at the Baron. "That may be true," she finally replied, "but I'm not into intentional physical pain."

"What about control?"

"I'm sorry," she replied, replacing the book, "I don't follow what you mean."

"The other night you did whatever I wanted. I was in control, total control of your actions. You let me do whatever I wanted."

"So?"

The Baron took a breath and considered what words he should say. "Eris, I think that you are a person who likes to be in power. You have such power over yourself that others freely give their power to you. You're always in control. Every once in a while it feels good to let go of the control, to do exactly what someone else commands you to do."

She looked at him but said nothing. It was true. She enjoyed power, over herself and others, but occasionally it felt good to follow someone else's orders, to be totally, completely possessed, to not be responsible for anything. She tilted her head and said, "Baron, you're a man of no small power yourself." She walked over to him, pulled out a chair from under the table he stood next to and put one foot on it imitating Marlena Dietrich in *The Blue Angel.* "Do you dare give up your power to the will of another? Do you dare let me be in total charge of everything and anything you do?"

He made no answer, Instead, he fell to his knees and rubbed his face against her booted foot on the chair. He started to lick it. "I didn't give you permission to do that," she said sternly, getting into her role in this new game.

He rose, his nostrils flaring with passion. He closed his eye and took a deep breath. "Certain games, games of power and dominance, of control and bondage can be interesting. I have a room specially designed for those kind of games. Would you like me to show it to you, or should we just return to the party?"

Eris picked up a pencil from a table and suddenly jammed it into the middle of the Baron's lower jaw. She had to stand on tip-toes so his head would be forced back and he would feel it. She stayed that way for a long moment. "Show me your room," she said, releasing the pencil. "I think we can have a nice… discussion about power."

The Baron rubbed his chin and they exited the room. They went further down the hall and the Baron unlocked a door. The room they entered was dark. He reached to the side and flicked on a switch. A light came on in a side room and Eris could barely make out that the room was large. The furniture, however, was draped and in shadows. "There are things you can change into, if you wish, in that side room. I'll light candles in here."

Eris entered the changing room There was a mirror with a row of make-up in front of it. Behind her were two cupboards. She opened one and the room quickly filled with the rich musk of finished leather.

She looked through the pieces of clothes until she found some she liked. When she was finished dressing she looked at herself in the mirror. *Wow!* She now wore thigh-high boots laced up the back with five-inch heels. This was topped by a black, silk G-string covered by a leather bustier. Attached to the bustier were belts and chrome rings that clattered and clanked as she moved. Spandex gloves with no fingers and a dog collar with small, hanging chains completed the image. She brushed her hair forward and sprayed it heavily. Then she brushed it lightly back, giving her a glowing halo of hair. She was ready to play.

When she came out of the changing room she could see the larger room was lit only by candles. Restraints, in the forms of chains, leather straps and even a pillory were everywhere. They were attached to the walls, ceiling, chairs, posts and tables. The Baron was not in the room.

Eris was both repulsed and attracted to the ambiance. She moved around, feeling the chains and leather restraints. Something about the room brought out deeply-buried feelings and she shivered. *Was it from the cold or…*

"It feels good, doesn't it?"

Eris turned to see the Baron and gasped. He was dressed now in spandex pants with stirrups. The muscles in his legs bulged under the elastic fabric. At his chest was a large circle of chrome. Five, two-inch wide straps came off if it. Two of the straps went over his shoulders, two around his chest and one between his legs. At his crotch there was another ring of chrome dividing the fifth strap. Behind the ring at his crotch were the long, hanging laces to his pants. On each forearm was a leather covering, marked by chrome studs. His biceps, which bulged beyond what she had imagined, looked like rocks.

He walked over to her and looked her over with such passion she blushed, something Eris had not done in many years. "Do you think you understand power? Prove it."

She slapped his face. Hard. "Prove it what?" she asked crossly, getting back into the game.

He felt his jaw and moved it around to check its soundness. He smiled. *She was certainly a perfect partner for this.* He quickly bowed his head in front of the dominatrix. "Prove it… *my lady,*" he replied with mock meekness.

"I am not *your* lady. You must pay for your insolence. Sit in this chair."

"Yes, mistress Eris."

He sat in the chair Eris was pointing to. She went behind the chair and tied a leather collar, which was attached to a vertical post on the chair, around the Baron's forehead. *This is going to be fun!* She strapped down his chest, arms, and legs. He gasped slightly as a tightened strap dug into his leg. Eris looked up. Her eyes glowed.

* * * * *

The Baron, drenched in sweat, rubbed his wrists where the leather restraints had scuffed them. "That was excellent," he said. "Nobody ever took me that far before."

Eris beamed. She was slumped on the floor next to the table that the Baron had been lying on. She was coated with a film of perspiration from her exertions. Eris had enjoyed her position of power over the strong man on the table above her. She had controlled him, pushed him to the limits of his ability to absorb servility. She had teased him, unfastening him, revealing his manhood and encouraging his excitement only to walk away and leave him frustrated, begging and meek.

"Shall we go back to the party?" the Baron asked.

Eris didn't answer. *I've always been in control. I wonder what it's like to give in totally to the whims of another?*

She didn't look at the big man. She just quietly asked, "What…is it like?"

The Baron smiled. "Ah, Eris, the freedom you can experience by totally giving up responsibility for just a few moments is incredible." He wiped some sweat from his upper lip. "If you want to, and *only* if you want to, I can take you farther on the road to ecstasy than you can imagine."

Eris felt herself begin to get damp between her legs. She had never been into this type of scene, but she saw the pleasant torture the Baron had received. She knew then that she had to find out what it was like. "Yes," she said.

"Are you sure this is what you want?" he asked.

"Yes, Baron. Take me all the way."

The Baron had seemingly regained his energy. He grabbed her long hair and pulled up. Eris yelped in surprise and grabbed at her hair to avoid it being torn from her skull. She rose to her feet to avoid the pain. He was sitting on the table and pulled her face close to his. "Then we will see how you take to the submissive role," he said quietly.

Something in his demeanor frightened her and she felt her heart pound. *Is this part of the thrill?*

He got off the table, still holding her hair. He pulled her over to a chair still covered with a cloth and pulled the cloth from it.

Her eyes widened. It was like the other restraint chairs in the room but with two additions: First, the seat of the chair was curved, made to fit the anatomy. Second, sticking up from the seat were two protuberances. She knew they were made to fit into her most tender parts. She struggled against him, but his strength was unbelievable.

He turned her to face him and held her by the shoulders, squeezing her painfully. He took her right wrist and strapped it to the chair, then did the same with the left. "You have two choices," he told her, "the gentle way or the painful way. Which do you prefer?" He grabbed her hair again with his left hand and ripped off her panties in a single move with his right. She gasped at the sudden feel of cool air on her skin where her panties had been. She was trapped in the game. There was no place to hide, no one to hear and no choice. She bit her lip and tried to relax. Eris took a slow, deep breath and lowered herself into the chair. It was designed so she had no choice but to be invaded. She groaned as the firm, cold, plastic projections entered her in front and in back. She was grateful both had been lubricated.

The Baron kneeled in front of her and fixed restraints around her ankles. Then he went behind her and fastened her forehead. Next he added restraints around her thighs, calves, chest, solar plexus and biceps. She literally could not move.

The Baron adjusted the chair so that it leaned back. He pulled down the top of her bustier and cruelly pinched her breasts and nipples. The movement was so hard and sudden that she couldn't scream, she could only suck air in response to the pain. But before she could complain he moved his hand down her body to her groin. At first the feeling was pleasurable, then painful, then pleasure, then pain. Suddenly, she exploded from being filled and manipulated. Her body arched against the restraints as she moaned her release. She closed her eyes and let her body relax as she regained her breath.

But she didn't have a chance to normalize her breathing. He was suddenly in her mouth, moving, plunging his huge size into her. She gagged and struggled for breath as he filled her mouth. It seemed to go on forever. Then he exploded, overflowing her mouth. She sputtered, coughed and again tried to catch her breath. She had not bargained for this much pain and humiliation. Tears came to her eyes and she started to sob.

"Nobody said you could cry, Eris. Now you must pay." The Baron took out a small rubber ball attached to the middle of a leather strap.

"What are you going to do with that?" she asked.

He said nothing, but forced the ball into her mouth and tied the strap behind her head. He went to the door and knocked twice. The people who were at the party filed into the room one by one. They were now dressed in plain black robes.

Eris' eyes grew in terror. This was no longer a game. She struggled to free herself from the numerous leather restraints, but it was hopeless. She had no choice but to wait. A chill filled her and her fingers and toes went numb. *Why is this happening? What is happening?*

The Baron readjusted the chair so that it was upright. He stepped on a metal bar and wheels under the chair rolled easily. "You wondered about my temple room, Eris. We're going to take you there now. Unfortunately, you won't see anything." Somebody brought out a hood and covered her head. She felt her chair being rolled.

Eris wanted to cry, but she just felt empty. *Oh My God, this has all been a trap! Oh God, oh God oh God. Will I get out of this with my life?*

The chair stopped rolling and she felt herself, still strapped to the chair, carried jerkily down some stairs. *I can't believe that it will all end now.* She couldn't see. She couldn't move and she was overcome with a wave of despair. The chair thumped to a landing on the floor of what Eris assumed to be the Baron's temple. The sudden shock changed her. *If it's going to happen I will not go easily. Simon and the Warriors must make the Baron and his followers pay.* She concentrated as best she could, sending her thoughts out to the void. *Simon, hear me. Call Allenda's machine. If I die I want you to avenge me.*

Avenge me, Simon, avenge me.

Avenge me.

Avenge me…

* * * * *

Allenda was terrified. *How can I "go through" a wall? That was insane. Sure, I can go through things that were astral in nature, but this wall is physical.* She hovered in her bee form for a few moments trying to set her mind to the task at hand. *Okay, Alli, concentrate, girlfriend, concentrate. The astral plane isn't a "higher" plane, it's a finer, more ethereal plane. Entities on the astral plane are so fine, their molecular structure so tenuous and widespread, they can effortlessly go through physical walls and buildings. Oh, God. I know it in my mind, but in my heart? I dunno. Will I bounce off the wall and pop out of the astral plane back into my body? What did Simon call that? An astral whiplash? I could stop and simply ease back into my body. I don't have to do this.*

She paused for a moment. *Damn it. I don't have a choice. I have to do this for Angelica. I have to do this for Simon...*

She looked at the building and steeled herself. ...*And most of all, I have to do it for me.* Allenda took a deep breath, closed her eyes and buzzed straight at the church. She went right through the walls of St. Lucy's in spite of the doors being boarded up. Suddenly the quality of the air changed and she knew she had made it. Allenda exhaled, opened her eyes and looked around.

The pews had been removed and a large table was in the center of the church. The walls were painted black. A white circle, perhaps twenty feet in diameter, had been painted on the floor. New black candles were placed around the rim of the circle. It was obvious to Allenda a ritual would be performed here soon.

In her astral bee form Allenda could still trace the pattern of energy she had followed. Now the energy pattern was more complex, as if more people were involved with it. The energy went down a hall and split in two directions. She followed one path and ended up in a small room. The energy went up to a large white freezer. Now more confident in her abilities she easily buzzed into it. To her horror, she found herself surrounded by body parts. Allenda shrieked in terror, but the ghastly display was everywhere she turned. Legs, arms, a torso, all the parts that were missing from the murder victims were there.

Allenda panicked and struggled to escape, but the display of death wouldn't allow it. She closed her eyes to block out the vision and regained her composure. Then she buzzed up and out of the freezer

Simon watched as Allenda's body writhed in the chair, struggling to escape from the freezer. When she calmed he held her hand and stroked it gently, lovingly. "Alli. Alli. Are you okay?

The stroking of her hand, as well as her escape from the body parts, had calmed her. " Yes. Yes. I'm okay. I Found the body parts. The evidence is here."

"Allenda, listen to me. Alli. Come back now. You've found the proof and we can tell the police. It's too dangerous. They'll discover you. You must come back…"

"More to see," was all she said.

"Alli! Alli!" he called, but she ignored him.

She flew back to where the energy stream had divided and took the other path. She followed it down a wide, well-formed, subterranean tunnel which connected the church to the house next door—the Baron's house. Soon she found herself in a smaller room under the Baron's mansion which, like the church, was painted black and had a white circle on the floor. In this circle were a large number of people. She knew that if she tried to enter the circle they would detect her, so she alighted on a wall and watched.

The group was in the midst of an orgy. In the center of the room was a woman in leather strapped to a chair. The figure in the chair wore a hood and was shaking as if sobbing. The robed women were servicing the men. She could tell the men were concentrating on the ritual at hand—she could see their thought forms surrounding the woman in the hood. The energy and the thought forms built in strength as the men's sexuality reached a peak. Soon, the men were exploding over the woman in the chair. When they were finished they all started circling the woman, chanting "Barra Edinnazu! Barra Edinnazu!" This built in speed and energy until a large man in a robe appeared. He pulled out a long, sharp knife. It glittered in the candlelight as the man waved it in the air. He moved toward the seated figure. There was no expression of regret or joy on his face. Allenda shuddered in horror as he slashed the throat of the woman in the chair.

A thin, red line magically appeared across her neck. Then it opened like a red sea, spilling life down the front of the hooded woman. The body in the chair shivered and quaked. Her fingers squirmed, seeking help, seeking escape. But there was none. Slowly her motions ceased.

Allenda/bee wanted to fly away, but like most people, she felt drawn to watch something that was horrible. The robed people closed in around the woman in the chair. They looked like wild animals as they licked and sucked at the blood dripping down her. On the astral she could see them draining what little remained of her energy, her spirit, her very soul along with the blood. Something seemed oddly familiar about the energy of the hooded woman.

Allenda watched the gruesome, vampiric ritual as the body was drained of both blood and energy. The large man, who had disappeared during the draining, reappeared with a two-handed broadsword. Bee/Allenda watched as the man cried, "For Barra Edinnazu," made a circle with his body to build up momentum and sliced through the woman's neck with a single, powerful stroke. The crowd roared its approval.

The large man held up a Tarot card. "Here is the final card," he said, "the Nine of Cups. It means complete success, pleasure, happiness and the fulfillment of wishes. Tonight we have the final part of the body, the perfect body, into which we will resurrect Barra Edinnazu. She will cleanse the world of poverty and ignorance, war and disease. We will all bask in her power."

He gave the card to one of the men. As if prearranged, that man and several others released the body from the chair and took it away. The large man released the head he had severed, removed the hood and held it by its long hair. He held the head so it was facing away from Allenda/bee. "Call Barra Edinnazu so She may approve of her future face. Behold the face-to-be of Barra Edinnazu!" He slowly turned so everyone could see the future appearance of She who was to be born. He continued to turn until the face of the dead woman could be seen by Allenda.

* * * * *

"It's Eris!" Allenda jumped up from the chair, screaming, her eyes wild and raving. She looked at Simon. "They've killed Eris! They sucked her dry and severed her head! Oh my God! She's dead, Simon, She's dead!"

Simon held her as she cried, her tears wetting his shirt. He stroked her hair, soothing her, until she was calm enough to speak. Through her tears Allenda told him everything she had seen and experienced.

Simon's face turned grim. "There's nothing we can do tonight. Besides, in a few moments you're not going to feel too well."

"Why not?"

"You snapped back to your body, leaving much of your astral substance along the way. You also shot out of a deep hypnotic trance. You can expect a bad headache." Simon left and returned with four aspirins and a cup of rose hips and hops tea to help her sleep. The headache had already started and she gratefully accepted them. "I have to make a couple of calls," he told her.

He went into another room where there was a phone. Simon was a real magician, and the first quality of a magician is that he or she should be a skeptic. Not a debunker or naysayer, but someone who needed all the information available before coming to a conclusion. He had no doubt Allenda shared exactly what she had experienced—she had no reason not to tell the truth. But was the reality of her experience mirrored in the actuality of the physical world? This he had to check out.

First, he called Eris' house. All he got was her answering machine. She was not at home. Then for some reason unknown to him he had a feeling he should call Allenda's home. Allenda had at one time given him the code so he could play back the messages on her answering machine while she was out of town. He had written it down and used it now to play back the messages. There was only one.

When it was over, he just held the phone and looked into the distance.

Not another. Dear Lord, not another! The phone line went dead, then buzzed repeatedly in his hand. He slowly hung up the phone.

He went back to Allenda. She was still crying. Simon held her tenderly. "I'll make the Baron pay," she said.

Here was the missing part of the puzzle. Allenda had been tracing Barton, and Eris had gone to visit the Baron. The Baron and Barton Mordus Oliver are one and the same. As he soothingly stroked Allenda's arm, anger and rage flew through him, not just in his mind, but in his heart, soul, being. It went beyond a desire for justice. Every fiber of Simon's being screamed for vengeance with a roar that could rend the universe. *This will not end here, Barton. You will pay for your crimes.*

The aspirins, tea and exhaustion had their effect. Allenda's cries turned to sobs, and then she slept curled up in the big, comfortable chair. Simon went to the window and looked out. He could see the Moon looking a sickly yellow through the dirty sky. Suddenly, the ground began to shake as the three-mile wide quake rumbled past his home. He could literally feel the evil moving through the ground. He fell to his knees and covered himself with his arms as if trying to keep the evil away. Nausea filled him and he fought the urge to vomit. The shaking of the house seemed to go on forever. Books toppled from shelves and decorations crashed down. The quake continued until there was nothing left to fall. Still the earth shook. Finally it eased and Simon, lying on the floor, slowly felt his stomach settle.

That was when he knew. The murders were just the preface to a novel of horror. They presaged the fact that *something* was coming. Something evil. "I will not let you accomplish this foul ritual. It ends, Barton," he said. "It *will* end." He got a light blanket and covered Allenda. Exhausted and drained, he laid down on a sofa and fell asleep.

* * * * *

The quaking earth moved from Hollywood past Simon's home and toward Venice. The spirit of Barra Edinnazu had come to approve of Her new face. Her energy smiled at the beautiful face and She sighed, Her breath was the real source of the foul gas that filled the air for miles around. *Yes, yes, this new face suits me. I am ready to be reborn.* Soon the rituals would be completed and Her resurrection would follow. Soon She would return to breathe the air, feel with flesh and control all that was in Her domain.

Soon.

Chapter Sixteen

Twelfth Afernoon

The ringing of the telephone dragged Paul from his sleep. "Yeah?" he answered groggily.

"Paul," Captain Minelli's voice said, "we need you to come to the station now. The earthquake..."

"Earthquake, what earthquake? What are you talking about?"

"Jee-zus, Paul, were you dead? It went on for ten minutes early this morning. It cut a three-mile wide path from Hollywood to Venice. The Governor has already declared a state of emergency and called in the National Guard. They're on the streets now."

Paul rubbed his eyes and slowly woke. His head throbbed and he couldn't focus his eyes. *Oh, God, I must have the world's worst hangover.* Slowly, Paul was able to make sense of what was going on. Earthquake. The Guard. "Why do you need me?"

"There's been another murder..."

"I'll be there as soon as I can."

Paul wrote down the location of the site where the victim was discovered. Then he put down the phone and rubbed his eyes. *How could I have missed an entire earthquake?* He never slept though one before. *Let's see, yesterday I went to the Baron's house and… damn!* Paul didn't remember anything after that. He had lost half a day. *What had happened? What had the Baron replied to my questions?*

Paul took off his suit. *How could I have fallen asleep in my clothes? I've never done that before either. Now I'll have to get my suit pressed again.* In the pocket on the inside of his coat was the note pad he had taken with him when he went to question the Baron. He took it out and as he looked at it his amazement at what he saw grew. His usual handwriting changed to circular doodles on the first page and continued to make meaningless doodles over five more pages.

Somehow the Baron had controlled me, perhaps hypnotized me! And Paul had lost half a day. *After I look into the latest murder scene I'll have to return and ask more questions of the Baron.*

Paul drove directly to the site of the murder. The evidence was the same as in the other murders. From a distance he could see how some trash cans, rocks, a bicycle and natural ground formations formed the "606" image. On the victim's thigh was the symbol from the *Necronomicon.* A Tarot card, the Nine of Cups, was discovered in her vagina.

Her head was missing.

Paul knew he would discover nothing new here, but he dutifully inspected the site while the body was tagged and bagged before transport to the morgue. From there he drove to the police station. As he drove he was shocked by all the damage to the streets and buildings caused by the quake. Some areas looked like they were a bombed-out war zone. People were camped in the streets and on sidewalks, tryiing to avoid any buildings that might fall during an aftershock. Twice he had to take side streets because the main streets had buckled and were impassable.

It suddenly dawned on him that he loved the city. It actually hurt to see the streets ravaged, the people in pain. *But L.A. would pull together. In spite of the politicians it always did. It pulled together after the Watts riots. It pulled together after the '92 riots. It will pull together after this, too.*

When he arrived at the station there were construction workers all over, skittering around like spiders in their webs, trying to clean up the mess and shore up weak sections of the walls and ceilings. The worst damage was in a room that flooded from a broken water pipe. He made his way to his office, crunching on broken glass as he went. Luckily, his office had been one of the least damaged, but the sound of power tools made work, and even thinking, difficult.

He looked around his desk to see if he had left any information from his missing day. He found nothing. An officer came in and dropped off a file. It contained some reports on the most recent murder. He tried to read the papers in the file, but the roar of the power tools made it impossible. He couldn't concentrate beyond a sentence or two. Finally, Paul put both palms over his ears and his elbows on the table. That helped, but not much. The sound was diminished, but everything was vibrating.

Paul sighed and started reading. *Maybe something new will show up.* "AAAHHHHHHHRRRRRRRRRR," sang out a power saw. *Then again, maybe not.*

* * * * *

When Simon awoke, Allenda was still sleeping. He slipped out of the room and made his way to the master bathroom where he shaved and showered. As he dried himself off, he smelled freshly brewing coffee. He dressed in black slacks, a black turtle-neck tee-shirt and cotton kung-fu shoes, then went to the kitchen. Allenda had risen, washed her face and made the coffee. Simon had never seen such an intense look on her face—he had rarely seen such an intense look on *anyone's* face. She had placed the telephone in front of her.

"Should I start the telephone pyramid?" Allenda asked.

"Why?" he asked.

Allenda looked at Simon with a puzzled look on her face. "I saw him kill Eris, Simon. That's something I'll never forget. He probably killed Angelica, too. He has to be stopped. No cop is going to investigate based on what somebody saw during an astral trip as a bee. If we want justice, we have to get it. We have to stop Barton or Baron or whatever his real name is. We're probably the only ones with enough knowledge of magic to stop him. And we have to stop him before he can kill again."

Simon looked at her and considered his response. "And if I say, 'No, let's give all the information we have to the police and leave it for them to handle,' what will you do?"

She stared in his eyes. Simon could sense her resolve. "I'll start the pyramid, assemble the Warriors and lead them against the Baron myself."

Simon had no doubt she meant exactly what she said. Somehow, the events of the last two weeks had turned the young, insecure Allenda into a self-assured woman. *But I still don't know why Barton is doing this. I don't know what he has planned. He can't really be doing this Barra Edinnazu thing.And the Warriors aren't developed enough for a magical battle. They've not had enough practice.* And as she had reported, there were at least twice as many in Barton/Baron's group as there were Warriors. *I don't want to be responsible for the death of any more Warriors of the Light!*

Simon knew that Barton, egotist that he was, would not have trained his followers to think independently. They would only do what they were told. Simon, however, had taught the Warriors to think and act according to logic, knowledge and instinct. They had a chance *if* they had a leader to provide encouragement, guidance, wisdom and added courage. The Warriors looked to him for that. That might give them a chance, but it would still be easier and safer if the police could take care of it strictly on their own.

"Alli, how about this? You start the pyramid and have everyone meet here at 8:00 P.M. promptly. We'll form car pools and caravan to St. Lucy's church. But as soon as you get off the phone, I'll call my contact at the police department and see if they can wind this up before there is any further danger to the Warriors. Agreed?"

Allenda was already dialing. "Agreed," she said firmly.

* * * * *

"Lieutenant Christian?" Paul jerked in surprise when an officer tapped him on the shoulder. He hadn't heard the man walk up because he still had his hands over his ears. "You have a phone call," the officer said, miming holding a telephone receiver to his ear. Paul nodded, thanking him.

He picked up the phone but just heard mumbling. "You'll have to speak up, I can barely hear you over the noise in here."

"Paul, it's Simon Raven."

"Do you have anything more for me?"

"Yes. There was another killing. The name of the victim is Eris. I don't know her last name. She was beheaded. The card was the Nine of Cups."

Paul sat back in his chair. "How did you know?" he asked in surprise. "What with the quake, this hasn't been reported in the media."

"One of my people… uh… did a ritual. She traveled on the astral plane and saw it. There's more. Barton Oliver is calling himself The Baron. He's the one who committed the murders."

Paul's jaw dropped. "I just interviewed him yesterday at his home in Venice."

"You did? What did he say? What did he tell you?"

Paul paused before he revealed what happened. "I… I don't know," he admitted. "I've forgotten what he said and my notes are just meaningless doodles."

Clever, very clever. "He may have put a forgetfulness spell on you, Paul, or maybe he drugged you. He certainly controlled you. You probably don't remember anything after you met him. In fact, you probably don't remember events that took place long after you left being with him."

Paul took a long breath and exhaled noisily through pursed lips. "You're right. Yesterday, my questions, the quake—it's a total loss. I don't remember a thing."

"Paul, he has a secret tunnel between his house and the church next door. There is a room in the church that has a freezer. In the freezer are the missing body parts."

"I need a motive, Simon. Why did he commit the murders? Why did he collect those body parts? What's he going to use them for?"

Simon ignored the questions and continued to talk. "He's got about fifty followers. If you can get there soon they'll all be there, preparing for or performing a ritual. Stop them now and they won't be using the body parts for anything."

"What is he going to use the body parts for?"

Simon took a breath, considering what to say. "Paul, you'd never believe me. But if he's not stopped the number of murders will multiply over and over and over."

"What's he going to use the damn body parts for?"

There was a long silence. Paul sighed and finally accepted that Simon was not going to answer his question. *It must be more of that damned magical mumbo-jumbo. There may be nothing there, but this is the only real lead I've had.* "I'll get there with some officers as soon as I can. Thanks for your help."

* * * * *

"You want how many officers?" roared Captain Minelli.

"At least ten, preferably twenty," replied Paul. "Raven says we'll be going up against fifty people."

"And this is all because somebody went, what did you call it, 'astral travelling,' and you can't remember yesterday?"

"Yes."

"Paul, there've been days when I've been so drunk I can't remember what happened the night before."

"If you give me the officers, Raven thinks we can catch all the perps and stop further murders."

Minelli just looked at Paul in amazement. " 'Raven thinks?' Paul, *you're crazy!* We just had an earthquake. Everyone's on overtime. We don't have any officers to spare."

"Can I ask for volunteers?"

"*No, Christian!* If they can volunteer they can damn well do work helping out with problems caused by the quake."

"There's nobody who can be spared?"

"Let me get this straight. You have no proof except for some wacky story by a phony wizard. Is that right?" asked Minelli.

Paul gripped the top rung on the ladder back of a wooden chair and squeezed it to control his anger. He looked down at the floor and said, "Sir, I've been assigned to find a serial killer. Each woman in this case has been slaughtered. Each one has been missing body parts. This is the only lead I've had in almost two weeks. I think this Simon Raven may have something. I really need to do this."

Minelli looked at Paul from where he sat, then he looked up at the ceiling and sighed. "Okay, Paul. I'll tell you what I'll do. There's a big drug bust going down. We've been working on it for almost a year and the lead officers didn't want to let the quake stop the bust. There are seven plainclothes and six uniforms working on it. When they come back they should be off duty. You can have any who will volunteer. That's the best I can do, take it or leave it."

"Thanks, Captain. I'll take it. When will they be back?"

"They should be here around 8:30 P.M."

"But that's three hours from now."

"I'm sorry, Paul. It's the best I can do."

Paul turned away for a moment, slapping his right fist into his left palm. Then he took a deep breath and let it out loudly. "Okay," he said, resignedly. He turned back and faced his superior. "Tell me when they come in."

Minelli looked at Paul and saw how serious he was. "The second they come in, Paul. The second they come in."

* * * * *

Paul slammed the door to his office closed. Immediately, the phone rang. It was Alexander Gardner. "Paul," he said, "I think I've finally found some answers to what's going on. That symbol is not from *The Grimoire of Armadel.* It's from a book called the *Necronomicon.*

"Yes, I knew that."

"Really? How did you find out?"

"From a man named Raven. Simon Raven."

"Yes. Well, I'm sorry it took so long for me to get this information, but like most people who might investigate this I kept looking in the well-known but spurious version of the *Necronomicon.* Now I've done research in the genuine book and in Himelhoch's *History of Magic.*

"The symbol drawn on the victims' legs is that of a goddess or demoness known as Barra Edinnazu. She was worshiped as a goddess in a pre-Sumerian culture. So little is known about that culture we don't even know its name. The method of Her worship was monstrous, grotesque. The most important ritual of that worship occurred on the same night each year. On that night the high priest would take some of the most beautiful women in the area, kill them and sever those parts of the victims' bodies he considered to be the most beautiful. He would then take those parts, skin them and sew the skins together into a costume. The high priest would then stretch this obscene cloak over his own naked skin. The followers would then worship the high priest as if he were the actual goddess. Some authorities think followers of this bloody cult believed on this night the high priest would actually *become* the goddess. Curiously, wearing the skin of a young girl was also practiced halfway across the world by the ancient Aztecs.

"In Sumer, somewhere around three to five hundred years after the height of this unnamed culture, Barra Edinnazu was considered a demoness. The high priests of Sumer captured the high priest of Barra Edinnazu, tortured him for weeks, then slew him. They dug a pit 'ten-thousand feet deep,' a symbolic phrase meaning very, *very* deep—a bottomless pit. Some have conjectured it may have been some sort of dormant volcano or vertical shaft in the earth. Into this they threw the body of the high priest of Barra Edinnazu. It was felt She went with him into the pit. Anyway, this act marked the end of activity by the Barra Edinnazu cult. They also killed the remaining people of that culture, eveery many woman, and child. They wiped the worship of Barra Edinnazu off the face of the earth.

"According to the *Necronomicon*, however, She is not dead. It says She is 'eternally dreaming,' and after 'strange eons' even Her death will cease to stop Her return. At that time She will move through the earth, from 'ten-thousand feet deep' to the surface, in order to be with Her worshippers and manifest in a body made for Her. And then, from a massive, golden throne laced with jewels, She will begin to rule the world."

There was a pause while Paul, incredulous, took in what Alexander had told him. "Are you saying somebody is going to use the missing body parts to bring back an ancient demoness? There's no way I can believe that."

"I told you before, Paul, it doesn't matter what you or I believe. The people who are doing this believe it. It's those believers whom you have to stop.

"Oh, Paul, there's one other thing…"

"Yes..."

"You know that night when the pre-Sumerian culture worshiped Barra Edinnazu?"

"Yeah..."

"Well, it was on what anthropologists refer to as a 'solar festival.' It occurred each year near the same date on their calendar. It's similar to what Catholics call a 'movable feast.' When I compared it with astronomical books I discovered that their night of worship each year was on the Summer Solstice."

He paused to draw attention to his next statement. "This year, the Solstice falls on June 21st, Paul, June 21st."

Paul looked at the calendar on his desk. The large number on the page was 21. The month read "June." "Do you mean tonight?" asked Paul.

"Tonight," replied Alexander. "If there is a group which intends to do it, the ritual for the resurrection of the demoness Barra Edinnazu would be held... *tonight.*"

His mind racing, he put down the receiver without saying goodbye. *I don't care about any ritual. I don't believe in this magical stuff anyway. But if I get there soon everyone involved will be there. I could round them all up and have the body parts as evidence.* He realized, though, the longer he waited the less likely it would be he could end this case tonight. He looked at the clock. It would still be two hours and forty-five minutes before he *might* get help.

He slammed his fist onto the top of his desk. Hard.

He didn't notice the pain.

* * * * *

Simon looked at the twenty milling people who had assembled in his yard. One Warrior could not be contacted, but all of the others had arrived. He held his hand up and the crowd quieted.

"Today is the Summer Solstice. Normally we would have had a ritual in celebration of this day. But events over the last two weeks have prevented this. As you know, Angelica was killed a week ago as part of a series of brutal murders. Last night, Allenda and I were doing some magical work on the astral plane. She discovered the murderer, but we were too late to save his latest victim…Eris is dead."

The assembled Warriors gasped. Alan Crawford's mouth hung open. He couldn't believe it.

Allenda stepped forward. She was dressed in a skin-tight leotard and a simple, elastic-waisted skirt. Her body, flabby and loose just weeks ago, was now firm and had a muscular sheen. Her posture was upright and proud. She held her shoulders back instead of hiding her figure by sagging them forward. Her posture was one of strength and an assured self-image. "My fellow Warriors," she began in a strong, confident voice, "while I was on the astral I saw Eris killed. I know who did it. I have no doubt he killed Angelica, too. I want justice for the murder of my friends and fellow Warriors. I am going to fight the murderer now. I want us all to go together."

The Warriors moved closer, shouting encouragement. Simon interrupted their enthusiasm. "It's not all that simple. The killer is named Barton Mordus Oliver. He calls himself the Baron. You may have heard of him or even met him. He advertises heavily to get people to join his group, the Barony. As a result he has at least twice the number of people we have." The Warriors grew silent.

"Barton is an egomaniac. He would not teach his followers to be independent, thinking individuals. They will only do what he says. That is their shortcoming. If we stop Barton the members of his Barony will give up. If we work together, if you use everything I've taught you, we can defeat them."

The Warriors started nodding and murmuring. They shouted, "Let's go. Let's do it."

"Wait," said Simon, "there's more. We will not merely be fighting a bunch of people. Oliver is in the middle of a ritual to evoke a demoness from pre-Sumerian times known as Barra Edinnazu. She is so old that no books I have ever seen reveal Her powers. We'll be going in blind. If he's successful with his ritual, if She is there, it's possible that She could simply kill us with Her stare or with a momentary thought."

It was Alan who spoke up. "When there's an attack on one of the Warriors the attack is on a brother or sister. The attack is on us all. We must defend our brothers and sisters. How do we get there?" Simon looked at him. Alan looked different, directed, driven, confident. *I guess my talk with him had an effect.* The others, lured by Alan's speech, roared their agreement.

"Okay, one last thing. None of you have ever been in a magical battle before. I would not take you into this battle if I did not think we could all get out alive. We can do this *only* if you do exactly as I say. Is that agreed to?"

The voices of the group murmured their yeses. They formed a caravan of six cars and started out toward Venice.

Tonight, the Warriors of the Light would earn their name.

If they did not, they would be dead.

Chapter Seventeen

Twelfth Night

The sun just finished dipping into the Pacific Ocean when the Warriors started their caravan and moved west on Venice Boulevard. It got darker and darker as they passed large, intersecting streets of Grand View, Centinella, Rose, Lincoln. By the time they turned up Pacific and parked near St. Lucy's, dusk was almost gone. It would be dark in ten minutes.

It was not merely the setting sun which caused the darkness where they stood. Few as they were in this area, the streetlights, which automatically kindled at dusk, should have broken through the dark. But they barely illumined the strange blackness that appeared around the church and the house next to it. A disgustingly filthy, orangish-brown cloud had oozed from some unholy pit to spread its evil around those two buildings. The cloud roiled and seethed. It was slowly spreading in all directions. A lone dog that had not fled with the other pets walked near the church and Barton's house. As it neared the ugly cloud the hair along its spine stood at attention. Then it suddenly arched its back, barked, and ran away howling, as if terrified.

When the Warriors exited their cars, they immediately started hacking and coughing. The air, thick with smog, humidity and foul stink, was almost impossible to breathe. Simon signaled them to assemble near the car where he stood. They surrounded him and looked to him for guidance. He led them through some simple breathing exercises until the terrible air became familiar to their lungs and at least slightly easier to breathe. Soon they could concentrate and feel more calm. Then he led them in a visualization of the ritual of the Rose Cross, linking themselves with the spiritual light of God.

"In your mind's eye, I want you to visualize at our east an enormous cross," Simon instructed. "There is a circle, the rose, around the junction of the vertical and horizontal bars. The cross is gold and the rose is red. Together, now, let us seal and empower the rose cross by chanting the Pentagrammaton."

"*Yeh-hahsh-oo-ah!*" the group sang. The gold and red image shimmered into visible appearance. They repeated the formulations of rose crosses at the west, north and south, and then half-way between each of these directions. Finally, they visualized rose crosses above and below them.

The performance of this ritual had two effects. First, it formed individual spheres of cleanliness around each of them, making it even easier to breathe. The second effect was explained to them by their teacher. "The rose crosses have surrounded your auras, giving each of you a type of invisibility. If somebody is looking for you they will discover you. But if there are people who are not specifically on the lookout for you your presence will be ignored." Simon hoped this would help in the invasion of Barton's territory which was to come.

In her astral/bee form Allenda had seen the main room of the church was prepared for the ritual. Barton will like the idea of using an old church for his rite, so I'm sure the ritual for the resurrection of Barra Edinnazu will take place there. Simon determined that with their semi-invisibility it would be safe to split the warriors into three groups. He would take five people into Barton's house and go through the tunnel that led to the church. Allenda would come with him because he would need her to guide them. The rest would form two groups. B-team would enter the front of the church and C-team would enter through the rear.

"I want to lead B-team," said Alan. Simon looked at him and saw a face carved with anger and determination, yet he was under total self-control. Simon nodded, and Alan picked the people to go with him. As a leader for C team, Simon asked Dominique Jef'ara if she would do it. Domi was a tall, Black woman who said little. She was also a weight lifter and probably the strongest member of the Warriors. If a physical fight developed Simon wanted her to be a back up. She knew why she had been chosen and nodded her assent. The remaining Warriors surrounded Domi. Simon instructed B and C teams to wait until they heard a commotion and the word, "now" repeated three times. Then they were to use tire irons taken from the cars they caravanned in to break into the church.

"When you break in, focus on Barton," Simon instructed. "I haven't seen him in years, but Allenda tells me he will be the biggest person in the place. He is huge and muscular. He will also be giving the orders. Don't try to attack him individually; work together. Good luck to you all. Now take your positions and watch out for guards. If they must be taken out do it as silently as you can. We don't want to warn the rest of the Barony we are here."

The three teams went to their assignments. Simon and his people went to the front door of Barton's house. He figured the easiest way to enter a place was in an unexpected manner, so he spread out his team on either side of the door and knocked loudly.

After a few moments steps were heard and a young man opened the door. "Can I help you?" he asked.

"Yes," replied an innocent-faced Simon. "I represent the Wesuck vacuum cleaner company and I would like to give you the opportunity of a lifetime! I want to talk with you about our wonderful, revolutionary, time-saving machine."

"Sorry, not interested," replied the man. He started to close the door.

"Ah," said Simon, "but let me tell you about some of our features." He took a step across the threshold to get closer to the man who was the door's guard. "We have the most powerful suction available..." Simon suddenly brought his right knee up into the crotch of the young man. The guard sucked in a huge gasp of air as he buckled forward, his eyes crossed in pain. Simon grabbed the man's hair and used it to slam the guard's head into the knee Simon had just used. The man crumpled to the floor, unmoving.

Simon looked around and saw the room was empty. *I guess I'm not the only one who's overconfident. But why would Barton not have more protection for a ritual he considers so important? Something else is going on here. He must have some other traps set up.* He waved the rest of A-team in, telling them to hug the walls.

Simon turned to Allenda. "Where's the entrance to the tunnel?" he asked.

"Uh... I don't know," she responded, with a half-smile, half-grimace on her face.

"*What?*"

"Well, on the astral plane things just happen. Besides, I came in from another direction. Wait a second, I remember it was in a large ritual room. When we find that room we should be able to find the door."

Simon's team slowly walked across the entry and through the door into the next room. Here was Barton's magical den and orgy room. The only exit to the room, other than the way they came, was through a hall. They quietly moved down the hall, carefully checking the doors on the sides of the hall as they went. The unlocked doors led to a bathroom, a spare bedroom, the library, a storage room, and a room that looked like a dungeon. The sight of it produced gasps from some of the Warriors. At the end of the hall was a door which had stairs leading down. Simon and his team slowly moved down the dimly-lit stairway. At the bottom was a large room. Allenda recognized it immediately.

"This is the room," whispered Allenda, with cold anger in her voice. "He killed Eris in here."

No other door was evident, so Simon pointed to his team of Warriors and they spread out in search of an exit. They examined the walls, feeling for trip levers and moveable panels. Finally, on the wall most distant from the church, a lever on the side of a bookcase was discovered. When moved, a section of the floor slid to the side. Although dark, Simon could make out that there were stairs leading down. In the distance he could just see flickering shadows, probably cast by a candle or a torch. Something was down there.

"Let's go," said Simon. But as he looked around at the Warriors he could sense their fear and see it in their worried expressions. He sat at the edge of the stairs and signalled them to come around him. They huddled in a small circle. "Look," he told them, "I'm not going to minimize the situation. There is danger ahead. But we have the element of surprise on our side. We have our training on our side. And Barton has become something terrible, a monster. He's killed again and again. He killed Angelica. He killed Eris. If we don't do something he will kill again. I have to do this, but you don't. Any of you should feel free to leave the way we came. Nothing will be said against you by any of the Warriors. Those who want to avenge the death of our fellow warriors and stop this madness should follow me." Simon slowly walked down the stairs. The A-team looked at each other. Simon could sense their conflicted emotions and their fear.

It was Allenda who broke the impasse. "We all know what we have to do," she said. "It's time for the Warriors to get to work." She started down the stairs. One by one the others followed into the unknown.

The stairs ended in a wide, well-formed tunnel. It was the same passageway through which Allenda had flown before. In the dim light they felt their way along the damp walls. Slowly they moved under the house and across the distance between Barton's home and the church. At the end of the tunnel was the torch which provided their flickering light. Here, too, was another set of stairs. This time Simon led the way up.

At the top of the stairs was a closed panel. Simon felt around until he discovered a button like one used for a doorbell. He pressed it and the panel that blocked their ascent silently slid to the side. Above was total darkness.

Simon and his Warriors quietly made their way up. It was Allenda who sensed something was wrong. "Wait," she said in a whisper. "The main room with the altar is just a few feet ahead. If the Barony is out there..."

It was too late. The lights suddenly came on and and at least twenty members of the Barony swarmed around the invading Warriors. Outnumbered four to one, surrender was the only option.

They were led to a wall where they were forced to kneel with their hands on the back of their necks, fingers interlaced. The hard surface was painfully uncomfortable on their knees. The people in the room, at least forty or fifty of them, said nothing. The quiet was eerie. Then they divided to make way for their leader.

For a moment, all that could be heard was the clopp-clopp of Barton's hard-soled shoes. The huge, robed figure approached, then threw back the robe's hood. "Hello, Simon," said the Baron, Barton Mordus Oliver, with a leer of satisfaction in his voice. "It was so good of you to come."

* * * * *

Paul looked at the six men and three women who stood in front of him. They all were exhausted. Each had already put in a grueling, twelve-hour day. They dealt with the effects of the quake and made a dangerous drug bust. Four of the officers Minelli had offered were so tired they said they would not be of any value on the raid Paul was planning. Paul looked at them and had to agree. He was lucky to get the remaining nine.

Only he and Minelli knew everything about this case. This had been to prevent leaks to the media. Paul explained the situation to the officers: "A weird cult has been committing the serial murders you've heard about. We know where they are. Tonight they're all together and we're going to capture them. Although they may have sharp knives, we have no reason to assume they have guns. Further, although they may number forty or fifty, we think that, as with all such cults, once we get their leader, they'll give themselves up. The leader's name is Barton Mordus Oliver, A.K.A. 'The Baron.' He is tall, bull-like and wears an eye-patch with a ruby in it.

"The site is in Venice, but since the victims of the murders show up in Hollywood, law enforcement in Venice has given us jurisdiction in this case. There are two buildings we will have to secure. One is at 117 Pacific. The other, adjacent to the first, is an abandoned church named St. Lucy's which we have reason to believe is connected to the structure at 117 by an illegal underground tunnel. Due to the small size of our numbers, officers Thomas and Clintock will secure the rear exits. Officers Langwell, Jordan, Clark and Prince will enter the structure at 117. Clark will be in charge. The rest of us will enter the church. I will be in charge. Thomas, Clintock, Clark and myself will be issued two-way radios.

"There are three of you who will be assigned wagons to pick up arrestees. The rest of us will ride over in two vehicles. It is now 8:20 P.M. We will assemble in the parking lot at 8:30 and caravan over. Any questions?"

There were no questions from the officers, so they prepared for the invasion.

* * * * *

Simon couldn't believe it. *Once again I've been so overconfident I've let myself fall into a trap. After all the times I've beaten Barton but let him break even, I made one of the worst possible mistakes anyone could make: I under-*

estimated my enemy. Simon glared at the big man towering over him. *Now I'll have to wait for Barton to make a mistake before I can call in the rest of the Warriors—if he even makes a mistake.*

Barton looked down the row of kneeling captives. He then walked down the row and examined each as he went by. Barton shook his head and laughed. "Is this all you could muster, Simon?" he asked. He looked back at Simon and frowned. "No, even you wouldn't be that stupid. You must have more followers outside, waiting to come in. Well, no matter. My guards will take care of them. Besides, in a few minutes it will be too late to change what *will* happen."

He continued to walk down the row but stopped in front of Allenda. There was a puzzled look on his face. "You. Get up," he said to her. She didn't move. Barton glanced at two male members of the Barony. They went over to Allenda and lifted her to her feet. Barton slowly looked her over. His leer made Allenda feel nervous, then dirty.

"I've felt your aura before, haven't I? What's your name?" he asked, although it was obviously a command. Allenda was still silent. "Of course, of course. You were the astral bee that watched our sacrifice to Barra Edinnazu. And you thought we wouldn't notice you. How silly. And you're so gorgeous, too."

He held out his right hand and with a "thwap," another robed figure placed the handle of a sharp knife in his palm like a nurse placing a scalpel in the hand of a surgeon. He came up to Allenda and slowly ran the tip of the blade from her stomach, up between her breasts, and to her throat. The blade bit into her flesh and a drop of red appeared at the tip. "Now—what *is* your name?" he demanded once again.

"Her name is Allenda, Allenda Henley," said Simon.

"Why thank you, Simon," replied Barton. "Allenda, eh? That's a beautiful name. Let's see if you have a body to match." He moved the tip of the blade to the top of her leotard. He tucked it inside and cut the neckline. Then he slowly brought the blade down, severing the material, until he came to the top of her skirt. He nodded to the men holding her and they pulled the material back, revealing Allenda totally from the waist up.

Allenda stared with venom at Barton. Just weeks ago she would have tried to hide her nakedness from these strangers. Now all that mattered was that this man, whom she had witnessed killing her friend just hours ago, not see any weakness in her. *Barton may be in control, but I have the power.*

"What spirit!" said Barton, admiringly. "Simon, you have picked this woman well. She should be honored. Tina," he called loudly. "Come here please."

Tina Drabeck, also dressed in a black robe, came forward. Her eyes had a glazed, faraway look to them. She was obviously drugged. "Yes Baron?" she asked.

"Take this dagger and hold it against Allenda's stomach." She took the dagger and put the tip in Allenda's navel. Allenda refused to flinch.

"I'm sorry, Tina, I was unclear. What I meant was for you to put the dagger in your mouth—hold it between your teeth—and press the sharp edge of it against Allenda's stomach." Tina took the blade in her mouth as she had seen them do in the movies. She bent over and placed the edge against Allenda's midsection.

"Excellent, Tina. Now Allenda, this is in honor of your pride and spirit. He lifted Tina's robe, revealing her bare derrière. Then he lifted his own robe and slapped his flacid manhood against the top of her buttocks. He started to move back and forth. Tina reached under herself to caress him, and spread her legs in preparation for his entry. Allenda refused to watch, and instead looked at Barton's face with anger and disgust.

Barton's rubbing action along with Tina's fingers had given him an erection and he entered the young woman. With his first thrust Tina grunted—not prepared for either the size or power of Barton's thrust moved forward. A thread of red appeared around the blade's edge. Allenda still refused to acknowledge that anything was happening. Only a slight twitch of her lip and shoulders showed her pain from the blade's kiss.

Barton continued to look at Allenda. Allenda stared back. Barton tried to get her attention by moving faster and with more exaggerated strokes. Tina was beginning to writhe and moan. As she did, the blade moved around against Allenda's skin. Allenda, feeling the bite of the blade, took some slow, deep breaths so that she could ignore the pain. Finally, she simply disregarded what was going on in front of her and looked away, a bored look on her face.

Her indifference to him infuriated Barton. He pulled out of Tina and re-entered her in another place, millimeters from where he had been. Tina was unprepared for this new attack. Her eyes opened wide from shock and pain and she moved forward and to the side. The result was a longer, deeper slice into Allenda's belly. Allenda buckled forward in pain, but swiftly regained her position. Again she looked away in boredom.

Simon struggled to rise and grabbed at one of the men holding Allenda. Barton nodded and two men grabbed Simon and pushed him back to the floor. He could really do nothing but watch and wait for any error Barton might make.

Barton grabbed Tina and pulled her toward him as his assault on her anus and bowels reached a climax. He made guttural sounds as he exploded. When he was finished he wiped himself clean on the hem of Tina's robe and told her to sit where she was. She folded her legs and followed Barton's command.

Barton's attention returned to the partially-clad woman standing before him. He looked at Allenda and said with mock concern, "You're bleeding." Still looking at Barton she shrugged off one of the men holding her and rubbed two fingers across the cut. She could tell that although it was wide, it was not very deep. She raised her fingers to her lips and licked the blood off of them.

"Ms. Henley, you are incredible. I stand in awe of your power," he said with a bow. "Please, kneel again with your friends." The two men holding her pushed her to the floor. "Simon, my old school chum, come with me."

* * * * *

Alan and the B-Team hugged the side wall of St. Lucy's church. He peered around the front of the church and saw two men walking around. *Guards.*

Alan pulled back and huddled with the rest of the members of the B-Team. "There are two guards walking around. Any suggestions on how to deal with them?"

"Yeah," said Nina Melchior. She was young, in her mid-twenties, and a fairly new Warrior. "We outnumber them. Let's just overpower them." The others nodded in agreement.

They're wrong, but how do I tell them and get them to agree with me without getting them mad at me? Alan thought quickly as he looked at their faces. "No," he said, "I don't think so. Nina, you're right in saying we have the advantage of numbers." Nina smiled at being told in front of the others she was correct. "But we need to keep our size a secret from both the guards and anybody who might be guarding on the inside. I think we can take care of the guards fairly easily, too. When the two guards come after me grab them and gag them."

"How are you going to get them to chase you?" Nina asked.

Alan smiled and picked up a couple of rocks. "No problem! Just watch."

Alan calmly started to whistle and walked around the corner of the church. "Hey bozos," he called to the guards. "Did you have plastic surgery or were you born that ugly?"

The guards looked at each other and ignored him.

"When they did the plastic surgery did they cut off your balls, too?" One of the guards started toward Alan with a gleam in his eyes. The second guard stopped him and whispered something to the first guard. The first guard, obviously quicker to anger than the second, continued to glare at Alan.

The leader of the B-Team threw a rock at them but missed. Alan threw the other rock and hit the second guard in the forehead. It made an audible "clunk," and the guard buckled over in pain. In order to anger them more Alan threw back his head and laughed.

The second guard straightened up and said, "Alright, let's get him." They ran after Alan who turned around and started to run away from them.

As Nina heard the guards near the corner of the church she threw herself flat on the ground in front of the two men. Unable to stop, they tripped over her prone body. The rest of the B-Team swarmed over the two guards.

When Alan came back to the crowd the guards were held in place and hands were over their mouths. "We have nothing to gag or tie them with," someone said.

"No problem," Alan said. "I'll just kill them with my bare hands." He went up to one of the guards and dug his thumbs into both sides of the man's neck. In a few seconds the guard started to wobble and went limp. The second guard, who had watched the killing, fainted dead away.

Alan sat down on the grass and laughed. The others stared at him in shock. "How can you laugh when you just killed a man in cold blood?" Nina asked.

"No. No," he gasped, trying to regain his breath from the laughter. "I didn't kill anyone. I just cut off the blood supply to his brain until he passed out. He'll be okay when he wakes up. But did you see that second guy pass out?" He started laughing again.

The rest of the B-Team started laughing, quietly, too. Nina held out her hand and Alan took it, getting up off the ground. "You did real good, Alan," she said, looking him in the eyes.

"So did you, Nina. I liked your football block." He looked back at her until she blushed and looked down. They held hands a little longer and Alan finally felt nervous and let her hand go.

"This isn't over yet," Alan told his team. "Let's move up to the porch and get ready to break in. Tonight the Warriors of the Light show what their name means." The B-Team moved near the front door of the church and waited.

We're all changing. I never knew I could do this. Suddenly Nina was next to him. She looked up at him. He saw trust in her eyes. *Is there something more, there, too?*

"Please," Nina whispered, "I feel safer next to you. May I stand here?" She quickly lowered her eyes, surprised at her own assertiveness.

Alan wanted to put his arm around her. Then he thought of Eris and his pain and loss returned. Still, the look in her eyes brought out feelings in him Eris had never caused. *Was I merely infatuated with Eris and not really in love with her?* Alan felt confused, his emotions tossed on a turbulent sea. *This is all happening too quickly; too soon. Still, Nina needs me…*

Alan said nothing. He tentatively put his hand on Nina's shoulder, then, protectively, let it rest there. She sighed and leaned her head against him.

* * * * *

Two men helped Simon rise, but he stayed where he was. "Simon, let me show you power. Tina, please stand." She did so. "Now take the dagger and cut off your robe." She took the knife and brought it to her throat. The young woman inserted the knife between the neckline of the robe and her skin. Then she bunched the fabric and cut the material in a line down to the hem. She shrugged her shoulders and the material fell off of her, leaving her naked.

"Now, give pleasure to those five men of the Barony," Barton told her. "You men may do as you will with her." She happily went off and joined the men whom Barton pointed to. Immediately they became a tangle of genitals and hands, mouths and moans.

"You see, Simon, my word is their command." Simon, following Allenda's example, said nothing.

"I know that you, of all the people here tonight, can appreciate what I am going to do, so let me show you something." Pushed by the same two men, Simon "followed" Barton to the large table that Allenda had seen when she travelled to the site as a bee. Simon reared back, revolted to see the body parts taken from the murdered women lying on the table. They were placed in the form of a person, a ghastly blue Frankenstein's monster that was still dead and in pieces. The head that had once been Eris' looked out with nothing in its soul, a grizzly reminder of what happened hours ago.

"Soon," said Barton quietly, "this body will be that of the goddess Barra Edinnazu."

"Uh Barton…"

"I am the *Baron,* Simon!"

"Alright, *Baron.* I hate to tell you this, but that body is dead. It's in pieces."

"Fool! Fool! You're such a fool, Simon. You've always been a fool. Of course it's pieces. Each piece is the most beautiful part of the woman from which it came. Together, they make the ideal womanly form. This will be the holy temple, the body for Barra Edinnazu."

"But why…?"

"Ahhh. Finally you're asking the important question. Simon, our world is a mess. Wars, crime, pollution, over-population, starvation and disease are rampant. Governments won't solve these problems. Individuals don't have the power to solve these problems. If the world is to be saved it must be saved in spite of itself.

"Rome became great due to the power wielded by individual leaders, the Caesars. The Roman Catholic Church became great because of the power wielded by individual leaders, the Popes. Germany became powerful under

Hitler, the Soviet Union under Stalin and China under Mao. Even the tiny island of Cuba under Castro was able to terrify the U.S. I determined that if the world is to be saved we need a powerful leader. For years I did research to discover an entity powerful enough to save the world. Finally, I found Her.

"Barra Edinnazu is a goddess from before Sumer. Her powers are unimaginable. Her priest feared Her and would not give Her an independent body, only his own with a beautiful skin cloak stripped from human sacrifices. She and Her priest, linked by ritual, were captured and thrown into a pit by Sumerian priests. But She came through the earth at our call. Yesterday She made the final journey across L.A.

"Now, She will have her own body and not be dependent on someone wearing a skin. Now, She can reign supreme. Through Her powers She will be able to take over this area. She will put us, Her faithful, at the head of a new government. With her behind us we will be able to control Southern California, then the whole state. From there we can take over the Southwest and then the entire country. With America's nuclear weapons Barra Edinnazu will control the world.

"The world will finally become the paradise every human has hoped and prayed for. Now those hopes and prayers will be answered. Barra Edinnazu, as the Earth's ultimate leader and goddess, will answer those prayers. We, Her faithful servants, will be Her first rank. I will be their leader. We will rid the world of pollution, crime, war and starvation."

"It won't work, Barton or Baron or whatever you want to call yourself," said Simon. "Utopias never work. Besides, Barra Edinnazu isn't a goddess, she's a demoness. The Sumerians were right to kill Her and Her priest and bury them in a bottomless pit. If you give Her a separate body there'll be nothing to stop Her or control Her. You'll make Her invincible. She'll do whatever She wants and have no need for you or your followers."

"Ridiculous!" said Barton, but there was a tiny hint of questioning in his voice.

Simon's jaw dropped as he understood the truth. "You don't even realize what's happening, do you?" he said. "You're not telling the truth to the Barony or even to yourself. The real reason you killed Angelica and Eris, out of all the people in the world, is not because you needed them for Barra Edinnazu. You sensed they were related to me and you wanted revenge for my humiliation of you 20 years ago. The real reason you attacked me and the Warriors was simply for your own petty revenge.

"The Barony doesn't follow you, they fear you. People follow leaders they think care about them and you've never cared about others. You only want power for yourself, the power you think Barra Edinnazu will give you. You don't care about humanity, you just want power. You just want to control. You just want to rule."

"That's not true!" Barton yelled angrily. "The only reason we'll rule is because we're faithful to Barra Edinnazu. We want to end world problems. We want to..." Barton suddenly felt confused. Triggered by Simon's words and his own inner demons Barton's instinctive objectivity, buried for years, came to the surface. *Have I mistaken my own intentions? In a dream Barra Edinnazu showed me how to prepare and perform the rites for her resurrection, and in return She offered me unlimited power to achieve my goals. But have I only lusted for that power?*

For a second Simon thought he saw turmoil in Barton's eye. But just as quickly, it faded. *No. Raven's wrong! It's not true. Simon's just trying to confuse me.* He cleared his throat and although shaken he tried to resume his previous demeanor. "Bring Tina here," he said loudly.

Tina had always been a sexual athlete. Her pleasuring of others tonight had resulted in her own pleasure. Now, a glow of ecstasy hung about her. She was covered with the sweat of pleasure mixed with the fluids of ecstasy. Her eyes were still glazed from drugs and the sex had only increased her trance. The five men who were with her stopped their activities and took her with them over to the table near Barton and Simon. "Hold her above the table," ordered Barton. Four of the men took either an arm or a leg and lifted her so that she was resting horizontally in the air above the gore on the table. Tina, drunk on drugs and sex, giggled.

"Now, let the ritual begin." The remaining members of the Barony, those who were not holding Tina or guarding Simon and the Warriors, started circling the table. They began a slow chant: "Barra Edinnazu. Barra Edinnazu." The chant started to get louder and the circling became faster. Soon the chant became a scream and the circling became frenzied. Faster and faster they went. Louder and louder went the cries. "Barra Edinnazu! Barra Edinnazu!"

"Can you feel it, Simon?" shouted Barton over the rising din. "The energy is everywhere. Now I will mix it with the sexual energy raised by our Lady Tina."

Tina had slowly roused from her sex and drug-induced haze and saw the gore below her. She started to squirm and struggle, her wide-eyed face a picture of revulsion and horror. Simon thought Barton was going to use his power of visualization to direct the magical energy from the circling crowd through the sexually charged body of Tina and into the dead flesh below her.

Simon was wrong.

Barton pulled a long knife from under his robe. Tina saw the knife and uttered an inhuman-sounding scream of terror. Simon fought against his captors and yelled, "Noooo!"

It was almost like a dance, both graceful and grotesque. Barton pushed the sharp blade into Tina's vulva, and with a smooth, slicing motion brought it up to her neck. Tina's hysterical shrieks and screams of pain faded into a gurgle as blood filled her throat and poured from her mouth. The gore on the table was showered with fresh blood and organs from above, leaving a steaming mess on the unholy altar. The men holding her arms and legs fought Tina's squirming until her eyes went lifeless and her struggling ceased. With a few more slices Barton freed the entrails from the lifeless shell of a corpse. Then the men holding what was left of Tina took her hollowed body to a corner of the room and, like a piece of useless garbage, unceremoniously discarded it.

Still, the people circled. "Barra Edinnazu!" they cried in a frenzy. "Barra Edinnazu!"

Chapter Eighteen

The Night of Barra Edinnazu

The crowd roared in approval. Simon stared, unbelieving, at the brutal scene. "Now!" he yelled, and the war began.

The guards who were supposed to be watching the Warriors in the room were distracte by the mad and bloody ritual going on. The Warriors leapt up to the surprise of their watchers and started yelling, "Now! Now! Now!" as they moved toward Barton.

Members of the Barony were at first surprised by the attack, but Barton yelled, "Jump them! Overpower them!" Immediately a dozen men attacked the Warriors who had come in with Simon. The Warriors were quickly outnumbered and flattened to the floor.

But the victors of the battle didn't know what to do next. Simon had shaken free from the men holding him and jumped Barton, tightening his fingers around the Baron's bull neck. Unprepared for the physical attack, the jump forced Barton several steps back. But he ended up just staring at his attacker. The muscles on his neck were so thick and powerful Simon's strong grip virtually had no effect.

Cracking noises sounded everywhere. Upon hearing the "Now! Now! Now!" signal, the two other teams of Warriors broke into the rite. Suddenly, the Warriors were everywhere, fighting and punching, making their way toward Barton. Members of the Barony, having a leader who was involved with an attacker, just milled around. They didn't know what to do. Against enormous odds, the Warriors were winning.

Barton finally shrugged Simon off as if his attacker was insignificant. "Clever, Simon, clever," he said. Barton strode to a side wall and yelled, "Barony, surround me!" Quickly, the many members of the Barony formed a semicircle, a human wall, to protect their leader from the Warriors.

Simon called out at his Warriors. "Use psychic energy. Get Barton!"

The battle changed from physical to psychical. The Warriors generated small balls of magical energy and threw them at the Barony. Quickly the air was filled with fist-sized spheres of magical power. The room lit up with an eerie, suffused glow. Each time a sphere struck a Barony member a crackling of energy, like sound effects from an old monster movie, could be heard. Then the person who was struck fell senseless to the floor for several minutes. Coupled with the screams of the people in the room, the fighters were surrounded by an atonal din.

The Warriors, now with some experience in the use of magical energy, were winning once again. Members of the Barony dropped senseless, their bodies littering the floor. The Warriors took their losses, too, but they were not nearly as severe as those of the Barony.

Bodies littered the floor around Domi. She had not yet begun to use psychic energy; she hadn't needed to. Domi frequently sparred with other fighters in the gym, but usually needed to pull her punches. Now she was enjoying beating on the Barony. Her eyes had a glazed look on them, her body filled with battle lust. Alan and Nina were fighting side-by-side. Together they shot out balls of psychic energy at their ebemies who toppled in front of them. "We're doing it!" shouted Nina. "We're winning!"

Simon fought his way through the scene on an unstoppable path back to Barton. He raised his right hand and a blue sphere, dripping sparkling energy, appeared. Just as he was about to attack Barton, his target mounted a counterattack. Barton used both hands to project a disk of reddish flame several feet in front of him. Simon threw his magical hand grenade, but when it hit the red, coruscating shield, both energy forms dissolved in a crackling of purple light.

Barton moved forward, shooting reddish energy out through his hands at Simon. The energy crackled around Simon who had his mind set on attacking Barton and was not prepared for a defense. Barton's crackling energy blinded him, confused him, and for a second Simon couldn't think straight. A second was all Barton needed, and by the time Simon's head cleared Barton was on him, punching, flailing, attacking.

Barton's size overwhelmed his foe. A powerful right cross to Simon's jaw resulted in a spout of blood from his mouth. "Fool!" Barton said toward the barely conscious Simon. "You won't even have a chance to see Her resurrection." Simon fell, lifeless, to the floor.

* * * * *

Through it all, Allenda simply stood there. She had never been in a fight, let alone an all-out war. Everything that had happened simply left her in a daze. She saw that her earlier false bravado had been meaningless.

The Warriors had been holding their own against the Barony, but once Simon fell, they began to retreat. Five members of the Barony overwhelmed Domi and Alan and Nina had been separated. Individually they were not able to fight effectively and Nina was soon unconscious on the floor. Alan jumped over two bodies to protect the fallen Nina. Three members of the Barony closed in on him. He laughed and jumped at the trio. In moments it would be over for him and the Warriors.

And then it happened. The enormity of the Warriors losing along with the fall of Simon was too much for Allenda. Something snapped. Something changed. Magical power surged through her. She started to walk slowly, directly toward Barton.

At first her body began to glow with a blue aura. Then she was covered in a shimmering, electric-blue flame. Red energy bolts from the Barony hit her but dissolved before they had any effect. Step-by-step she walked slowly toward Barton, her fixed eyes intently staring under furrowed brows. Barony members jumped at the bare-breasted woman, only to fall, shivering in a *grand mal* seizure near her feet. Finally, they just separated as she approached Barton.

Her face set and power crackling all around her, she looked at the huge man in front of her. "I knew Angelica. I knew Eris. *Simon was my friend!* Now, you're going down."

Barton laughed at the young woman in front of him. He carelessly threw a red energy bolt at her, expecting her to fall. It dissolved at the edge of her aura without her even making a motion. She kept coming at him.

He pointed his palms at Allenda. A beam of magical energy, powerful enough to fell an elephant, shot out of his hands straight at her. She raised her left hand and pulled the energy into her, ignoring the negative impact it should have had. Instead, it made her stronger. Now it was Allenda's turn to laugh at what she considered a feeble attack. Barton paled. She continued coming at him.

Barton took a deep breath and directed a huge flurry of red energy at Allenda. This time she merely waved her hand and it vanished before it got near her. *Would nothing stop this madwoman?*

"I told you," said Allenda. "I told you. Simon was my friend. You're going down." She put both hands by her waist, her fingertips down, fingers separated and slightly curved, and her palms forward. The blue energy increased around them.

Barton's eyes opened wide. He couldn't believe this woman could overpower him. *If magic doesn't work, physical strength will.* He roared like an attacking Viking in the throes of a berzerker rage and came at her. Allenda didn't waiver.

Just before he reached her, the power exploded out of her hands. It hit Barton on the chest and shoulders, lifting him six feet into the air and driving him back to the wall. He hit so hard he lost consciousness for a second. He slipped down the wall leaving a red smear behind him.

Allenda shrugged her shoulders and a beam of glittering, blue energy flew from her hands. The powerful beam of energy lifted the awakening Barton into the air and held him there. *This can't be happening. I have to defeat this stupid woman. I have to…* He couldn't think of a defense.

"Angelica was my friend," she shouted. "This is for her." Although ten feet from the floating Barton, she made a motion toward him with her right hand as if she were a tiger or lioness attacking her prey. Lines like claw marks opened on Barton's left cheek, spraying blood and muscle and revealing bone. Barton screamed in pain.

"Eris was my friend. This is for her." She repeated her action but with her left hand. It had the same result on his opposite cheek. The floating Barton screamed again. When he stopped, his eyes were almost lifeless. All of his fight was gone.

"Simon was my friend. *You wanted to be a big man. Be big!*"

Allenda held her hands out in front of her, shooting a different shade of blue energy at Barton. He started to spin in the air, his arms and legs flailing in helplessness and excruciating pain. His skin began to ripple, distorting his appearance. The rippling, as if mice were running under his skin, got more and more exaggerated. Soon, Barton was unrecognizable, looking more like a Macy's Thanksgiving Day Parade balloon than a human. His voice, a painful moan, rose into a high-pitched scream.

"*Be big!*" Allenda screamed. Suddenly, there was a loud "plop." What had once been the Baron, Barton Mordus Oliver exploded, covering the room in large splatters of blood and ripped pieces of skin, muscle and gore. The bones, each separated at their joints, sounded like dominoes as they dropped from the air and scattered all over the hard floor.

* * * * *

Silence filled the room. Everyone realized the battle, the magical war, was over. The threat of Barton and his Barony was finished. There would be no more murders. Members of the Barony who had fallen to the Warriors' attack slowly recovered and rose from the floor. Leaderless, they milled around. The Warriors helped their fallen comrades revive. Dominique walked with a limp and Alan helped revive Nina and get her back to her feet. Some of the Warriors moved near Allenda with questioning looks on their faces. Was she to be their new leader?

Allenda continued to look in the air, where she had destroyed Barton. She had made her decision and used her power. Eris was gone. Angelica was gone. Simon was gone, too. But she had ended the threat of Barton and his Barony. She also knew that she had achieved the goal of her training: *Now I can truly say I am a magician, a true Warrior of the Light.*

"Well done, Allenda," came the familiar voice from behind her.

Allenda whirled to see Simon standing, brushing himself off. She ran over and threw her arms around his neck, almost strangling him with her hug. "I thought you were dead," she cried.

"Nah. I've always been able to defeat Barton."

"Then how did he defeat you? Did you fake what happened?"

"Well," he said, rubbing his bruised chin, "I didn't *entirely* fake it." He spoke more loudly so that all of the Warriors could hear him. "My goal has always been to help each Warrior of the Light develop a strong self-image and become a powerful magician." He looked at Allenda. Pride shown in his eyes. "Tonight you realized your personal and magical power. Tonight you took a stand for what you believed in. Tonight you demonstrated you have the power to make your will a reality. Allenda, you *are* a magician."

Allenda looked at Simon and smiled slightly. He did not have to tell her she was a magician, she already knew it. She also realized by becoming a magician she had accepted a terrible burden. Others may talk about it, but she knew from now on she was responsible for every action she made, even the destruction of Barton. She also knew that destroying Barton was something she had to do, no matter the consequences.

"Alan, too," said Nina.

"What?" asked Simon, turning to seek the source of the voice.

Alan smiled uncomfortably as Nina recounted his exploits. Simon looked at him with a slight smile on his face. *More has been accomplished here tonight than I thought.*

The other Warriors came up to Allenda and Alan, some in awe, and congratulated them. Nina hung close to Alan. One of the Warriors gave a jacket to Allenda so she could cover her breasts. She left it hanging open.

Simon looked around to make sure all the Warriors were together. "It's time to go," he said.

They started to walk out in silence. All that could be heard was their feet moving against the floor. The members of the Barony stayed near the table/altar that remained covered with gore.

As the Warriors neared the door, a sound like the electric spark of a Jacob's Ladder came from the table. They turned and looked. Blue, white and red flashes, like technicolor lightning, shot through the air from the table. Then the ground began to quiver and shake, as if vomiting up something poisonous. People screamed and fell to the floor.

Barra Edinnazu was no longer coming.

She was here.

* * * * *

When Paul and his officers arrived, they could see the door to the church had been broken down. Paul called out to the officers, changing plans. "Thomas and Clintock go in through the rear of the church.

Everyone else, let's go through the front door." As they approached, lights of red, blue and white started shooting like rockets through the church. They broke holes through the boarded-up windows and like searing comets burst through the shingled roof, sending boards flying 30 feet into the air. The officers stood, looking at the flashes of colored light that lit up the muck-enshrouded sky. The bottom of the church's steeple burst into fire. Like a Titan missile, the flaming spire rose about ten feet into the air. Just as quickly it collapsed and fell to the roof, shattering and sending pieces of emberous wood in all directions, eventually falling off the angled roof and showering the ground below.

Then the ground began to shake.

Inside the church, everyone stared at what was happening on the table. The pieces of the murder victims started to wiggle and squirm as if each had a life of its own. They moved together. When they met, a blinding light exploded at the juncture. When the light faded, the pieces of bodies were joined. No scars could be seen. Barra Edinnazu was preparing a perfect body to be Her body.

The building began to groan as the ground continued to shake. A large timber broke away from the ceiling, smashing two members of the Barony as it landed. Smoke began to fill the church as more fires erupted in the structure.

It only took a few moments for the action on the table/altar to be finished. The shaking stopped.

Paul and the officers came in, guns drawn and pointed out in front of them. An unearthly quiet hung over the room with only the crackling of burning wood paneling breaking the silence. As they watched in awe, the parts on the table, now conjoined, levitated horizontally into the air. Paul, gape-mouthed, pointed his weapon straight up and held up his free hand. The other officers, following his lead, moved their guns from the ready stance to a safety position of pointing straight up or down. Paul and his officers watched the transpiring events. They knew what was happening here was out of their league.

Barra Edinnazu's naked body, still covered with the gore of Tina and Barton, sharply pivoted into an upright position. Her head moved stiffly, then opened its eyes for the first time, looking at those around her. She looked down at her new body. An unearthly voice, a voice not meant to come through human vocal cords exulted, "Free from my imprisonment at last!" She stretched her body and smiled, however there was no joy in her eyes or facial expression. "Barra Edinnazu is satisfied with this body. She thanks those who brought her here. Whoever would worship Barra Edinnazu may now kneel and join me. As one we will take over this world."

My God! She can't mean it. "Out! Out!" he yelled at the Warriors. As they moved toward the door, Simon saw Paul and his officers. "Get out, Paul. Hurry!"

Paul signaled his officers to leave, but moved slowly himself so he could watch what was happening. As if in an hypnotic trance instead of leaving he stood where he was. The officers started to leave but, like Paul, stayed to watch.

The leaderless members of the Barony were now more than willing to follow a "goddess" who offered them power. First one kneeled, then another. Soon they all were kneeling. None of them realized the impact of the demoness' statement as had Simon.

Barra Edinnazu was not human. Mere things like life and death were meaningless to Her. She was beyond comprehending each human had a separate consciousness, life and existence; nor did She care. All that mattered was each body had energy. She had used most of Her own energy to move through the earth, and enliven and inhabit the body which had been prepared for Her. To Her, humans had no value other than to supply Her need for energy. She felt no remorse or passion in taking it. She merely absorbed what She felt She was entitled to.

The demoness' eyes glowed purple. A beam of light flashed out from them and struck one of the kneeling worshippers. He flew up into the air, held aloft by the beam of energy. Screaming, he kicked his arms and legs wildly. *Why is he fighting joining with me?* Then he just stopped moving and hung there. His body crumpled up and shrank in on itself. Every bit of energy and fluid had been sucked from it and the body looked like a dried-out apple cut into a caricature of its former owner. Worthless to Her now, Barra Edinnazu released the body and let the lifeless, empty husk fall to the ground. Barra Edinnazu sighed as one might sigh after eating a delicious meal.

The beam shot out from Her eyes again and hit a kneeling woman. The result was the same. Before the members of the Barony realized what had happened, five dried-up bodies were on the ground. The people who were kneeling started to rise, screaming, but more and more beams shot out. More and more bodies dropped to the floor.

Paul screamed, "Shoot that thing!" The officers raised their weapons and fired at the floating figure. Dozens of shots struck Her body, but the volley of bullets had no effect on the demoness. Most of the bullets missed or passed through Her. She caused the bullets that remained in Her patchwork body to rise to Her throat. Then She spat them from Her mouth with a laugh. They clinkled against the hard floor as they fell. Paul signaled the officers to meet against a wall. The demoness made no move against them. The metal pellets they fired at Her could do Her no harm.

Allenda had moved toward the door, but looked backwards to see what was causing the screams. the building was so filled with smoke and fire it was difficult to see and breathe. She and Simon were the last of the Warriors to exit the church. Paul and the officers, none of whom had left, just watched, not believing what they saw.

Once all of the Warriors were outside, Simon turned to re-enter the battle and finish what he knew had to be done. As he moved, Allenda grabbed his arm. "I'm coming with you, Simon."

"No," he said, "it's too dangerous."

"It doesn't matter. We have to end this now."

"You're not ready for this type of battle."

"I *am* ready. Besides, look at how strong She is. No one person can finish this. *Let's do it!*"

Simon knew Allenda was right. He bent and kissed her forehead, took her hand and moved in toward the beast.

When they re-entered the room it was again eerily silent. All of the members of the Barony were lifeless blobs on the floor. Paul and the officers stood near a wall. They had not volunteered to become one with Her so She would not give them the privilege. She left them alone. Barra Edinnazu, strengthened with the energy She had absorbed, started to move through the clouds of smoke toward the front door. She floated a foot above the ground. Walking was beneath the pride of a goddess.

Simon and Allenda stood at the door. "Visualize a circle as we move around Her," Simon instructed. They slowly moved apart. Simon went to the left and Allenda moved to the right. It looked as if they were allowing the demoness room to pass between them.

Barra Edinnazu ignored them. To Her they were humans and insignificant. When She neared the door a flash of blue prevented Her from moving forward. "What is this?" said Her unearthly voice. "Who dares?"

The creature turned, but it was too late for Her to stop what was happening. Allenda and Simon had completed the circle, locking Her inside. She moved around, trying to get out, but each time She came to an edge of the circle of blue light She was thrown back.

"Now, Barra Edinnazu, it ends," said Simon. He focused his energy and shot a blue beam of psychic power at the demoness. She fell backward a few feet, recovered and laughed.

Simon continued to pour out power at her. She fought Her way closer to him. Allenda stood next to her mentor. She, too, fired out energy. Again the demoness fell back, only to recover and come at them.

"I know not who you are," She said, "but Barra Edinnazu shall overpower you."

In an instant it was clear that She was right. Even Simon and Allenda's combined power was not enough to stop Her. Inch by inch She moved toward them and deflected their magical beams. Simon and Allenda, both drenched in sweat from the exertion, knew the end was inevitable. The protective blue circle was fading, too. But the creature wanted more than just victory. She wanted to crush those who had the audacity to attack Her. She wanted to make an example of these two.

The demoness sneered, then waved Her arm. Her appearance changed until She looked completely like Eris. "Why are you doing this to me?" She asked in Eris' voice. Allenda started to falter in her attack.

Suddenly a loud cracking sound was heard. The fire had eaten some supporting timbers and the north side of the building collapsed. Smoke and dust exploded into the air, but Simon kept his focus. Allenda brought her attention back to the attack on the creature.

The demoness waved Her arm again. Her appearance changed to the likeness of Angelica. "Guys, please stop. I need your help. You're hurting me." This She said in Angelica's voice. Allenda, who had never seen such transmogrifications before, put her hands down and stopped her attack. Simon did not have the power to support his own attack and keep the circle strong.

The magical circle began to fade. Seeing Her chance, the creature moved toward them. Her face changed into an obscene mixture of the faces of all the women who had died to make up Her body. Each part seemed to move independently, screaming in anguish. Simon and Allenda watched in horror. The two Warriors renewed their attacks, but Barra Edinnazu's psychological ploy had distracted them enough from their concentration to cause the circle to lose most of its strength.

Barra Edinnazu's face took on a look of ecstasy as a living *something* wriggled beneath the skin of Her lower abdomen, trying to escape the monstrous body of the demoness. Her lip curled in the pleasure/pain of orgasm as two, eight-inch thick tentacles unfurled and fell from the demoness' vagina. Covered with a smoking, greenish slime, they plopped to the floor along with quarts of filthy, sticky green ichor and shot across the polished surface, wriggling and shaking like grotesque, obscene serpents. They broke through the weakened circle. One looped around Simon's neck, the other around Allenda's. The pointed ends of the tentacles moved toward their victims' mouths.

Allenda stopped her attack on Barra Edinnazu and used both hands to prevent the writhing protuberance from entering her. She fought it as it squirmed to escape her hands. With a tenaciousness that surprised even her, she held the protrusion at bay. "You can't beat me you bitch!" she called out. The creature merely smiled. Allenda's eyes widened as three smaller tentacles came out of a side of the one she held and entered her mouth and both nostrils. Her eyes took on a look of terror as she felt them wiggle inside of her, slowly moving deeper and deeper.

Simon continued his magical attack. His only defense against the attacking demoness was to keep his gritted teeth closed. This proved to be of little use as the thick tentacle forced itself between his teeth. Simon gagged as the obscene thing started to slither down his throat.

Allenda was on the floor, pounding at her invader with her fists. Simon, unable to breathe, fell to his knees. *We can't lose now, we can't!* But his consciusness began to fail and darkness was rapidly creeping upon him.

Suddenly, Barra Edinnazu screamed in pain. The invading tentacles shot back inside of Her, freeing Allenda and Simon who fought to regain their breath. The demoness turned to see what had assaulted Her. There stood Alan Crawford, confident magician. Energy streamed from his hands. "That was for Eris!" he told Her. The demoness laughed, a deep, non-human echo, and came for him. Alan had given Simon and Allenda the few seconds they needed to recuperate. They renewed their attack on the creature. For the first time the demoness looked puzzled. She did not know what to do.

She shouted and squirmed in pain. Nina came in and stood next to Alan. She added her energy to the attack. Dominique limped back into the church and moved half-way between the other four. She pointed her hands at the demoness and shot psychic energy at the creature. As if She had been a boxer who had just received a powerful punch, Barra Edinnazu's head flew back, teeth falling to the floor as a splattering of blood rained from Her mouth.

One by one the Warriors, true to their name, re-entered the church. They surrounded the creature and attacked it sending magical energy charged to harm and destroy.

Barra Edinnazu cried out in agony. She flew around the circle, looking for a way out. There was none. She moved to the middle of the circle and looked for a means of escape. There was none. *How could these worthless humans, these nonentities, cause me such pain? How can these insignificant beings defeat me?*

Her appearance changed. She flashed back and forth between Her current body and Her true appearance. Feet of a chicken with bony legs sprouting tiny, wiggling, sucker-covered tentacles, the body was covered with a thick mat of gorilla-like hair. The head had a gaping, circular maw with row after row of razor-sharp, pointed teeth. High on the front of the head was a group of seven, emotionless, shark-like eyes. Two useless, short arms flapped from Her sides while a large pincher came from the front of Her torso. A prehensile, hairless tail whipped from behind and danced through the air in pain.

Still the Warriors attacked. Finally, She just hung in the air in Her assumed body. A glittering of lights appeared about Her, shining through the brownish-grey smoke. There was a blinding light as the parts of the dead which had housed Her spirit separated at the points where they had been joined and fell to the floor.

The earth shook once and the room went silent except for the sound of the smoldering building. Barra Edinnazu was gone.

* * * * *

For long moments they stood there. It was as if no one dared move lest the demoness return. Finally, Simon said, "It's over. Let's get out of here before the place burns down. Let's go home." The scream of a fire engine's siren could be heard in the distance.

The victorious Warriors of the Light started to leave the scene as did Paul and his officers who had holstered their useless guns. Paul looked at Simon. "Did you kill Her?"

Simon shrugged. "How do you kill a goddess?"

"I thought she was a demoness."

"The gods of one society become the demons and devils of the society that follows it."

"Are you telling me that murderous thing could come back?"

"Maybe," said Simon. The mage continued to walk away. "But not tonight, Paul," he added, "not tonight."

The screams that came from the sirens of several fire engines came to a stop as the fire-fighting machines arrived. But it was too late to save St. Lucy's church. The old building, which had been engulfed in flames for the better part of a half hour, collapsed in on itself, leaving only a cloud of dust and a rising spire of golden embers that glittered 100 feet into the night sky. The fire fighters, unable to stop the destruction, watered the remains to prevent the fire from spreading. A wind, coming off the ocean, was quickly dispersing the fire's smoke.

The Warriors were mostly in their cars when Paul ran over and stopped Simon. "What happened here, Raven? What should I put in my report? What should I tell the media? They'll never believe me if I tell what I saw."

Exhausted, Simon Raven entered the back seat of a car in order to be driven home. He leaned heavily on the door and looked at Paul. "Then tell them any damn thing you please, Lieutenant Christian. Tell them any damn thing you please."

Simon got into the car, closed the door and leaned back against the seat. He rolled down the window and called out to Paul, "How do you like the air?" The car started off for the trip back to his home. Simon didn't look back.

Paul scratched his head as he watched Simon drive off. He pulled some Tums from the packet in his pocket, but before he could put them in his mouth he took a breath and realized what the magician had meant. The stink in the air was gone. The humidity was gone, too. Paul didn't even feel any smog. For the first time in many nights he could see stars. Paul rolled the Tums between his fingers, looked at the pills in his hand then threw them away.

The air smelled like L.A. after a rain; clean, refreshed, new. That was the best time to be in L.A.

Paul felt clean, too.

Epilogue

It was sunset, and Simon sat near the ocean waves at his favorite location, a hundred yards north of the pier at Venice beach. The clean, onshore breeze made his longish hair slightly dance. Simon looked out across the waters toward the Sun.

Simon stayed on the beach for hours. He was lost in thoughts about and memories of the last two weeks. He knew he should speak, to call Mother, but felt no real need to do so.

Finally, within the hiss of a retreating wave, Mother spoke to him first. Her voice, for the first time in weeks, was strong and filled with energy. There was also joy in her voice. "*Hello, Simon, my son.*"

Simon still said nothing. "*Simon, what is wrong? You have won. The soil is fertile, the air clean and the water clear. I feel better than I have for some time.*"

Simon pursed his lips. "Eris and Angelica are gone. Did they have to die?"

"*Allenda and Alan have proved themselves under fire. They have become magicians…"*

"They would have probably become magicians sooner or later. There is a difference between making a powerful change in your life, such as becoming a magician, and dying."

"Is that so? Look around you, my son. Everything is born, grows, dies and is reborn. Eris and Angelica will be reborn, too."

There was silence between them for several minutes. "Mother, I miss them…"

"As I will miss you."

"What? What do you mean?"

"You are not my only son, Simon. Nor are you my first. I have been here for a long time. Many of my sons and daughters have come and gone. Physical death is just a part of life. Their spirits did not die. They live on."

Simon sighed. He disliked word games. "I do not want to have those I love leave me on the physical plane. I loved them, mother, and they're gone. It hurts."

"Allenda, Alan and the Warriors need you. You are at a point of change in your life. You do not need me any more. They need you for what is to come."

"What do you mean? You're stronger. That means the evil is gone. Barra Edinnazu is gone. Or do you know something that you haven't revealed?"

"My son, you have prevented a great evil from taking over the land. But one victory does not win a war. Evil still exists. The battle continues. You are still needed, but you no longer need me. Goodbye."

"Do you mean I'll never be able to talk with you again Mother? Mother?" There was no response.

It feels like I have the weight of the world on my shoulders. Why me? Why me? He walked away from the beach but stopped after fifty paces. Just ahead of him on the Venice boardwalk were a couple of teenagers. They were sitting on a bench, kissing. Simon watched discretely as they kissed and caressed each other, their hormones driving them into a passion.

Simon felt tears come to his eyes. New love was being born. *This is why I'm needed. This is why the Warriors are needed.* He looked up at the Moon and stars. With a deep sob/sigh, he said, "Goodbye, Angelica. Goodbye, Eris. May you find peace and happiness." He suddenly felt as if a huge weight had been lifted from his shoulder. The tears flowed, releasing his pain.

It was time for the healing to begin.

Everywhere.

To order additional copies of this book,
please send full amount plus $5.00 for
postage and handling for the first book and
$1.00 for each additional book.

Send orders to:

8490051R00215

Printed in Great Britain
by Amazon.co.uk, Ltd.,
Marston Gate.

CW01623990

Also available by Christian Henning

Golf: How to Break 90 in 42 Days or Less

Golf Fitness Training: Core to Score

Golf Fitness: Shed Pounds to Shave Strokes

Golf Fitness: 30 Yards or More in 30 Days or Less

Kettlebell Golf Body

CHRISTIAN HENNING,

NASM-CPT, PN1, ONNIT ACADEMY CERTIFIED TRAINER

GOLF
AGGRESSIVE
MAKE YOUR OWN LUCK

Golf Aggressive Publishing

ISBN: 9780692323601

"The results of physical fitness are the direct opposites of those that follow from unfitness.

The fit are healthy and strong, and many as a consequence save themselves decorously on the battle-field and escape all dangers of war; many help friends and do good to their country and for this they earn gratitude, glory and honor that leads to a better life and provide their children a better means of achieving a livelihood".

~ Socrates

Disclaimer

You must get your physician's approval before beginning this exercise program. The following recommendations are not medical guidelines but are for educational purposes only. You must consult your physician prior to starting this program or if you have any medical condition or injury that contraindicates physical activity. This program is designed for healthy individuals 18 years and older only.

The information in this book is meant to supplement, not replace, proper exercise training. All forms of exercise pose some inherent risks. The editors and publishers advise readers to take full responsibility for their safety and know their limits. Before practicing the exercises in this book, be sure that your equipment is maintained, and do not take risks beyond your level of experience, aptitude, training, and fitness. The exercises and fitness routine in this book are not intended as a substitute for any exercise routine or treatment or dietary regimen that may have been prescribed by your physician.

Don't lift heavy weights if you are alone, inexperienced, injured, or fatigued. Don't perform any exercise unless you have been shown the proper technique by a certified personal trainer or certified strength and conditioning specialist. Always ask for instruction and assistance when lifting. Don't perform any exercise without proper instruction. Always do a warm-up prior to strength training and interval training.

If you are taking any medications, you must talk to your physician before starting any exercise program, including Kettlebell Golf Body. If you experience any lightheadedness, dizziness, or shortness of breath while exercising, stop the movement and consult a physician.

You must have a complete physical examination if you are sedentary, if you have high cholesterol, high blood pressure, or diabetes, if you are overweight, or if you are over 30 years old. If your physician recommends that you don't use Kettlebell Golf Body, please follow your doctor's orders.

DO THIS FIRST! (BONUS)

As one of the Kettlebell Golf Body bonuses, you get FREE support via our private Facebook group.

Our private Facebook group has been proven to help our clients stick to the workout program. The group is where you'll get positive social support from like-minded golfers from around the World. You can even ask Christian Henning, the author, all your diet and exercise questions. The private group is also a great place to find an accountability partner.

Step 1 – Unlock access to the private member's area where all the video demonstrations and bonus materials are located.

You just need your Amazon order ID number and contact details so our team can verify your order:

https://kettlebellgolfbody.com/amazon-4322

Once verified, they will send you an email with your login details and the URL to the Member's Area.

If you do not receive the email within 24 hours, please contact us via the Facebook group listed below. Please check your SPAM folder first, as sometimes the welcome email falls into those.

Step 2 – Join the PRIVATE Facebook group at https://www.facebook.com/groups/kettlebellgolfbody, you'll need to provide your Amazon Order ID# and the email address you ordered under. You can get faster support via the group and gain access to our quarterly Power and Distance Challenge where you can win prizes.

Table of Contents

CHAPTER 1: WHY THE KETTLEBELL?

SIMPLICITY, EFFICIENCY, RESULTS

Simplification and efficiency are paramount to time management for the busy golfer who wishes to improve their game. As such, the kettlebell delivers on this simplification and efficiency.

The kettlebell is also perfect for golf fitness training.

Let's talk about why I believe that to be a true statement.

The design of the kettlebell itself is simplistic... nothing more than a handle on a cannonball that can replace an entire gym full of equipment.

However, don't let the kettlebells simplicity fool you...

THE SHAPE OF THE KETTLEBELL MAKES IT INCREDIBLY VERSATILE

For starters, the shape of the kettlebell allows it to fit into the body and around the hand ergonomically. The ergonomics allow us to move our body through our available range of motion utilizing the weight of the kettlebell to force muscle adaptation.

The handle allows us to manipulate the bell and control it easily, changing direction and stopping and starting while in fluid motion. This type of movement is difficult with a dumbbell or barbell.

As you know, the golf swing is fluid and dynamic employing virtually every muscle and joint in the body. The great thing about kettlebells is that we can design our training to build and improve our golf game with fully body exercises that mimic various aspects of the swing.

Most importantly, the kettlebell is versatile and can be used in place of a barbell, dumbbell, Bulgarian bag and many more workout tools. This opens the entire playbook of exercise selection and allows us to create many different styles of workouts.

There is nothing more versatile than the kettlebell when it comes to exercise selection.

And this versatility allows us to train more athletically than we can on machines...

THE KETTLEBELL MAKES YOU MORE ATHLETIC

Perhaps the most important reason to use the kettlebell is to improve your overall athleticism. Golf is an athletic sport that requires excellent balance, coordination, strength, flexibility, and power. In short, the kettlebell can make you more athletic when used properly.

Athletic kettlebell training solidifies the mind-body connection, improving our proprioception. Proprioception is described as the "sixth sense" and is our sense of movement and body position. In short, kettlebells will help you improve your proprioception and that improves athleticism.

If you haven't viewed yourself as an athlete, it's time to change your mindset!

Viewing yourself as an athlete raises the bar on your expectations and thus your training. And if you want to get better at the sport of golf, it's time to deploy the kettlebell and kettlebell training to improve your athleticism.

In fact, we'll be developing your athleticism in the 'How To' section of this book as we learn to move weight more efficiently and dynamically.

The kettlebell allows us to replicate the acceleration and deceleration of the golf swing in a controlled environment. As we build our strength, endurance, balance, and flexibility that will begin to transfer over to your golf swing.

Training with the kettlebell will force our muscles to adapt both in force generation, but also force deceleration… athletic qualities we need to create power and promote consistency.

And perhaps one of the least discussed benefits of kettlebell training is injury prevention…

THE KETTLEBELL HELPS BULLETPROOF YOU AGAINST INJURY

Training athletically with the kettlebell also has a carryover effect of bulletproofing your body against injury.

As you know, golf isn't a sport on rails like a train. Your stance is never the same and usually uneven which can create the potential for injury. And the clubhead sometimes has a mind of its own… and it's important we have the strength to tame the club's arc.

Taming the arc is a term used not only for the golf swing, but kettlebell exercises too. Taming the arc simply means controlling the club or bell instead of letting it control us. When the club or bell control us, our balance is off, and we perform poorly.

What I mean by this is that we must be in control of the kettlebell and the golf club at all points during movement. Control comes from our core for both the kettlebell and golf swing.

If we are weak anywhere along the path of a golf swing or a kettlebell exercise, we open ourselves up to potential injury. Therefore, taming the arc is best done through strengthening our posture through dynamic exercises and working on our proprioception.

By training dynamically and athletically with the kettlebell, we can prepare the body for uncertain circumstances on the golf course and life in general.

Fighting the bell through swings, snatches, presses, squats, and figure 8's develops instinctive balance and coordination that machines and barbells are incapable of.

The kettlebell forces you to tame its rebellious behavior by developing a strong posterior chain as well as core... valuable tools in creating power but also longevity to be able to play golf well into your golden years.

Perhaps the most important aspect of an athletic golf swing is your ability to stay balanced...

KETTLEBELLS DEVELOP INSTINCTIVE ATHLETIC BALANCE

There's an old saying that you can't fire a canon from a canoe. If you did, well, the canoe would tip right over tossing you into the water. The same is true for the kettlebell and your golf swing.

Recall the last time you swung a club out of balance. The forces owned you and pulled you at their will. Chances are your shot was a big slicer or a duck hook. Not good!

When the club pulls you off balance, your only course of action is to strong-arm the swing. And I don't have to tell you what happens when you try to steer the club... woods, water, ditches, long stuff.

Deploying the kettlebell and training more athletically will help you tame the club and keep things more consistent. Consistency means more greens and fairways.

Further, it is impossible to create consistently accurate power when you are off balance. The kettlebell will not only make you strong, but it will also force you to stay balanced. When you combine strength and balance - only then you can generate maximal power swing after swing. And keep in mind, a 300-yard slice isn't what I'm talking about here. By maintaining our balance and taming the arc, we will improve our ball-striking through better contact and improved accuracy.

The goal of the program in this book is to increase your strength and balance for maximal and accurate power. Power comes from strength and balance. We simply cannot be powerful if we are not strong and stable.

The kettlebell is the perfect tool because it forces you to be more athletic as most KB exercises are athletic in nature. The kettlebell seamlessly builds coordination, balance, strength and power.

Kettlebell training will turn your canoe into a battleship, complete with a powerful canon capable of delivering power into the back of the golf ball consistently!

We'll be mixing up our own 'Effortless Distance Cocktail' using the kettlebell and the kettlebell golf body program.

But what good is all this power if you are too deconditioned to play a full 18 or 36 holes?

KETTLEBELLS ALLOW YOU TO KEEP IT UP

You are familiar with the little blue pill? Imagine the kettlebell doing the same for your golf game. There's nothing worse than the 'back 9 fade' in golf... playing fantastic until you just run out of gas on the 12th, 13th, or 25th hole only to implode.

Perhaps your back begins to get tired from getting in and out of the cart and all the walking? Maybe, you get worn down and mental fog begins to set in, leaving you disengaged and frustrated.

If this sounds familiar, these are common side effects from not being conditioned properly. A lot of this has to do with our modern lifestyle, which has left us weak physically and mentally.

Whatever the cause, the kettlebell can resolve these issues.

Many a good round has been lost to the back 9 fade! No more.

The strength endurance that kettlebell training delivers will allow you to easily play 18 holes or even 36 leaving the course fresh as a daisy.

Kettlebell swings will build your core strength and protect your lower back.

And one of the reasons the kettlebell translates so well to golf is that we can move our body through its normal range of motion with additional weight. When we build the muscles up with a kettlebell, movement becomes much easier without the kettlebell.

However, we must stay away from 'fluff' exercises that permeate much of the celebrity Instagram trainer's feeds today. We are not working out to show off, we are going to work out for tangible results.

A good example of a fluff exercise for golfers would be the bench press. Now, if you are a bodybuilder, the bench press is not a fluff exercise... it is an essential exercise.

Imagine a bench press where you are laying on a bench and pressing up... not real transferable to golf.

Don't get me wrong, I love being macho and knocking out some bench presses! It's just that this type of exercise doesn't really help us play better golf.

Instead, we would use the kettlebell like a dumbbell and press with one hand laying on a bench. The offset in weight would challenge our core to resist rotating to maintain stability. The bench press would not offer this torque building benefit that the single arm bench press does.

My point is we will train smarter and for the specific purpose of golf performance.

And to eliminate the back 9 fade we need to make our body stronger, more durable, and improve our cardiovascular output.

ALL OF THIS WILL TRANSLATE to better golf because you are able to move better, more easily, and more powerfully.

Strength endurance will keep you pounding drive after drive with consistency, until the 18th hole and beyond.

Another reason the kettlebell is so good for golf is it trains us instinctively to cycle our tension...

CYCLING TENSION AND RELAXATION

The golf swing is a blend of tension and relaxation. A little bit of relaxation here and a little bit of tension there mixed with explosive movement. To be honest, the golf-swing is a complex beast that requires the most powerful computer in the world to perform - our brain. That's why kettlebell training is so good for golfers, it teaches instinctive proprioception.

I don't think we fully understand the extent to which tension and relaxation play a role in the swing, and it's hard to consciously control these actions during your golf swing. As we all know, thinking too much will create a bad result. :)

The good thing is, we only need to understand that the golf swing and kettlebell are similar in terms of training for tension cycling. Our brain takes this up instinctively but as humans we aren't perfect - we can always get better. That's where the kettlebell comes into play with exercises like the swing and snatch.

Training with the kettlebell swing will help us learn to control our bodies better and this will translate to your golf-swing by improving your posture from beginning to end of your golf swing.

Let's compare both:

The single arm kettlebell swing starts from a stopped position much like the golf swing. We hike the kettlebell back into position (back-swing) to prepare for the explosive hip pop that pushes the kettlebell forward until the kettlebell reaches our mid-line straight out in front of our chest (downswing and impact).

The downswing in golf begins with a power move that loads the club into the right slot to deliver power into the back of the ball. The body also fights to maintain its posture during this move so that you don't come up and out of the shot. I won't go into the complexity of the downswing here, but you can imagine that as we swing, our body is constantly tensing up and relaxing to maintain an optimal path.

Similarly, the 'downswing' of the kettlebell begins with a quick pop of the hips that propel the kettlebell up and forward towards its target (straight ahead of us).

As the bell floats up and forward, we maintain just enough body tension, so the bell doesn't pull us forward... using a strong base to maintain our balance.

Once the kettlebell reaches the finish position (straight in front of us opposite our chest) we can sense that our core, glutes, and shoulders are firm. At the start of the hip pop, the muscles other than the glutes (used to pop the bell up) are relaxed. It is only when the kettlebell reaches the finish point that the glutes, core, shoulders, and grip firm back up.

As the kettlebell begins to drop thanks to gravity, we again relax slightly while increasing tension at the bottom of the kettlebell swing to slow the kettlebell down and prevent injury. The follow through in golf is much the same where we tense our core and glutes slightly to slow the club-head down.

At the same time, a single arm kettlebell swing works much like the single arm bench press we discussed earlier... by building a rock-solid core. During the entirety of the kettlebell swing, your body is fighting to maintain control and balance. This resistance bulletproofs your core for the backswing as well as downswing while protecting your back on the follow through. As you can see, tension is never constant with a kettlebell swing.

But there's more to the kettlebell than just fitness, it can also save you money and time...

THE MOST PRACTICAL TRAINING TOOL THAT EXISTS TODAY

A handful of kettlebells are more practical than a rack of dumbbells.

Most dumbbell exercises can be done with a kettlebell. And the way the kettlebell fits into your hand allows it to orbit the body much like a golf club... something a dumbbell isn't capable of.

Owning a set of a few kettlebells is more than enough to keep you in shape the rest of your life, without ever visiting a gym again. Think of the money you could save by investing in a set of quality kettlebells!

Put simply, you will not get more bang for your buck than a good set of kettlebells.

I often joke that my set of kettlebells are family heirlooms that will long outlive me and those I pass them down to.

All you need are three or four kettlebells to replace an entire gym of equipment.

Most kettlebell junkies like yours truly have a range of matching kettlebells... but you don't even need matching sets when you are just starting out.

Don't get me wrong, barbells and dumbbells are fantastic, and you can get similar results using them versus kettlebells. Barbells are expensive and require a lot of room to store.

And while I love training with barbells, the kettlebell is a great tool to build up strength to make barbell training even more effective. The kettlebell is on par with the barbell in building grip strength.

Let me be clear though, I am not saying we should replace Olympic training, bodyweight training or anything of the sort. These are fantastic and complimentary training methods that should be used in conjunction with the kettlebell. In fact, if you complete Phase II of Kettlebell Golf Body and join us for Phase III, you'll see that we begin to introduce tools such as barbells, dumbbells, sandbags, etc.

In fact, in future Kettlebell Golf Body phases, we'll mix things up by using kettlebells, bodyweight and barbells together. If this is interesting to you, make sure to join our mobile app where we will deliver a year cycle of training to keep you motivated, engaged, and challenged.

For the scope of this book though, we will focus on mixing the kettlebell with bodyweight and flexibility exercises to create a solid foundation for better golf.

Oh, and barbells don't travel well...

YOU CAN TRAIN ANYWHERE WITH A HANDFUL OF KETTLEBELLS

And my final reason on why the kettlebell is perfect for golf training is space!

All you need is a 3-foot by 3-foot square will do just fine to not only use as your workout area, but as your storage area. This is commonly known as a 'courage corner'.

I just keep mine lined up in front of my dumbbell rack in my garage gym. In my indoor gym, they line the wall, taking no space at all.

If you are sold by now on the kettlebell - let's move on to what you can expect in terms of results for your personal golf game.

All of this sounds good, but I can here you asking me... but what can I do for me?

RESULTS LIKE THESE ARE HARDER WITH FAD WORKOUTS

You purchased this book with one goal in mind - to play better golf.

You want more distance, better accuracy, eliminate the back 9 fade, and perhaps even reduce your risk of injury while increasing the number of rounds you can play.

These are all great things taken by themselves, but to get all from one tool - I don't blame you if you are skeptical!

First off, you WILL get RESULTS if you STICK TO THE PROGRAMMING. You may find the workouts difficult at first but do what you can. Over time, you will gradually improve and get better, and you will fall in love with the kettlebell.

If you need proof that the program works, you probably saw the testimonials on the sales page for this book. They are all true and performed during our various tests. In fact, many of the results listed were in just SIX WEEKS, not the eight weeks of programming that this book delivers.

In full disclosure, you simply can't expect to do one or two workouts a week and get results like our test subjects. That is unrealistic.

Don't half-ass and expect full-ass results. This is like buying a toothbrush and tooth paste and using them half of the time and then getting a cavity. What did you expect?

So don't be that golfer, instead be one that starts strong and finishes even stronger.

For those of you that stick to the program and DON'T get results - just contact us and we'll refund your money with no hassles and no questions!

The key for me with this program is to put you in the best possible position for success with your personal swing and game. If you show up every day and work on flexibility, strength, and balance you WILL get results… and if you don't, I'll refund every dime you paid for this book.

Let me be clear though, you can't expect a refund if you aren't brushing your teeth.

Sound complicated? It can be, but don't worry about the minutia, that's my job. I just need you to show up and put in the effort.

Now let's talk about the average results my clients have received with our programming model.

YOUR EXPECTED RESULTS AND PROVEN CLIENT RESULTS

If you complete the entire 8-week cycle as written… and you've made good progress in your strength, power, and flexibility - you can expect to add roughly 10 to 15 yards to your driver. On average, you'll see 10 yards across every club in your bag. Obviously, the longer the club, the more distance you'll see.

The distance is also accompanied with improved ball striking consistency.

That is not a misprint.

The proof is in the pudding as they say and I'm positive the workout system in this book will unlock your body, create more balance and strength, and tap into more athletic power than you ever imagined.

What good is a golf fitness program if it doesn't back up its claims? Sure, we can tell you about our students like Paul and Brian who have added 20 yards to their drives, well into their 40's and 50's.

Another one of our die-hard students is Tom who routinely blasts 300-yard drives and consistently shoots in the low 80's and high 70's as a result… and did I mention Tom is 65 years old?

My sincere expectation is that if you follow the program consistently you will see a BIG difference in the distance you hit your clubs. And I'm not talking about just your driver, but every single club in your bag.

A huge carryover to improving your balance, coordination and strength is increased accuracy as well. While we won't be asking you to measure that, I encourage you to do so!

In full disclosure, our clients listed in the results also received my Distance Accelerator program. The Distance Accelerator follows a 6-week program of my proprietary Greasing the Groove (GTG) method to refine your existing swing, distance specific drills, and tempo swing drills.

If you are interested in adding the Distance Accelerator, there is a link at the end of this book.

TAKE MY DISTANCE CHALLENGE

How much distance can you add? This depends on how consistent you are with the training, how well you stick to proper form, and recover properly.

As mentioned previously, the range of distance gains to your driver are 10 to 30 yards with the average somewhere in the middle. On your irons, depending on the length of the iron we see increases from 5 to 10 yards per club, across the entire bag.

If you are game, take my Distance and Accuracy Challenge and let's see how many yards you can gain.

A nice side effect of Kettlebell Golf Body is that you will be feeling better and moving better off the course after your rounds of golf. The mix of flexibility training and strength will see to that just fine... you'll have to measure that by how you feel.

And if you tighten up your nutrition, it would not be impossible to lose 10 to 15 pounds... I've seen it time and time again with my new students. This one is easy to measure with a scale and mirror. Perhaps this is more of a couch to gym story than it is about anything else, but nutrition has always been king to fat loss and weights queen.

Why not go for a few pounds of fat though? Eating better will give you more clarity, better health, and you'll just feel better on the course.

You can measure your body changes as well if you wish during the challenge.

Kettlebell Golf Body will also help you build superior strength endurance to that of your competitors. Strength endurance delivers a repeatable swing - even late into your rounds - virtually eliminating the back 9 fade many golfers experience.

Stick to the plan, don't quit, and be consistent in your training and your golf practice.

I can tell you all day about the success of my students, but it only matters if YOU get results, right?

So, here's how the challenge works...

HOW TO THE CHALLENGE WORKS

The Distance and Accuracy Challenge is 8 weeks total and consists of measuring the distance you hit each your clubs at the beginning (before your first workout) and the end (after your last workout - preferably a day or two after). You'll measure your starting distance and final distance and the accuracy of each shot.

Don't worry, we've created a nice little PDF you can print and take to the range to plot your accuracy and distance on.

It's really that simple!

For example:

- Measure distance the day before your workouts begin in Phase I.
- Once you complete Phase II, you'll take the Distance Assessment again, again after a day or two of rest.

Report your results each time here:

https://kettlebellgolfbody.com/distance-assessment

INSTRUCTIONS

Measure your distance on a non-windy day (may be difficult in some regions) ... or at the very least where the wind is similar in direction and speed if this is not possible.

Indoor shot monitors will work too and may provide more precise details like clubhead speed and more. Write all this info down for each shot if known.

On our printable PDF, write down all the clubs in your bag on the left side of the page. Above the clubs at the top of the page, write down the numbers 1 through 6 (these are the individual shot distances for each attempt).

- At your practice facility, start with your lob wedge and work your way backwards through your bag until hitting your driver. Use a laser range finder to gage the carry of each shot. Do not count the roll.
- Hit 6 balls with each club. Fill in each slot next to the club with the distance the ball flew in the air. Do not count roll.
- If you have access to a flight monitor and know the clubhead speed, write this in the available field. If not known, we will just be using distance as our gage.
- Mark where the ball lands on the imaginary fairway, not where it runs out to. It is not necessary to notate the club used (but you can if you wish). This will give us a rough indication of you hitting or missing the fairway… in addition, we'll know if you consistently miss left or right
- It is most helpful to have someone mark the sheet for you so you can get in a groove of hitting shots and be more consistent.
- When complete, add up all the total shot distance for each club. Then divide by 6. This will give you the average.

All useful information when on the course and you should be doing this anyway!

IMPROVE YOUR RESULTS

Like any program, you are going to face challenges and roadblocks. One way of eliminating roadblocks is by joining our 1-on-1 coaching program.

You can learn more at https://golff.it/kgb-coaching, where you can work directly with Christian and his team through your mobile device or PC.

Get the 'Follow Through' you need to implement the Kettlebell Golf Body. You'll be held accountable, so you break bad habits and build great habits – which almost guarantee your success.

You'll implement everything inside of this book and eliminate any potential roadblocks you may face. You'll receive a customized fitness program crafted just for you and based on the Kettlebell Golf Body through our new app (iOS, Android, Web).

In full disclosure, 1-on-1 Coaching is a paid program... but VERY affordable!

Next, we need to make sure we have everything we need to take the Distance and Accuracy Challenge and perform the workouts.

PROGRAM OVERVIEW

In this section, I'll breakdown our mission for Kettlebell Golf Body as well as some specifics of the program.

I'm not going to spend a ton of time here; I want to provide you with enough information so that you believe in the program and understand how it works and why we are doing what we are doing.

This is not a science book and I'm not going to convince you with words - that's why I've thrown down the gauntlet so to speak with the Distance and Accuracy Challenge.

If you want to prove if this program can work for you, take the Distance and Accuracy Challenge, measure your results, and see for yourself.

To be even more clear, here's our Mission Statement...

KETTLEBELL GOLF BODY MISSION STATEMENT

Build a stable foundation that allows for more consistent bal striking. Build strength and athleticism that is translated through an increased balance and acceleration for more accurate power. Increase our range of motion through flexibility, stretching and proper recovery techniques. Finally, by bulletproofing the acceleration and deceleration stabilizer muscles used in the golf swing to prevent ourselves from injury and promote longevity.

WHY WASTE TIME WITH EGO-CENTRIC WORKOUTS?

We will be direct and cut to the chase. There are no 'vanity' pop star workouts or exercises. Every exercise, rep, set, and workout have a clear outcome associated with them.

Know your mission and know the outcomes you want to achieve from the training.

Anything else that does not add to achieving the mission is left out.

PROGRAM HIGH LEVEL OVERVIEW

When the military is given a mission to attack a target, they custom build a plan of attack. The leaders will review all their available assets, the target, and the manpower required to overcome the enemy. But first, they assess the enemy and learn the enemy.

I view golf training in the same way. We must train for the outcome we wish to achieve.

Unfortunately, the Internet is full of fitness pop stars brainwashing people that they need to be laying on the floor in a sweating heap of heavy breathing after each workout.

Worse, they distract their fanboys with impressive feats of strength or fancy challenging exercises the average golfer has no business trying. While impressive and great for social media – these types of ego-centric workouts don't help much with golf.

Instead, why don't we build up our body for golf instead of breaking it down with relentless insanity type workouts? I only care about improving your golf game and building you up instead of breaking you down.

Our training will be more like that of power lifters.

Power lifters, kettlebell lifters, and Olympic lifters know that mastery is the key to success. It's hard to master something when you are like a pinball, moving from program to program or exercise to exercise. Instead, powerlifters vary their training with cycles... either changing the programming up a bit or changing the weights, reps, time under tension, and even lifting principles.

Don't get me wrong here, I'm not saying to do the same workout repeatedly... that leads to burnout and overuse injuries. Rather, I'm saying we will cycle our training to keep your body fresh and progressing while also eliminating boredom and burnout. .

We'll focus on the following outcomes (goals):

1. Improved Balance

2. Increased Strength

3. Better Endurance

4. More Power

5. Bulletproofing Against Injury

We may put emphasis on some of the above as we change phases. This is normal and how to balance our fitness, prevent injury, and avoid burnout.

Think of the Kettlebell Golf Body system as a circle. We begin in one phase and move around the circle to return to the origin position. This leads to mastery and improvement. Complete a full cycle and repeat. This is how to master the kettlebell and your performance. Our current system is a 12-month circle designed to change each month to focus on different aspects.

Over time, you gradually raise the bar on your fitness and golf game using this method. And the best thing is, you'll never be searching YouTube for 'what's next?'.

So how much time does the program take?

TIME REQUIREMENTS

This book is split into two four-week phases for a total of eight weeks. You'll need to finish the first phase before progressing to the second phase. You'll workout three to four days per week, depending on the phase you are in.

Each workout in Phase I will take you approximately 40 minutes from beginning to end including the warmup and decompression (cool down). Two strength workouts are prescribed with one optional conditioning workout.

There are four workouts in Phase II. It will take you roughly 40 to 45 minutes from warm up to cool down to complete each workout.

If you complete Phase I and Phase II and wish to continue, we have the entire year cycle available for you through our Mobile App.

And if you are wondering about flexibility, stretching and recovery - each session is roughly 10 to 15 minutes long, performed on off days. You are encouraged to go to the driving range or play golf on these recovery days and perform your recovery AFTER your round.

The early morning flexibility program is 15 minutes and should be done every day when you roll out of bed. For best results, go through it twice for a total of 30 minutes.

Every Sunday is a total rest day where no recovery or workout is performed.

PROGRESSION

Do not skip ahead.

Do not pass go.

Complete each phase one after the other.

There is no 'advanced' workout as they are all 'advanced' workouts. The difficulty level is adjusted with the kettlebell size, time, and reps. If an exercise is too difficult, reach out to me in the Facebook group or the mobile app - I'll give you a workaround.

Remember, we are re-building you from the ground up brick by brick. Each phase builds upon the other. Each phase is four weeks

Each phase builds upon the previous phase. You will be challenged as you change from Phase I to Phase II, this is how we get better and improve.

This forces your body and mind to adapt through 'forced progression'.

Phase II builds upon Phase I by adding more challenging exercises and turning the heat up on cardio demands. Phase II also expands your flexibility.

Just remember, you can't fire a canon from a canoe. Kettlebell Golf Body is going to build a battleship foundation for you in Phase I. In Phase II, we'll mount the canon to the battleship and start firing away.

The programming is designed to work from the ground up. Primarily to deliver stability through motion, which in turn, allows you to be more accurate and deliver more power to the golf ball. Everything below supports this mission.

Let's break down the recipe from the ground up.

BREAKING DOWN THE WORKOUTS

Let's go just a bit deeper into the thought process behind each workout. I'll break the body down part by part so you can see the things we will be working on in the program.

First, losing stability or balance in any aspect of the swing will rob you of power, accuracy, and consistency. Losing balance is unacceptable.

The programming is designed to put you in a position of strength and control in an unstable environment.

If the stance determines there could be balance issues, I want you to be able to adjust on the fly… instinctively. While we can address some of this balance in your fitness training - you'll need to supplement it with good practice as well. Just remember, no two stances in golf are the same on the course - yet we practice for the most part from a very stable environment on the practice tee. Your fitness training will help bridge this gap (although you should be training different lies too).

To be balanced through motion, we need to train separate parts of our body to work together and provide the ability and coordination to deliver center of the club power.

The closer we can get to the center of the clubface, the more power we can transfer to the ball. The more consistent we get with making solid contact, the more accurate our shot will be.

FROM THE GROUND UP - BUILDING THE WHIP

The golf swing begins from the ground up - requiring a good and balanced setup position. Most tour pros begin the swing with their lower body and move the club back and forward through a series of chain reactions. One leading to the other… just like this program will provide to you.

I'd like you to train with kettlebells in your bare feet or socks. The reason for this is that your feet can make subtle adjustments with direct contact to the floor - adjustments you just can't make when wearing shoes.

Flat shoes like Vans will work fine too but you won't develop the fine motor control training in your bare feet provides.

And don't worry, you are NOT going to break your foot with the kettlebell! I've trained for a decade and never had an incident. Just make sure if you lose control of the kettlebell, you get out of its way with quick feet!

We'll cover proper form on all movements in detail later in this book.

FEET, ANKLES, CALVES

Barefoot training will help you improve your stabilization muscles by removing the shoe which is artificially giving you support.

Perhaps the most common issue I see in older golfers is a lack of range of motion in the ankles. This can hinder power transfer, balance, as well as backswing and downswing so it is important, we zero in on this problem area.

Next in the chain are the calves which are vital to your balance and adjusting your balance on the fly. The calves have various roles in the backswing and downswing. In fact, you can see the calf activation in many top golfers when they wear shorts. Most golfers also have decent calf strength from the amount of walking that they do.

We'll zero in on the calves and work on ankle mobility as well as ankle stabilization with various exercises. We'll be breaking each down into chunks, so you understand not only the why but the how.

KNEES

What would a solid foundation be without strong knee position?

Weak knees can wreck your golf game causing instability. Basically, if you have weak knees, you do not have enough strength to support your rotational resistance (building up torque in the backswing) or stability to unwind that power and resist the force on the downswing (allowing you to make consistent contact).

The knee though is just a big joint that depends on muscles, ligaments, and tendons for stability. We'll work on your hamstrings, IT band, quads, glutes as well as your lower trunk core muscles.

Squats, kettlebell swings, single-leg exercises, and a multitude of lunges are just a few of the techniques we'll deploy to build your solid foundation. The good news is, many of these exercises over-deliver and we get more out of each exercise which means less time in the gym by being more efficient.

THIGHS

As we learned about knee stability, the knee joint is dependent upon many other muscle groups. I won't get too technical here, but we'll be working the anterior, posterior, medial, and lateral areas on your thigh region.

We'll be getting more value from efficient compound exercises that carry over here as well. Think of one stone, five birds.

We'll also incorporate deadlifting as well as some single-leg movements to ensure we are well developed to protect knee stability.

HIPS

Perhaps the biggest trouble spot for most of my male students. You need good flexibility and mobility in the hip joints if you want power. Most males are challenged in this area, but I've developed special flexibility and mobility routines designed to unlock tight hips.

Your warmups and cool downs will also open the hips up and prepare you for better golf as well as performing better during the workouts themselves.

Tight muscles such as the IT band, glutes, piriformis, and quads can affect your hips - for that reason we'll pay special attention on stretching these areas to ensure we can apply all our new strength and power to the golf swing.

CORE

The core is a group of muscles connecting your upper body to your lower body. The core is where you'll store up energy on your backswing and then unwind back into the ball. The core also will protect your back on the follow-through by allowing a controlled deceleration.

The core is crucial. We need to work on building a strong core to support our back, store and create power, and improve our overall endurance.

The good news is the kettlebell delivers in spades in core work. We won't need to waste time on useless sit-ups here.

Once we have a strong base can we apply power from our core efficiently. The easier we can make it on our body to deliver a powerful swing, the more swings we can do without fatiguing. Think of a professional boxer and how efficient they are at punching. There is no wasted movement, straight in and straight out. Sure, they may have to get creative to land on target, but the movement is still efficient.

The more movement, the more energy it takes, and the less efficient we are - and displays itself in a lack of accuracy and power.

Most importantly the core helps us to maintain a proper hinge (posture) on the backswing and downswing. Coming out of the shot will not be a problem once you develop your core with kettlebell training.

Our upper body connects to the mid-section and is vital. Slumping at setup can create a cramped environment, so we'll be working on maintaining a good posture through many different rowing exercises, squats, swings, and more.

There's also a certain amount of force that will try to pull you off balance and out of your posture... after all, you are holding a golf club and swinging it around your body. To control this diagonal force, we'll need to bulletproof our abs and obliques.

The programming will deploy single leg and single arm movements to help build your smaller stabilizing muscles. You'll be forced to resist rotating and turning to keep your alignment and posture, all fantastic for building a solid core.

SHOULDERS AND BACK

As mentioned above, slumping can be disastrous for your golf swing - and it's avoidable for the most part.

I can't tell you how many golfers suffer from 'slouch syndrome' (SS) thanks to the modern era. If your shoulders round forward and you must force yourself to stand up straight and pull your shoulders back, you probably suffer from SS.

Slouch syndrome comes from desk jobs, binge watching tv, playing on your phone, and basically neglecting your posterior chain. It's not your fault and you are not alone, it's a side effect of the modern job.

The training programs are designed to strengthen your 'pull' muscles (weak muscles that allow SS). Better posture allows you to hold the club at address position with enough room for a proper backswing, but also creates the room for a powerful downswing.

We will also dial in on your shoulder mobility. Stretching and mobility routines come to the rescue here, working to unlock tight shoulders and increase your range of motion.

As we unlock tight shoulders, it is not uncommon to increase your backswing length. In fact, I personally suffer from tight shoulders that have hindered my backswing ... gradually shortening it over the years.

A few years ago, I was reviewing my swing on video and noticed this. Immediately, I began stretching and working on shoulder and upper back mobility... gradually improving my swing and giving me a few extra yards. It's still not what it was in my youth... and that's why it is important to keep or improve what we have now in terms of range of motion.

WRISTS AND FOREARMS

It's common for golfers coming into our programs to have wrist issues... many have difficulty doing pushups without pushup bars. Compromised wrists deliver a lack of mobility and strength, which can cause a multitude of issues like golfer's elbow.

Bad wrists can also make it a chore to practice golf as much as we would like.

Kettlebells in general are fantastic for improving grip strength and reversing this trend over time.

Kettlebells are also great in terms of building mobility in the wrists. Better mobility coupled with stronger forearms helps protect your elbow joints... and protect your wrists at impact on the downswing.

We do not need to program any additional forearm exercises to strengthen them thanks to the kettlebell. We'll be using presses and swings that will bulletproof your wrists and forearms.

BALANCE AND COORDINATION

Finally, we'll put it all together in athletic exercises that train our body to work in sync.

What good is strength, rotation, and mobility without balance? Without balance, you cannot have power or accuracy (lack of consistency). Without strength you cannot have power.

If you are swinging out of balance, you have a power leak or multiple power leaks. A power leak will kill your consistency.

Again, the more efficient we are with the club, the more power we can generate and more consistently strike the ball.

The kettlebell will naturally be helping us develop balance and coordination. So, if you feel out of sorts and not grooving with the kettlebell - give it time - this is a skill that develops over time.

See how that all works together? The kettlebell is the yin and yang of better golf.

What you'll find is that consistent kettlebell work makes you a better athlete. Your body parts will start working together better. When your body is 'in sync' you'll have a natural athleticism with superior balance and coordination.

To get all these benefits from barbells and dumbbells is difficult... and I may be a bit biased, but I believe that 50% of your training throughout the year should be kettlebell focused. Further, an athletic kettlebell exercise should be incorporated at least once a week into any training program you are doing.

LONGEVITY

It is vital that we incorporate acceleration and deceleration movements in our kettlebell training. These movements such as the swing and snatch and many others are designed to generate power while also bulletproofing your core.

Power is two-sided.

When you generate force, you need to be able to decelerate this power. The kettlebell is superior for this type of training. This brings in a whole new range of stabilizing muscles and really challenges your core. A bulletproofed body means more golf for longer.

In addition, Kettlebell Golf Body delivers flexibility and mobility programs for you to keep your joints oiled up and muscles supple and flexible.

Now let's learn about everything you need to get set up and using kettlebells.

CHAPTER 2: SET UP

YOUR COURAGE CORNER

As I mentioned in the previous chapters, the kettlebell is simplistic... and you just need the bare minimum to get started.

The first thing you need is a safe place to use the kettlebell.

For our purposes, our 'safe place' is not a room on a college campus with counseling and teddy bears. Our safe place is where we'll do work and re-build our body from the ground up. This space is meant to keep others safe from us and our kettlebell.

Most kettlebell junkies call their workout spaces 'courage corners'.

A simple 3-foot by 3-foot area will do. If you plan on moving into the advanced phases of Kettlebell Golf Body (Phase III and beyond), you'll need a 5-foot by 3-foot area. This will allow you to lay down to perform Turkish Get Ups and other exercises. We won't be learning these yet, but we will if join our 1-on-1 coaching in Phase III.

BUILD YOUR COURAGE CORNER FOR GOOD AND BAD TIMES

The courage corner is a minimalist's dream come true. Particularly adept at stepping in and providing an equal, if not superior, workout on-demand in difficult times such as a pandemic.

For example, when the recent pandemic brought everything to a crawl, including gyms... those with a courage corner at home were able to keep fighting without disruption. In fact, we in the kettlebell sub-culture had a running joke that "everyone used to make fun of us kettlebell guys, until now".

And that was a true statement!

The kettlebell geeks got the last laugh... and hundreds of thousands of people around the world soon bought out all kettlebells available for sale. This was a silver lining because the kettlebell is now a common sight to see in many homes - opening a world to people who never would have considered the kettlebell before.

All kidding aside, the kettlebell provides us with a full gym of challenging exercises. The courage corner is always on duty - in good times and bad.

With that said, you will need a few things for your safe space and to protect you from potentially angry partners (we don't want to destroy walls, furniture, floors, pets, kids).

DESIGNATE A PLACE

The first thing you need is a designated space for your courage corner.

You'll need a ceiling height of at least 8' (more depending on how tall you are). I am 6'3" tall and my ceiling is 8 feet tall. This is plenty of headroom for me to perform snatches with my biggest bell I named 'The Demon' in tribute to Gene Simmons. I even painted him to match the Demon. A 10-foot-tall ceiling is better.

You don't have to put your courage corner inside your home, it can go in a garage or even outside. Just make sure you have plenty of room to swing the kettlebell overhead without putting a hole in your ceiling.

THERE'S ONLY ONE RULE FOR THE COURAGE CORNER - DON'T DESTROY THE HOUSE. :)

Next, you need enough open space around your courage corner, so you do not damage furniture or nearby items. Usually a 3' by 3' square will do for standing kettlebell work. If you plan on doing the Turkish getup and groundwork like stretching, a bit more space will be required... like I mentioned earlier, I recommend 5 feet long by 3 feet wide.

An easy way to test your space to see if it will work is to stand in the middle of the proposed courage corner. From here extend your hand straight out in front of you as if you were going to punch someone, fingertips extended. Then simply rotate in a circle all the way around, you should find you have plenty of space in doing so.

Next, extend your arm straight above your head in the same fashion... now, here's where it gets tricky. If you can touch the ceiling (like I can) it may be too short if your technique is not good on the overhead snatch. If your technique is good, you should be just fine like I am.

Also, if you have a kettlebell... do a slow-motion press above your head, that will tell you if the overhead space is adequate.

Further, you need to place your courage corner out of heavy foot traffic areas. The last thing you need is a distraction when handling a kettlebell. This protects others from you, rather than you from them.

CHOOSE THE RIGHT FLOORING

The kettlebell is nothing but a canon-ball with a handle on it. Made of iron. Let me repeat myself here... the kettlebell is a canon-ball with a handle on it and it is 100% iron.

If you loaded it into a canon and fired it, it would behave the exact same way a cannon ball would. :)

As such, we need to take in to account accidents. Everyone drops the bell from time to time, although it is quite rare to see an experienced kettlebell geek drop the bell even under dire circumstances. BUT IT CAN AND DOES HAPPEN.

To protect your flooring, even concrete flooring, we need to ensure we have a good base of operations.

I've got two courage corners in my home. One outside is a cheap golf mat with a rubber bottom. Nothing fancy, but it does provide protection to the concrete patio. Be careful that your mat isn't too thick, as it can affect your balance when doing work. Take my word for it, the kettlebell also doubles as a wrecking ball on concrete, prepare accordingly. I can't tell you how many chunks I've taken out of my back porch when I didn't use the mat.

My second courage corner is in my office right next to where I am writing this book. The Bowflex mat under my indoor courage corner is made for a treadmill. The nice thing about this mat is not only does it have the right amount of padding, but it is also exactly 5 feet long and 3 feet wide, allowing ground movements such as the Turkish get up.

You can also get by with 3' by 3' horse stall mats from Tractor Supply. Those will work just fine, they are cheap, thick, and tough, best suited for your garage or outdoors. You'll need more than one of those for full body work. The only problem with them is that they do not interlock, and the two mats may slip when moving between them. I prefer the solution below...

Probably the best solution is interlocking judo mats which many experts recommend that provide good padding and give you enough room to operate.

Regardless of what you choose, you need to choose something that can protect your beautiful floors. Worst case scenario, workout on your lawn or in the park... no mat needed!

CHOOSING YOUR KETTLEBELLS

If you have not purchased any kettlebells, that's fine! In fact, we'll go over a few things I wish I had known when I first was introduced to the iron.

Probably the most common thing I hear from people new to kettlebells concerns the weighting. To be honest, these not much uniformity here...

KETTLEBELLS ARE WEIRD

Kettlebells do not go up in weight like dumbbells. Instead of going up by 2.5 pounds or 5 pounds, kettlebells often go up 8 to 12 pounds from one size to the next. They even vary in weights from one manufacturer to another. Even more confusing is that some kettlebells are marked in pounds and some in kilograms... and some are marked with both!

The beauty of the 8-to-12-pound range is it makes things easier by requiring less bells. Instead of an entire rack of dumbbells that can cost thousands of dollars, you just need a few kettlebells and can get fully equipped for a few hundred dollars... never having to spend a dime again!

Further, we don't need tiny increments with the kettlebell. This is due to its design because we can make the kettlebell challenging by varying the exercise difficulty, time under tension, and intensity.

When buying your kettlebells, look for ones made by the same manufacturer that are weighted 8 to 12 pounds apart. This will give you a good variety to choose from.

I've created a handy chart below to help guide you on picking your weights. But let's cover a few more things I've learned from experience that will help you pick your starter set of kettlebells.

DO I NEED TWO KETTLEBELLS?

Not yet.

But...

It can't hurt to buy them in matching pairs. For example, I bought a kettlebell I absolutely loved around 2010. The handle was smooth and fit perfectly into my grip. The bell was of high quality. Finally, when I was skilled and strong enough to handle two kettlebells at the same time - I went to purchase the matching bell. Unfortunately, they stopped making them! This didn't stop me from buying something similar, but it was just weird for my brain to process as the handles varied slightly.

One more item to consider for getting matching kettlebells at purchase is the COVID situation. When COVID first hit, exercise equipment was hard to find. COVID was hopefully a once in a lifetime situation, but it is best to always be prepared.

Starting out, you could begin with three bells total - each of different weights. A relatively light bell, a medium bell, and a heavy bell. As you advance, you'll want to add a fourth bell that's heavier than our heaviest.

As you can see, this could get expensive if you were to buy matching bells at each weight. If you have the money though, it is well worth it! You're basically done with your gym once you have a variety of weights and will never need to spend a dime again.

In terms of the Phase I and Phase II, we will only be using a single bell for our exercises. Quite simply, we need to build a solid base with one bell before we upgrade our training to two bells.

Phase III will introduce double kettlebell work but only on select exercises. First things first, we need to build that solid foundation to enable double bell capability. Double bells step up the difficulty level tenfold.

My current configuration of bells spans from matching pairs of 20kg all the way up to 2.5 pood (90 pounds).

One more thing, NEVER get rid of a kettlebell - even if you think you've outgrown a lighter one. As we cycle programming, we will be utilizing the full range of kettlebells in our courage corner. Light bells can be made to feel heavy depending on different factors.

Perhaps the most important factor is the handle...

THE HANDLE MATTERS

The handle on a kettlebell can make or break it. You want a bell with a smooth handle that fits into your hand properly. Otherwise, you are headed for uncomfortable sessions.

Steer clear of bells with rubber grips or rough handles. We're going to be working with our hands on bells and they will be slipping, sliding, and moving around when we are working. A rough handle or a rubber grip will eat your hands alive.

I'll cover hand care in the next section, and trust me, you'll want to read that section a few times. If our hands are beat to hell, it's hard to do work and play golf.

Now that we understand what we are looking for, let's look and building your starter set...

BUILDING YOUR KETTLEBELL COLLECTION

As I mentioned above, kettlebells are marked on the iron with their weight in kilograms. In Russia, kettlebells are weighed in 'pood'. A pood was originally the system used to weigh crops in Russia. If you live in the United States, some kettlebells are weighed in pounds. And of course, some are marked in both.

For men, we like them to begin with 1 pood, which is 16kg or 35 pounds. You may see kettlebells in athletic stores with the US Imperial weighting on them. These are perfectly fine.

All the different measurements can be a bit confusing so I created a chart so you can cross reference the weights:

Pood	Kilograms	Pounds
.25	4	9
.5	8	18
1	16	35
1.25	20	44
1.5	24	53
1.75	28	62
2	32	70
2.5	40	88

Keep in mind, those weights are approximate and vary slightly depending on the manufacturer. Therefore, it might be a good idea to buy matching pairs, to ensure you have equal weights for your matched pairs.

Now that you understand the variety available, you can now start to determine what you want in your courage corner...

WHAT DOES A GOOD STARTER SET CONSIST OF?

The following chart will help your plan your starter set or expanding your current collection. Remember, you just need one of each so as you get stronger, you can progress - but it is a good idea to buy matched pairs.

Starting Kettlebell Size		
Person	**Start With**	**Recommended Set**
Average Female	8kg	8kg, 16kg, 20kg
Average Male	16kg	16kg, 20kg, 24kg, 28kg
Strong Female	16kg	16kg, 20kg, 24kg
Strong Male	20kg	20kg, 24kg, 28kg, 32kg
Very Strong Male	24kg	24kg, 28kg, 32kg, 40kg

If you want to add a fourth kettlebell, always add the next heaviest one.

Now that you've decided on your starter set, you'll need to find a reputable place to purchase them.

WHERE SHOULD I GET MY KETTLEBELLS FROM?

A place I'd suggest picking your bells up from is RogueFitness.com. These kettlebells are made in the United States and are top quality. Further, they have a few different lines depending on your budget. One thing is for sure, they are built to last and will outlive you.

Avoid cheaper bells you'll find at sporting goods stores. I've found that the handles are just awkward and some like I mentioned above, some are even covered in rubber! The weights seem a bit off and the casting is just not as good as the ones you'll find at Rogue.

Another strike against your local sporting goods stores is that you will rarely find the same type of bell at the same weight down the road. This can lead to mixed pairs. You won't have this issue with Rogue Fitness as their kettlebells have been consistent for the past ten years.

A big plus for your local sporting goods store is that you'll only pay sales tax. Shipping can get rather expensive when you are moving 70 pounds from one end of the country to the next. The strike against the Internet retailers is you'll probably be paying sales tax AND shipping.

Please buy quality bells, they will last a lifetime. Buck up and swallow the added expense here - you will thank me later.

Once you get them ordered, you'll need a few extra's that will make your life much easier in your courage corner and on the course...

EVERYTHING ELSE YOU NEED

WRIST GUARDS

Many of the old schoolers in the kettlebell sub-culture prefer that you work without wrist guards or gloves. Their argument is that your form improves much faster without gloves or guards... as you are forced to improve your technique or suffer the consequences.

This is true, but it is also bad advice... here's why:

Movements like the clean and snatch done with less than perfect form are going to bruise your forearms making these moves painful. I've never seen anyone nail these movements on their first try with perfect form.

I can tell you, the bruising felt from poorly done cleans and snatches is not pleasant. In fact, bruised forearms can keep you from improving your form because you'll waste time healing. And this can impact your golf game as well.

The fastest way to improving your form is not injuring yourself which will only delay improving. As we know, no one is perfect... and movements like the clean and snatch take time. Eventually, you'll get to the point where you do not need wrist guards.

I use wrist guards every time I use kettlebells and feel no shame. Mainly, they help keep sweat from getting onto my hands which can create more friction and in turn blisters. They are also there for the inevitable slip or bad rep. No one is perfect.

Don't feel shame when using wrists guards, I'd rather be able to play golf and enjoy life than sit around feeling like a tough guy.

The key here is to get the form right so that you eventually do not need the guards... but use them just in case of a bad rep and help keep the hands dry.

Like learning the golf swing, learning the kettlebell is a work in progress. No one steps into the courage corner and has perfect form their first day. There is no shame in this... once your form is solid - ditch the wrist guards if you wish.

HOW TO BUY WRIST GUARDS

Wrist guards are like sweat bands except that they have plastic inserts in them. These inserts are fantastic at protecting your wrist and forearm bones.

You can use sweat bands, but they suck. Sweat bands alone are better than nothing. In a pinch, they will be fine, but you'll still feel the bell make contact on bad form. The plastic inserts provide a bit more protection.

When hunting down wrist guards, make sure they have the plastic inserts in them.

Your best bet is from KettleGuard.com. Don't skimp here and get a good pair of wrist guards.

Your hands will take a beating too...

FINGERLESS COTTON GLOVES

For gloves, I usually opt to go gloveless. In Kettlebell Golf Body, we won't be doing a large amount of volume sets, which is where you can really beat up your hands.

When I am getting ready for a certification event, I will use gloves on exercises I am doing a lot of reps on. This is only done as a precaution to ensure I can get in all my reps to be prepared.

For example, when doing long sessions such as 100 snatches in a row, I'll often use fingerless cotton gloves. Some call them military gloves. The only reason I'll use them on long snatch sessions is to prevent blisters and no other reason.

In addition, I've discovered these gloves make gripping the kettlebell MORE difficult - and help strengthen my forearms. This is great because the gloves are helping improve my gloveless snatches.

Starting out, you might find them helpful learning proper form. Many newbies to kettlebells often struggle with grip strength and over-grip which causes all sorts of issues. Cotton military gloves make it hard to get a blister even if you do use improper form or over-grip. Again, moving is better than waiting around to heal.

The best place I've found for fingerless cotton military gloves is Amazon. I also have found them at Military Surplus stores here locally for $5.

BENCH

A solid adjustable weight bench would be beneficial as there are a few exercises that use it. It is not necessary though and we can work around if required. Just let us know on the Facebook group.

A non-adjustable bench would work just as well too. However, if you are adding a bench and don't have one - go for an adjustable one - it will make Phases III and beyond much easier.

I have an old Bowflex bench that is probably 10 years or more old. It's held up very well and is a solid brand. Bowflex is generally not cheap, but you do get what you pay for.

The only real rule of thumb here is that the bench should be able to hold your weight plus your heaviest kettlebell.

And that's really all you need.

Keep it simple but keep it safe!

Now, it's time to get our hands dirty and start using our kettlebell.

CHAPTER 3: HOW TO

HOW TO STAY SAFE

TREAT THE BELL AS IF IT'S FULLY LOADED

1. Consult with your Physician before you begin the Kettlebell Golf Body program. Do not start this program if you have an injury. Consult with your doctor on when to begin.

2. Treat the kettlebell like you would a gun and assume it is always loaded when in movement. Once in motion, the kettlebell can be extremely dangerous to you as well as others in your immediate range.

3. Make sure your Courage Corner is free of objects that may be hit by the bell. In addition, make sure the surface you are training on is not slippery. Ensure there are no people or small animals or breakables in or near your Courage Corner.

4. If possible, train barefoot or with shoes that are flat like Converse or Vans. Barefoot and flat shoes allow us to spread our toes for the forces the bell will be placing upon us. Running shoes are not good for kettlebell training as they can throw you off balance.

5. Respect the kettlebell by getting out of its way if you lose control of it. Do not try to save bad reps, this is how you can injure yourself. Simply guide the kettlebell out of your body space and allow it to fall where it wishes. Stay light on your feet in such cases.

6. If you are unsure how to perform a movement – ask us! If an exercise hurts or doesn't feel right – STOP. We can provide alternative movements or regressions to any exercise listed in the Kettlebell Golf Body workouts. Simply ask for a substitution.

Regressive exercises may be needed if you are unable to perform some of the exercises listed in our program. In many cases, this will IMPROVE performance. Don't be afraid to use a regressive movement.

7. Focus on QUALITY and not quantity. This is not a CrossFit competition based on reps and time. First, understand what proper form is for each exercise before attempting. Bad form will most assuredly result in injury.

Expert coach Gray Cook offers that motor control (proper form) falls as you fatigue and that your body will always "sacrifice quality". If you notice your quality failing, STOP.

Here are a few warning signs:

- RPE (Rate of Perceived Exertion) exceeds an 8 out of 10.
- You are gasping for air.
- Your technique noticeably changes for the worse.
- Rep speed or tempo drops, or you are taking too long between reps 'resting'.

If the rep is not PERFECT because of any of the above, you are DONE. Stop. Aim to beat your rep count next time with perfect form.

8. Once your heart rate is up, do not lay down or rest. Stay standing. Keep moving.

9. Most importantly, do not place your spine into flexion after training. We do not want to be doing a forward bending stretches or slouching after training. These may seem harmless but can injure your back.

10. Build your weights and training gradually by listening to your body! Common sense is your best teacher here, do not listen to your ego or other people. We are looking to master the kettlebell and get stronger by doing so. We are not looking to set world records. Always remember that strength is a skill, and it takes time to build that skill.

HOW TO PROTECT YOUR HANDS

Your hands are going to be tested when you use the kettlebell.

Priority must be taken when caring for your hands when you are training. The handle of the kettlebell moves around in your hand as you move through each exercise and creates friction.

This friction can come from rough bell handles, sticky handles, too tight of a grip or all of these.

Blisters = downtime.

If you get blisters from your kettlebell training, you are either going to have painful sessions or missed days... and these issues will carry over to your golf game.

The name of the game then is to reduce this amount of friction as much as possible.

There are a few things to look out for:

1. Rough or pitted kettlebell handle.

One easy solution is to ensure the kettlebells you buy have smooth handles. Some bells come with grips that are rough or pitted. I've got a few of these bells and there are two solutions.

- Smooth the handles out with a metal file.
- Use fingerless military style gloves.

Either one or both solve the issue of the rough handle.

You may have a kettlebell you bought before reading this book that has a rubber coated handle. This is not going to work well for you. Replace it with a quality all iron bell.

2. Not enough time under the kettlebell.

It takes time to toughen the hands up. If when starting out you have issues with blisters, it may simply come down to not enough time using the kettlebell.

If this is the case and you have chosen to train without gloves, take your time building your hands up.

Another common issue with beginners is they grip the bell too tightly. Gripping too tight will cause more friction and make movements more difficult, often compromising your form too.

Start light and grip the bell only as tightly as needed. To put your mind at ease, make sure you have your courage corner setup, and a drop won't matter.

3. Too Much Chalk.

Too much is a bad thing. Use sparingly, if ever, as too much can cause your skin to tear. I've found chalk can also cause some added friction when you get sweaty.

4. Thick Calluses.

If you do manual labor, chances are you may have calloused hands. And working a lot with Olympic weights and kettlebells will build callouses as well.

Thick callouses are no bueno for kettlebell work. These are like speedbumps and will blister up and tear.

An easy way to get them under control is to work on them in the shower or bath. Once you get them moistened up, you can usually peel some of the thickness that could get pinched between the bell and your hand.

If this does not work, then you can soak them in warm water.

Be careful as you don't want to get rid of them totally. A little callusing is needed to protect the hands.

5. Over-gripping the kettlebell.

Using a proper grip will go a long way to preventing blisters. Make sure you are 'hooking' the bell handle with your fingers and not pinch the calluses at the base of fingers. As you advance, you'll get better at your grip.

This is much the same as your golf grip. My grandad used to say grip the club like you were holding a baby bird.

The kettlebell will challenge your grip - but one thing is for sure - you can't hold it with a death grip, or you are going to shred your hands and you are going to have bad form which can cause injury.

Start light and get reps under your belt, your grip will grow stronger over time.

TIPS FOR HAND CARE

1. Moisturize your hands with lotion or as my mentor Pavel Tsatsouline recommends, with Cornhusker Lotion.

2. If you have a blister or just created a new one - take care of the blister and rest that day. No reason to make a bad situation worse, it will just delay your training.

3. Wear fingerless cotton military gloves. These go a long way in protecting the hands, but you can still get blisters wearing them if your grip is improper.

4. A little bit of chalk.

5. Smooth your kettlebell handles if they are rough!

6. Use the right grip for the exercise.

Next, let's look at proper form which will keep you safe and moving instead of on the sidelines...

HOW TO PRACTICE PROPER FORM

The Warmups (at the beginning of each workout) will contain several 'practice' movements that are designed to improve your form and unlock your body for better performance.

Proper form is the key to getting the most bang for your buck with your workouts... and the best preventative medicine possible. Keep in mind, learning the kettlebell, like learning the golf swing will always be a 'work in progress'.

Perfection is the goal but is never attainable. However, perfect form is the standard we will measure ourselves by.

Each workout and each rep therefore should be recognized as 'practice'. No different than the driving range or putting green where you work on your swing and stroke.

With each successive practice session and rep, you improve (or regress) a tiny bit.

As such, we will go over the proper form for our big four exercises. We'll cover each exercise in detail and focus on breathing techniques, grips, grunts and groans and everything in between on all our primary mover exercises in Kettlebell Golf Body.

We'll start from the ground up just like the golf swing and work our way to the toughest exercise of them all... the snatch!

And please, don't get too down on yourself if you are having difficulty in any one exercise or movement - we are practicing!

Each rep and each session you'll improve and become more flexible, stronger, and more comfortable with the kettlebell.

Now, it's time to graduate from absorbing this information mentally and put everything to work...

Athletes move from the hips first, never from the back or knees. This generates to most power and is best for your knees and back.

We must first start with the hip hinge to program our brains to work from the hips first with the kettlebell.

HOW TO GRIP THE KETTLEBELL

How do you grip a kettlebell?

IT DEPENDS

Just like we can adapt our grip on the golf club depending on the type of shot we will be hitting, we can do the same with the kettlebell.

We use an 'it depends' on mentality when selecting a grip. Depending on the lift that is...

I've created a chart of a few below for you to easily reference:

GRIP	EXERCISE(S)
45-Degree	Racking, Pressing, Single Arm Squatting
Double Over Hand	Swings, Deadlifts, Sumo Squatting
Single Over Hand	Swings, Snatches, Rows, Clean
Corner Grip	Rotational
Goblet	Squats, Lunges, Pressing

The chart above is to give you an understanding that we will be varying our grip using the ‘it depends’ on method. The ‘it’ being the exercise.

There are others, but for our purposes, I won’t waste your time with them.

GRIP PRESSURE

We will not be squeezing the life out of the kettlebell. Instead, like the golf grip we only want to use enough pressure to hold the bell as we work. Too much pressure or too little and we won’t be able to maintain athleticism.

Some grips simply rest on our palm while others are hooked with our fingers.

45-DEGREE

Usage: The 45-degree grip is the one we'll use when we work into the rack position. From the rack position, you have access to overhead presses, squats.

How: The handle should be fitted into your hand at a 45-degree angle. The handle will fall along the slow you palm naturally makes when you close your thumb and index finger.

This grip will keep your wrist straight, meaning that the back of your hand is in line with your forearm. When you use heavier weights, a broken wrist position can cause all sorts of trouble.

When the wrist breaks back or forward, this is called the broken wrist position. Either forward or backward broken wrist position will make pressing the bell difficult if not impossible. Further, a broken wrist position can result in injury. The biggest fault to look for here is that the bell is not fitting into the palm groove naturally created but is instead following your finger line.

When you are first starting out, you'll need to pay particular attention to your wrist position when using the 45-degree grip. It can be difficult to get at first, but very important.

You may notice that your wrists feel weak in the 45-degree position, this is simply because they are de-conditioned. Work with a lighter bell and your wrist will strengthen over time.

I'll cover this grip in a lot more detail shortly.

DOUBLE OVER HAND

Usage: Two-handed swings, deadlifts, sumo squats, upright rows

How: Grip the bell with both hands with an overhand grip. You'll do this by gripping the bell in your fingertips and closing the grip with your thumb. The bell will be held in place with this hook of four fingers and the lock is the thumb. The handle will only slightly touch your palm, this is mainly a finger hook grip.

Keep the grip light throughout your movement. Be aware of where you tighten the grip. Remember, an overly tight grip will cause friction and blisters.

If you have large hands, your grip may encompass the curve of the handle.

On long runs with the swing, you'll find that your grip may struggle, it is ok to adjust your grip tightness as you move through the swing. Keeping the tension at the same strength for too long can cause burnout. By loosening the grip slightly when the bell is in motion will help you push longer.

SINGLE OVER HAND

Usage: One-Handed Swing, Snatches, Dead Clean, Rows

How: Grab the bell near the corner furthest away from your body. The bell handle will stay in your fingers, just below your palm. You'll create a thumb lock with your index finger but keep this very light.

Like the double over hand grip for single arm exercises.

This grip is used as a starting point in certain exercises before we slowly migrate the grip to the 45-degree position.

For example, when pulling a bell off the floor into the clean, we start with a corner grip and then transition to the 45-degree grip at the end of the clean.

CORNER

Usage: Around the body, figure 8, rotational exercises.

How: Hold the kettlebell at the corner of the handle with an overhand grip. You can go with a thumb lock or not on this one.

You can grip from either corner with this grip. For presses, you'll grip the corner furthest away from your body. For figure 8's or around the body, I like to grip the corner closest to my body.

GOBLET

Use: Squats, Lunges, Presses

How: You won't be using the handle in this grip, instead, you'll be turning the kettlebell upside down and cradling it like a giant goblet.

You'll press into the kettlebell with both of your palms. The more under the bell you go, the easier this grip is. And the reverse is true as well, the higher up you go, the harder it is... and you also risk losing your grip. So, try to stay slightly under for best results.

Your elbows will be close to your body for the goblet squat, helping solidify your base to grip under the kettlebell. You'll maintain constant tension by pressing your opposing hands into the ball and into each other.

HOW TO BREATHE

Let's talk about breathing now... You should never fully exhale during the swing. By maintaining some air in your lungs, your core remains tight and protective of your back.

Imagine you are going to be punched, this is the type of firmness we wish in the core.

The general rule is that you inhale through your nose when the bell has almost reached the fully loaded position of the hike pass.

You give a quick exhale the moment you explode from the hips... like a martial artist throwing a punch. The breathing syncs with the explosion and provides firmness in the core and helps with generating power. Some people combine a grunt and exhale at this point.

As we get more advanced, we'll introduce suggested breathing patterns for you to try.

Next is probably the most important proper form technique you can learn for your golf game and the kettlebell...

HOW TO PROPERLY HINGE

Whether it is the golf swing or the kettlebell swing, you'll need a solid hip hinge. You'll also need to be able to maintain this hinge while fighting and producing force to maintain control of the kettlebell and club.

This section is perhaps the most important aspect of this entire book when it comes to proper form and improving your golf game. Spend time working on your hip hinge and you'll be rewarded big time.

The hip hinge is very similar to how we get setup properly to strike a golf ball. Also known as your posture in golf, we hinge at the hips. Hinging at the hips and maintaining that hinge position into impact is important. When we round at the back or adjust ourselves with the knees, we run into big problems with the golf swing.

You've heard golf professionals mention "coming out of the shot" or "standing up" or even "dipping"? This is the loss of your hip hinge.

Generally, when you lose this position your consistency, accuracy and power go out the window. And if you have a rounded back at impact during your golf swing or in your kettlebell swing, this drill is going to cure that once and for all. Not only will getting rid of the rounded back help your game, but it will also help protect your back from injury.

Please do not confuse the hip hinge as a static position, it is dynamic.

However, we maintain proper hinging through our swing, be it a golf swing or a kettlebell swing. Let's go through the step-by-step process here and nail this before moving on in the book.

HIP HINGE DRILL

The hip hinge drill is no different than the hip hinge you set when you address the golf ball.

Once you learn this movement, you'll notice quick if you have good or bad posture with your golf swing. So please pay extra attention to the proper hip fold.

1. Stand up and place the edge of your hands into the crease at the top of your thighs. Picture the place on your body that is the most like a hinge. Press your hands in hard and stick your rear end out.

NOTE: One difference between the golf hinge for proper setup posture and the kettlebell hinge is you'll put your weight on your heels in the kettlebell version.

2. Keep bending over as if you are going to sit on a chair behind you. Your knees are bent slightly, and your shins remain upright. The biggest area I see this go wrong is when the knees are brought in too much. The knees must be flexed in much the same way as your golf posture. They are not straight, but they are not overly bent. They are more like shock absorbers.

3. Keep the back straight as you fold over. Your eyeline tracks with your back and neck. Simply put, your vision will move like a pump and not be focused on a single spot here. The spine, neck, and head all remain in a straight line as you move up and down.

4. On the way up, imagine pushing your hips forward as if strings were attached to your hands, simply reversing this process. A good squeeze from your glutes and hamstrings (and no help from the back) will push the hips forward and drive your spine up to a standing position.

A good way to practice hips first and program your mind for perfection is through the wall squat.

Practice this hip hinge for ten reps randomly throughout the day before moving on to the next skill... the wall squat.

WALL FACING SQUAT

This squat is fantastic for first-time kettlebell students. The very beginning of the wall facing squat is much like your golf stance... we just stop before going too far.

The wall facing squat was popularized by John Du Cane in his 'The Qigong Recharge' book.

This squat is fantastic for first-time kettlebell students. This is because it teaches the proper hinging we'll need for squats, pulls, and swings.

First, you'll need a wall. Stand close to it, with your toes just a couple of inches away. As we get better at this squat, we'll inch our feet closer and closer until our toes are directly against the wall. Trust me, this is possible with good form.

Next, your feet are slightly wider than shoulder width. A good way of finding the 'slight wider than shoulder-width' is to allow your arms to hang down with a proud chest. The insides of your feet should be directly under your fingertips. From here, I like to point my toes out at roughly 15 to 30 degrees.

The goal is to lower yourself without pushing your face or knees into the wall. Instead, we want to slowly lower ourselves and learn the proper movements to reach the bottom of a squat without touching the wall. Also, the knees track over the feet and don't flare out. The feet stay flat and planted. Your face should move straight up and down like an elevator.

As you descend, feet remain planted and do not roll in our out. If you roll your feet to the sides, your knees will flare out and you will lose the form. This is called 'frogging'. If you find yourself doing this, your butt needs to be pushing out further behind you, following the floor in parallel.

If you lean back onto your heels too much, you will tip backwards and your back will not fold forward, staying more vertical.

If you are leaning too much onto the balls of your feet, you will tip forward and smack your face into the wall.

Move in a controlled fashion as you descend, using your core and strength in your legs for control. This is not a speed exercise.

Let your arms hang naturally straight down as if you were going to pick up a kettlebell handle between your legs. Keep a proud chest without shoulders rounding forward.

Once you feel your hips can go back no further and your knees start to bend, this is the bottom of your hip hinge. Take note, this position will be like the hike position in the swing I will teach you later.

Now, squeeze your butt cheeks and hamstrings and push the hips forward.

Inch closer and closer to the wall and repeat until your toes are against the wall.

This first exercise is important to practice over and over as it will protect you from injury down the road. So, take your time with it. Once you've nailed it, progress onward to our next practice exercise - the Sumo Deadlift.

HOW TO PICK UP THE KETTLEBELL

Let's pick up a kettlebell now using the wall facing squat we just learned.

SUMO DEADLIFT

The next progression we'll need is to learn how to pick the kettlebell off the floor with good form. This is the same exercise as the wall squat you've been practicing except; we will be picking a kettlebell off the ground.

With a stance slightly wider than your shoulders, you'll turn your feet outward at roughly 15-to-30-degrees.

The kettlebell is situated in the center of your stance. Next your kettlebell will fall upon an imaginary line between the balls of your feet.

From here, you will begin to squat down by pushing your rump backward on a parallel line to the floor, as you would to sit in a chair. You'll keep a proud chest while doing this and not letting it fall forward.

Your arms will hang straight down thanks to gravity, and you'll grab the kettlebell by the handles using the Double Over Hand Grip. Then, stand back up reversing the movements. Maintain the same core intensity throughout the lowering and raising phases.

The weighted hinge movement we learn from the Sumo Deadlift translates to the kettlebell squat and the swing, snatch, clean, etc.

The sumo deadlift should not be ignored as our first practice exercise.

SUMO DEADLIFT CHECKPOINTS

1. Your arms are always straight. The legs will do all the work other than gripping the bell. Keep a proud chest and don't slump forward with the shoulders.

2. The knees track over the feet on your way down and up.

3. Heels remain planted firmly on the ground, your weight does not fall forward over the toes. You don't put too much weight on your heels.

4. The back is straight and not rounded, this does not always mean straight up. Your shoulders should always remain over your knees through this lift. Think of a scissor-lift machine where the basket always remains over the base even though the scissors underneath may be going opposite directions.

5. The neck is relaxed though and not tense and your eyes will track along the natural path your hinge brings.

Practice the sumo deadlift and when you feel you've got it locked down, let's move on to the swing.

HOW TO DO THE TWO-HAND SWING

The next step in using the kettlebell is to learn how to properly swing the bell.

When you see someone with good swing form, it looks as if they are barely using any muscles at all. The flow is simple, clean, and powerful.

For the beginner, proper form is challenging...

KNOW WHAT BAD FORM IS FIRST

I can't tell you how many times I walk into my local gym and see people using all kinds of bad technique for the swing.

Perhaps the two most common things wrong I see are:

#1. Too much knee bend. The swing is not a squat and your lowest position in the swing (the hike pass) is the same as your lowest position in the wall squat. Just as in the wall squat, using too much knee bend puts you in a weak position not just from a power standpoint, but an injury standpoint.

#2. Pulling the bell up with the upper back and arms. This is a big no. You are looking to get injured quick here. The power comes from the hips, always remember HIPS FIRST.

And there are countless other issues I've seen, but these are the most common and usually the person who has too much knee bend also pulls the bell up with the arms out of the hike pass position.

LEARN BY PROGRESSING

Getting the proper technique down can take some time for the swing. However, this movement will do more for your golf game than any other exercise. I won't cover all the benefits, but let's just say your game will never be the same again after deploying the swing.

And while the experts make it look easy, it can be challenging to find your swing groove. So, we'll start by breaking the swing down like we did picking up the kettlebell… by improving our hinge.

STEP 1: BOX SQUAT

The box squat is used by powerlifters to improve their squats. We will use the box squat to improve our swing. A by-product will be the improvement of our squat as well.

Remember the Hip Hinge Drill and how to pick up a kettlebell?

Good, now let's put those to work.

First, you'll need a sturdy chair or box to sit on. Don't use a chair with wheels, the object must be stationary and able to hold your weight.

Next, stand with your heels about one foot away from the box or chair… and perform the hip hinge drill. If you have not practiced the hip hinge drill, do not pass go, and practice it all the way through to the sumo deadlift.

Now, sit back with the hips, your knees will only move at the appropriate time. Don't let your knees move forward, they need to stay over your feet and your shins upright.

You should feel your glutes and hamstrings tighten as you lower, this is good. If you are not feeling your hamstrings, you are doing this wrong.

Your knees should not bow out or in, they remain stable and track over your feet.

This will be very similar to the wall squat, but more extreme in terms of your butt sticking out and the forward fold from your hips. You can use your arms to counterbalance this movement.

Continue sitting back until you are sitting on the box or chair.

Now you must stand up.

Do not replant your feet, keep them in the same position as when you began.

As you sit back, roll your upper body back while maintaining a straight spine, then with your momentum roll forward and push the hips forward. You will stand up straight.

Pretend that you are stuck in cement as you stand.

As you roll forward, reach forward with your arms. The counterbalance will make standing easier. Push your feet and heels into the ground.

Squeeze your butt cheeks and drive the hips forward, the knees remain steady.

Once you've got this movement down, it's time to learn how power is generated in the swing... and where I see MANY people in the gym making a big mistake.

STEP 2: BOX SQUAT TO VERTICAL JUMP

Now we'll combine the box squat and a vertical jump. This will teach you where the power from a swing comes from.

Most people I see in the gym performing the swing are not generating power. Instead, they are pulling the bell up with their upper body.

A pull swing as I call it, is not really a swing at all. Instead of creating power and making the bell weightless, the person is pulling the bell up.

Imagine that we want to jump to reach the rim of a basketball goal. From the hike pass position, we will then explode from the hips by pushing them forward. As we explode with the hips, we drive with our legs vertically and uncoil our body to create lift.

The swing will utilize the same mechanics for the swing to generate power.

Remember, hips first!

The hips are the first to move back and load the bell into our hike pass position. The hips are first to push the bell forward.

I cannot stress enough how important it is to be explosive with the hips here. While we practiced with the hip hinge drill and the box squat by being slow and deliberate… we were working on proper form.

Once we have form nailed, it's time to build our power component… and once you nail this movement, the swing is a piece of cake!

We'll begin by performing the box squat drill. However, once we reach the bottom we are going to explode from the hips.

The big mistake I see here is people swing their arms. Keep your arms in front of you and power yourself up with nothing but your hips.

Drive the hips forward and catch some air. As you propel yourself up, it's ok to let the arms drive you up into the air… your hands finishing by your hips as you are off the ground and body is vertical as if in a standing plank.

Reset yourself each jump. Load your hips and drive all the way up to a jump position. This is the swing!

Now, we've got to dial in our technique a bit more to protect our wrists, elbows and back.

STEP 3: TOWEL SWING

Now it is time to learn how to handle the weight of the kettlebell. As the swing is a dynamic exercise, the kettlebell is going to be moving around as we fight gravity and try to maintain control.

The easiest way to teach you the proper kettlebell flow is by using a towel. Specifically, you are going to need a kitchen towel.

You will be able to feel how the bell should move from this highly efficient drill.

Imagine that your body is the handle of a bullwhip, and your hips are your wrist. Now imagine cracking a whip... you won't get a crack if your wrist is limp, and your movement is all arms. There is a rigidity to the arm and a loading of your wrist. This stored up energy is then released with a pop as the arm releases the stored-up energy in your wrist.

The kettlebell swing will work the exact same way.

You'll need your kitchen towel and your lightest kettlebell.

Next, place the kettlebell about a foot and a half in front of your toes, middle of your feet. Turn the kettlebell so the handle is pointing straight in front of you like an arrow. Run the towel through the handle by the horn farthest away from you.

Now, you are going to do the good old box squat here without the box. Reach out in front of you and grab the towel so that you feel the weight of the bell. Now, tip the bell backwards toward your body while maintaining tension. Remember how this position feels.

Your arms will form a straight line from your shoulders through your wrists and into the bell. Everything should be tied together with no slack. Slack is bad here!

Your next move is called the hike pass. From here, you are going to elevate your hips slightly. As you do so, the kettlebell will move under you. Push the bell back behind you with your shoulders.

It is very important to maintain tension in your core, glutes, shoulders, arms, hamstrings. Do not let the bell move you around. Resist!

As the bell reaches behind you and your arms are still straight, including your wrists and the kettlebell you will now be in the hike pass position.

Now, explode from the hips just like we did with the vertical jump. Be careful here, don't pull with the arms. This IS ALL HIPS.

The hips will push forward, and your arms will be propelled forward as well as the kettlebell. The bell should remain in a straight line with your arms the entire way and finish in front of you at chest level.

Throw the kettlebell behind you as if you are descending into an explosive start position for a jump.

The towel will give us instant feedback on improving your form. If you are doing the movement improperly at any point - the kettlebell will not be in a straight line with your wrists and arms.

If your wrists are floppy and not firm on the hike pass, the bell will fly up and try to hit you in the butt.

If you are using too much of an arm movement (the pull I see in the gym), the kettlebell will be below your hands at full extension.

If the kettlebell pulls you forward and out of balance, drop the bell. Don't fight it. Start another clean rep.

We will not worry about breath control here, just breathe as you do but do not hold your breath. We will get into breath later one during the kettlebell. First, we must master the basics!

Continue with this until you can do 10 to 15 quality reps. Remember this feeling as you will now replicate it with the two-handed swing.

STEP 4: PUTTING IT ALL TOGETHER

Now it's time to dance.

Stand a foot and a half (depends on your arm length) behind the kettlebell. Feet are a little wider than your hips, toes angled out slightly.

Perform your Box squat and grab the handle of the bell.

Tilt the bell back towards your body. The bell will be on its side and in a straight line with your arms and wrists (just like the towel swing).

Put your weight onto your heels and slight push your hips forward. The bell will swing back, and you will push it behind you into the pike pass position.

The handle and your hands will pass closely by your groin.

Once fully loaded, the bell handle will remain in a straight line with your wrists and arms.

From here, it's time for that explosive hip pop. Push the hips forward and power the bell forward and in front of you at chest height. Again, at the chest position the handle of the bell and your wrists and arms form a straight line.

HOW TO DO THE ONE-HAND SWING

All that we learned in the two-handed swing applies to the one-hand swing. The only difference here is that the bell will try to twist you during the one-hand swing because you are only using one-arm due to the weight. This is good for our golf game because this twist resistance builds our ability to store and release torque in our swing.

You must resist this twisting action by stabilizing your core and shoulders.

Also, you will notice your grip may feel weak. This is normal, just make sure you are hooking the handle with your fingertips, your grip will get stronger and stronger the more you swing.

Just as we learned the two-handed swing by progression, we will do the same with the one-hand swing. The main difference is how we begin the swing. Instead of using two hands to move the bell off the ground, we will just be using one arm.

HOW TO DO THE KETTLEBELL CLEAN

Now, we need to learn how to clean the kettlebell off the ground from a dead position. This will be the pre-cursor to the very mportant press and squat exercises.

WARNING

Leave the ego at the door when learning the kettlebell.

Wrist guards are a form of training wheels and eventually you will not require them. But starting out learning the clean, we don't want to lose time from bruised forearms... use them if this is your first rodeo.

Knowing how to properly clean the kettlebell will not only save your wrists, but also put you into proper setup for presses, squats, swings, etc.

The clean is a technique used to pick the kettlebell up off the ground with one arm. If you are familiar with kettlebell cleans.

Earlier, we learned how to pick the kettlebell off the ground using our sumo deadlift with two hands. That's good for goblet squats, deadlifts, and the sort where we need to use two hands to secure the kettlebell. However, we also need a technique for single arm exercises.

That's where the clean comes in for us. A well-done clean will place the kettlebell into a pocket that allows us to perform squats, swings, and presses among many other single-arm exercises.

The goal of the clean is to take the weight off the floor and place it into a pocket formed by our core, shoulder, forearm and upper arm. This 'pocket' and the placement of the kettlebell into the pocket is called the rack position.

From this rack position, we can squat or press or begin a swing or snatch.

Let's begin to learn the clean step-by-step...

STEP 1: THE RACK POSITION

Learning the clean in reverse is the easiest way. Therefore, we'll start with the rack position and the grip. From there, we reverse engineer the clean, going from the rack to the drop. From the drop we will then bring the bell back up to the rack position.

The handle should rest in your palm, almost to the point where it would slide down onto your forearm. Your thumb and index finger grip the handle at the corner of the horn.

Your forearm is almost vertical to the ground. The kettlebell rests in the pocket formed by your upper arm and forearm. Your elbow rests against your body. The kettlebell feels tight to the body and the overall position feels compact.

Practicing this position is easy, just grab a kettlebell with two hands and work your left hand into the grip, focusing on keeping a straight wrist and forearm. Support the bell with your opposite hand and place the bell into the pocket of your forearm and upper arm. Once you are in the right position, let go with the supporting hand.

Your arm, body, hand, and kettlebell should feel as one single unit. Tight, against the body, palm supporting the kettlebell and the elbow on hip supporting your hand. A firm chain.

Hold this position awhile, switch hands… get used to how it feels and memorize it. Much like the golf grip, this is an important feel to automate in our mind.

When you are done practicing the grip and rack position, put the bell down with both hands. We'll learn the proper way with one arm next.

The next stop in our reverse learning method is called the 'drop'.

STEP 2: THE DROP

To perform the drop from the rack position we reverse the clean from finish to beginning.

Let me explain first what the drop is. When we are in the rack position, we need to be able to put the kettlebell into motion for swings, snatches, high pulls and hang cleans.

You must drop the bell close to your body with a loose arm. At the bottom of the drop your arm will be completely straight. Your hips will work as shock absorbers to carefully slow the momentum.

Do not try to stop the bell from dropping by 'bicep curling' the weight on the way down, this is called negative curling. Negative curling will result in elbow issues.

As the kettlebell moves down and your arm fully extends the weight will need to be pushed behind you into the hike pass position. To get the bell into the hike pass position your thumb will rotate to point behind you.

At the top of the rack position, your thumb will be pointing at your body, primarily your neck. Imagine pouring out a drink by simply rotating your thumb down and letting the straight arm push the bell behind you.

In addition, you will transition the bell from the heel of your palm supporting the weight into your fingers forming a hook to support the weight at the bottom of the drop. Don't worry, this movement will become second nature and I ask you use your lightest kettlebell to practice.

For me, I visualize the kettlebell adjusting on its own as it moves downward until my thumb is pointing behind me and the bell is held firm by the hook my fingers create.

And remember tension we discussed earlier? You are not allowed to be tense during this movement as that will restrict the kettlebell handle repositioning itself on its downward track.

Pay special attention to your elbow, it must not flare out to the side, this will create a jerking motion at the bottom of the drop and hurt your elbow. The elbow tracks down and close to your body.

At the same time all the above is happening we are also transitioning into our box squat position. This will provide our shock absorbers and load the kettlebell for the hip extension when we reach the end of the hike pass position.

A good way to learn this is by visualizing the drop first.

Imagine you are wanting to hike a football between your legs from the rack position. You'll feel as if you are throwing the kettlebell behind you. There is a slight arc on the drop, it is not a straight down movement. We need a bit of arc to use momentum to swing the bell behind us.

Now that we have a high-level overview, let me simplify your practice for you:

1. Start in the rack position.

2. At the same time, push your butt back, relax your arm, and start pouring out the drink by turning your thumb down.

3. The kettlebell will roll off your forearm and your grip will begin to shift from heel supported to finger hook supported. The arm is not tense other than the hook of your fingers.

4. Do not flare the elbow and let the weight of the bell swing into the hike pass position. The forearm will encounter your groin. This is good! For me personally, my forearm touches the inside of the leg the kettlebell is on all the way back into the hike pass position. Interestingly, when I pop my hips, the hips push my forearm forward, moving the bell out of the hike pass.

This reads as a highly complex move, but it is not, it will feel natural to you after practicing.

Keep practicing.

My mentor Pavel says not to attempt the full clean until your drop is as loose as a whip.

STEP 3: PUTTING IT ALL TOGETHER

How did practice go?

When your drop is relaxed and you are calm, it is time to pop those hips from the pike pass position. The hips will push the bell back up into the clean position.

Do not pull with the arm.

Simply retrace the drop in reverse.

As the bell becomes light, near waist level, you will spear your hand through the handle like you are performing an uppercut. The weight of the bell rolls back into the heel of your palm.

This uppercut move rolls the bell around your forearm instead of over. At the top, form a fist and the bell will fall into perfect placement for the rack.

Remember, on the clean the kettlebell orbits around the forearm and not over your hand.

Another handy visualization is to imagine cleaning the bell to your waist. This ensures you begin the rotation early to avoid slamming the bell against your forearm. Many visualize cleaning to the shoulder, which causes all sort of bad movements.

As a final note, you need to brace your body as if in a standing plank when the bell begins to move into the pocket known as the rack. Squeeze your glutes, abs, and brace against the weight to stand firm.

Make sure you have your kettlebell wrist guards on. :)

If you struggle, we've got a neat little drill for you.

STEP 4: WALL CLEAN (ADVANCED)

Remember our friend the wall squat? Let me introduce you to another friend, the wall clean!

The wall clean is all about keeping the arc tamed and near the centerline of your body.

Too far away is bad news for our shoulders, back, and elbows.

The wall clean also helps us refine our movement and reduce unnecessary movement.

Just as in the wall squat, stand with your toes a few inches away from the wall and practice your cleans top to bottom.

Use your opposite hand as a guard in case the bell bangs off the wall. Block and move out of the way!

If the weight bangs into the wall, figure out where you went wrong, and try again.

I think you can understand this move appears simple, but there are many things going on here.

Do not pass go until you have a solid clean movement.

HOW TO DO THE PRESS

Our next progression in learning the basic movements for Kettlebell Golf Body is the press.

The press is performed from the rack position.

You'll pick the bell off the floor with your clean and place it into the rack position. Then you'll press the kettlebell over your head.

If you've been lifting weights for a while and used dumbbells, you may know the Arnold Press. Made famous by Arnold Schwarzenegger, the Arnold press works in a corkscrew manner to the top lockout position and then reverses neatly back down in the same fashion. SIDE NOTE: 3-time Mr. Olympia Frank Zane claims that Larry Scott was first to perform the 'Arnold Press'. Too late to rename it to the Larry Press? ☺

The resting position of the dumbbell in an Arnold press is very similar to how the kettlebell sits in the 'pocket' of the rack position.

If you know the Arnold press, you are good to go!

LEARN BY PROGRESSING

For those of you who are not familiar, let's break down the press like we did the hip hinge, swing, and clean... one step at a time, starting with the loaded clean.

STEP 1: THE PUSH AWAY

The first drill we'll use to develop the proper feel of the press is called the Push Away.

The push away will teach us how to release tension on our shoulder and develop a solid pushing motion.

The push away should feel like you are pressing against a pull up bar overhead. Think the opposite of a shrug. With a shrug, your shoulder pulls up towards the ceiling. With our press, it will feel close to the body and as if it is pushing into the floor.

A good way to gain this feeling is to stand underneath a pull up bar or door frame. From here, push your palms into the bar or top of the door and press. You'll feel the sensation we are looking for at the top of the press.

Further, I want you to create a solid base with your quads, glutes, and abs. Feel as if you are bracing to receive a punch. You'll breathe throughout the press while maintaining a firm core section.

Squeeze your quads and glutes while keeping the knees flexible and not straight... this is an athletic feeling here overall and bracing through the press.

The shoulder position from beginning to end during the press will remain relatively the same, down low.

After you've gained a basic feel for the push away, let's tweak how we think about the press for better performance.

Instead of trying to press the door or pull up bar away from us, try to push your body away from the bar. You'll notice something very odd - your shoulder will maintain the proper positioning we desire for the press.

This technique will increase the amount of weight you can press and will protect your shoulders. Instead of lifting the shoulders, we are pushing away the shoulders.

It's important to practice this line of thinking when doing high intensity or long cycle sets. As we fatigue, we get sloppy, and you will be tempted to lift the kettlebell instead of pushing it away. If you feel you are lifting the bell, park it. Regroup. Try again.

Once you nail the push away feeling and technique with two arms, try it with one arm. The process is the same, but you'll notice how you feel off-balance. Tense your obliques more with the single arm to prevent the natural tendency for the body to sag and twist.

This dynamic tension you create for the press is athletic, not static. You'll be tense but not stuff. Allow the body to move but fight to maintain your form the entire movement.

Keep practicing the push away with two arms and one arm. Monitor your body for weak points in your pressing chain. You should have dynamic but athletic tension from top to bottom. Eliminate weak points by practicing the push away technique and using the mental queue of 'push away'.

Now let's learn how to move the kettlebell out of the rack position into a full overhead press.

STEP 2: THE GROOVE

Practicing with dumbbells is a good way to learn the proper mechanics of the press. Specifically, using the Arnold press. Named after Arnold Schwarzenegger, this press follows the natural movement of the body and is better for your shoulders. Arnold used it to build definition and mass for his entire shoulder.

During the press, your starting position has your thumb gripping the kettlebell pointing at your neck. As you push the bell overhead, your thumb will rotate about 45 degrees in a nice corkscrew motion as you press up. At the top of the press your thumb will now be pointed roughly at an imaginary line that raises vertically out of your opposite shoulder.

The kettlebell begins in the rack position, with the bell positioned neatly into your pocket and the bell in front of you. As you push the bell overhead, you'll notice that there is a distinct groove formed naturally when you rotate your palm to face forward.

At takeoff, the bell will push slightly out from your body and not up, this is perfect. As you continue pushing away from the kettlebell and rotating your palm forward, you'll notice the corkscrew.

Practice this motion with no weight. Add in the door or pull up bar and ensure you are finishing with the proper push away technique we learned earlier.

The forearm stays vertical the entire press. If you lose the bell forward or back, let it go and get out of the way. Your wrist is also firm and straight using our 45-degree grip and supporting the bell on the heel of our palm. The fingers grip the bell loosely with no tension.

If you attempt to press straight up without the Arnold press motion, you are putting your shoulders in danger. The bell starts in front of your body but finishes in line with the body in a stacked position.

Ensure that the kettlebell is stacked over your body. In a side shot of the lock out position, you'll notice the bell is in line and stacked on top of the shoulder, the chest, the core, the hips, the knees, and your feet. It is NOT behind this line or in front of it. A good way of visualizing this is that the kettlebell is always over the feet during the press.

Visualize this first, then practice this without a kettlebell.

The movement is slow when pressing up and many kettlebell guru's slowly exhale as they press overhead, like a leaking bicycle tire. They do not fully exhale though and fill the lung back up and maintain dynamic tension the entire time. Remember, we need to keep some air in our lungs to build strength, stability, and tension.

Now, there is one slight variation from the Arnold press that occurs at the top of the press. In the Arnold press, we do not lock out our elbow. With the kettlebell press, we do lock out our elbow. In fact, the elbow will be facing inward toward our ear at the very top locked out position. If the elbow is too far forward or back, this is bad for the shoulder.

As for your eyes, do not watch the kettlebell. Keep your eyeline straight in front of you.

Now, we've got a cannonball overhead, how to bring it down safely?

STEP 3: THE PULL

We learned the push away to get the bell overhead properly. Now we will learn the 'Pull In' to lower the bell safely.

As the push away is opposite from conventional thinking, so is the pull in. With the pull in, we will be visualizing doing a pull up. The bar just happens to be the handle of the kettlebell.

Now practice this line of thinking by going through your push away, groove press, and then pretending you are doing a pull up with your kettlebell as the bar.

Lower it with a firm but loose arm, brace your abs, tense your glutes, firm the core, maintain your breathing slowly without fully exhaling. As the weight comes down, use your knees as shock absorbers. Trust me on this one… when you are lifting a heavy bell you will need the dynamic and athletic tension the knees provide to slow the bell calmly.

Much as a load of rocks being dumped into the back of a pickup truck, your legs will perform the same as the shocks on the truck. You'll feel as if you are catching the bell with your knees.

Once done, you can park the bell on the ground like we learned earlier.

Now that we've mastered the press, here's how we can use it…

STEP 4: PUTTING IT ALL TOGETHER

There are three types of presses we will be using.

1. Clean and Press - you should be familiar with this by now. This is where we clean the bell off the ground, press it, and then return the bell back to the ground.

2. Military Press - We clean the kettlebell to the rack and press. We do not place the bell down, rather, we keep pressing it until we hit a set number of reps.

3. Push Press - Clean the bell, and then we will use that dynamic and athletic tension from the knees to give us a running start on the press. You'll dip with the knees and then explosively press overhead. This is done with a heavier weight than we can handle with a strict clean and press or military press.

The clean and press is a great full body exercise. Once that recruits every muscle in the body and develops conditioning.

HOW TO DO THE SNATCH

The final progression in our series is the snatch.

The snatch works your back, shoulders, hips, fingers, forearms, and develops your cardio like nothing else available. The snatch is a truly athletic exercise, and it carries over to running, jumping, fighting, and even golf.

There's a good reason we left the snatch for last, it can be difficult to achieve. Everything we have learned up until this point will be used. If you are weak on any area like the clean, swing or press, please revisit those sections and improve them before moving into the snatch.

The snatch will closely resemble the swing for most of the movement with one difference, your arm will not remain straight the entire time. You'll be using a high pull to bring the bell in closer to the body on the way up and then punch your hand through the bell to finish at the top.

The snatch is a great exercise that improves your power and athleticism for golf.

LEARN BY PROGRESSING

Performing the snatch is a lot like a multi-stage rocket launch.

The first stage for the snatch comes from the hips. The hip hinge and explosion will push the kettlebell to chest level.

On the second stage, you'll pull back on the bell like starting a lawnmower. It will feel a lot like a rear elbow strike (someone standing behind you). This stage guides the bell closer to the body (more efficient).

The third stage begins when the kettlebell is weightless (thanks to the hips and elbow strike), you will now punch as if you are performing a jab in boxing. This subtle jab will guide the kettlebell overhead and simultaneously wrap the bell around your wrist, protecting it from injury. The bell will also shift from your hook grip (fingers) to the 45-

degree grip as you punch. Don't think too much here, it will happen naturally.

The fourth stage is the finish, here you will lean into the kettlebell as it moves overhead. This should feel like a standing plank pressing forward against the bell as it works itself overhead and back in line with your body's centerline. Your elbow will be locked, and the weight of the bell will be resting on your palm with the 45-degree grip.

By now, you should be proficient with the hip hinge, hike pass position, and exploding from the hips for the kettlebell swing. If you are not, do not pass go.

We'll begin putting our rocket together by starting with stage two, the high pull.

STEP 1: THE HIGH PULL

The second step in learning the snatch (with the swing being #1) is called the high pull. Master the high pull technique and the snatch becomes easy.

The high pull is simply a swing with an elbow strike feeling.

Now, imagine you perform the first part of a swing and load the bell into the hike position. From here you explode your hips (**remember hips first**) and then perform an elbow strike on the ride out of the hike position. You'll perform the elbow strike roughly when the bell is between your knees and hips. This will pull the bell closer to your body.

At the top of the high pull, your body will be firm just like it is during the top portion of a swing. The main difference here is that you will be resisting (a feeling of pushing) the bell when it reaches shoulder height.

Lean into the kettlebell here as if someone was pushing against you, and you wanted to maintain your balance.

As with the swing, your arm will be parallel to the ground and the kettlebell is in line with your wrist at the top of the high pull. Do not allow for a weak grip here or allow your wrist to break back or down. The forearm, wrist, and bell form a straight line out of the hike pass into the top of the high pull. Your elbow will be bent at a 90-degree angle.

At the finish position of the high pull, the bell will be opposite your shoulder and should feel completely weightless. You will push against the weight with your shoulder blade as the bell tries to knock you off balance.

Once you reach the top and the bell becomes weightless momentarily, push the bell out with a slight push forward and allow the bell to follow a natural arc back into the hike pass position. Repeat until perfected.

I suggest going with a medium weight when learning this... but ONLY after you've nailed your swing. Remember, the kettlebell is going to try to knock you off balance, so when you perform your elbow strike, lean forward into the bell.

The high pull is the halfway position of our snatch. Developing a solid high pull is paramount to developing monster core, shoulder, and hip strength. This will pay huge dividends in your golf game.

The next step in the snatch is what I call the jab the sky exercise.

STEP 2: THE JAB

The third stage begins when the kettlebell is weightless (thanks to the hips and elbow strike), you will now punch as if you are performing a jab in boxing. This subtle jab will guide the kettlebell overhead and simultaneously wrap the bell around your wrist, protecting it from injury. The bell will also shift from your hook grip (fingers) to the 45-degree grip as you punch. Don't think too much here, it will happen naturally.

We'll use the jab the sky drill to perfect this movement. Our third stage is roughly the 75% position of the snatch.

STEP 3: GUIDING THE BELL

We're talking a lot about your arms here, but make no mistake, the kettlebell is being pushed up mainly with our hips. On the second stage we are using our shoulder to drive our elbow behind us and pull the bell closer to the body (protecting our elbows from injury).

On the third stage, the jab the sky drill will guide the kettlebell into the proper 45-degree grip position (saving our wrists from a painful kettlebell re-entry).

This punch will guide the kettlebell into place for the final stage.

Think jab, not a cross or uppercut. Jab when you feel the bell is weightless.

The jab travels at a slight upward angle here rather than straight in front of us. Pretend you are going to jab Shaq with the kettlebell. Our jab will place the kettlebell about eye/forehead level in front of you while moving the bell into the perfect grip for the overhead lockout.

The jab only works if you are braced against the kettlebell. Remember earlier in the book when I mentioned you can't fire a canon from a canoe? The same is true here, we need a firm platform (our standing body plank and firm shoulders) to jab against. Otherwise, we lack power and stability and risk injury.

A good mental cue is to pretend you are starting a lawn mower (stage two) mixed with a jab once the kettlebell becomes weightless from the hip explosion and elbow strike.

I can't stress enough how important the jab the sky drill is in keeping the kettlebell from banging into your forearm while shifting the grip of the bell to mimic the overhead press. Use your wrist guards and practice with your medium bell. Too light doesn't force the bracing you will need to power your jab.

For our jab the sky drill, aim to lock out your jab and elbow at about a 45-degree angle from your shoulder. We'll save the fourth stage for next; we just want to work on jabbing. Skipping through this drill will result in bad form - it is important to nail your jab down with both arms which can be challenging before moving ahead. Remember, I am trying to save your elbows and a potential bloody nose here.

Once we nail this jab the sky drill, the kettlebell will flow naturally to the top using the momentum generated from the hips, elbow strike, and jab. From here, we go to the lockout position.

STEP 4: THE LOCKOUT

We can reverse engineer the quality of our snatch on the fourth stage of our rocket, the lockout position.

Do you remember practicing the press when we pushed against the pullup bar? If not, revisit as that is the feeling we are looking to achieve when we are fully locked out with the snatch.

Push away is a good mental cue here because we do not want the shoulder to pull away from the body.

In the push away drill, we learn that strength comes from a straight wrist, locked elbow, and pushing into the shoulder socket.

As the bell travels to its final position and we firm up to stop its momentum, we then can relax the arm and wiggle our fingers. Maintaining the firm wrist, locked elbow, and powerful shoulder position, we build a little base to allow some relaxation in the muscles.

A good mental cue here is to visualize the arm straight out while pushing hard into your shoulder socket. Many beginners try to extend the shoulder socket away from the body to catch the bell, this is bad, do the opposite.

Your elbow should be opposite your ear and the bell should be straight over your shoulders which are straight above your hips, knees, and feet.

It is common for the kettlebell practitioner to attempt to bicep curl the bell in here. Do not do this, as it is bad for the elbow joint and shoulder socket.

Right before full lockout, suck your shoulder into the socket and lock your elbow. This will protect you from a jarring the bell will deliver.

The bell is now locked out over our stacked body, how do we get it down?

You can use the reverse Arnold Press to return it to the rack position and then use your drop to place it on the ground safely.

However, when we are doing back-to-back snatches, we need a way to keep firing off snatches. Next, we will learn the drop from the lockout position.

STEP 5: THE DROP

This movement is serious business and please read this section a few times before attempting.

Doing this improperly is bad news for your elbows or back. If you suffer from tennis elbow, you need to pay special attention and take care.

You've already learned everything you need to know for the drop.

The hip hinge and the hike pass position are the brakes for the drop from lockout.

At the top of the lockout position, I like to push the bell away in front of me, but not too far, I want the bell to drop close to my body but with a natural arc. The push is very slight and is done against a braced shoulder and body.

A good mental cue is to pretend there is a wall in front of you, but DO NOT practice the drop in front of a wall. I am only trying to get across that close to the body is the way to go for the drop.

Dropping the bell in this manner helps us to tame the arc so to speak. By keeping the bell closer to the body on the way up and down, we are saving energy and improving performing... at the same time, we are also reducing our risk for injury to our shoulders, low back, wrists, elbows, and parts unknown.

As the bell drops thanks to gravity, I will catch it using my hip hinge and hike it behind me into the hike pass position. Once here, I can either park the bell or perform a swing to slow the momentum of a heavy kettlebell.

The drop is more of feeling of being a human shock absorber.

Practice with bodyweight only first, then move to a light dumbbell. Once you feel you've nailed it, try with your lightest kettlebell.

And that's the stage four rocket known as the snatch!

Nail this exercise and you've conquered not only the best exercise for power, but for conditioning as well... and that's going to deliver a massive arsenal to your golf game.

STEP 6: PUTTING IT ALL TOGETHER

Now it's time to perform the snatch from beginning to end. Remember the rocket stages because there are so many different things going on at once.

Let's go back over the stages and now introduce the final component to the rocket launch... re-entry and landing.

The first stage for the snatch comes from the hips. The hip hinge and explosion will push the kettlebell to chest level.

On the second stage, you'll pull back on the bell like starting a lawnmower. It will feel a lot like a rear elbow strike (someone standing behind you). This stage guides the bell closer to the body (more efficient).

The third stage begins when the kettlebell is weightless (thanks to the hips and elbow strike), you will now punch as if you are performing a jab in boxing. This subtle jab will guide the kettlebell overhead and simultaneously wrap the bell around your wrist, protecting it from injury. The bell will also shift from your hook grip (fingers) to the 45-degree grip as you punch. Don't think too much here, it will happen naturally.

The fourth stage is when we reach orbit, here you will lean into the kettlebell as it moves overhead. This should feel like a standing plank pressing forward against the bell as it works itself overhead and back in line with your body's centerline. Your elbow will be locked, and the weight of the bell will be resting on your palm with the 45-degree grip.

Now, we need to bring the bell back down safely. Re-entry involves the drop. Catch the bell by enabling your shock absorbers and the hip hinge. Allow the kettlebell to drop following a nice arc so there is no sudden jerk at the bottom which can strain your elbow.

Allow momentum and gravity to take the bell back into the hike pass position. Once here, you either park the bell or perform another snatch.

If you decide to stop, park the bell by simply reversing the beginning of the swing.

You'll allow the bell to be loaded in the pike pass position, then retain your hinge and guide the bell to the starting position about a foot and a half in front of you.

Stay tensed during this process until the bell is fully parked and its weight resides on the ground.

And that's the snatch... if you've been practicing and learning our big movements, you are ready to start the workouts.

CHAPTER 4: THE WORKOUT

PHASE I

PHASE I WORKOUT GUIDELINES

- Perform PHASE I for 4 weeks and then transition to PHASE II of Kettlebell Golf Body.
- Morning workouts are recommended (THIS WAY, YOU GET IT DONE). If you are not currently exercising, take it easy until you adapt.
- If there is a 4-digit number beside an exercise, it represents the lifting tempo.
- Start every workout with the warm-up circuit and specific warm-up sets if required.
- You will notice throughout this book that there are mainly 2 types of workout structures – Supersets and Circuits.
- Superset exercises are to be performed back-to-back. That is, perform one set of exercise "1a" and then immediately perform one set of "1b". Then rest for the required amount of time and repeat for the recommended number of sets.
- Circuits are to be performed in such a way that you go through the list of exercises to completion and only rest when you have completed a full round of all exercises. These will have the same number in front such as 1a, 1b, 1c, etc.
- Finish each workout with the decompression set to improve recovery.
- Make sure to perform the Grease, Flex and Roll mobility programs (in that order) on your days off.
- **For a full description of how to perform any exercise in this program, please see the Exercise Library chapter.**

Alternatively, you can access the free exercise demo video's here:

Step 1 – Unlock access to the private member's area where all the video demonstrations and bonus materials are located.

You just need your Amazon order ID number and contact details so our team can verify your order:

https://kettlebellgolfbody.com/amazon-4322

Once verified, they will send you an email with your login details and the URL to the Member's Area.

If you do not receive the email within 24 hours, please contact us via the Facebook group listed below. Please check your SPAM folder first, as sometimes the welcome email falls into those.

Step 2 – Join the PRIVATE Facebook group at https://www.facebook.com/groups/kettlebellgolfbody, you'll need to provide your Amazon Order ID# and the email address you ordered under. You can get faster support via the group and gain access to our quarterly Power and Distance Challenge where you can win prizes.

If you want 1-on-1 Coaching to improve your results:

Get the follow through you need to fully implement the Kettlebell Golf Body. You'll get motivation and accountability so you can fully realize adding consistently accurate distance. In addition, this level of coaching is shown to build good habits and break bad habits - which carry over to your day-to-day life off the golf course too.

WHAT'S INCLUDED:

Full 1-to-1 coaching with Christian with CUSTOMIZED workouts based on YOUR unique situation and needs. Includes an additional 3 workouts (for 12 weeks total), exercise tracking, video demo's, meal tracking, group accountability, and direct access to the coaches. You'll get the workouts from the book PLUS an additional 4 weeks for a total of 90 days of workouts.

HOW IT WORKS:

You'll be given a survey that will tell the coaches where you are currently in your fitness, what you wish to achieve, as well as difficulties you may face.

A coach will then custom design a program based on the Kettlebell Golf Body system that systematically helps you reach your goals by the end of the 90 days.

After that, you'll be sent instructions on how to access your custom program and get started!

Sign Up Here: https://golff.it/kgb-coaching

PHASE I CALENDAR

KETTLEBELL GOLF BODY - PHASE I						
MON	TUE	WED	THU	FRI	SAT	SUN
EMF W/O A ASSESS	EMF GREASE FLEX	EMF W/O B	EMF GREASE FLEX	EMF W/O A	EMF W/O C	OFF
EMF W/O B	EMF GREASE FLEX	EMF W/O A	EMF GREASE FLEX	EMF W/O B	EMF W/O C	OFF
EMF W/O A	EMF GREASE FLEX	EMF W/O B	EMF GREASE FLEX	EMF W/O A	EMF W/O C	OFF
EMF W/O B	EMF GREASE FLEX	EMF W/O A	EMF GREASE FLEX	EMF W/OB	EMF W/O C	ASSESS

WARM UP

DO NOT SKIP THE WARMUP!

Warming up is important, especially as we get older. We are all guilty of passing on the warmup of our workouts - but I'm here to tell you that your performance will INCREASE with a warmup.

Better performance, better form, injury risk reduction, more energy... all good reasons to perform a solid warm up before you get to work.

In addition, we'll be programming in neural work with certain exercises to get your CNS (Central Nervous System) primed and ready to rock for more difficult moves. In terms of performance, you'll lift more weight, use better form, and be able to do more work starting out. Most people use their first set or two to warm up, and that is perfectly fine when you are crunched for time.

Here's a few considerations to consider:

1) PHYSICALLY - Getting the body warm is the purpose of the warmup, right? But really, it's a dry run of the workout that follows. Not only do we want to get our body warmed up, but we also want to prepare for what's to come. That's why my warmups resemble mini workouts.

2) HORMONALLY - A good warm up has benefits such as releasing IGF-1, Growth Hormone, Testosterone - all of the hormones we want circulating. A good warm up is also mental, setting the mood of the body by increasing our adrenaline - and when the adrenaline flows, our workouts deliver better results.

3) JOINT HEALTH - As we age, joint mobility issues seem to start popping up. As your coach, I want to keep your joint greased up and moving smoothly. By getting the blood pumping we will get 'loose' and lubricate our joints and soft tissues. Keeping tendinitis at bay is easier when you do your warmups.

Most importantly, the warmup should be in-line with your training. For example, when power lifters have dedicated days, such as doing squats… guess what they warm up with? YES, with squats! That only makes sense, and that will get you prepped and ready to attack your workout.

Perform your warmups right before the workout and don't skimp. If it helps to mentally view the warmup as 'the workout' then do so. Our mobile app doesn't distinguish between the warmup and regular workout.

WORKOUT A

Warm-Up

1A) Deadbug - :40 seconds

1B) Around the Body - :40 seconds

1C) Halo - :40 seconds

1D) Inchworm - :40 seconds

1E) Wall Facing Squat - :40 seconds

No rest between exercises. Rest 1 minute after completing each circuit. Repeat the circuits twice more for a total of 3 rounds. Rest 1 minute and move onto the next superset.

2A) Plank w/Kettlebell Pull Through – 2 sets of 10 reps / side

2B) Shoulder Elevated Hip Bridge (2L)– 2 sets of 10 reps per side

3A) Goblet Squat – 3 sets of 12 reps with slight pause at bottom

3B) Bent Over Row (2H) – 3 sets of 12 reps / side

4A) Sumo Deadlift – 3 sets of 12 reps

4B) Pushup – 3 sets of 12 reps

Decompression (OPTIONAL)

5A) Hip Pry Squat - :60 seconds

5B) Kneeling Hip Flexor - :60 seconds, :30 per side

5C) Sleeping Pigeon :60 seconds, :30 per side

5D) Downward Facing Dog - :60 seconds

5E) Backswing Angel - :60 seconds

WORKSHEET A

DATE:	SET 1	SET 2	SET 3
WORKOUT: A	REPS / TIME	REPS / TIME	REPS / TIME
2A) Plank w/KB Pull Through (2x10/side)			
2B) Shoulder Elevated Hip Bridge (2L) (2x10/side)			
Complete one superset and rest 60 seconds. Complete two more rounds for a total of three supersets. Rest 60 seconds and continue to 3A.			
3A) Goblet Squat (3x12)			
3B) Bent Over Row (2H) (3x12/side)			
Complete one superset and rest 60 seconds. Complete two more rounds for a total of three supersets. Rest 60 seconds and continue to 4A.			
4A) Sumo Deadlift (3x12)			
4B) Pushup (3x12)			
Complete one superset and rest 60 seconds. Complete two more rounds for a total of three supersets. Finish up with Decompression to speed recovery.			

WORKOUT B

Warm-Up

1A) Deadbug - :40 seconds

1B) Around the Body - :40 seconds

1C) Halo - :40 seconds

1D) Inchworm - :40 seconds

1E) Wall Facing Squat - :40 seconds

No rest between exercises. Rest 1 minute after completing each circuit. Repeat the circuits twice more for a total of 3 rounds. Rest 1 minute and move onto the next superset.

2A) Deadbug Resurrected – 2 sets of 10 reps / side

2B) Side Plank on Elbow – 2 sets of :40 side

3A) Dead Stop Clean (1H)– 3 sets of 6 reps / side

3B) Half Kneeling Press – 3 sets of 12 reps / side

4A) Goblet Split Squat – 3 sets of 12 reps / side

4B) Flat Back Pullover – 3 sets of 12 reps

Decompression (OPTIONAL)

5A) Hip Pry Squat - :60 seconds

5B) Kneeling Hip Flexor - :60 seconds, :30 per side

5C) Sleeping Pigeon :60 seconds, :30 per side

5D) Downward Facing Dog - :60 seconds

5E) Backswing Angel - :60 seconds

WORKSHEET B

DATE:	SET 1	SET 2	SET 3
WORKOUT: B	**REPS / TIME**	**REPS / TIME**	**REPS / TIME**
2A) Deadbug Resurrected (2x10/side)			
2B) Side Plank on Elbow (:40 sec/side)			
Complete one superset and rest 60 seconds. Complete two more rounds for a total of three supersets. Rest 60 seconds and continue to 3A.			
3A) Dead Stop Clean (1H) (3x6/side)			
3B) Half Kneeling Press (3x12/side)			
Complete one superset and rest 60 seconds. Complete two more rounds for a total of three supersets. Rest 60 seconds and continue to 4A.			
4A) Goblet Split Squat (3x12/side)			
4B) Flat Back Pullover (3x12)			
Complete one superset and rest 60 seconds. Complete two more rounds for a total of three supersets. Finish up with Decompression to speed recovery.			

WORKOUT C

Beginning to end, this workout should only take you roughly 20 minutes. The goal of this workout is to develop power and cardiovascular endurance. Both are important factors in the strength endurance required to play a round of golf at your best.

Equipment required: Bodyweight, Kettlebell (SUGGESTED: 24kg men / 16kg women)

Warm-Up

Go through the following with no rest between exercises. Stick around an exercise if you feel a bit tight. The time is only a suggestion.

1A) Deadbug - :40 seconds

1B) Around the Body - :40 seconds

1C) Halo - :40 seconds

1D) Inchworm - :40 seconds

1E) Wall Facing Squat - :40 seconds

Workout

This workout focuses on strength endurance, which will help us on the course to maintain consistent swings in tough conditions or slow play. We'll keep things simple and only be using 1 kettlebell and bodyweight. You can choose between pushups or bodyweight squats for the bodyweight component. You can even alternate between pushups or squats if you wish. The goal here is to pre-fatigue your muscles and cardio system so that we build strength endurance.

The workout is a descending ladder. A descending ladder is where we start with the most reps (when we are our strongest) and work our way down. In this case we will start with 10 kettlebell swings followed by a matching number for a bodyweight exercise (pushups or squats).

We perform the prescribed repetitions every minute on minute (EMOM). Once we hit our prescribed repetitions, we rest the remaining time. For example, if 10 kettlebell swings take us 25 seconds, we would rest 35 seconds until it is time to do our 10 squats. As we move through the workout down the ladder, our kettlebell swing reps and bodyweight exercise decrease by 1 rep. You'll continue this pattern until you hit the last rung on the ladder, 5 reps for this workout.

Set a timer to beep Every Minute on Minute (EMOM) for 12 minutes (or 11 minutes if you are starting your reps with the timer on zero). Give yourself a few seconds to get set, and then get rolling. Some timers allow you to set them for a few seconds to allow you to get situated.

I suggest using a heavier bell to really tax your strength and cardio. The key is maximal power output for your repetitions. Go hard with good form and knock out your reps as fast as you can. Do not get sloppy, sloppy reps do not count.

The faster you do your reps, the more recovery time. This is ideal for building power and strength endurance.

NOTE: Don't dismiss this workout - it is the base for a more challenging follow up in Phase II.

Decompression (OPTIONAL)

5A) Hip Pry Squat - :60 seconds

5B) Kneeling Hip Flexor - :60 seconds, :30 per side

5C) Sleeping Pigeon :60 seconds, :30 per side

5D) Downward Facing Dog - :60 seconds

5E) Backswing Angel - :60 seconds

WORKSHEET C

WORKOUT C		
Minute By Minute	**Exercise**	**Reps / Weight**
1	2H Swing	10 /
2	Squat	10 /
3	2H Swing	9 /)
4	Pushup	9 /
5	2H Swing	8 /)
6	Squat	8 /
7	2H Swing	7 /
8	Pushup	7 /
9	2H Swing	6 /
10	Squat	6 /
11	2H Swing	5 /
12	Pushup	5 /

PHASE II

PHASE II WORKOUT GUIDELINES

- Perform PHASE II for 4 weeks and then transition to PHASE III of Kettlebell Golf Body.
- Morning workouts are recommended (THIS WAY, YOU GET IT DONE). If you are not currently exercising, take it easy until you adapt.
- If there is a 4-digit number beside an exercise, it represents the lifting tempo.
- Start every workout with the warm-up circuit and specific warm-up sets if required.
- You will notice throughout this book that there are mainly 2 types of workout structures – Supersets and Circuits.
- Superset exercises are to be performed back-to-back. That is, perform one set of exercise “1a” and then immediately perform one set of “1b”. Then rest for the required amount of time and repeat for the recommended number of sets.
- Circuits are to be performed in such a way that you go through the list of exercises to completion and only rest when you have completed a full round of all exercises. These will have the same number in front such as 1a, 1b, 1c, etc.
- Finish each workout with the decompression set to improve recovery.
- Make sure to perform the Grease, Flex and Roll mobility programs (in that order) on your days off.
- For a full description of how to perform any exercise in this program, please see the Exercise Library chapter.
- Alternatively, you can login to the member’s area and watch the videos there. You’ll need your logins you were sent when you ordered your copy of the Kettlebell Golf Body.
- Here’s a link over to the member’s area: https://members.golfaggressive.com

Once you complete PHASE II and want to keep going,

that's where 1-on-1 coaching comes in and keeps you moving forward day in and day out.

You'll get expert coaching as well as customized workouts, based on your skill level and ability.

Please visit the 1-on-1 Coaching Sign Up to join.

PHASE II CALENDAR

KETTLEBELL GOLF BODY - PHASE II						
MON	TUE	WED	THU	FRI	SAT	SUN
EMF W/O D	EMF GREASE FLEX	EMF W/O E	EMF GREASE FLEX	EMF W/O D	EMF W/O F.1	EMF GREASE FLEX
EMF W/O E	EMF GREASE FLEX	EMF W/O D	EMF GREASE FLEX	EMF W/O E	EMF W/O F.2	EMF GREASE FLEX
EMF W/O D	EMF GREASE FLEX	EMF W/O E	EMF GREASE FLEX	EMF W/O D	EMF W/O F.3	EMF GREASE FLEX
EMF W/O E	EMF GREASE FLEX	EMF W/O D	EMF GREASE FLEX	EMF W/O E	EMF W/O F.4	EMF ASSESS

WARM UP

DO NOT SKIP THE WARMUP!

Warming up is important, especially as we get older. We are all guilty of passing on the warmup of our workouts - but I'm here to tell you that your performance will INCREASE with a warmup.

Better performance, better form, injury risk reduction, more energy... all good reasons to perform a solid warm up before you get to work.

In addition, we'll be programming in neural work with certain exercises to get your CNS (Central Nervous System) primed and ready to rock for more difficult moves. In terms of performance, you'll lift more weight, use better form, and be able to do more work starting out. Most people use their first set or two to warm up, and that is perfectly fine when you are crunched for time.

Here's a few considerations to consider:

1) PHYSICALLY - Getting the body warm is the purpose of the warmup, right? But really, it's a dry run of the workout that follows. Not only do we want to get our body warmed up, but we also want to prepare for what's to come. That's why my warmups resemble mini workouts.

2) HORMONALLY - A good warm up has benefits such as releasing IGF-1, Growth Hormone, Testosterone - all of the hormones we want circulating. A good warm up is also mental, setting the mood of the body by increasing our adrenaline - and when the adrenaline flows, our workouts deliver better results.

3) JOINT HEALTH - As we age, joint mobility issues seem to start popping up. As your coach, I want to keep your joint greased up and moving smoothly. By getting the blood pumping we will get 'loose' and lubricate our joints and soft tissues. Keeping tendinitis at bay is easier when you do your warmups.

Most importantly, the warmup should be in-line with your training. For example, when power lifters have dedicated days, such as doing squats… guess what they warm up with? YES, with squats! That only makes sense, and that will get you prepped and ready to attack your workout.

Perform your warmups right before the workout and don't skimp. If it helps to mentally view the warmup as 'the workout' then do so. Our mobile app doesn't distinguish between the warmup and regular workout.

WORKOUT D

Warm-Up

1A) Deadbug - :40 seconds

1B) Around the Body to Hold - :40 seconds

1C) Halo - :40 seconds

1D) Figure 8 - :40 seconds

1E) Hip Pry Goblet Squat - :40 seconds

No rest between exercises. Rest 1 minute after completing each circuit. Repeat the circuits twice more for a total of 3 rounds. Rest 1 minute and move onto the next superset.

2A) Spiderman Pushup – 2 sets of 8 reps per side

2B) Plank with Kettlebell Pull Through – 2 sets of 8 reps per side

3A) Squat (1H) – 3 sets of 8 reps per side

3B) Strict Press (1H) – 3 sets of 8 reps per side

4A) Flat Back Pullover – 3 sets of 8 reps

4B) Romanian Deadlift (1L) – 3 sets of 8 reps per side

5) Swing (1H) – 3 sets of 8 reps per side

Decompression (OPTIONAL)

6A) Hip Pry Squat - :60 seconds

6B) Kneeling Hip Flexor - :60 seconds, :30 per side

6C) Sleeping Pigeon :60 seconds, :30 per side

6D) Downward Facing Dog - :60 seconds

6E) Backswing Angel - :60 seconds

WORKSHEET D

DATE:	SET 1	SET 2	SET 3
WORKOUT: D	REPS / TIME	REPS / TIME	REPS / TIME
2A) Spiderman Pushup (2x8/side)			
2B) Plank w/KB Pull Through (2x8/side)			
Rest for 60 secs after each superset and do a total of 2 supersets.			
3A) Squat (1H) (3x8/side))			
3B) Strict Press (1H) (3x8/side)			
Rest for a total of 60 secs after each superset and do a total of 3 supersets.			
4A) Flat Back Pullover (3x8)			
4B) Romanian Deadlift (1L) (3x8/side)			
Rest for a total of 60 secs after each superset and do a total of 3 supersets.			
5) Swing (1H) (3x8/side)			
Rest for 60 secs after each set and do a total of 3 sets.			

WORKOUT E

Warm-Up

1A) Deadbug - :40 seconds

1B) Around the Body to Hold - :40 seconds

1C) Halo - :40 seconds

1D) Figure 8 - :40 seconds

1E) Hip Pry Goblet Squat - :40 seconds

No rest between exercises. Rest 1 minute after completing each circuit. Repeat the circuits twice more for a total of 3 rounds. Rest 1 minute and move onto the next superset.

2A) Half Turkish Get Up – 2 sets of 5 reps / side

2B) Side Plank - Elbow – 2 sets of :30 seconds per side

3A) Suitcase Deadlift (1H) – 3 sets of 8 reps per side

3B) Bent Over Row (1H) – 3 sets of 8 reps per side

4A) Goblet Split Squat – 3 sets of 8 reps per side

4B) Waiters Walk (1H)– 3 sets of 20 yards down and 20 yards back per arm

5) Snatch (1H) – 3 sets of 8 reps per side

Decompression (OPTIONAL)

6A) Hip Pry Squat - :60 seconds

6B) Kneeling Hip Flexor - :60 seconds, :30 per side

6C) Sleeping Pigeon :60 seconds, :30 per side

6D) Downward Facing Dog - :60 seconds

6E) Backswing Angel - :60 seconds

WORKSHEET E

DATE:	SET 1	SET 2	SET 3
WORKOUT: E	REPS / TIME	REPS / TIME	REPS / TIME
2A Half Turkish Get Up (2x5/side)			
2B) Side Plank (:30 seconds / side)			
Rest 60 secs after each superset and do a total of 2 supersets.			
3A) Suitcase Deadlift (1H) (3x8/side)			
3B) Bent Over Row (1H) (3x8/side)			
Rest 60 secs after each superset and do a total of 3 supersets.			
4A) Goblet Split Squat (3x8/side)			
4B) Waiter's Walk (1H) (3x/20yards down and back/side)			
Rest 60 secs after each superset and do a total of 3 supersets.			
5) Snatch (1H) (3x8/side)			
Rest 60 secs after each set and do a total of 3 sets.			

WORKOUT F

Warm-Up

1A) Deadbug - :40 seconds

1B) Around the Body to Hold - :40 seconds

1C) Halo - :40 seconds

1D) Figure 8 - :40 seconds

1E) Hip Pry Goblet Squat - :40 seconds

No rest between exercises.

2A) Swing (2H) - 60 seconds, 10 reps / rest remainder

2B) Swing (2H) - 60 seconds, 10 reps / rest remainder

2C) Pushup - 60 seconds, 10 reps / rest remainder

2D) Pushup - 60 seconds, 10 reps / rest remainder

REST 1 MINUTE. REPEAT SPECIFIED AMOUNT ROUNDS IN SCHEDULE.

Decompression (OPTIONAL)

3A) Hip Pry Squat - :60 seconds

3B) Kneeling Hip Flexor - :60 seconds, :30 per side

3C) Sleeping Pigeon :60 seconds, :30 per side

3D) Downward Facing Dog - :60 seconds

3E) Backswing Angel - :60 seconds

WORKSHEET F

DATE:	
WORKOUT: F	INSTRUCTIONS
2A) Swing (2H) (60 secs/10 reps)	10 reps in 60 seconds. Rest remaining minute.
2B) Swing (2H) (60 secs/10 reps)	10 reps in 60 seconds. Rest remaining minute.
2C) Pushup (60 secs/10 reps)	10 reps in 60 seconds. Rest remainder.
2D) Pushup (60 secs/10 reps)	10 reps in 60 seconds. Rest remainder.
Rest 60 seconds at the end of each round. Each round takes 5 minutes when factoring in the 60 seconds rest.	
SCHEDULE	
WEEK 5 (F.1)	3 ROUNDS
WEEK 6 (F.2)	4 ROUNDS
WEEK 7 (F.3)	5 ROUNDS
WEEK 8 F.4)	6 ROUNDS

RECOVERY

This section is perhaps the most important for the golfer over age 40. As we age, our mobility starts to drop off. Mostly, this is due to lack of use.

As a wise old man once told me, "USE IT OR LOSE IT!" ... and he wasn't wrong.

When you stop movement patterns, your body will tighten up and eventually you will lose the ability to perform movement patterns that were once easy for you.

For that reason, my recovery system outlined in this book is aimed at maintaining or restoring movement patterns for you.

The best way to recover is to keep your muscles primed and ready for action. Besides sleep and nutritious food, you need a system that restores your muscles, joints, ligaments, and tendons.

You are welcome to use four methods for recovery:

Method #1 - Joint Mobility. We'll go after stiff joints and work on improving range of motion.

Method #2 - Flexibility. Tight muscles, tight ligaments and tendons will be put through their paces through static stretching and dynamic stretching.

Method #3 - Myofascial Self Release. Also known as foam rolling, MFR aims to restore damaged muscles (adhesions) back to their original form. These adhesions are felt in the form of painful knots where your muscle forms to prevent further injury. These adhesions restrict proper muscle function and can lead to further injury in your movement chains. As such, it is important to work on these on a continual basis.

Method #4 - Preparation and Decompression. Before every workout we will do a workout specific warm up aimed at prepping the body for more intense work. After each workout, we'll perform what I call

'Decompression'. Simply, we'll just stretch out the muscles we used during our workout.

Here's how the recovery model works…

MAP THE BODY

First, you need to become an expert in listening to your body. Many people ignore the messages their body sends them in the form of pain, restricted movement, or stiffness. These messages are warnings that something needs repair or recovery.

Instead of avoiding problem area's when the body sends a message, we will work on them to restore proper movement. If the problem area needs a doctor or surgery, we will seek professional help for advice on returning to 100% range of motion.

Of course, not everyone will be able to recover lost range of motion. This may be due to severe injure or conditions outside of our control like arthritis.

However, by deploying the recovery system in this book, we will become the "best that we can be" and work towards improved range of motion.

I call listening to your body, 'mapping the body'.

For example, if I'm doing my routine and know my shoulder is a bit tighter than normal - I know I need to work on my shoulder with stretching, joint mobility, as well as foam rolling. I may even get a massage to help repair the body.

Perhaps I am performing foam rolling and run across a few painful knots… I'll make a mental note of this problem area and devote more attention to it.

Make it a habit to write down or make mental notes of the weak points you find.

Our body will heal itself and injure itself, so mapping your body is an ongoing mission.

In addition, we need to craft our workouts so that we build durability…

STAY CONSISTENT

The most important benefit golfers receive from our recovery system will be longevity.

According to Merriam-Webster, longevity means:

Long continuance: permanence, durability.

While nothing is permanent, we can improve our enjoyment of the game of golf into our golden years. We can also make life easier off the course by improving our overall health.

Golf can really put wear and tear on your body, and it is important for us to improve our durability.

Without consistency, you won't get long-lasting results.

For golf, we need to consistently work on our durability which will allow us to play more rounds of golf.

Durability leads to less injuries. Durability leads to more consistency.

You must become more durable if you want longevity.

Working on greasing your joints, ligaments, tendons, muscles and fascia is built into the recovery system. All you need to do is show up and make the effort consistently.

Consistency is the key to health, golf, work, relationships, really anything in life you want to improve at.

And of course, our workouts are designed to build the body up and create even more durability by improving strength, balance, and power.

All of this sounds good right? So how do we do the recovery system?

1) WARM UP

2) DECOMPRESS

3) GREASE

4) FLEX

5) EARLY MORNING FLEXIBILITY

Done in the right order and at the right time, each of the above moves us along the path to improved longevity.

The recovery system is designed to:

- Increase your ability to withstand wear and tear on all systems of the human structure.
- Improve your ability to repair damaged tissues and joints.
- Map and test your body's state and see where you need to improve or potentially seek help.
- Relieve tension, mobility-restriction, and pain from such.
- Improve movement capacity for increased performance on the course and off.
- Warming you up before your workouts to prevent injury.
- Decompress your body mentally and physically after working out so recovery is accelerated.

Remember the old man that told me to "use it or lose it"? We'll be 'using it' quite a bit in the recovery system with the aim of not 'losing it'.

Here's a breakdown of each component in the recovery system:

WARM UP

Warming up is part of recovery as well, helping to prevent injury and prepare the muscle for optimal work.

Each warmup is designed for the movements you will be doing in that workout.

Some warmups may be the same as we are working the same basic movements patterns.

Other workouts may use different warmups... again, we are doing specific warmups for the specific work we will be performing.

DECOMPRESS

Performed at the end of each workout, decompression allows us to address the specific areas targeted during our workouts.

Decompression allows us to address muscle imbalances as well and set us up for better sleep and better performance the next workout.

It is important to note that the workouts have a general time recommendation for your decompression exercises... however, please extend these times as needed if you find rough spots.

Many of our golfers perform this while watching TV, seven nights a week. This is one you can do to your hearts content.

GREASE

Joint mobility work. To keep our joints moving well, we need to make sure we are not neglecting them.

One of the issues with modern life is that we stop moving in certain ways. And if you don't use it, you will lose it!

However, we can start to reclaim our joint mobility by performing the GREASE routine on our recovery days.

FLEX

In addition to the decompression you'll do after workout days, you'll perform a basic full body flexibility routine. As mentioned above, if you find any difficult areas that need more stretching - take the time to dial in and improve those areas. A little goes a long way here.

EARLY MORNING FLEXIBILITY

Also known as EMF, this routine if done daily can help reduce tight spots, stiff joints, and improve your movement patterns. In addition, the EMF works as a wakeup call of sort that gets you moving, mentally focused, and feeling prepared to attack the day.

The flexibility program alone is good, but the EMF is great. Done together you've got a cocktail that will unlock your body and have you feeling better than ever.

Just take it slow and easy when starting out.

SUMMARY

Don't get overwhelmed here, we will guide you on the when, where and what. Remember, we do recovery in a very distinct order for best results.

I wanted to give you a high-level overview of the programming, so you understand why we are doing what we are doing. The science can be quite confusing and really isn't required here - perform the recovery programming and you'll feel the science at work.

All in all, you'll be feeling better and moving better if you don't skip recovery!

That wraps up the instructional portion of Kettlebell Golf Body.

Let's get to work!

RECOVERY GUIDELINES

The cornerstone of adding distance AND consistency is to increase joint mobility and range of motion. Without an increased range of motion, you will NOT be as good as you can be. Simply, you will be 'limited' much like a race car with a governor enabled.

By limited, I mean the arc of your golf swing could be compromised (shorter). I don't care what swing you use; you won't be able to add and maintain distance if your mobility is limited.

Think of the Grease, Flex, and EMF program to be the gears in your race car whereas the workouts are the engine. We need both primed and optimal to be effective.

To increase your range of motion (gears), it is vital we perform certain movement daily – even on off days. These movements do not take very long and will help the body to recover and thus add valuable yards to your game. I can promise you one thing... if you DON'T USE IT, YOU WILL LOSE IT!

Strategic Recovery performed on off days will prime your body for gains every single day and allow us to work out to our fullest potential... building golf horsepower into our engine.

TIP: Perform joint mobility and dynamic warm-ups each morning when you wake up if you are not working out. This ensures your body stays loose and pliable and gets you ready for the day.

EMF

Each morning, I'd like you to build in the habit of the emf. The Early Morning Flexibility is quite simply a short bodyweight routine designed to gradually unlock stiff joints, tight muscles and wake you up.

You'll do the circuit two times. The first time through is called the 'body audit' and this is where we consider all our tight spots, sore spots, stiff spots and gradually work to grease our joints and loosen up tight muscles.

The second round you'll notice a major improvement in your range of motion.

Feel free to go through for a third round as well, as this is all preventative maintenance... much like an oil change.

I've broken it down into three distinct sections, and you can do them all or pick and choose.

The sections are upper body and shoulders, spine and lower body, and hips and low back. I know hips can be considered part of lower body, but as a golfer, I felt we needed to target them specifically.

Now, if you stick to this program every single morning, you'll quickly discover that your range of motion improves dramatically. This is perfect for your golf game and your body.

There's a lot of exercises here, and feel free to take your time when you find a rough spot to spend an extra moment or two smoothing those spots out.

The goals of the EMF:

1) Boost Metabolism (which helps burn fat)

2) 'Wake Up' our nervous system

3) Re-enforce/practice movement patterns

I'll break down each of these now for you as I feel it's important to understand how vital the EMF is to your quality of life.

BOOST METABOLISM

One of the better benefits of the EMF is that getting up and moving early in your day helps boost metabolism. A higher metabolism helps burn fat. This is a nice benefit, but not our primary goal with the EMF.

PRACTICE MOVEMENT PATTERNS

One of my sneakier methods is to get clients to 'practice' more complex movement patterns in part of whole, using bodyweight only. As you coach, my motive for doing this is to give you new movements and give you time to get better at them before they re incorporated into your monthly training programming. You get to work through mobility and flexibility issues and develop good form before we put these moves 'into the game'.

WAKE UP NERVOUS SYSTEM

Equally important as 'Practice Movement Patterns' is the goal of waking up our mind body connection. In addition to feeling more energetic after performing the EMF, you'll wake up the nervous system. A more fired up nervous system helps us improve our neurological efficiency in our workouts and everything else. I've been delivering this to my clients for years and many have described the EMF like "drinking an entire pot of coffee" without the caffeine crash later.

WHEN SHOULD I DO THE EMF?

It can be done at any point before your workout. However, for best results, and a fast-start to your day - I HIGHLY RECOMMEND DOING IT FIRST THING. Before the gym, before work, before breakfast, before your shower.

Perform this entire program once, every morning. A I told, it should take you anywhere from 15 minutes if you are short on time to the full 30 minutes if you do both rounds.

EARLY MORNING FLEXIBILITY (EMF)

1A) Chin Wave x 8 reps

1B) Gunslinger x 8 reps

1C) Clasp Hand with Neck Roll x 8 reps

1D) Arm Screws

1E) Arm Circles

Continue to 2A.

2A) Hip Sway with Reach x 8 reps per side

2B) Hip Hinge x 8 reps

2C) Bootstrapper x 8 reps

2D) Standing Forward Fold x 8 reps

2E) Inchworm x 8 reps

Continue to 3A.

3A) Prone Knee to Chest x 8 reps per leg

3B) Knee Side Drop Out x 8 reps per leg

3C) Side Frog Leg x 8 reps per leg

3D) Double Frog Leg x 8 reps

3E) Hip Pry Squat x 30 seconds

The first time through is the 'body audit'. Go through a second time to measure the improvement and push the benefits even further.

GREASE

Equipment required: Bodyweight

Instructions

Go through the following with no rest between exercises. Stick around an exercise if you feel a bit tight. The time is only a suggestion. When you complete the first round, immediately start a second round. You should feel refreshed at the end of the circuit.

1A) Three Plane Neck - :30 seconds

1B) Shoulder Circles - :30 seconds

1C) Fist Exercise - :30 seconds

1D) Wrist Rotations - :30 seconds

1E) Elbow Circles - :30 seconds

1F) Arm Screws - :30 seconds

1G) Arm Circles - :30 seconds

1H) Hula Hoop - :30 seconds

1I) Standing Spinal Rotation with Club - :30 seconds

1J) Knee Circles - :30 seconds

1K) Ankle Circles - :30 seconds

FLEX

Equipment required: Bodyweight

Instructions

Go through the following with no rest between stretches. Stick around a stretch if you feel a bit tight. Exhale and relax when you find a spot of discomfort. The time is only a suggestion.

1A) Backswing Angel - :60 seconds

1B) Standing Forward Fold - :60 seconds

1C) Hip Pry Squat - :60 seconds

1D) Kneeling Hip Flexor - :60 seconds

1E) Sleeping Pigeon - :60 seconds

1F) Downward Facing Dog - :60 seconds

1G) Cobra Pose - :60 seconds

1H) Child's Pose - :60 seconds

CHAPTER 5: EXERCISE LIBRARY

IMPORTANT: While a picture is certainly worth a thousand words, a video is worth a million. I chose specifically to leave out step-by-step photographs in the book and instead place demonstration videos into a private member's area for you.

Unlock access to the private member's area where all the video demonstrations and bonus materials are located.

You just need your Amazon order ID number and contact details so our team can verify your order:

https://kettlebellgolfbody.com/amazon-4322

Once verified, they will send you an email with your login details and the URL to the Member's Area.

If you do not receive the email within 24 hours, please contact us via the Facebook group listed below. Please check your SPAM folder first, as sometimes the welcome email falls into those.

Once you receive your logins, you can view the demonstration video's here:

https://members.golfaggressive.com

PHASE I

WARM UP

Deadbug

1) Lay on your back. If you have a small towel, place it under your lumbar spine. This will help you maintain neutral spine and give you something to push against while performing the exercise.

2) Initiate the exercise by extending one leg, straightening the knee and hip to bring the leg towards the ground. Only go as far as you can to maintain your back against the ground. And move the opposite hand towards the ground above your head.

3) Your lumbar position must be maintained against the towel throughout the exercise.

4) Keep your abs drawn in and tight and return the moving leg and arm to the starting position.

Around the Body

1) Stand up straight with your feet shoulder-width apart. Hold the kettlebell with a corner grip in one hand.

2) Use momentum to swing the bell across the front of your body and pass it to your other hand.

3) Continue the momentum and swing the kettlebell behind your back and pass it to your other hand.

4) As the bell changes hands bring the bell in front of your body and catch it with your opposite hand. Now, reverse direction. After you've returned the bell back to your start position, this counts as one repetition.

5) Brace your body against the momentum by engaging your glutes, core, and back muscles.

Halo

1) Pop the kettlebell up from the center of your stance and grip the handles. Use a light weight until you master this movement.

2) Turn the bell upside down so that the handles are on bottom, and the bell is on top. This is not a goblet squat grip; we are holding onto the horns of the kettlebell with our hands. The bell is in front of your chest but close to the body, without touching it.

3) Stand with your feet shoulder-width apart and knees slightly bent.

4) Raise the kettlebell to the side of your head, move it behind your head, to the opposite side and then back to the front. The kettlebell should naturally move into a bottom-down position as your move it around.

5) Brace your body against the momentum by engaging your glutes, core, and back muscles. Imagine pinching a coin between your glutes - to protect your back.

6) Once you complete one orbit around your head, reverse directions. Once you complete the second orbit in the opposite direction that is one repetition.

Inchworm

1) Stand tall, your feet roughly hip width apart. Your ears should be aligned over your shoulders, hips, knees, and ankles, your core engaged.

2) Look down at the ground and start reaching your hands toward the floor in front of your feet. Allow your back to bend forward, as if doing a spinal roll. Allow the knees to bend, as needed, letting your hands to touch the ground.

3) Once your hands reach the floor, begin walking them forward keeping your weight pressed into your palms. Allow your heels to lift off the floor as your body begins to straighten. When your hands are directly under your shoulders, you will be in the plank position with your core, chest, quads, triceps, and shoulders engaged, your body forming a straight line from heels to head. Don't let your body sag.

4) The next step is to walk your feet forward to meet your hands. Try to keep your legs somewhat straight as you begin to walk your feet forward. Step forward, one foot at a time, toward your hands. This should provide a nice stretch through your hamstrings, calves, and glutes as your hips start lifting toward the ceiling.

5) Stop walking the feet forward your feet are as close to your hands as you can comfortably step. Bending your knees as you walk forward is just fine but fighting to keep them straight will help provide a nice stretch to your hamstrings.

6) Now, we just return from where we came and do a reverse spinal roll back to a full standing position. When you reach the top, engage your core and glutes. Then turn around and go back to where you started.

Wall Facing Squat

1) Stand close to a wall, with your toes just a couple of inches away.

2) Feet are slightly wider than shoulder width. A good way of finding the 'slight wider than shoulder-width' is to allow your arms to hang down with a proud chest. The insides of your feet should be directly under your fingertips. From here, I like to point my toes out at roughly 15 to 30 degrees.

3) Lower yourself without pushing your face or knees into the wall. Instead, we want to slowly lower ourselves and learn the proper movements to reach the bottom of a squat without touching the wall. Also, the knees track over the feet and don't flare out. The feet stay flat and planted. Your face should move straight up and down like an elevator.

4) As you descend, feet remain planted and do not roll in or out. If you roll your feet to the sides, your knees will flare out and you will lose the form. If you find yourself doing this, your butt needs to be pushing out further behind you, following the floor in parallel.

If you lean back onto your heels too much, you will tip backwards and your back will not fold forward, staying more vertical.

If you are leaning too much onto the balls of your feet, you will tip forward and smack your face into the wall.

5) Move in a controlled fashion as you descend, using your core and strength in your legs for control. This is not a speed exercise.

Let your arms hang naturally straight down as if you were going to pick up a kettlebell handle between your legs. Keep a proud chest without shoulders rounding forward.

6) Once you feel your hips can go back no further and your knees start to bend, this is the bottom of your hip hinge. Take note, this position will be like the hike position in the swing I will teach you later.

Now, squeeze your butt cheeks and hamstrings and push the hips forward to stand.

WORKOUT A

Plank with Kettlebell Pull Through

1) Begin with a normal push up plank position with a kettlebell by your left side. The bell should be positioned underneath your left pectoral about 2" outside your body line.

2) Do not allow your chest to cave in during the movement and resist your body twisting by squeezing your glutes and tensing your body. Some twisting is normal.

3) Slide your right arm underneath yourself to grab the kettlebell handle and drag the kettlebell across your body to your right side.

4) Pull the kettlebell back to your left side with your left hand. This completes 1 repetition.

Shoulder Elevated Hip Bridge (2L)

1) Lie with your upper back resting on a bench and your feet flat on the floor.

2) Raise your hips until your body forms a straight line from your shoulders to your knees.

3) At the top of the rep your thighs should be perpendicular to the floor.

4) Hold for a count and then slowly return to the starting position.

Goblet Squat

1) Hold a DB/KB with 2 hands at chest height keeping your shoulders down and back and your elbows tucked in using the goblet grip.

2) Brace your abs, push your hips back and bend your knees descending into a squat.

3) Stop your decent when your thighs reach just below parallel to the ground. HOLD THIS POSITION for the time prescribed or 1 second.

4) Push your feet into the ground and drive yourself back up into a standing position, squeezing your glutes at the top.

Bent Over Row (2H)

1) Start off with the kettlebell placed on the floor slightly to your left side. Stand in the split squat position with your foot back on the kettlebell side.

2) Bend and flex your knees slightly, driving your hips back and placing your body weight on your heels. Hinge your hips and lean down with a straight back at a roughly 45-degree angle, picking up your kettlebell with your left arm. Fight to maintain square shoulders through the rowing movement.

3) Once you're in position, make sure that your back is straight, and your chest is pushed out, so your shoulders are not rounded. Using your back muscles, pull the kettlebell up towards you pulling with your elbow and back before slowly dropping back down in a rowing movement. Imagine a string linked from your lats to your elbow and pull the string using your lat.

4) Once you've completed a satisfactory number of repetitions, hinge your hips back to lower the bell to the floor safely. You may also flex your knees to help return the bell back to the floor. 5) Switch sides and repeat.

Sumo Deadlift

1) With a stance slightly wider than your shoulders, you'll turn your feet outward at roughly 15-to-30-degrees.

2) The kettlebell is situated in the center of your stance. Next your kettlebell will fall upon an imaginary line between the balls of your feet.

3) From here, you will begin to squat down by pushing your rump backward on a parallel line to the floor, as you would to sit in a chair. You'll keep a proud chest while doing this and not letting it fall forward.

4) Your arms will hang straight down thanks to gravity, and you'll grab the kettlebell by the handles using the Double Over Hand Grip.

5) Then, stand back up reversing the movements. Maintain the same core intensity throughout the lowering and raising phases.

Pushup

1) Keep the abs braced and body in a straight line from toes (knees) to shoulders.

2) Place the hands on the floor slightly wider than shoulder-width apart.

3) Slowly lower yourself down until you are 2 inches off the ground.

4) Push through your chest, shoulders, and triceps to return to the start position.

5) Keep your body in a straight line at all times.

WORKOUT B

Deadbug Resurrected

1) In a seated position on the floor, grab a light to medium kettlebell using the goblet grip. Slowly roll back until your back is flat on the floor. If you have a small towel, place it under your lumbar spine. This will help you maintain neutral spine and give you something to push against while performing the exercise.

2) Now press the kettlebell overhead and keep your arms locked. Maintain this position during the entire exercise.

3) Initiate the exercise by extending one leg, straightening the knee and hip to bring the leg towards the ground. Only go as far as you can to maintain your back against the ground.

4) Your lumbar position must be maintained against the towel throughout the exercise.

5) Keep your abs drawn in and tight and return the moving leg to the starting position. Repeat on the other side for 1 repetition. Your goal with this exercise is to do one swing at a time from start to park (placing the bell where we started). This is so we can master the beginnings of the swing.

Side Plank on Elbow

1) When performing the side plank, ensure that your body is in a straight line and your elbow underneath your shoulder.

2) Squeeze your glutes to keep your hips forward in line with your body.

3) Once in position and you have a nice straight line down your body, hold.

Dead Stop Clean (1H)

Dead Stop just means we will be resetting every rep. We will bring the KB from the floor to the rack and then back to the floor, resetting the repetition.

1) Stand about one foot behind the kettlebell. Your feet hip-width apart and a slight bend in your knees. Your shoulders should be directly over your hips with a neutral head and neck position, and your chin should remain tucked throughout the movement as if you were holding an egg under your chin.

2) Perform your hip hinge to get into position and grab the right corner of the kettlebell handle with your right hand using an overhand grip.

3) Engage your lat and upper back by rotating your arm outward. Your shoulder blades should be higher than your hips, and your hips should be higher than your knees. Your shins should be in an upright position. There should be no 'slack' between the bell and the body and arm, everything is tight like a board. Your grip on the kettlebell should be loose and relaxed to allow the kettlebell to move smoothly in your hand (remember: no blisters!).

4) To initiate the movement, slightly raise your torse and pull the kettlebell between your legs into the hike pass position. As you pull backward, keep your palm facing the floor. The kettlebell handle should pass above your knees. Your shins should be vertical, and your glutes and hamstrings should be stretched and prepared to initiate the hip action of the clean.

5) Once the kettlebell reaches the hike pass position, your hand should be under your pelvis. While maintaining a neutral spine, start your upward movement by driving your hips forward to swing the kettlebell to the rack position of the clean.

6) As your hips push the bell out of the hike pass position, you will begin to stand up. Quickly rotate your hand outward while keeping your upper arm connected to your ribcage as you begin to pull the kettlebell up toward your body. Rotate your hand around the kettlebell while maintaining a neutral wrist position. The kettlebell should stay close to your body. Your hand should travel upward as if you were zipping up a coat, and the thumb side of your hand should be pointed toward your chest.

7) Engage your core and squeeze your glutes and quads to keep your body stable as the kettlebell travels to the rack position. The kettlebell should finish in the rack position with your wrist neutral and your forearm vertical. Your elbow should be under the kettlebell, and you should engage your upper back to help support the kettlebell.

8) To initiate the drop, hip hinge and drop the kettlebell from the rack position by turning your hand slightly inward as if you were giving a thumbs down to keep the kettlebell close to your body. Your upper arm should stay connected to your ribcage.

9) The hip hinge acts as a shock absorber. Make sure your upper arm maintains connection to your body to protect your elbow and wrist.

10) Swing the bell back into the hike pass position and then park the bell in front of you.

Half Kneeling Press

1) Kneel on one knee like you were going to perform a runners stretch, with a kettlebell opposite your planted foot.

2) Clean the bell to the rack position. Press the handle directly upwards over your head without letting your torso rotate.

3) At full extension, your elbow should be opposite your ear.

4) Slowly return to the start position, complete your remaining repetitions.

5) Lower bell to the ground using a reverse bicep curl. Repeat on other side by changing your foot plant.

Goblet Split Squat

1) Grasp the bell using your goblet grip, holding the bell close to your chest. Your elbows are fine to touch the body as added support.

2) Take a hip-width stance and step out with your right leg, only as far as necessary. No need to take a giant step.

3) Keep your spine tall and do not round your back or fall forward. This is an up and down movement. Think proud chest!

4) Squat down by flexing the knee and the hip of the front leg. Allow the heel of the rear foot to rise while the knee of the rear leg bends slightly until it almost contacts floor. Stay tall and do not allow the rear hip or the low back to flex forward. Perform this movement slowly - there is no slamming the knee into the ground!

5) Return to the original standing position by extending the hip and knee of the forward leg. Repeat for the desired repetitions and then switch legs.

Flat Back Pullover

1) Keep the bell close to your bodyline during the movement. Do not overextend the arms.

2) Sit on your rump, feet shoulder width apart and knees about 90 degrees. Drive the heels into the ground during the movement.

3) Grip the kettlebell upside down by the handle, holding close to chest without touching the chest.

4) Roll backward onto your back without letting the kettlebell touch the ground, and while not allowing your arms to straighten out. Keep a slight bend in the elbows.

5) Engage and begin the movement by squeezing your tailbone and pushing it into the ground while engaging your core and back muscles. Exhale and pull the bell down over your chest while squeezing your core and crunch up slightly.

6) Maintain tension and engage your core the entire time of the movement. Return to start position and maintain tension.

WORKOUT C

Swing (2H)

1) Stand with feet a little wider that hip-width apart holding a kettlebell with two hands. You may see this notated as 2H in the workout, which just means two-handed.

2) Brace your abs, push your hips back with a hip hinge and move the bell from the parked position through your legs to the hike pass position.

3) Staying braced, thrust your hips forward and swing the KB up, the arms are along for the ride and simply grip and guide the bell along its natural arc.

4) When the kettlebell reaches the top, the kettlebell will be directly in front of you and your arms straight. Ensure that you maintain a proud chest and do not allow your shoulders to be pulled out of their sockets.

5) Gravity will now force the kettlebell to drop. Keep your abs braced and your arms straight, allow the bell to drop quite a bit before your hips will be pushed back naturally into the hip hinge and finally pushing the bell back into the hike pass position. To complete another swing, just execute another hip explosion. To park the bell, use the technique taught in the Deadstop Swing in workout B.

***NOTE: It's important to note that your hips are the prime mover in this exercise and are responsible for bringing the KB up. The harder your thrust your hips, the higher the KB will go. DO NOT attempt to lift the KB up with your arms/shoulders. Your arms are "just along for the ride".

Bodyweight Squat

1) Stand with your feet just greater than shoulder-width apart.

2) With your abs braced and glutes squeezed, start the movement at the hip joint and push your hips backward and "sit back into a chair".

3) Make your hips go back as far as possible and keep your knees in a straight line.

4) Keep your low back tensed in a neutral position. Don't let your lower back round.

5) Push with your glutes, hamstrings, and quadriceps to return to the start position.

Pushup

1) Keep the abs braced and body in a straight line from toes (knees) to shoulders.

2) Place the hands on the floor slightly wider than shoulder-width apart.

3) Slowly lower yourself down until you are 2 inches off the ground.

4) Push through your chest, shoulders, and triceps to return to the start position.

5) Keep your body in a straight line at all times.

PHASE II

WARM UP

Deadbug

1) Lay on your back. If you have a small towel, place it under your lumbar spine. This will help you maintain neutral spine and give you something to push against while performing the exercise.

2) Initiate the exercise by extending one leg, straightening the knee and hip to bring the leg towards the ground. Only go as far as you can to maintain your back against the ground. And move the opposite hand towards the ground above your head.

3) Your lumbar position must be maintained against the towel throughout the exercise.

4) Keep your abs drawn in and tight and return the moving leg and arm to the starting position.

Around the Body to Hold

1) Stand up straight with your feet shoulder-width apart. Hold the kettlebell with a corner grip in one hand.

2) Use momentum to swing the bell across the front of your body and pass it to your other hand.

3) Continue the momentum and swing the kettlebell behind your back and pass it to your other hand.

4) As the bell changes hands bring the bell in front of your body and catch it with your opposite hand. Now, reverse direction. After you've returned the bell back to your start position, this counts as one repetition.

5) Brace your body against the momentum by engaging your glutes, core, and back muscles.

Halo

1) Pop the kettlebell up from the center of your stance and grip the handles. Use a light weight until you master this movement.

2) Turn the bell upside down so that the handles are on bottom, and the bell is on top. This is not a goblet squat grip; we are holding onto the horns of the kettlebell with our hands. The bell is in front of your chest but close to the body, without touching it.

3) Stand with your feet shoulder-width apart and knees slightly bent.

4) Raise the kettlebell to the side of your head, move it behind your head, to the opposite side and then back to the front. The kettlebell should naturally move into a bottom-down position as your move it around.

5) Brace your body against the momentum by engaging your glutes, core, and back muscles. Imagine pinching a coin between your glutes - to protect your back.

6) Once you complete one orbit around your head, reverse directions. Once you complete the second orbit in the opposite direction that is one repetition.

Figure 8

1) Place a light kettlebell on the floor with the handle positioned diagonal depending on which side you'll start from. Grab only half of the kettlebell handle at the part that is furthest from you. I like to grab it at the corner of the handle, so I give myself plenty of room on the handle to pass it between hands.

2) Stand close to the kettlebell with feet roughly shoulder-width apart.

3) Bend at the knees, hinge at the hips with the back flat and rounded, tighten your core, then pick up the kettlebell with your corner grip.

4) Swing the weight between your legs toward the opposite arm and grab the handle using the empty hand. Your empty hand moves behind you and meets the open portion of the handle of the kettlebell.

5) After the pass the bell is behind you, swing the bell around the outside of the leg, pop your hips forward slightly without fully extending. Maintain a shock absorber stance throughout. This tiny pop from the hips will push the kettlebell on an arc in front of you.

6) Now, with the kettlebell in front of you, guide the kettlebell back through your legs and meet the handle with your empty hand behind you. That's one full rep!

7) Repeat the process and keep the figure 8 moving non-stop for the total amount of reps or time listed.

Hip Pry Goblet Squat

1) Focus on prying your hips open at the bottom of your squat, wherever that is. Don't force this stretch. Lower is not necessarily better. Lengthen the spine and maintain tension the entire time.

2) Grab a light kettlebell with a goblet grip and hold the kettlebell at chest height. Your elbows and upper arm will be pressed against your body.

3) With your goblet grip secure, feet shoulder width apart, and toes pointing 15 degrees outward, maintain a proud chest as you squat.

4) Lower as far as you can without folding over. When you begin to fold over, this is the point where we want to begin our hip prying action. You may find this more difficult with the addition of the kettlebell. If you find it too difficult, back off and go bodyweight only.

5) Maintain tension in your quads and glutes and push against your knees with your elbows. Push your knees against the kettlebell and create an isometric tension as you slightly move from one side to another as you focus on loosening up your hips. Allow the weight of the kettlebell to provide an assistance with your stretch.

6) Stand up and park the kettlebell.

WORKOUT D

Spiderman Pushup

1) Start by getting into a regular push-up position. As you come down, bring your knee up to your elbow, back down, and then alternate sides.

2) Try to keep your body in a straight line and minimize the rotation in the hips. You should have good mobility in your hips which will allow you to do this exercise.

3) This is a very difficult push-up when done with proper form because when you bring your elbow to your knee you are going from 4 stabilizing points to only 3. Therefore, you are increasing the stress load on your body, as well as working your abdominals

Plank with Kettlebell Pull Through

1) Begin with a normal push up plank position with a kettlebell by your left side. The bell should be positioned underneath your left pectoral about 2" outside your body line.

2) Do not allow your chest to cave in during the movement and resist your body twisting by squeezing your glutes and tensing your body. Some twisting is normal.

3) Slide your right arm underneath yourself to grab the kettlebell handle and drag the kettlebell across your body to your right side.

4) Pull the kettlebell back to your left side with your left hand. This completes 1 repetition.

Squat (1H)

1) Hold the kettlebell with your forearm as vertical as possible and your wrist straight. Turn your toes to point out slightly—more if you have trouble squatting deeply, and less if you're mobile in your hips. Take a deep breath into your belly, and actively twist your feet into the floor, but don't let them move. Think of your legs as screwdrivers, or that you're standing on grass and trying to twist it up beneath you. You should feel the arches in your feet rise and your glutes tighten, creating tension in the lower body.

2) Squat as low as you can while keeping your head, spine, and pelvis aligned, and pushing your knees apart. If you feel your tailbone beginning to tuck under, stop there, and come back up. Keep your torso as vertical as possible—you shouldn't have to lean forward or work extra hard to hold the bell upright. Avoid bending or twisting to either side.

3) Come back up, extending your hips and knees. Complete your reps on that side, and then switch sides and repeat.

Strict Press (1H)

1) When performing this exercise, you want to ensure your shoulder's safety. When you lockout your arm overhead, keep your bicep close to your ear.

2) Clean the kettlebell to your shoulder by extending through the legs and hips as you pull the kettlebell towards your shoulder. Rotate your wrist as you do so, so that the palm faces inward. This will be your starting position.

3) Press the kettlebell up and out until it is locked out overhead.

4) Lower the kettlebell back to your shoulder under control and repeat.

5) Complete one arm before starting the other, then do the other arm.

Flat Back Pullover

1) Keep the bell close to your bodyline during the movement. Do not overextend the arms.

2) Sit on your rump, feet shoulder width apart and knees about 90 degrees. Drive the heels into the ground during the movement.

3) Grip the kettlebell upside down by the handle, holding close to chest without touching the chest.

4) Roll backward onto your back without letting the kettlebell touch the ground, and while not allowing your arms to straighten out. Keep a slight bend in the elbows.

5) Engage and begin the movement by squeezing your tailbone and pushing it into the ground while engaging your core and back muscles. Exhale and pull the bell down over your chest while squeezing your core and crunch up slightly.

6) Maintain tension and do NOT sit up, engage your core the entire time of the movement. Return to start position and maintain tension.

Romanian Deadlift (1L)

1) Place a kettlebell slightly to the front of the foot you will be starting with. For example, let's start with your right foot. Place the kettlebell directly in front of your toes.

2) Distribute your weight onto one foot, stabilize, and then lift your other foot off the ground.

3) Keep your pelvis pointed forward, push your hips back, pull your pelvis down, and lean forward. You should feel your hamstring on your standing leg lengthen and your glute activate.

4) If you do not feel your hamstring and glute activate you might be rounding into your lower back or leaning too far forward. Remember to hip hinge and not just round forward into this movement.

5) Come back up with control and keep the integrity of your form before returning to your starting position.

Swing (1H)

1) Stand with feet a little wider that hip-width apart holding a DB/KB with 1 hand.

2) Brace your abs, push your hips back and bend your knees bringing the KB between your legs.

3) Staying braced, thrust your hips forward and swing the KB up with your arm squeezing your butt tight as you fully stand up.

4) Keep your abs braced and your arms straight, push your hips back and bend your knees bringing the KB between your legs again to repeat the movement.

WORKOUT E

Half Turkish Get Up

1) Start with the kettlebell right at the shoulder. Hand goes right through the handle of the 'bell, pull it up to the frame and roll to the back.

2) Punch the kettlebell up towards the ceiling. You want it right above your shoulder. Elbows locked out; shoulders sucked down into the socket. Your shoulders should be nice and stabilized and your lats are engaged. All those muscles that surround the shoulder should be nice and tight.

3) Your right heel is flat on the ground and knee in the air. Your left leg is extended and flat on the ground. Right heel, same leg as your arm is up. Your left arm is roughly 45 degrees off your body.

4) Drive through the right heel and punch the bell straight up as you roll onto your left elbow.

5) Continue moving through the elbow position by bridging up and rolling from your elbow to your palm.

6) Reverse back to the elbow and shoulder back to a flat back position. Repeat other side.

Side Plank on Elbow

1) Lie on a mat on your right side.

2) Support your bodyweight with your knees and on your right elbow.

3) Raise your body in a straight line so that your body hovers over the mat.

4) Keep your back straight and your hips up. Hold your abs tight. Contract them as if someone was about to punch you in the stomach, but breath normally.

5) Hold this position for the recommended amount of time.

6) Switch to your left side and repeat.

Suitcase Deadlift (1H)

1) Position kettlebell(s) on the floor beside the outside of your feet and take a stance that is shoulder width apart.

2) Engage your core and begin a hip hinge to lower yourself to pick up the kettlebell(s) by the handle. Keep your shoulder(s) down and back. Do not round your back. This is not a squat, but a hip hinge.

3) Keeping your core engage, squeeze your glutes, and push your hips forward to move the bell(s) up. Do not overextend your hips.

4) Return bell to the ground, this is 1 rep.

.

Bent Over Row (1H)

1) Start off with the kettlebell placed on the floor slightly in front of you. Stand with your feet shoulder-width apart and your toes pointing forward.

2) Bend and flex your knees slightly, driving your hips back and placing your body weight on your heels. Hinge your hips and lean down with a straight back at a roughly 45-degree angle, picking up your kettlebell with slightly bent arms.

3) Once you're in position, make sure that your back is straight, and your chest is pushed out, so your shoulders are not rounded. Using your back muscles, pull the kettlebell up towards you so that the handle is level with your sides before slowly dropping back down in a rowing movement. Imagine a string linked from your lats to your elbow and pull the string using your lat.

4) Once you've completed a satisfactory number of repetitions, hinge your hips back to lower the bell to the floor safely. You may also flex your knees to help return the bell back to the floor.

Goblet Split Squat

1) Grasp the bell using your goblet grip, holding the bell close to your chest. Your elbows are fine to touch the body as added support.

2) Take a hip-width stance and step out with your right leg, only as far as necessary. No need to take a giant step.

3) Keep your spine tall and do not round your back or fall forward. This is an up and down movement. Think proud chest!

4) Squat down by flexing the knee and the hip of the front leg. Allow the heel of the rear foot to rise while the knee of the rear leg bends slightly until it almost contacts floor. Stay tall and do not allow the rear hip or the low back to flex forward. Perform this movement slowly - there is no slamming the knee into the ground!

5) Return to the original standing position by extending the hip and knee of the forward leg. Repeat for the desired repetitions and then switch legs.

Waiter's Walk (1H)

A waiter's walk is performed by simply holding a weight overhead and walking. With one kettlebell, the obliques and spinal erectors get extra work stabilizing the body.

1) It is important to take care of the wrist in this movement. If you push heavy weights overhead, your wrist should be as straight as possible. Allowing it to bend back can lead to wrist injuries.

2) Getting the weight overhead can be a limiting factor. Any way you can get the weight overhead will work. However, I recommend using a weight you can clean and press overhead. Ensure your wrist is straight at the top.

3) Once the weight is overhead, lock out your elbow and maintain a strong wrist position. Do not allow the weight to bend your wrist forward or backward.

4) Engage your lats and shoulders. Pull your shoulders back and down.

5) Begin slowly walking in a controlled fashion and feeling the tension in your shoulder, core, and legs as you move. As this is an unbalanced move, your body will brace itself as you walk.

6) DO NOT WALK FAST. Feel the movement and resist against any changes as you move.

Snatch

1) Start in the hike position by hinging your hips, bell 12 - 18 inches in front of feet. Feet are hip width apart with a slight angle.

2) Hike the bell back by engaging your core.

3) Power the bell forward and up with an explosive movement from your hips while pulling the bell up along your body line.

4) As the bell reaches above your chest, punch through the bell handle allowing the bell to rotate around your wrist. This will keep the bell from slamming into your wrist and bruising it. Wear a guard until you master this process as it can take time.

5) When the bell is overhead and your arm fully extended, you can return the bell back to the hike position by slightly leaning backward and allowing gravity to follow the natural arc back to the hike position. From here you can park it or continue with another rep.

WORKOUT F

Swing (2H)

1) Stand with feet a little wider that hip-width apart holding a kettlebell with two hands. You may see this notated as 2H in the workout, which just means two-handed.

2) Brace your abs, push your hips back with a hip hinge and move the bell from the parked position through your legs to the hike pass position.

3) Staying braced, thrust your hips forward and swing the KB up, the arms are along for the ride and simply grip and guide the bell along its natural arc.

4) When the kettlebell reaches the top, the kettlebell will be directly in front of you and your arms straight. Maintain a proud chest and shoulders sucked into your shoulder sockets.

5) Gravity will force the kettlebell to drop. Keep your abs braced and your arms straight, allow the bell to drop quite a bit before your hips will be pushed back naturally into the hip hinge and finally pushing the bell back into the hike pass position. To complete another swing, just execute another hip explosion.

***NOTE: It's important to note that your hips are the prime mover in this exercise. The harder your thrust your hips, the higher the KB will go. DO NOT attempt to lift the KB up with your arms/shoulders. Your arms are "just along for the ride".

Pushup

1) Keep the abs braced and body in a straight line from toes (knees) to shoulders.

2) Place the hands on the floor slightly wider than shoulder-width apart.

3) Slowly lower yourself down until you are 2 inches off the ground.

4) Push through your chest, shoulders, and triceps to return to the start position.

5) Keep your body in a straight line at all times.

RECOVERY

EARLY MORNING FLEXIBILITY (EMF)

Chin Wave

1) Start by pushing your chin forward while keeping your neck and shoulders stable.

2) When your chin is fully extended, tuck the chin into your chest.

3) Return to the chin extended position and then pull the chin back.

4) Once you have fully retracted your chin, slowly tilt your head back. Do not lose your balance here, and if you do feel as if you are losing balance, you can skip this step.

5) Return back to chin extended and repeat.

Gunslinger

1) Extend arms at chest level, fingers interlaced, index fingers extended forwards, like pistol.

2) Roll shoulders forward. Tilt pelvis back and thrust mid back backwards. Imagine the letter C from pelvis to shoulder. Bend legs slightly.

3) Exhale through the mouth and stretch more.

4) Inhale through nose and stand straight, chin down, lifting chest up and back. Repeat.

Clask Hand with Neck Roll

1) Take your hands behind your back and press palms together while interlocking your fingers. Keep this handshake relaxed.

2) Begin to roll your shoulders back as you stand taller, driving your handshake down towards the ground.

3) When you hit your low point, let your chest stretch and expand in this position for a moment.

4) Now, let your head drift to one side looking over to the ground next to you. Keep your head relaxed as you do this. Keep your head moving and begin to look sideways and then upward. Your head should move in a circular fashion.

5) Keep moving your head in the circular fashion onto your opposite side now. Move from upward to side to floor and back to the start position.

6) Move your head back the opposite direction now.

7) It is important to flex and push your hands down during this entire process while breathing comfortably. You can improve the stretch by squeezing your pecs and shoulders and holding all of this in an isometric fashion.

Arm Screws

1) Start with arms out straight and your palms facing down.

2) Pivot and turn to one side while keeping your arms in the same spot in space.

3) Both hands should turn up as much as possible.

4) Switch sides keeping your shoulders in line.

Arm Circles

1) Draw maximal circles with both arms.

2) Move in oppcsing and random directions.

Hip Sway with Reach

1) Stand with your feet shoulder width or even like you were going to do a sumo squat.

2) Kick your left hip out to the left.

3) With your right-hand reach down and across your body, trying to touch your left knee. Don't strain too hard, your body will loosen up.

4) Your left hand reaches above you reach over the left side of your body over to the right. Try to keep your left arm in line with your body for best results and so you don't lose your balance.

5) Repeat to the other side. You can get a good rhythm here, just be gentle and slow.

Hip Hinge

This is also known as a bodyweight good morning exercise.

1) Stand with your feet hip-width apart and and place your fingertips into your hip crease where your body folds.

2) Keeping your back flat and core braced, push your hips back, lowering your torso until it is nearly parallel to the floor.

3) Pause, and then return to the starting position.

Bootstrapper

1) Stand with your feet about shoulder width apart.

2) Bend your knees and squat down so that your butt is almost sitting on the back of your calves.

3) Lean forward on your toes and place your hands on the ground. It's ok to reach under your shoe or toes and grip. This will help the stretch on the way up.

4) Stand up and push your heels down against the floor and straighten your legs out.

Standing Forward Fold

1) With your arms reaching overhead, sweep your arms down on either side of your body to come into a forward fold from your hips. This is often called a Swan Dive.

2) Point your fingertips towards your toes. Work your palms flat to the floor if possible. If you can't, cross your arms and let the weight of your arms relax your hamstrings.

3) Maintain a slight bend in your knees so that they are not locked.

4) Engage your quadriceps muscles and tighten them up. The more you use your quads, the more the hamstrings (the muscles on the back of the thighs) will open.

5) Bring your weight a little bit forward into the balls of your feet so that your hips stay over your ankles and let your head hang.

6) Come up slowly, placing your hands onto your hips. Press your tailbone down and contract your abdominal muscles as you rise slowly.

.

Inchworm

1) Stand tall, your feet roughly hip width apart. Your ears should be aligned over your shoulders, hips, knees, and ankles, your core engaged.

2) Look down at the ground and start reaching your hands toward the floor in front of your feet. Allow your back to bend forward, as if doing a spinal roll. Allow the knees to bend, as needed, letting your hands to touch the ground.

3) Once your hands reach the floor, begin walking them forward keeping your weight pressed into your palms. Allow your heels to lift off the floor as your body begins to straighten. When your hands are directly under your shoulders, you will be in the plank position with your core, chest, quads, triceps, and shoulders engaged, your body forming a straight line from heels to head. Don't let your body sag.

4) The next step is to walk your feet forward to meet your hands. Try to keep your legs somewhat straight as you begin to walk your feet forward. Step forward, one foot at a time, toward your hands. This should provide a nice stretch through your hamstrings, calves, and glutes as your hips start lifting toward the ceiling.

5) Stop walking the feet forward your feet are as close to your hands as you can comfortably step. Bending your knees as you walk forward is just fine but fighting to keep them straight will help provide a nice stretch to your hamstrings.

6) Now, we just return from where we came and do a reverse spinal roll back to a full standing position. When you reach the top, engage your core and glutes. Then turn around and go back to where you started.

Prone Knee to Chest

1) Lie down on the ground on your back with your feet flat on the floor and your legs straight.

2) Bring one knee towards the chest by lifting the foot off the ground. Use your hands to pull the knee into the chest and increase the intensity of the stretch.

3) Hold this position for recommended time and repeat.

Knee Side Drop Out

1) Lie flat on your back with legs extended in front of you. Arms at your side.

2) Raise one leg and use your leg muscles and core to bring the knee as close to the chest as possible. Do not pull the knee in with your hands.

3) When the knee reaches the point where you cannot move it any closer to your chest, push it to the side towards the ground. Push as far as you comfortable can and when you can go no further straighten the leg out.

4) Extend the leg fully without touching the heel to the ground and repeat for recommended time or reps.

Single Frog Leg

1) Lay on your back, knees bent with feet flat on the floor (1 foot from buttocks). This move combines the Knee to Chest and the Knee Side Drop Out.

2) First perform the Knee to Chest.

3) When your knee is as close to your chest as you can get it, perform the Knee Side Drop Out.

4) When knee is close to the floor, extend your leg until it is parallel to the floor.

5) Pull knee back into chest and repeat movement. 6) Perform all reps on right side before performing on the left side.

Double Frog Leg

1) Lay on your back, knees bent with feet flat on the floor (1 foot from buttocks). This move combines the Knee to Chest and the Knee Side Drop Out.

2) This is done with both legs at the same time. First perform the Knee to Chest.

3) When your knee is as close to your chest as you can get it, perform the Knee Side Drop Out.

4) Try to touch your soles together when both knees are close to floor.

5) When knee is close to the floor, extend your leg until it is parallel to the floor.

6) Pull knee back into chest and repeat movement.

7) Perform all reps on right side before performing on the left side.

Hip Pry Squat

1) We will focus on prying our hips open at the bottom of our squat, wherever that is. Don't force this stretch. Lower is not necessarily better, what we are working on maintaining and active squat. Lengthen the spine and maintain tension the entire time.

2) With your arms out ahead of you, feet shoulder width apart, and toes pointing 15 degrees outward, point your thumbs up and maintain a proud chest as you squat.

3) Lower as far as you can without folding over. When you begin to fold over, this is the point where we want to begin our hip prying action.

4) Maintain tension and place your elbows inside of your knees by praying your hands together. Push your hands down and pray that you can stand up. Resist the motion slightly with your hips.

5) Stand up and reset your feet, repeat.

DECOMPRESSION

Hip Pry Squat

1) We will focus on prying our hips open at the bottom of our squat, wherever that is. Don't force this stretch. Lower is not necessarily better, what we are working on maintaining and active squat. Lengthen the spine and maintain tension the entire time.

2) With your arms out ahead of you, feet shoulder width apart, and toes pointing 15 degrees outward, point your thumbs up and maintain a proud chest as you squat.

3) Lower as far as you can without folding over. When you begin to fold over, this is the point where we want to begin our hip prying action.

4) Maintain tension and place your elbows inside of your knees by praying your hands together. Push your hands down and pray that you can stand up. Resist the motion slightly with your hips.

5) Stand up and reset your feet, repeat.

Kneeling Hip Flexor

1) Kneel on floor and face forward.

2) Place your left leg forward in front of you so your left shin is upright, leaving your right shin parallel to the floor and balance on your toes. Your torso is upright, and your hips squared.

3) Flex your abs to protect your back. You will not extend the hips forward, rather you will keep your glutes flexed.

4) Flatten your right foot to the floor, squeeze your entire right leg as you push forward. Maintain this squeeze and breathe.

5) As you exhale, you will feel your muscles relax and you will sink a bit lower.

Sleeping Pigeon

1) Cross one leg in front of your body on the floor.

2) Lean your chest over the top of your front leg while you sit back on your hips.

3) Straighten out your back leg and bring it across your body to increase the stretch.

Downward Facing Dog

1) Really focus on calf muscles and try to get heels to touch floor. This may take time, but is integral in helping to create more power, length, and tension in your swing.

2) Come to your hands and knees with the wrists underneath the shoulders and the knees underneath the hips.

3) Curl the toes under and push back raising the hips and straightening the legs.

4) Spread the fingers and ground down from the forearms into the fingertips.

5) Outwardly rotate the upper arms broadening the collarbones.

6) Let the head hang, move the shoulder blades away from the ears towards the hips.

7) Engage the quadriceps strongly to take the weight off the arms, making this a resting pose.

8) Rotate the thighs inward, keep the tail high and sink your heels towards the floor.

Backswing Angel

1) Stand with your back against a wall or any flat surface.

2) Have your feet a few inches away from the wall. Keep your belly tight throughout.

3) Have your butt, shoulder blades and back of head touching the wall. Keeping these 3 points of contact, put your arms up, as if someone were pointing a gun at you.

4) Squeeze your shoulder blades back together until your elbows touch the wall. If you can, try to get your wrists to touch the wall also.

5) Keep these 5 points of contact with the wall at all times, slowly slide your arms up and down to the count of 4 seconds. When pulling your arms down, think about squeezing your elbows in tight to your sides.

GREASE

Three Plane Neck

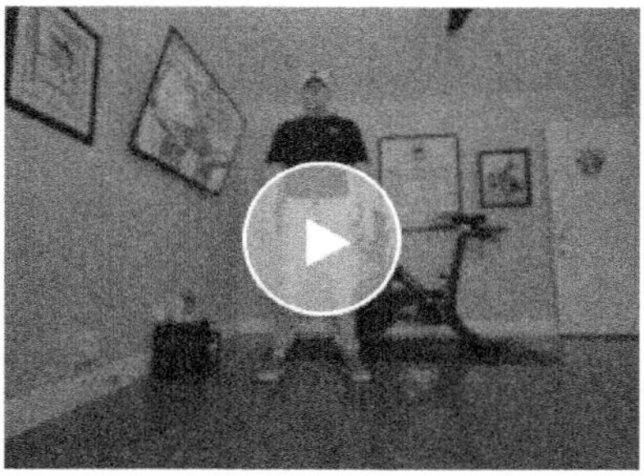

1) Slowly turn head left, then right, gradually increasing range of motion.

2) Tuck your chin in, then tilt your head back.

3) Tilt your head strictly to one side, then to the other (no twisting).

Tip: Perform this movement in a slow, controlled manner. Do not combine the 3 movements into a head roll.

Shoulder Circles

1) Draw circles with your shoulders, as big as possible.

2) Inhale & expand ribcage as shoulders are moving back.

3) Do 10 circles one direction, then switch directions and do 10 more.

Fist Exercise

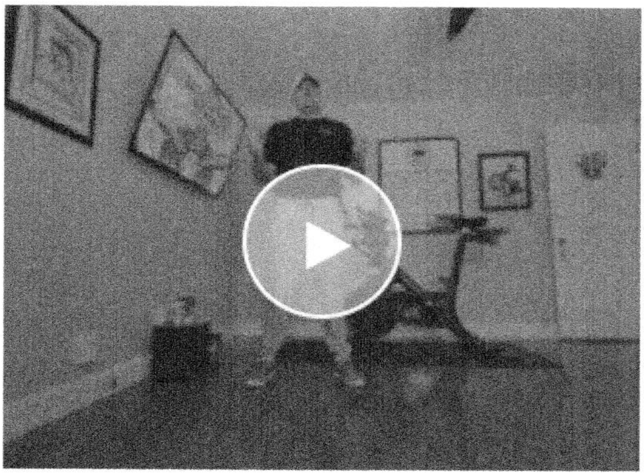

1) Extend fingers from closed fist, then clench your fist again.

2) Perform a total of 20 repetitions

Tip: Try to perform this movement as quickly as possible.

Wrist Rotations

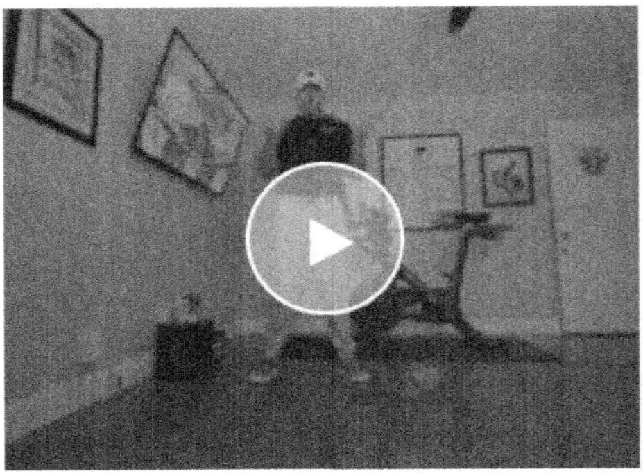

1) Sit on a bench or other surface and hold a dumbbell by the end.

2) Brace the elbow of the arm that is holding the weight against your thigh.

3) With your opposite hand, hold firmly against your thigh the wrist of the hand that is holding the weight.

4) Lower the weigh to one side, rotating at the wrist. Slowly rotate your wrist to the other side. This is one repetition. It will be tempting to move the elbow; limit the movement to your wrist and forearm.

Elbow Circles

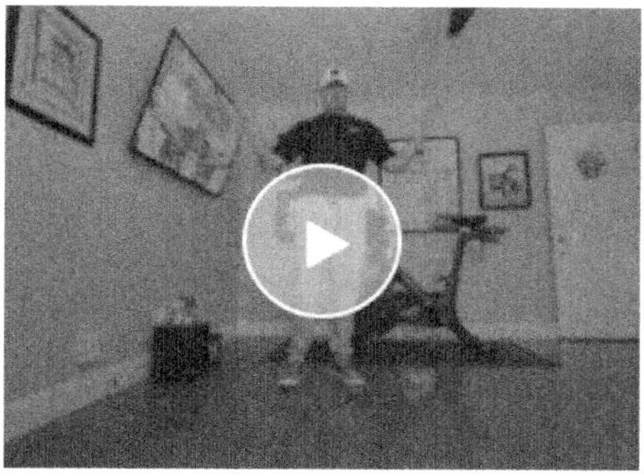

1) Make circles with your elbow maximally bending and straightening it out.

2) Outward circles are more awkward than inward ones.

Arm Screws

1) Start with arms out straight and your palms facing down.

2) Pivot and turn to one side while keeping your arms in the same spot in space.

3) Both hands should turn up as much as possible.

4) Switch sides keeping your shoulders in line.

Arm Circles

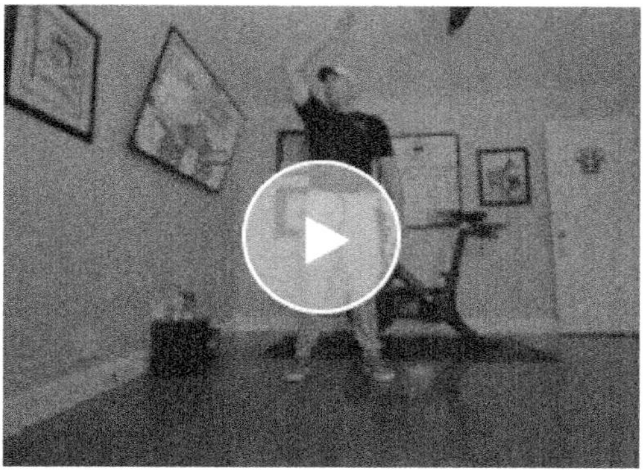

1) Draw maximal circles with one or both arms.

2) Repeat in opposite direction.

Hula Hoop

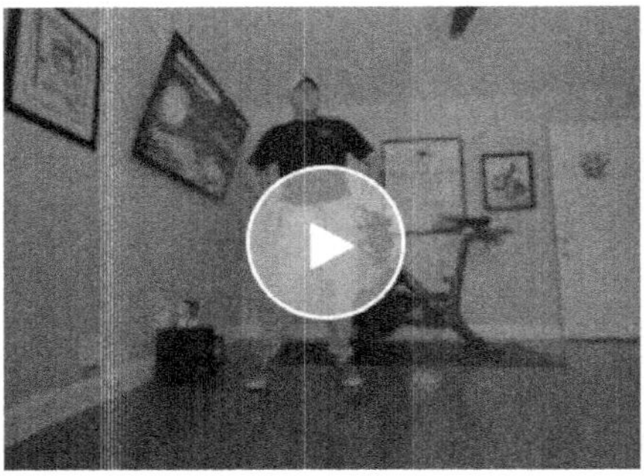

1) Imitate a hula hoop motion.

2) Keep shoulders stationary and make big circles with your hips.

Standing Spinal Rotation w/Club

1) Plant your feet & hips solidly.

2) Slowly turn your trunk clockwise and counterclockwise.

3) Make sure your head moves with your torso.

4) It is important to not turn too far. Resist the turn with your hips until you feel a slight stretch. This is a fluid motion so keep moving.

Knee Circles

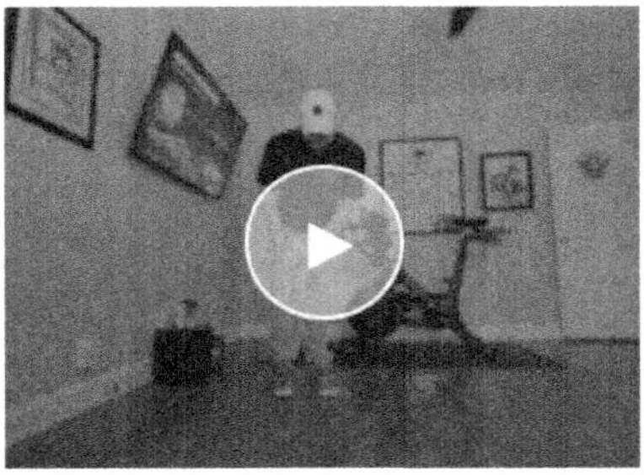

1) Place your hands above your knees – not on kneecaps.

2) Make small circles, NOT large.

Tip: Knee was designed for only minimal lateral motion, so keep your circles tight and small.

Ankle Circles

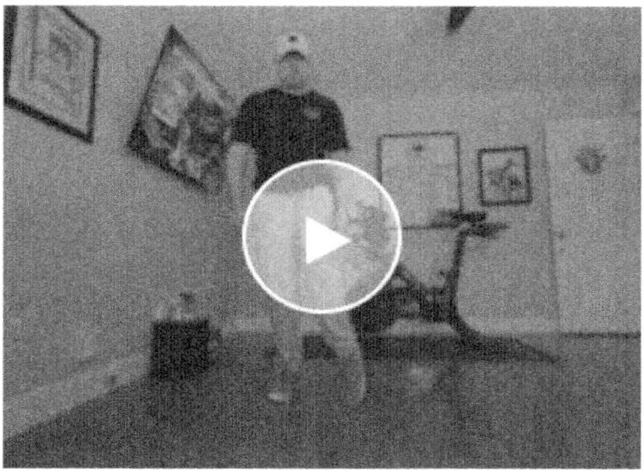

1) Draw circles with your toes while making a point of achieving a maximal range of motion in ankle.

2) Pointed toes, toes to nose, and in and out motion.

FLEX

Backswing Angel

1) Stand with your back against a wall or any flat surface.

2) Have your feet a few inches away from the wall. Keep your belly tight throughout.

3) Have your butt, shoulder blades and back of head touching the wall. Keeping these 3 points of contact, put your arms up, as if someone were pointing a gun at you.

4) Squeeze your shoulder blades back together until your elbows touch the wall. If you can, try to get your wrists to touch the wall also.

5) Keep these 5 points of contact with the wall at all times, slowly slide your arms up and down to the count of 4 seconds. When pulling your arms down, think about squeezing your elbows in tight to your sides.

Standing Forward Fold

1) With your arms reaching overhead, sweep your arms down on either side of your body to come into a forward fold from your hips. This is often called a Swan Dive.

2) Point your fingertips towards your toes. Work your palms flat to the floor if possible. If you can't, cross your arms and let the weight of your arms relax your hamstrings.

3) Maintain a slight bend in your knees so that they are not locked.

4) Engage your quadriceps muscles and tighten them up. The more you use your quads, the more the hamstrings (the muscles on the back of the thighs) will open.

5) Bring your weight a little bit forward into the balls of your feet so that your hips stay over your ankles and let your head hang.

6) Come up slowly, placing your hands onto your hips. Press your tailbone down and contract your abdominal muscles as you rise up slowly.

Hip Pry Squat

1) We will focus on prying our hips open at the bottom of our squat, wherever that is. Don't force this stretch. Lower is not necessarily better, what we are working on maintaining and active squat. Lengthen the spine and maintain tension the entire time.

2) With your arms out ahead of you, feet shoulder width apart, and toes pointing 15 degrees outward, point your thumbs up and maintain a proud chest as you squat.

3) Lower as far as you can without folding over. When you begin to fold over, this is the point where we want to begin our hip prying action.

4) Maintain tension and place your elbows inside of your knees by praying your hands together. Push your hands down and pray that you can stand up. Resist the motion slightly with your hips.

5) Stand up and reset your feet, repeat.

Kneeling Hip Flexor

1) Kneel on floor and face forward.

2) Torso and front shin should remain upright for the duration of the stretch and hips should remain squared.

3) Flex your abs to protect your back.

4) Once the tension is released you will begin to sag down.

Sleeping Pigeon

1) Cross one leg in front of your body on the floor.

2) Lean your chest over the top of your front leg while you sit back on your hips.

3) Straighten out your back leg and bring it across your body to increase the stretch.

Downward Facing Dog

1) Really focus on calf muscles and try to get heels to touch floor. This may take time, but is integral in helping to create more power, length, and tension in your swing.

2) Come to your hands and knees with the wrists underneath the shoulders and the knees underneath the hips.

3) Curl the toes under and push back raising the hips and straightening the legs.

4) Spread the fingers and ground down from the forearms into the fingertips.

5) Outwardly rotate the upper arms broadening the collarbones.

6) Let the head hang, move the shoulder blades away from the ears towards the hips.

7) Engage the quadriceps strongly to take the weight off the arms, making this a resting pose.

8) Rotate the thighs inward, keep the tail high and sink your heels towards the floor.

Cobra Pose

1) Lie face down on your chest on a mat with your hand's palms down next to your armpits.

2) Press your hands into the floor and raise your upper body up away from the mat while keeping your hips on the mat.

3) Relax and breathe in this position for desired amount of time.

Child's Pose

1) Get onto your hands and knees on the floor, with your hands slightly in front of your shoulders.

2) Sit your hips back towards your feet, while keeping your hands planted on the mat.

3) Hold this position while breathing and relaxing.

Q & A

Q: How can I make sure I stay on course and complete the program?

A: Social Support. Take a moment and join our free Facebook group at:

https://www.facebook.com/groups/kettlebellgolfbody

In addition, take the Distance and Accuracy Challenge by measuring your before and after distance measurements and reporting them here:

https://kettlebellgolfbody.com/distance-assessment

The combination of the two will provide additional motivation for you to see the program through.

Q: Which phase should I start with?

A: Everyone should start with the Phase I work out. The workout difficulty is relative to the amount of weight you will use - you can adjust the difficulty level based on weight alone.

Phase I builds a solid base and prepares us for every phase that follows.

After four weeks you will progress to the Phase II workouts.

Q: What I am finding it difficult to perform certain exercises or staying motivated?

A: One of the biggest challenges golfers faces who start a new fitness program is follow through.

By follow through, I'm not talking about your golf swing... I'm talking about having good intentions, even great intentions, and then falling off the wagon...getting little to no results.

I'm guilty of it myself. I have purchased many self-help books in the past where I started out the first few chapters fired up and excited... only to fizzle out before I got any meaningful results.

The sad thing is, I know if I had stuck to the book or course, I WOULD have achieved some success... maybe even a LOT of success.

Sometimes I hit a section of a book I don't totally understand or agree with, and I just quit. Instead, I should figure out a way around or a way through the obstacle. After all, I bought the book for a reason and it's a shame to just leave my dreams and goals behind.

So, what am I driving at?

First, I'd like to work with you personally on implementing the Kettlebell Golf Body.

I want you to crush the ball and get results... and I'd like to get to know you better and learn from you as well... after all, that's how we improve our programs here at Golf Aggressive.

Second, I'd like to make you an offer you can't refuse:

Work with me for the next 90 days to increase your clubhead speed. If you don't increase your clubhead speed, just reach out and we'll either extend the coaching until you do... or you can cut your losses and be issued a full refund... no questions asked.

Here's how it works:

You'll be given access to our iOS or Android coaching app that works on just about any phone, tablet, or computer today.

Once you are set up, we'll figure out where you are currently physically. Based on what you tell us, we'll customize the Kettlebell Golf Body program to your unique situation. This will take out any of the 'road bumps' I mentioned earlier.

After you are up and running with your customized program, you'll be kept accountable through direct communication with me personally. And it's proven that being accountable to a partner or a coach improves your 'follow through'. In addition, the new coaching app allows you to view exercise demo's, track your meals, track your workouts, follow along on certain workouts, and communicate with other Kettlebell golfers inside our private group... It really is amazing and easy to use. It even works with the Fitbit and Apple watches to track caloric expenditure. And the great thing is, we've slashed over $1500 off our normal pricing to work with myself and my team.

If you want to follow through and guarantee success, you can join us here:

https://golff.it/kgb-coaching

Add Even MORE Speed?

Q: I've seen some of your programs that blend golf fitness and golf lessons into one program. Would that help me add even more consistently accurate distance?

A: Yes. The Distance Accelerator is the perfect 'Distance Cocktail' because it mixes perfectly with the Kettlebell Golf Body by helping you refine your golf skills for additional speed boost.

The Distance Accelerator is a blueprint with lessons, drills, and our GTG skill grooving system that literally programs your golf swing for repeatability and consistency... in just minutes a day - at home or at the course.

The Distance Accelerator is normally $47, but you can add it to your Member's Area for just $10

You can unlock access to the Distance Accelerator by clicking the link below:

https://golff.it/da

About The Author

I am a certified personal trainer, former golf pro, and Internet entrepreneur.

It is my sincere belief that anyone who devotes 30 minutes per day a few times a week can become a single digit handicap golfer or better.

I've written several golf fitness books such as Core to Score, 30 Yards or More in 30 Days or Less, and Shed Pounds to Shave Strokes. I've also co-authored How to Break 90 in 42 Days or Less.

And I created the Single Digit Blueprint, it was... and still is... the only complete game transformation system blending golf fitness as well as tried and true foundational golf skill improvement.

My Mission: Help 1 million golfers by the year 2024 to improve their health and performance by blending golf fitness with complimentary golf lessons, drills, and playing tactics through my Single Digit Blueprint.

And build a supportive and competitive community of like-minded golfers who enjoy fitness as much as the game of golf.

Aid golfers in eliminating pain and injuries, so they can comfortably play golf into their golden years without the aches and pains many golfers suffer from as they get older.

Printed in Great Britain
by Amazon

17772533R00129